Night Rain

by *New York Times Bestselling Author*

JOE HILLEY

A MIKE CONNOLLY MYSTERY

Dunlavy + Gray
HOUSTON

Dunlavy + Gray ©2021 by Joe Hilley

Library of Congress Control Number: 2021909757
ISBN: 978-1-7364105-2-3
E-Book ISBN: 978-1-7364105-3-0

This book is a work of fiction. Names, characters, businesses, organizations, places, events, and incidents either are the product of the author's imagination or are used fictitiously. Any resemblance to actual persons—living or dead—events, or locales are entirely coincidental.

Typesetting and cover design by Fitz & Hill Creative Studio.

But if I had just one more try

I would be yours alone until the day I die

And we would have a love so divine ...

Turn Back the Hands of Time, Tyrone Davis

PROLOGUE

Dibber Landry stood at the window and stared into the darkness, waiting for the next flash of lightning. When he looked out earlier in the evening, he saw nothing but the stand of pine trees on the far side of the yard. Four rows, tall and straight, with trunks so large a grown man couldn't reach his arms all the way around them. But the wind had been blowing since the afternoon, as a hurricane made landfall and tore its way across the island.

It rained, too. Constant rain. Heavy rain. Soaking the ground. And now, the steady blow of the storm surely had taken its toll. The ground, saturated with water, let go of the tree roots, relaxing the grip it had held on them for decades, releasing the trees to the wind and sending them crashing to the ground. Dibber was certain he'd heard the sound of it a few minutes ago. He was at the window hoping for confirmation.

Then a sudden flash lit up the sky. Followed by another. And one more. Three in a row. Brighter than any Dibber had seen in a long time. And in those moments, the yard was like noon and he could see the house next door and the one beyond, which meant only one thing. The pine trees really were on the ground, splintered and ruined. He smiled. That was a good sign. The storm was a bad one. Maybe the worst in years. He'd gone out in smaller ones when the wind wasn't as strong and the rain wasn't as great, and he had done alright. But a bad one … that was a special opportunity.

After another flash to confirm what he already knew, Dibber moved away from the window and eased into a worn and tattered recliner. Around him the house shuddered against the wind, resisting with all its might the hurricane's attempts to smash it to splinters, too. Like those pine trees that grew nearby. But Dibber didn't mind. No, sir. Not tonight. He pushed against the back of the chair and a footrest popped out as the chair reclined. He propped his feet on the rest, folded his hands across his lap, and closed his eyes. Better rest a while, he thought. Before long, the eye of the storm would pass over. The wind would disappear and for a while, everything would be calm and still. And then there would be work for him to do. He smiled at the thought of what he might find.

Two hours later, the wind slackened and the house, still cloaked in darkness, became quiet and still. Dibber's eyes popped open and he sat up. Awake. Alert. "The wind," he whispered. "The wind is gone. The eye is passing over."

Dibber hauled himself up from the chair and hurried across the room to the door, then stepped outside to the porch. Around him the night air was thick and humid. Rainwater dripped from the eaves of the house in a steady, rhythmic cadence. Above him, stars shone bright against the dark sky but around him there was not a light to be seen in any direction. He grinned. "The power's out all over the island." And indeed, from Pelican Point all the way to the west end, the electricity service was down.

From the porch, Dibber moved down the steps to the yard and started across to the dock. Even without a light he knew how to find it. He'd been there thousands of times. On the mantle in the house there was a picture of him in his daddy's arms, standing near the end of the dock, looking across the pass to Heron Bay. But that was a long time ago. Before that day, his aunt came and took him out of school. He remembered her bloodshot eyes and the way her nose dripped. She took him by the hand and led him outside under the oak trees on the playground. They sat on the swings, the ones with the big, thick chains that hung down with bottoms made of rubber cut from Mr. Vann's old truck tires. They sat there for a long time, her staring at the ground, him staring at her—and then she told him. A carload of kids skipping school. The car swerved across the centerline on the road to Mobile. Hit his daddy's pickup head-on. His daddy was dead. Dibber was seven. In Mrs. Williams' second grade class. That day, on the swings with his aunt, was as far back as he could remember.

But his feet remembered, and they took him through the night to the dock without the need of conscious thought. In less than a minute, he felt the toe of his sneaker strike the first board. He reached into the darkness with his left hand for the first piling, a telephone pole driven into the ground where the yard ended and the dock began. His hand found it without searching and he moved forward at a confident, purposeful stride.

Twelve paces out, he knelt at the first cleat and found the line that was wound around it. He grasped the line and gave it a tug. By then, his eyes had adjusted to the darkness and he could see the faint outline of the boat. It was two-thirds full of water, but it had survived the first half of the storm without sinking. He steadied himself against the dock and stepped into it.

Dibber sloshed his way to the bow of the boat and opened a storage compartment, took a five-gallon bucket from it, and started bailing water. In no time at all, he scooped out enough to make the boat usable—the bilge pump could handle the rest. He untied the boat from the pilings at the dock and pushed it back with both hands. As the boat drifted free, he moved to the seat behind the steering wheel and felt along the console for the switch. "Let's hope this still works," he said, and he pressed a button to start the engine.

The outboard motor turned over once but didn't catch. Then again. And again. On the fourth try, it sputtered to life. Dibber let it run a moment to make sure, then flipped on the bilge pump and checked to make sure it was working. Then, with a quick scan of the shoreline, he put the engine in gear and bumped the throttle with his hand. The boat started across the water.

On the leeward side of the island, where the house and dock were located, the waves were not too large, but still the boat struggled to climb over them and wallowed from crest to crest. He glanced over his shoulder toward the engine. The water that had been around his feet had moved to the back and splashed against the transom. A steady stream came from the bilge pump outlet. He thought about scooping more with the bucket but chose to ignore it. The pump would take care of it. Eventually. The calm at the center of the storm wouldn't last long. He had to make the most of it while he could.

Minutes later, he made the end of the island. As he rounded the point and headed west, the boat plunged headlong into six-foot waves. The first one crashed over the bow of the boat, sending spray into the air and drenching Dibber to the bone. He tossed back his head and laughed out loud as he followed the shore along the seaward side. To the right, the hulking remains of mangled beach houses lurked in the shadows. What remained of their frames stood just above the water that flooded most of the island. He slowed the engine and surveyed the damage.

A Category Three hurricane, the storm had pushed a wall of water ahead of it, sending the Gulf across the beach and running the surf all the way to Bienville Boulevard. Many of the beach houses were gone, swept away as the storm blew ashore. Most of the ones that remained were severely damaged. Most, but not all, and Dibber focused his attention on a small frame house that stood on pilings a few feet above the water. It was damaged but mostly intact. Exactly the kind of place he was looking for.

He pointed the boat in that direction and slowed the engine to an idle. Waves coming from behind carried the boat forward, and he used the engine to keep it pointed in the right direction. Pilings that supported the house loomed ahead, coming closer and closer. Dibber watched patiently. Coaxing the boat this way and that. Keeping it pointed for the house.

Right before the boat would have slammed into the pilings, Dibber threw the engine into reverse and pushed the throttle to full power. The engine screamed as the prop churned the water, dug in against the waves, fought with all its power, and at the last moment overcame the momentum of the waves, bringing the boat to a full stop. Dibber slowed the engine, knocked it out of gear, and the boat drifted beneath the house. He ducked to avoid banging his head on the floor joists that passed above him.

From a compartment beneath the steering wheel, he took out a spotlight and flipped it on, confident that no one would notice the glare, or care if they did. With his free hand, he grasped one of the floor joists to steady the boat. "Water must be up seven ... eight feet," he observed. "Not quite as high as they predicted."

In the glare of the light, he saw boards and bits of debris sloshing in the chocolate brown water around the boat. A jet ski bobbed a few feet away. He worked the boat in that direction, grabbed the jet ski, and tied it to the stern with a heavy rope.

At the far corner of the house was a storage closet. The door flopped back and forth with the waves. He pushed the boat over to it and held open the door. Inside he found half a dozen fishing rods, the tops poking above the water. He pulled the first one up and found a deep-sea fishing reel attached to the other end. With a freshwater bath and a little oil it would be good as new. He placed the rod and reel in a rack along the gunnels of the boat. He took the others from the closet and put them in the boat, along with a tackle box from a shelf above the water.

When he finished with the closet, he moved the boat from underneath the house to a stairway on the landward side. He tied the bow to the railing by the steps that led up from the driveway and took a large flashlight from beneath a seat along one side of the boat. Steadying himself against the gunnel railing, he put one foot on the bottom rung and tested it to make sure the steps would hold his weight. Satisfied it wouldn't give way, he shifted his weight to it and swung free of the boat.

The steps led up to a deck at the back door of the house. When he reached the top, Dibber leaned his weight against the door and pushed. It didn't budge. He tried again, but it still didn't open. Then he stepped back and gave it a hard kick. The bolt of the lock tore through the facing as the door flew open and crashed against the wall on the inside. Dibber stepped inside and found himself standing in the kitchen.

To the right was a refrigerator and sink. Farther around was a stove. A countertop separated the kitchen from the living room. Across the living room, a large sliding glass door offered a view of the beach. A sofa sat facing the view with chairs on either end. Between the sofa and the counter, a hallway opened through the center of the house. Dibber moved around the end of the countertop and started up the hall. A few feet from the living room he came to a bedroom on the left. He leaned through the doorway and glanced inside.

In the center of the room was a bare bed frame. Across from it was a dresser. There was a closet in the corner. He moved around the bed frame and opened the closet door. The closet was empty. He stepped back to the dresser and opened the top drawer. There was nothing inside it, either.

At the end of the hall was a second bedroom. Along the wall by the door was a dresser. A bed sat to the right. Blankets and sheets on the bed were wadded and tossed in a mess. On the dresser top was a wooden box. Next to it was a blue vase. Scattered around them were bits of paper, loose change, and pieces of this and that deposited there over time. He raked through it with his finger, picking up loose change as he moved things around. With the flick of a wrist, he sent a can of spray deodorant tumbling to the floor. Behind it he found a class ring. He picked it up and held it between his fingers. In the glare of the flashlight he could see the inscription. "Class of 1985." The ring was heavy. Maybe gold. He bounced it in the palm of his hand, then deposited it in his pocket.

In the corner of the room beyond the dresser was a closet. The door was ajar and inside he could see clothes hanging from a bar. Holding the light with one hand, he raked the clothes aside with the other. Behind them he found an automatic shotgun propped against the wall. He picked it up and held it under the light. Convinced it was in good shape, he tossed it on the bed behind him, then checked the closet shelf.

A shoe box sat to one side. He took it down and knocked the top off with the flashlight. In it were pictures and a handful of seashells. He dropped the box on the floor and ran his hand over the shelf. A pair of boots. A folded sweatshirt. Behind the shirt was a cigar box. He took it down and raised the lid. Inside was a one-inch stack of twenty-dollar bills bound with a rubber band. "Bingo," Dibber exclaimed. "What have we here?" He took a seat on the bed and took the money from the box, fanned through it with his thumb, then shoved it in his pants pocket.

Beneath the money were dozens and dozens of money order receipts. The ones on top were made payable to Southern Nursery Supply, but near the bottom he found one that caught his eye. He took it from the box for a closer look.

The money order had been purchased at the Snack In A Bag, a convenience store on Halls Mill Road in Mobile. Whoever filled it out had included the name of the person who bought it in the lower left corner. As his lips whispered the name, his heart sank. He knew the …

Bam! A noise came from the front of the house and Dibber jumped at the sound of it.

"The boat," he said to himself. "That's all."

He glanced out the window and noticed the stars were gone from the sky. The wind was picking up again. The eye of the storm was moving past. In a few minutes the back half would hit, and it would be the worst part. He closed the box and slipped it inside his shirt. As he reached for the shotgun that lay beside him, the beam of the flashlight swept across the bed. Two eyes peered at him from the tangled sheets.

Dibber gasped. Was someone there? Had they been there all this time? Did they see him? What would he …. Then he noticed the eyes were open wide. And the mouth was open in a look of terror. Dibber caught his breath.

Bam! The boat banged against the steps once more. Dibber bolted for the door.

CHAPTER 1

Mike Connolly stood before the judge's bench, a little to one side. Watching. Waiting. At the age of fifty-five, he thought he had seen all there was to see of life. Drug dealers. Prostitutes. Pimps. Thieves. As an attorney, he had defended all kinds and heard stories no one would ever believe. Now he was witnessing something he never thought he would see. Hollis Toombs. Getting married.

Hollis was a different sort. As an enlisted man in the army, he survived three tours in Vietnam. After discharge, he came home to find his uncle had died and left him a shack in the swamp off Fowl River along with a few hundred acres of marsh. The bequest was quite unexpected and rankled several of Hollis' cousins, who thought they should have it. The cousins contested the uncle's will, which is how Hollis and Connolly came to be acquainted. Connolly defended Hollis' claim to the property and after they were successful, Hollis became his investigator.

That morning, though, Hollis stood in the courtroom a few feet to Connolly's left, locked arm-in-arm with Victoria Verchinko, a petite, dark-haired woman with large brown eyes and beautiful olive skin. Hollis gazed at her with a look that seemed both intense and soft. Happy. Almost giddy. She in a blue silk dress, he in a gray suit. Hollis in a suit. Connolly smiled. He had never seen Hollis cleaned up before.

Mrs. Gordon stood behind them. Seventy-five now, she still beat Connolly to the office every morning and somehow managed to keep him organized and out of trouble. Next to her was Barbara. Connolly glanced at her. It had been six years since they divorced. Six years. It hardly seemed like a moment. It didn't even seem like they were divorced at all. Not now, anyway. Just a bad fight and a long, slow make-up.

On the far side of them was Raisa. All the way from Croatia … or Bosnia … sometimes he couldn't remember which. But he remembered the first time he saw her, living with Victoria and the others in a makeshift apartment in that warehouse down by the river. Penned like animals. Taken out each morning. Forced to sell themselves every day. Well, at least that wouldn't happen anymore. Now, all but Victoria and Raisa had been resettled with new identities and new lives in new places.

Raisa glanced over at him, a sad look in her eye. He knew what she was thinking. What she was hoping. But it was the one thing he couldn't give her.

A door opened behind the bench and Judge Bolin appeared. Barbara caught Connolly's eye and waved him over with a snap of her finger. He moved closer and stood beside her. "Act interested," she whispered.

"I am interested," he mumbled beneath his breath. "But I know a bookie on Dauphin Street who's taking bets on how long this will last."

"Hush." She punched his thigh with her fist and clinched her teeth, trying not to laugh.

Judge Bolin took a seat at the bench. "Okay," he began. "I see we have a wedding today."

Victoria grinned nervously and looked away. Hollis smiled proudly. "Yes, Your Honor."

Bolin glanced at the marriage license, then looked up and noticed Connolly. "Mike, good to see you. Haven't seen you in my courtroom in quite a while."

"No, Your Honor," Connolly replied. "I don't get to probate

court much anymore."

Bolin nodded. "Are you still living in Lois Crump's guesthouse?"

"Yes, Your Honor."

"Did y'all have much damage from the hurricane?"

"A few trees down. A little roof damage. That's about it."

"You got off easy." Bolin glanced at the license again, then looked to Hollis once more. "You're Hollis Toombs?"

"Yes, Your Honor."

Bolin looked to Victoria. "And you are Victoria Ver...."

"Verchinko," she said, helping with the name.

"Yes. Verchinko. And the two of you want to get married." Hollis and Victoria nodded in reply. Bolin cleared his throat. "Very well. Victoria, will you have Hollis to be your husband?"

"Yes."

"And Hollis, will you have Victoria to be your wife?"

"Yes."

Bolin smiled. "Very good. Then by the power vested in me by the State of Alabama, I pronounce that you are husband and wife." He nodded to Hollis. "You may kiss your bride."

Hollis kissed Victoria lightly on the lips. Mrs. Gordon and Barbara gave her a hug.

Connolly shook Hollis' hand. "Congratulations."

"Thanks," Hollis replied. "You need to sign the license."

"Oh. Yeah. Sure." Connolly moved between the women to the judge's bench. The license lay in front of Judge Bolin. He took a pen from the pocket of his jacket and scrawled his signature across the document. Barbara slipped in beside him. He handed her the pen. She signed her name below his. Judge Bolin reached across from the bench and shook Hollis' hand. "I wish you much success in your marriage."

"Thank you, Your Honor."

Victoria flashed him a smile. Bolin gathered the papers and disappeared through the door behind the bench. Connolly checked his watch, then said to Raisa, "We better get you to the airport. You have a plane to catch."

"Yes," she said. "I suppose I do."

Connolly tried to sound hopeful. "In a few hours, you'll be back home in Bosnia."

She rolled her eyes. "Ah, yes. Lovely Bosnia. Land of opportunity at the pickle factory."

"But it's home."

"This should be my home."

Barbara touched Connolly on the elbow. She smiled at Raisa. "We better get going."

Connolly came alongside Hollis. "Okay," he said. "You're on your own for now."

Hollis grinned. "We'll be back in a few days. See if you can stay out of trouble 'til then."

Connolly placed one hand on Hollis' shoulder. He pressed the other against Hollis' palm. In the exchange, Connolly slipped him a handful of cash. Hollis leaned closer and whispered. "Thanks."

Connolly patted him on the back. "Have a good time on the trip."

Barbara and Raisa said goodbye to Victoria. Connolly moved beside her and kissed her on the cheek. Tears filled Victoria's eyes. "I don't know what to say."

"Don't worry." Connolly gave her a hug. "After two weeks alone with Hollis, you'll have plenty to say." She grinned. Everyone chuckled. Connolly stepped aside and said his goodbyes to Mrs. Gordon. By then, Barbara and Raisa were down the aisle and headed toward the door. He followed them out and gave Hollis a final wave as he stepped outside to the lobby.

CHAPTER 2

Connolly escorted Barbara and Raisa from the courthouse and down the steps to the street. Heat and humidity engulfed them as they walked up the sidewalk to Connolly's car, a blue 1959 Chrysler Imperial parked at the curb in the next block. He opened the front passenger door for Barbara, then held the rear door for Raisa.

From the courthouse downtown they drove west through the urban clutter on Airline Highway and made their way toward the airport. Raisa gazed out the window as they passed the purple building that had once housed the tanning salon where she and the others had been forced to work. "What will they do with the building now?" she asked.

Connolly glanced at her in the mirror. "The bank sold it to an investment group from Jackson. I think they're going to convert it into a restaurant."

Raisa shook her head. "They should burn it to the ground. What about the warehouse?"

"I don't know. They'll probably find a tenant for it, eventually."

Raisa sighed and rested her head against the back of the seat.

Twenty minutes later, they reached the airport. Connolly took Raisa's suitcase from the trunk of the car and carried it to the ticket counter. He stood with her while the ticket agent checked her in, then he and Barbara walked with her as far as the security checkpoint at the entrance to the concourse. There, Raisa faced him. "Well, I guess this is goodbye for good."

Connolly was sad to see her leave but knew there was no other choice. "I hope you have a safe trip," he said. It was a silly thing to say. She could do nothing for her own safety now and neither could he. At least, not until she reached Bosnia.

Tears ran down Raisa's cheeks. "Thank you for everything," she whispered.

Connolly put an arm around her and pulled her close. She rested her head on his shoulder. He spoke to her in a quiet voice. "Everything will be alright. Someone from the State Department will meet your plane and take you to the hotel. An FBI agent will go with you when you speak to the Bosnian authorities. They will do everything possible to keep you safe."

She pulled away and wiped her eyes. "I think it is futile." Connolly offered her his handkerchief. She used it to wipe her nose. "But someone has to speak up." She looked him squarely in the eye. "At least Victoria will have a good life."

"Yes." Connolly nodded. "She will. And the others, too." He squeezed her shoulder. "You have the phone card?" She nodded. "Do you remember how to use it?" he asked.

She nodded again. "Yes. I remember."

"If something happens, you call me."

She looked at him and forced a smile. "I will."

He guided her toward the security officer. "You better get going. Your plane is already boarding."

Suddenly, Raisa leaned toward him and before he could react, she kissed him full on the lips. Then, just as suddenly, she pulled away and stepped through the checkpoint. Connolly could only watch.

Barbara came to his side. "What was that all about?"

"She's scared." He stared after Raisa and wiped her lipstick from his lips.

Past the checkpoint, Raisa glanced back at them one last time and gave a forlorn wave. They waved and watched as she disappeared around the corner.

When she was gone Connolly offered Barbara his arm. She took his elbow and they started toward the door. As they stepped outside, Connolly's cell phone rang. He took it from his pocket and checked to see who called.

"Mrs. Gordon," he grumbled. He pressed a button and answered the call. "Yeah."

"Carl Landry is here."

"Where?"

"At the office."

"Did he have an appointment? I don't remember having anyone this afternoon."

"Said it's an emergency. He says he knows you."

"What kind of emergency?"

"His nephew was arrested yesterday."

"Check my calendar and give him an appointment sometime tomorrow. I can't come down there now."

Connolly switched off the phone and shoved it in his pocket. He and Barbara walked to the Chrysler. As he opened the door for her, the cell phone rang again. Barbara took a seat in the car. The call was from Mrs. Gordon. "What is it now?" he asked.

"He says he doesn't want to see you tomorrow. He needs to see you now."

Connolly sighed. "Alright. I'll be down there after lunch." He switched off the phone and glanced at Barbara. "Sorry about that." He closed the door and moved around the car to the driver's side. Barbara glanced over at him. "Trouble at the office?"

"Carl Landry."

"Isn't he the guy who came to you that time about his nephew? The one they caught stealing a highway sign from the interstate?"

"That's him." Connolly grinned. "Caught him cutting down the stop sign at the end of the Broad Street exit ramp."

Barbara frowned. "I've always wondered about that. What was he going to do with the stop sign?"

The grin on Connolly's face grew wider. "It wasn't the stop sign he wanted. It was the pole."

"The pole?"

Connolly started the car and backed it from the parking space. "Wanted it for an exhaust pipe on his pickup truck."

Barbara laughed. "Would that really work?"

"He said they worked great. Had one on the left side already. Needed one for the right. That's when they caught him."

Barbara shook her head. "Whatever happened to that boy?"

Connolly put the car in gear and started toward the exit. "He was arrested yesterday."

"What's the charge?"

"I don't know, but I think I'm about to find out."

"Now?"

"Right after we go to lunch."

She looked over at him. "We're going to lunch?"

"Aren't you hungry?"

"Yes. I am. But it would be nice if you asked, first."

"Sorry," he said. "Would you have lunch with me?"

She grinned. "I would be delighted."

CHAPTER 3

After lunch, Connolly took Barbara home to her house on Ann Street, then drove downtown. His office was located in the Warren Building, a 1920s style high-rise on Dauphin Street across from Bienville Square. It was after one when he arrived. He parked the Chrysler up the street near the Port City Diner and walked to the lobby entrance.

Inside the building, he crossed the lobby to the elevator and pressed the button for the third floor. As the doors closed, he leaned against the back wall of the elevator and thought of Raisa. Her body pressed against him as he held her for one last goodbye. The smooth skin of her cheeks against his. The look in those brown eyes. A sense of sadness came over him and he wondered if he'd done the right thing by sending her away. She would have been glad to stay. Glad to....

A bell sounded and the doors opened on the third floor. Connolly stepped out and made his way down the corridor to the office. Mrs. Gordon was seated at her desk when he entered. She pointed down the hall. "He's waiting," she droned.

Connolly glanced at his watch. "I hope this doesn't take long."

Mrs. Gordon brightened. "Plans?"

"I planned on not being here right now."

"Well get moving and you can still get to Barbara's in time for dinner."

Connolly gave her a look to say she was meddling. Mrs. Gordon ignored him. "Go on." She waved him past her desk. A little way down the hall he could see Carl Landry sitting in a chair in front of the desk.

Carl was a short man, about five and a half feet tall, and though he had a slight build his body formed a perfect V with broad shoulders and a narrow waist. Lean and hard, he looked like a construction worker, or a boxer, or one of those guys on a crew who moved heavy machinery by hand. He looked like anything but what he was, the owner of a dozen low-end, discount grocery stores. He stood as Connolly entered the office. "Mike. It's good to see you." They shook hands. Carl had a nervous smile. "Thank you for seeing me on short notice."

"No problem," Connolly replied. He took off his jacket and hung it on the coat rack by the door, then moved behind the desk and took a seat. "What's this all about?"

Carl sat in the chair and propped an arm on the armrest. "Dibber's been arrested," he said.

"What for?"

Carl raised his eyebrows. "Capital murder."

Connolly frowned. "Murder?"

"Yeah."

"What happened?"

Carl shrugged. "I don't know, for sure. He's been living down at our place on Dauphin Island for the last few months. Had a good job on a construction crew up in Virginia but he got in a fight. Hit the foreman a couple of times." He sighed. "That was the end of that."

"So, he's working for you now?"

"No." Carl shook his head. "I tried that once before. He ran off half the customers." A wisp of a smile crossed his face. "And that's pretty tough to do in my stores. I got a lot of customers who don't have anywhere else to go."

Connolly nodded. "So, how did he get charged with murder?"

"They say he broke into a house on the Island during the hurricane. Looting, I guess. Only someone was inside. They say Dibber shot him. Something about murder during a robbery making it a capital charge."

Connolly nodded again, but his face quickly clouded in a question. "They think he was in someone's house during a hurricane?"

"Yeah."

"Sounds a little strange."

"Not really," Carl replied. "Wouldn't be the first time that's happened."

"He's done this before?"

"Not Dibber." Carl paused a moment as if giving his answer a second thought. "At least, I don't think so. I meant looters. Wouldn't be the first time somebody tried to steal something in a hurricane. Those people you hear about riding out storms on Dauphin Island, or in Coden, or Grand Bay ... they aren't crazy like the news reports make it seem. They got people down there who come around right after the storm and pick through the houses. Go right in and take whatever they want before anyone can get back to see about their stuff. Sometimes they don't even wait for the storm to end. I caught a guy trying to get into my house down there one time."

Connolly shook his head. "So, that's what they think Dibber was doing?"

Carl shrugged again. "I guess."

"Who do they say he killed?"

"They don't know yet. They haven't been able to identify him."

Carl reached into his pocket and took out an envelope. "Look, I know you don't come cheap, but maybe this will get you started. Dibber ... he doesn't have any money and he's one big aggravation. But he's my sister's boy and I have an obligation to look after him." He laid the envelope on the desk. "You'll take his case?"

Connolly glanced at the envelope. Through the fold of the flap he could see it was stuffed with hundred-dollar bills. "Sure," he said. "I'll take his case."

"Good." Carl stood. "You're a busy man. I won't take any more of your time. Dibber's down at the jail. He can give you all the details. He tried to tell me about it, but I told him he should wait and speak to an attorney and not talk about it to anybody."

Connolly stood. "That's pretty good advice."

"Yeah, well, I've seen how they work down there. You never know who's listening." Carl gave him a sober look. "Call me after you talk to him. Let me know what the fee is. I'll find a way to take care of it."

Connolly came from behind the desk and scooped up the envelope as he followed Carl out. They walked up the hall in silence. When they reached Mrs. Gordon's desk, Connolly moved ahead and opened the door to the corridor. Carl paused and looked Connolly in the eye. "Dibber's done a lot of things in his life, but he isn't a murderer."

Connolly nodded as if to agree. "We'll get to the bottom of it," he assured.

Carl stepped outside to the corridor and walked toward the elevators. Connolly closed the door behind him and handed Mrs. Gordon the envelope of cash. "Take care of this," he said. She took it from him, pulled the flap open with her finger, and glanced inside. Her eyebrows lifted. "Carl Landry is a nice guy."

"Yes, he is." Connolly walked up the hall to his office and retrieved his jacket from the rack by the door, then came back toward Mrs. Gordon. "But I'm not so sure about Dibber," he offered.

Mrs. Gordon set the envelope aside and took out the receipt book. "Dibber," she chortled. "How'd he get a name like that?" She opened the receipt book and began writing a receipt.

Connolly slipped on his jacket. "I'll ask him."

"You're going to see him now?"

"Yes." Connolly straightened the jacket across his shoulders. "Why?"

"I thought you and Barbara were going to dinner."

"Stop worrying about that."

"I'm not worrying. I just think the two of you—"

"Myrtice," Connolly interrupted.

Her eyes narrowed in a scowl. "That's the second time you've called me that."

Connolly smiled playfully. "Your mother gave you that name." He opened the door. "You should wear it like a badge of honor."

With the flick of her wrist Mrs. Gordon sent the pen in her hand sailing toward him. He ducked out the door as the pen flew past his ear and struck the wall across the corridor. He laughed and closed the door behind him.

CHAPTER 4

From the office, Connolly drove across town to the county jail. Ten stories high, it stood near the end of Water Street across from the banana wharfs that lined the Mobile River. Built of dark brown brick, it had a hulking, formidable appearance. Steel bars, rusted from the salt air that drifted in from the bay, covered the windows and added to the building's imposing character. Built in the 1950s and never remodeled, it was dirty, worn, and cramped.

The door from outside opened to a lobby. Worn and tattered chairs lined the wall. Opposite the entrance was a desk. Beyond it was a metal detector and the door to the booking area. The elevator to the upper floors was behind all that.

A guard sat at the desk reading a paperback novel. She looked up as Connolly approached. "May I help you?"

"I'm here to see a prisoner."

"Name?"

"Landry. Dibber Landry."

The guard checked a list of prisoners. "Don't have any Dibber." She glanced at the list once more. "Got a Dilbert." She looked up. "Is that him?"

"Yes," Connolly replied. "I'm sure it is."

She pointed to a basket on the desk. "Empty your pockets and step through the metal detector."

Connolly put his car keys and cell phone in the basket, then walked through the detector. The guard checked the scan, then handed him his keys and shouted in a shrill voice, "Visitor coming in!" The door to the booking room opened automatically and Connolly stepped through, then took the elevator to the eighth floor. Dibber was waiting for him in the interview room.

Like his uncle, Dibber was short with broad shoulders, but he was much heavier, with a thick neck, a muscular chest, and a stomach that spilled over the waistband of his pants. His hair was long and stringy, hanging almost to his shoulders. His face was scruffy and unshaven. He was standing in the center of the room as Connolly entered. They shook hands, then moved to a table on the far side of the room.

"Uncle Carl talked to you?" Dibber asked.

"Yes."

The table was made of stainless steel with benches that were bolted to the floor. Connolly laid a yellow legal pad on the table and took a pen from the pocket of his jacket. "They have charged you with capital murder."

"They're crazy," Dibber snorted. "I ain't never killed nobody in my life."

"Why don't you start at the beginning and tell me what happened."

"Everything?"

"Yes," Connolly said. "Everything. The advice I give you is based on what you tell me. So make sure you tell me everything. It will come out one way or the other anyway and it's better if I find out now rather than on the witness stand in court."

"Okay." Dibber nodded. "Well, I guess it begins with the storm."

"The storm?"

"Yeah. The hurricane." Dibber leaned away from the table and rested his back against the wall. "I was down on the island, Dauphin Island. I live in a house down there. Belongs to Uncle Carl. Used to be my grandparents' house. They died. He got it." Dibber paused. Connolly jotted down a note on the pad and nodded for him to continue.

"I was down there when the storm hit. Eye passed right over the house. When it went over, I got in my boat and rode around to the south side to see what I could find. Uncle Carl's house is on the north side. Faces toward Heron Bay. I rode around to the south side, the Gulf side. Lot of beach houses around there. Storm was pretty bad. Worse than they expected. I figured there'd be a lot of stuff floating around out there. So, I went to see what I could find."

"You were looting."

Dibber frowned. "I ain't no looter." His breath escaped in a long, heavy sigh. "Storm like that comes in, stuff's just floatin' around all over the place. All you got to do is ride along and pick it up. Ain't no way of telling whose it is. People that owned it don't even know. Half the time, nobody even comes for it. I got a friend lives in Bayou La Batre, found a boat after the last storm before this one. Nobody ever claimed it. He peeled the numbers off the side, got new ones, been using it ever since."

Connolly nodded. "You went around to the south side of the island to see what you could find."

Dibber glared at him. "I ain't no murderer and I ain't no looter, neither." He took a deep breath and continued. "I come around the east end. Came up the beach a little way. First couple of houses were gone. Nothing but pilings sticking out of the water. Water was way up past the road. About three or four houses up, I come to one that was still there. It was in bad shape, but it was still pretty much in one piece. Water was underneath it. I floated the boat under the house. Found a little bit of stuff."

"You went inside?"

"Yeah. I found a little stuff underneath it. A jet ski came drifting by. I got it. Then, I went inside to look around."

"What did you find?"

"Not much, really. A shotgun in the closet. A few trinkets. Then I seen that fellow on the bed."

"Someone was in the bed?"

Dibber shook his head. "Not in it. On it. Sort of rolled up in the sheets. Eyes staring at me." He chuckled. "Spooky. Especially after I seen the blood."

"Blood?"

"Yeah. Looked to me like the mattress was soaked."

"What did you do then?"

"I started to leave, then I seen he had on a nice watch."

"You took his watch?"

Dibber gave a nervous smile. "He was already dead. Looked to me like he'd been dead a while." He rested his hands on the bench. "I mean, if I didn't get it somebody else would."

"You're sure he wasn't alive?"

"That man was stone cold dead," Dibber insisted. "Maybe even a little stiff. Most of the blood was dried."

"Then what happened?"

"I took the watch and the other stuff and high-tailed it out of there. Back half of the storm was coming in. Waves was starting to kick up. I got back to the boat and went straight back to the house. My house. Carl's house where I was staying."

"Which way did you go?"

"Same way I come. Back around the east end. Too rough to go on around the other way. By then there was white caps three foot high in the road."

"In the road?"

"Yeah. Water was five foot deep all the way to the road."

"What did you do with the things you took?"

Dibber shot a look across the table. "Found."

Connolly glanced up from his notepad. "Excuse me?"

"The things I found. I didn't take nothing. I found it."

"Alright."

"I ain't no looter."

"Okay," Connolly replied. "What did you do with the things you found?"

"Took most of the jewelry to a guy in Chickasaw."

Connolly was puzzled. "Jewelry? You called it trinkets before."

"There was some in the bedroom. You know, the watch, stuff

like that."

"Who did you take it to?"

"A guy I know."

"What's his name?"

Dibber shifted positions on the bench. "I'd rather not say."

Connolly folded the pages of his notepad back in place and closed his pen. "Then I'd rather not represent you." He moved to stand.

Dibber gestured for him to stop. "Wait. It ain't that big a deal. I'll tell you." Connolly paused. Dibber waved him toward the table. "Sit down. I'll tell you."

Connolly stared at him. "I'm waiting."

"Lutie Shaw." Dibber sighed. "His name is Lutie Shaw."

Connolly wasn't sure Dibber was being honest, but the irony of the name struck him as humorous. "Lutie?" He chuckled as he dropped onto the bench. "You took this stolen loot to some guy named Lutie?"

Dibber's face was red. "That's what they call him. I don't know his real name. And like I told you, it wasn't stolen. I ain't no thief."

Connolly was still grinning. "Lutie?"

"I think he pronounces it Loo-Tay now."

"Okay." Connolly opened his notepad and took the pen from his pocket. "You took some of the stuff to Chickasaw."

"Yeah," Dibber said. "But he didn't want the jet ski. I held on to it for a week or two and took it to a pawn shop in Saraland."

"They didn't have a problem taking it?"

"No. I'd cleaned it up by then."

"Cleaned it up?"

"Scrubbed off the license numbers. Waxed it. Made it look good as new. I could have got fifteen hundred for it on the street, but I didn't want to worry with it."

"Which pawn shop?"

"Golden Nugget."

"What did he give you for it?"

"Three fifty."

"Alright," Connolly said. "You pawned the stuff. What happened after that?"

"Nothing, at first. Then the other morning I was asleep at the house—"

"What day?"

"Day before yesterday. Cops came in, rolled me out of bed. Put me in cuffs and hauled me down here."

"Did they tell you what you were charged with?"

"Not when they arrested me." Dibber seemed to stop and think. "I can't remember, actually. Might have. They brought me in, put me up here, came back later and took me downstairs. It was late that night after they brought me in. A judge was there. Told me I was charged with capital murder. Said I killed some guy in a house on Dauphin Island."

"What did you say?"

"I said I ain't never killed nobody in my life."

"Has anyone try to question you?"

"Yeah. When they brought me in, they put me in a room down-stairs where they fingerprint you. Came in with a tape recorder. But I told them I didn't have nothing to say about nothing. One of them started to ask me about the jet ski and I told him I was waiting on my lawyer. They left me alone after that."

Connolly glanced over his notes, then looked up at Dibber. "Is that it?"

Dibber nodded. "Think I got a chance?"

"There's always hope." Connolly stood.

Dibber seemed surprised. "Well, wait a minute. What do we do next?"

"I'll talk to the DA's office. See what they have. Check on some details about what you've told me. Maybe a few more things, depending on what I find from them. I'll get back to you in a day or two."

Dibber stood and followed Connolly toward the door. "How long am I gonna be in here?"

"Have they set a bond for you?"

"No." Dibber shook his head. "Told me I wasn't gonna get no

bond."

"Then you'll be in here until your trial, if the case goes that far."

"How long will that be?"

"It'll take about a year to get your case to trial."

Dibber frowned. "I'll be in here a year?"

"If your case goes to trial."

Dibber shook his head. "That ain't right."

They were in front of the door by then. Connolly rapped on it to get the guard's attention, then glanced back at Dibber. "Don't talk to anyone about this except me. You understand?" Dibber nodded. "And don't get discouraged," Connolly added. "We'll know a little more about what you're facing after I talk to the DA."

Dibber nodded again. The guard opened the door. Connolly stepped into the hall and started toward the elevator. Dibber followed the guard toward the cell block.

CHAPTER 5

The afternoon was gone by the time Connolly drove away from the jail. Evening was fast approaching. In the distance beyond the buildings the sun was sinking below the horizon, setting the blue sky ablaze with streaks of purple, orange, and red. For a moment he considered going to the guesthouse, having an early dinner—surely there was something in the refrigerator he could eat. Maybe get to bed early for a change. He'd had a long and—

Suddenly, he remembered Barbara. Their plans for dinner. They had worked hard to get past being divorced and angry. That led to the divorced but civil stage. And now they'd made it to the standing-dinner-date phase. No need to call ahead. Just show up and eat together. It had been awkward at first. Did he kiss her good night? They hadn't worked all of that out but eating dinner with her had become the highlight of his day. His week. His life.

"Damn," he whispered. "How could I forget that?" He made his way to Government Street and drove toward midtown.

A few minutes later, Connolly brought the car to a stop at the curb in front of Barbara's house on Ann Street. Their house until the divorce, it was a two-story white frame with dormer windows on the second floor. A porch ran across the front and down the side next to the driveway. The first time he saw it he knew it was home. But that was many memories ago. Now, the house seemed like a trap. A black hole of memories waiting to suck him down and down and down into the despondent nothingness of regret. He wanted none of it.

When the car came to a stop, Connolly switched off the engine, then opened the door and climbed from the seat. He paused long enough to slip on his jacket, then started up the sidewalk toward the front steps. On the porch he rang the doorbell and waited.

In a moment, the door opened, and Barbara appeared. She smiled at him. "Wasn't sure you'd make it." He smiled back at her. "It wasn't that important." She held the door for him. "Come on in and have a seat. I'm not quite ready."

Connolly hesitated. Barbara looked puzzled. "What's the matter?"

"I … ahh."

"Are you alright? Has something happened?"

"Nah." He shook his head. "I'll wait out here."

"Out here." She frowned. "On the porch?"

"Yeah."

"Don't be ridiculous. You can sit on the sofa."

He shook his head again. "I … I can't come inside."

She had a quizzical expression. "What do you mean? You've been in this house thousands of times. Maybe millions. Come in. It won't take me long. You can sit in the living room."

Connolly backed away. "I'll wait for you out here." He retreated to the edge of the porch and sat with his feet resting on the front steps. Behind him, he heard the door close and from inside, the sound of footsteps as Barbara went upstairs.

He knew it was strange, acting that way about the house. He loved the house. Loved Barbara, too. But inside—the look, the feel, the smell—right then, it felt … like a trap. Lethal. Deadly. Too many memories. Most of them, the recent ones, little more than reminders of how much he'd failed. How much he'd lost. How much he'd missed.

Alone on the porch, with only his thoughts for company, Connolly propped an elbow on his knee, rested his chin in his hand, and stared across the front yard. The house had been a wonderful place to settle as a couple. Raise their daughter. Meet the neighbors. Grill out in the back yard. Those were the days. The good days. Not all the memories were bad.

As he sat there, staring blankly ahead, waiting, the light changed, and it was the middle of the day. Rachel appeared as a young girl rolling a ball across the lawn. The ball was almost as big as she, her head just high enough to see over it. Her chin bumping against the top with every step. Pushing. Running. Giggling. "Daddy. Daddy. You see me, Daddy?" A smile crept over his face. Then tears filled his eyes. "I see you," he whispered. "I see you."

Something soft brushed against his cheek. A fragrance filled the air. Sweet. Clean. Nice. And the ball faded from view. The steps reappeared beneath his feet and Barbara was beside him. Smiling. "I'm ready now," she said.

He stood and took her hand. "You look nice."

"Thank you."

At the sidewalk, she placed her arm in his and glanced over at him. "Are you alright?"

"Yes," he replied. "I'm fine."

"What were you saying?"

"When?"

"Just now. When I came out? You were saying something. What was it?"

"Nothing," he replied.

"It seemed like you said, 'I see you.'"

Tears filled his eyes once more. "Yeah."

She squeezed his arm. "Memories again?"

"Always."

They reached the car and he opened the door for her, then came around to the driver's side and got in behind the steering wheel. "Where are we going?" she asked.

He started the car. "How about The Silver King?"

"Great," she said. He knew she would like the choice.

The Silver King was a restaurant located on the causeway at the northern end of Mobile Bay, about a ten-minute drive from Barbara's house. Connolly brought the car to a stop near the valet attendant's stand. Someone opened the door for Barbara. Connolly stepped out and caught the valet's eye. "Take it easy with my car."

"Yes, sir." The valet slipped in behind the steering wheel. "I'll treat her just like she was my own." Connolly rolled his eyes. "That's what I was afraid of." He watched as the car moved away. Barbara came to his side. "That car is like a girlfriend for you."

"We've been a lot of places together."

"I remember the day you got it."

Connolly smiled. "Remember that first drive?"

"How could I forget?" She took his arm and they started toward the restaurant door. "You and me in front. Rachel in back."

Connolly nodded. "And she spilled ice cream everywhere." They both laughed.

The restaurant had two dining rooms. The one upstairs was Barbara's favorite and the reason she enjoyed coming there. Its large windows afforded a stunning view of the bay, the Mobile skyline, and the bluffs along the eastern shore. They made their way in that direction but when they arrived at the top of the stairs, they found the room was packed and Connolly wished he'd made a reservation.

The maître d' approached. "How many tonight, sir?" He seemed to recognize Connolly, but Connolly had no idea why. "Two," he said. "How long is the wait? It looks like you're full."

"Busy night. Convention in town. Summertime."

Connolly pointed across the room. "Any possibility you could get us by the window?"

The maître d' looked in that direction, then glanced back at them. "Just a minute." He stepped away and disappeared through a door at the back of the dining room. A few minutes later he appeared with two men from the kitchen carrying a table and chairs. They scooted a table of vacationers aside and squeezed the new table in a spot by the window. When it was ready, the maître d' caught Connolly's eye, and waved them over.

After they were seated Barbara gave Connolly a questioning look. "How'd we get a table so fast?"

Connolly had a mischievous grin. "I think the guy up front thinks he knows me."

Barbara smiled at him and shook her head. A waiter appeared. "Could I get you something to drink?"

Connolly looked to Barbara. "Just water," she said.

He looked up at the waiter. "She'll have water. I'll have a cup of hot tea."

"Very good, sir." Barbara glanced across the table at Connolly. "That sounds good." Connolly caught the waiter's eye. "Make that two cups of tea." The waiter nodded and moved away from the table.

Barbara looked over at him. "When did you start drinking hot tea?"

Connolly shrugged. "I don't know. Tonight?" Barbara laughed. Her eyes sparkled. He glanced out the window. "Nice view." The lights of the city glowed against the night sky and reflected off the dark water of the bay.

"And good to be inside," she noted. "Where it's cool and not so muggy." A moment passed, then she said, "So, tell me what's bothering you."

He avoided her gaze. "What do you mean?"

"At the house. Refusing to come inside. What was that all about?"

Connolly stared out the window for a moment. "That place is like a trap for me," he said, finally.

"A trap?"

He nodded. "Like every time I get around Rick."

"Rick?" She seemed perplexed. "What's your brother got to do with the house?"

"Nothing. But he still sees me as a little boy on a bicycle and he keeps bringing up all the stupid things we said and did when we were kids. And the next thing I know, I'm talking and acting like that kid he remembers."

"That's the way people are," she said. "Memories are how we know each other."

"And that's the way that house is for me. I love that house. I liked it the minute the realtor showed it to us. But every time I come over there now, I feel it pulling me back to what I used to be. I see what I used to be. I hear what I used to be. I think about what I used to be." He ran his fingers through his hair. "All these …"

"Memories, Mike," she said, finishing his sentence. "They're just memories."

"No." He shook his head. "They're more than that. I don't even think it's the memories so much. It's more of a feeling. Like there's some kind of … momentum in that place. Pushing me back to where I don't want to go."

Barbara looked hurt. "I didn't realize—"

"It's not you," he said, cutting her off. He reached across the table and took her hand. "It's not you. It's that place."

The waiter appeared with their tea and set it on the table. "Are you ready to order?"

Connolly let go of Barbara's hand and reached for the menu. "Give us a minute, if you don't mind."

"Certainly," The waiter said and moved away.

Barbara picked up a menu, too. "What looks good?" Connolly asked.

"I think I'll have the crab jubilee."

"That does sound good." Connolly glanced across the room and gave the waiter a nod. The waiter came to the table.

"Yes, sir."

After they ordered and the waiter was gone from the table, Barbara picked up their conversation once again. "So, if you're uncomfortable with the house, what else are you uncomfortable about?"

"Living apart from you."

"Well…."

"I'm not asking you to change things," he said quickly. "I understand what that would mean." He looked her in the eye. "But you asked and that's the answer. The house bothers me. At least, it does right now. But you are the most perfect thing in my life. And you always have been. And being away from you bothers me more than anything."

Connolly looked out the window again. They sat in silence. After a while she said, "Did you ever find out why Dibber is named Dibber?"

"Dilbert." Connolly took a sip of tea. "That's his name. When he was young, he couldn't pronounce it and that's how it came out. Dibber."

Barbara grinned. "That makes sense. And it fits." She took a sip of tea. "In a twisted sort of way."

Connolly glanced at his watch with a playful expression. "What do you suppose Hollis and Victoria are doing now?"

"I'd rather not think about that. Where were they going?"

Connolly chuckled. "She wanted to see Disney World."

Barbara's eyes opened wide. "Disney World?"

"She said she'd heard about it all her life. Dreamed of going there as a little girl. That was all Hollis needed to hear."

"How would Hollis Toombs have enough money to take her to Disney World?"

Connolly took another sip of tea. The waiter appeared with their food. Barbara waited until he was gone, then said, "Mike? How did Hollis get the money to go to Disney World?"

Connolly gestured toward her plate. "How does the crab taste?"

"I saw you give him something when we were in the courtroom."

"Hollis is a good guy."

"You two are very different."

"Not so much when you get to know us."

"Why did they get married at the courthouse? Father Scott would have married them."

"I told Hollis that, but they didn't want that."

"Did she feel guilty?"

Connolly nodded. "I think that was part of it."

"She shouldn't."

"No. She shouldn't. We're all just trying to get through life the best way we can."

"Is that what you're doing?"

"It is now."

CHAPTER 6

After dinner Connolly drove Barbara home and walked her to the door. She had a playful look. "Do you want to come inside?"

Connolly felt nervous. "I don't think so."

"Just for a minute?" Connolly shook his head. Barbara's countenance changed. Her shoulders slumped. "Alright."

He leaned forward and kissed her warmly. "I better go," he said, and he moved across the porch to the steps, then waited while she opened the door.

She glanced at him over her shoulder. "Mike." Their eyes met. "I enjoyed dinner."

His face softened. "I did, too," he said.

Connolly made his way down the steps to the sidewalk and out to the Chrysler. As he moved around the rear bumper, he looked across the car toward the house. A light came on in the kitchen. He moved to the driver's door and got inside.

A few minutes later, he arrived at The Pleiades, a four-story mansion built in 1901 by Elijah Huntley, a broker who made a fortune importing bananas from Costa Rica. In its day, the house had been an architectural marvel and a showplace for the city's elite. Now owned by Huntley's great-great-granddaughter, Lois Crump, the house and grounds still evoked wonder and awe but it was not a practical residence. By the time it passed to Lois, she was living in Birmingham and had little time or money for maintenance. To make the place more affordable, she rented out the guesthouse that sat near the rear of the property. Connolly was the latest in a succession of tenants.

He brought the car to a stop at the end of the driveway and got out. Standing there, he glanced up at the night sky. Haze and the glow of city lights obscured most of the stars, but behind the trees on the far side of the garden the moon was rising, full and round with an orange hue. It looked huge and seemed so close he could touch it. He stared at it a moment, enjoying the beauty, then flipped the key ring around to the guesthouse key, unlocked the door, and went inside.

Built as an afterthought at the insistence of Huntley's third wife, the guesthouse was larger than many suburban homes. It had a kitchen, three bedrooms, two marble bathrooms, and a wine cellar. The door from the driveway opened at the end of the house, between the living room on the left and the kitchen on the right. Beyond the kitchen was a dining room and beyond it, a hall that led through the center of the house.

A lamp was on in the living room. It sat on a small table at the end of the sofa next to the wall. The telephone sat next to it and beside that was an answering machine—Connolly still had a landline that he refused to give up. A red light on the machine blinked indicating he had received a voicemail.

Connolly crossed the room to the table and pressed a button on the answering machine. While it replayed his messages, he wandered to the kitchen. The first message was from Mrs. Gordon, reminding him he needed to be in Judge Pearson's court the following morning. When it ended, the machine beeped and began another. In the kitchen, he flipped opened the refrigerator door and took out a bottle of Boylan ginger ale and twisted off the top.

The second message described a free vacation he had won, three nights at any Royal Hotel in the country. It could be his for only a ninety-nine-dollar processing fee. He took a drink from the bottle. The message came to an end and beeped again. Connolly swallowed. The next message began. This one was from Raisa.

"Hello, Mike," she said. The sound of her voice struck deep in his soul. A tingle ran across his shoulder and down his arm. He froze with the bottle of ginger ale still at his lips.

"This is Raisa. I'm in Atlanta. The plane is delayed so they sent us to the restaurant for dinner. They say I will still make the one in New York. I miss you. I'll call you later." The machine beeped and went off.

Connolly took another drink from the bottle, then crossed the room to the answering machine and pressed the button. Raisa's voice played again. Sadness crept over him. Then, worry.

He hadn't wanted her to be alone in the Atlanta airport. Hadn't wanted her there at all. Mrs. Gordon had tried to get her on a direct fight to New York. When that didn't work, they tried to route her another way but there was no other choice. The best they could do was a layover of about an hour. Now, even that had fallen apart. A frown wrinkled his brow. "No telling who will see her there."

He pressed the button on the machine and listened to her voice again. Images of the first time he saw her filled his mind. Her petite frame. Those brown eyes. Standing there in the darkness of that warehouse where she and the others were kept. Forced to—

The message ended for the third time and he reached to press the button again, then hesitated. There was nothing more he could do about her now. He rescued her from the warehouse. Rescued all of them. He and Hollis. And he had kept them in Rick's beach house for as long as he could manage. But the prosecutors needed a witness they could use in court and Raisa wanted to become a US citizen. To make that happen, she had to leave the country and file a claim from home.

Connolly shook his head. "It's a stupid system." He took a seat on the sofa, kicked off his shoes, and propped his feet on the coffee table. "Ridiculous to send someone like her back to a country like that." He took another sip of ginger ale and remembered her again. The first time he put his arm around her. How small she felt. How nimble. How vulnerable. He knew he shouldn't think of her that way, but he was tired of struggling to resist the thoughts.

CHAPTER 7

Throughout the night, Connolly dreamed of Barbara and Raisa. Crazy dreams that made no sense. Dreams that kept him on the verge of being awake. Never quite sound asleep. He rolled out of bed the following morning more tired than the night before. It was after eight when he left the guesthouse. Judge Pearson was halfway through the docket call when Connolly arrived in court. By the time he reached the office he was feeling grouchy and tense.

Mrs. Gordon glanced up as he entered the office. "You look rough," she said. Connolly groaned in response. Mrs. Gordon looked concerned. "Is something wrong?"

"Just tired," he replied.

She handed him a stack of phone messages. He paused long enough to take them from her. "Any of these important?"

"Only to the people who left them. How was Barbara?"

Connolly started up the hall toward his office. "She's fine."

Mrs. Gordon called to him once more. "Are you sure you're alright?"

"I'm fine," he said as he reached the door to his office. "We're fine. Everything's fine. We had a wonderful time last night. Just had a tough time getting to sleep."

"How did she sleep?"

Connolly scowled. "It wasn't that kind of evening."

Mrs. Gordon laughed. Connolly hung his jacket on the coat rack beside the office door, then moved to the chair behind the desk and took a seat. In a moment, the sound of Mrs. Gordon's fingers moving across the keyboard drifted down the hall.

Connolly spent the morning returning phone calls and working through the files that had gathered on his desk. Business was better than it had been in a long time, or so Mrs. Gordon seemed to think. He couldn't remember much about how things used to be, except the way the floor felt when he awakened from sleeping on it. And the clanking sound the gin bottles made as they rolled together when he opened the bottom drawer of the desk.

At noon, Connolly took a notepad from the desk and stepped to the coat rack by the door. He slipped on his jacket and started up the hall. Mrs. Gordon glanced at him as he passed her desk. "You've been mighty quiet back there."

"Working." He stopped to straighten the sleeves of his jacket. "Pushin' paper."

Mrs. Gordon frowned. "More likely you were sleeping."

He smiled at her. "I'm finished with the files on the desk. I left notes for you."

She grimaced. "It'll take me all day to decipher your scribble."

He chuckled as he started out the door, then made his way toward the elevator.

From the lobby on the first floor, Connolly slipped out through the service door to Ferguson Alley. At the end of the alley he crossed Government Street to the courthouse in the middle of the block and went up to the fourth floor where he came to a reception area outside the district attorney's office.

A row of chairs lined the wall to the left. Windows to the right gave a view of the atrium and the lobby below. Along the far wall was a counter that stood chest high. Hidden behind it was a desk and Juanita, the receptionist. She raised her head just high enough to glare at him over the countertop as he approached. Her eyes were piercing, and they rolled up to the top of the socket as she looked over the reading glasses she kept perched at the end of her nose. "May I help you?" she asked.

Connolly stepped to the counter. "I need to see Henry McNamara."

"What about?"

The tone in her voice put him on the defensive. It wasn't her place to screen Henry's visitors. "A case," he said.

"Which court?"

Connolly frowned. "Which court? How many courts is he handling these days?"

"Mr. McNamara supervises all three district courts."

"Supervises?" Connolly chuckled. "Henry got a promotion?"

Juanita tilted her head even lower and her eyes grew dark. "Which court?"

Connolly grinned at her. "Judge Cahill, I guess. I haven't checked the file. It's a …"

Juanita punched some numbers on the telephone keypad. "That would be Ms. Underwood. I'll see if she has time to meet with you."

While he waited for an answer, Connolly moved to the opposite side of the room. A moment later he heard Juanita hang up the phone. "Ms. Underwood will be out in a minute." Her voice was loud and flat. "Have a seat." Connolly took a drink from a water fountain in the corner, then found a seat as far from the counter as possible.

In a few minutes, a door opened near Juanita's desk and a petite woman appeared. About five feet tall, she wore a gray suit with a white blouse. She was older than most of the prosecutors Connolly had dealt with in the past. Older, but not old. And the expression on her face seemed all business, but not her eyes. They sparkled with irrepressible laughter. She was … different and Connolly liked her before she even said a word. She caught his eye. "Mr. Connolly?"

"Yes." Connolly rose from his seat and crossed the lobby.

She offered him her hand. "I'm Gayle Underwood."

They shook hands. "Mike Connolly," he said. "Glad to meet you."

Gayle held the door for him as he stepped passed, then led him down the hall. "I'm handling the cases in Judge Cahill's court," she said. "What case do you have?"

"Dibber Landry."

"Landry?" She glanced at him with a questioning look. "I'm not sure I have that one. I don't remember it." Her face brightened. "But that's not unusual. I have a lot of cases."

Connolly liked her sense of humor. "It's a capital murder case."

"Oh." She seemed startled. "I haven't handled a murder docket yet."

At the end of the hall, they came to a small conference room. Sparsely furnished, even by county standards, it held only a plain folding table and four chairs. The walls were bare and windowless. And a florescent light in the ceiling above the table made the room seem even more stark. Gayle paused when they reached the door and gestured for him to enter. "Have a seat," she said. "Let me check with Henry and see what we're doing with this case." She stepped away from the door. Connolly took a seat at the table and waited.

In a few minutes, Gayle returned. Henry McNamara was with her, carrying the case file. Gayle took a seat across the table from Connolly. McNamara closed the door. "Mr. Connolly." McNamara tossed the file on the table. He and Connolly shook hands. "Good to see you again. I understand you have this Landry case."

"Yes."

McNamara took a seat at the end of the table to Connolly's right. "Ms. Underwood is handling most of the cases in Judge Cahill's court now, but I'll still have the murder cases for a while. What do you want to know about Landry?"

"Well." Connolly shrugged. "Everything."

"Ha." McNamara laughed. "I can't tell you my secrets."

"Then tell me what you think happened."

McNamara opened the file and leafed through the papers inside. "Let's see." He paused a moment, checked another page, then said,

"It looks like the sheriff's office got a call from somebody down on Dauphin Island who found a body inside a house down there."

"Who made the call?"

McNamara seemed wary. "I'll give you the name and address if you won't tell your client. Some of these people are a little worried about getting harassed by criminals. Especially murderers."

"Nobody's going to harass your witnesses. What's the name?"

McNamara glanced at the file. "The call came from Amy Wilburn. Address we have is 4155 Yorkhaven Road. She and her husband own a house on Dauphin Island. The body was found at 8925 Bienville Boulevard. That's way out on the west end of the island. The Wilburns were down there cleaning up after the hurricane. Smelled something. Started searching for the source. Found the body in a neighboring house. Called 911."

Connolly scribbled the address on his legal pad. "Who's the detective?"

"Brian Hodges. He's with the sheriff's office."

"What's the victim's name?"

McNamara shook his head. "We don't have a name. Body hasn't been identified yet." He read from the file. "White male. Mid-thirties. Took him to Mobile General." He glanced up at Connolly. "Looks like he died from a single gunshot to the head. I don't think we have an autopsy report yet."

"So, the dead person was a man?"

"Yes. Male. Mid-thirties."

"And how did you connect this to Dibber?"

"Dilbert Landry." McNamara grinned. "Good ol' Dilbert pawned a jet ski at the Golden Nugget Pawn Shop in Saraland." His voice had a sarcastic tone. "The owner of that fine establishment filed the proper paperwork like all good pawn shop owners do. The sheriff's stolen property unit checked the numbers from it against the list of stolen property. They called us. The person at the pawn shop is …" He checked the file for the name. "Tommy Porter. You want the address?"

"I know where it is."

"The jet ski was registered to Inez Marchand. She owns the house where the body was found. You want her address?"

"Sure."

"She lives at 125 Upham Street."

Connolly wrote down the address. "So, the Wilburns own a house on Dauphin Island. They were down there after the storm. Noticed a rank odor. Tried to find out where it was coming from. And—"

"And found the dead guy in a neighbor's house."

"And the owner of that house is Inez Marchand."

"Yes."

"And she doesn't know who the dead man is?"

"No. Hodges took a statement from her. She said she'd never seen him before. Didn't know who he was. Didn't know why he was in the house and didn't know anything about what happened to him."

Connolly gave him a 'so what' gesture. "And your theory about this is…?"

"Squatter."

Connolly's forehead wrinkled in a puzzled frown. "Squatter?"

"Yeah. My theory is, he was a squatter. It's a bigger problem down there than you might think. Lot of those houses aren't used that often. Drifter comes along. Needs a place to stay. Finds an empty one. Breaks in. Stays until the owner throws them out."

"So, what makes this capital murder?"

"The dead man was living in the house. Landry was out there looting houses after the storm. Broke into the house. Surprised the man. They got in a fight. Landry shot him." McNamara flipped through the file to the warrant and handed it to Connolly. "Murder during the course of committing a burglary."

Connolly glanced at the warrant. "Squatter, huh?"

McNamara leaned back in his chair. "Doesn't matter if the dead guy had permission to be there or not. He could have been Landry's accomplice. Wouldn't make any difference. Landry was committing a burglary. Someone was killed during the burglary. That's all it takes."

Connolly laid the warrant on the table. "Do you have the gun?"

"Not yet."

"What kind was it?"

"Thirty-eight caliber."

Connolly thought for a moment. "How do you know Dibber was in the house?"

"Prints. His fingerprints were all over the place."

"And how do you put him there at the time this man died?"

McNamara cut his eyes toward Connolly. "I don't have to prove it to a mathematical certainty."

Connolly glanced at Gayle. A wisp of a smile appeared on her face. Connolly ran his fingers through his hair. "Got any physical evidence at all?"

McNamara leaned forward and flipped through several pages in the file. "I'm sure we do." He scanned across a page. "Looks like they found a small pseudoephedrine bottle in the kitchen. Point 125 grams of meth in it."

"Dust."

McNamara shook his head. "Not angel dust. Methamphetamine."

"I know what meth is," Connolly replied. "I'm saying, the amount you found was dust. In the bottle. Point 125 is residue. Residue in a Sudafed bottle. Could have been residue from the pseudoephedrine."

McNamara chuckled. "I don't think so."

"You think Dibber was doing meth?"

"I don't know, yet."

"Because you didn't find his prints on the bottle." Now it was Connolly who leaned away from the table. "You don't know much at all about this case, do you?"

"I've read the file."

Connolly sighed. "Henry, Henry, Henry."

"What?"

"This is thin, Henry. Mighty thin."

McNamara closed the file. "Seems like a good case to me."

"Did anybody see Dibber at the house?"

"Not that we know of, yet."

"You want to plead him out to first degree theft?"

McNamara shook his head. "I'll let him plead to straight murder. Take his chances on a sentence with the judge."

Connolly smirked. "He'll never go for that."

"Beats the death penalty."

Connolly felt the muscles in his neck tighten. "I can't …." He stopped himself and gestured toward McNamara's file. "Give me a copy of the reports and the warrant and whatever inventories you have and I'll get out of your way."

"Gayle will give you what you're entitled to." McNamara handed her the file and stood. "Tell Landry to think about my offer." He stepped to the door and disappeared up the hallway.

As McNamara disappeared, Gayle stood and picked up the file. "Come on," she said. "I'll get your copies for you."

CHAPTER 8

Connolly left the courthouse and retraced the route up Ferguson Alley to the office building. He entered through the service door, moved past the elevators, and crossed the lobby to Dauphin Street. There, he made his way to the Port City Diner in the next block. It was after one when he arrived. Most of the lunch crowd was gone. He took a seat in the back at the end of the counter.

A waiter appeared. "Hello, Mr. Connolly. Having your usual?"

"Yeah."

The waiter scribbled on an order pad. "Turkey on whole wheat. Swiss cheese. Mayo. Mustard. No onions. Sweet tea."

As the waiter walked away, Connolly had a second thought and called after him. The waiter came back. "Change that," Connolly said.

"You want something else?"

"Yeah. Give me a muffuletta instead." He was thinking of Hollis and it just seemed right.

"No problem." The waiter changed the order, then disappeared through the door to the kitchen.

Connolly stared at the napkin dispenser on the counter and thought of Hollis. A smile spread across his face. Hollis. With Victoria. On their honeymoon. In Disney World. Hollis on a honeymoon with anyone was a reach but seeing him in Disney World was more than Connolly could imagine.

Then he thought of Raisa. The last time he heard from her, she was in the Atlanta airport. He took the cell phone from his pocket and dialed the office. Mrs. Gordon answered. "Has Raisa called?"

"No. Was she supposed to?"

"She called yesterday from Atlanta. Left a message on the machine at the house. Said her flight was delayed."

"And you don't like it."

"No."

"Not much you can do about it. Certainly not now."

"Leave me a note to call somebody and find out where she is."

"They won't tell you."

"Maybe not. But leave me a note about it anyway." He switched off the phone.

The waiter appeared with the sandwich and a glass of tea. He set the plate on the counter in front of Connolly and put the tea beside it. "Best muffuletta in town," he said. He took a knife and fork from under the counter and arranged them on either side of the plate. "Enjoy." The waiter stepped away. Connolly took a bite of the sandwich.

After lunch, Connolly walked from the diner toward the office. As he approached the building, he noticed a girl out front, smoking a cigarette. She was not more than five feet tall and her skin was pale and chalky. Her short blonde hair was dull and lifeless and laid flat against her head. She was dressed in blue jeans and a pink tank top that exposed her shoulders. On her feet she wore a pair of black Converse high tops.

As Connolly drew even closer, he saw a diamond stud in her nose and a silver ring in her eyebrow at the corner of her left eye. When he was a few feet away, she tilted her head to one side and exhaled cigarette smoke from the corner of her mouth. Her left shoulder rolled forward and from under the strap of her shirt he saw the edge of a tattoo just below the neckline. She stepped toward him as he passed. "Mr. Connolly?"

He was surprised she knew his name. "Yes."

"We need to talk."

A frown wrinkled Connolly's brow. "How do you know who I am?"

"I seen you on TV. And at the Pig."

"The pig?"

"Yeah. The Whistlin' Pig."

The Whistlin' Pig was a barbeque restaurant on Holcombe Avenue. It had been around since Connolly was a little boy, but he hadn't been there in …. He couldn't remember ever being there. She continued. "Buster makes sure the local news is on every night. I seen you on there when you got that guy off on killin' that lawyer."

Connolly nodded. She took another puff on the cigarette. "Everybody says you're the man to see if you're in trouble."

"Are you in trouble?"

She shook her head. "Not me. But we need to talk."

"About what?"

Her eyes darted around warily, as if checking the street. "Dibber," she said softly.

"What about him?"

She glanced around again. "Not out here."

Connolly gestured toward the building. "Come up to my office. We can talk there."

She nodded. "Alright."

Connolly waited while she took one more drag from the cigarette, then dropped it on the sidewalk and rubbed it out with her foot. As she started toward the building entrance, he saw more of the tattoo and realized the part he'd seen before was the tip of a wing that stretched across her back from shoulder to shoulder. A dark outline was visible through the thin fabric of her shirt. From the look of it, the tattoo went all the way down her back.

He watched her as she walked ahead of him to the front entrance of the building, trying to decide how old she was. One minute she looked fifteen. The next he was sure she was thirty. He'd seen girls like that before. And he'd taken one home with him a time or two. The thought of those days made him shudder.

They rode the elevator to the third floor and walked down the corridor to Connolly's office. Mrs. Gordon was in the break room when they arrived. Connolly ushered the girl down the hall and pointed her toward a chair in front of the desk. "Have a seat," he said.

Connolly reached to close the office door, then thought better of it and left the door open. He took a seat in the chair behind the desk. "So, you know Dibber?"

"Me and him's been datin' for the last year or two. I didn't know—"

"Wait." Connolly held up his hand to stop her. "How about if we start at the beginning. What's your name?"

"Tiffany."

"And the rest of it?"

"Tiffany Previto."

He jotted the name on a legal pad. "You and Dibber have been dating?"

"Yes."

"How did you meet Dibber?"

"He come in the Pig one day. Me and him got to talking. First one thing then another."

Connolly nodded. "And what did you want to tell me?"

"I didn't know what they was doing, really."

"Who?"

"Them people in that house."

"What people?"

"Nick and those guys he has working for him."

"What are you talking about?"

"Tinker asked me to help him. I helped him. Now they think I put Dibber up to breakin' in."

"Wait a minute." Connolly leaned forward and propped his elbows on the desk. "Start over. Who's Nick?"

"Nick Marchand."

"Marchand. Is he related to Inez Marchand?"

"I don't know." She shrugged. "He runs a nursery in Wilmer."

"Okay. And you know Nick."

"Sort of. I know Tinker. Tinker knows Nick."

"Who is Tinker?"

"Tinker Johnson. One of them guys that works for Nick."

"At the nursery."

"Yeah."

"How do you know Tinker?"

"We …" She hesitated. "We been friends a long time."

"And why do you think Nick thinks you put Dibber up to breaking into that beach house?"

Tiffany sighed. "Look, I was helpin' them out. Okay?"

"Helping who?"

"Nick and them," she said.

"Helping them do what?" Connolly asked.

"Tinker come to me one day and asked me if I wanted to make some extra money. I got a kid. I can use all the help I can get. So, I said 'Sure.' All I had to do was go to the store and get some money orders. They'd give me some money. I'd go buy money orders."

"So, you did it?"

"Yeah. Sure." She said it in a matter-of-fact tone as if the answer was obvious. "I mean, it ain't nothing illegal about buying no money orders."

"How many did you buy?"

"At first it was maybe two or three a week."

"And later?"

"Last week, before the storm, I bought twelve."

"For how much?"

"A thousand dollars."

"Each?"

"Yeah."

"And what did you make out of it?"

"My cut?"

"Yes. What did you receive for buying the money orders?"

"Started out at twenty dollars apiece. Last week it was forty."

"They paid you forty dollars for each money order you bought?"

"Yeah."

"And you gave the money orders to Tinker?"

"No. I gave them to Nick. Tinker didn't handle the money. He just got me the job."

"How do they know about you and Dibber?"

Her eyes darted away. "Tinker come by the house one day. Dibber was there. Nick's boys was with him. I guess Tink told them who he was."

"When's the last time you saw Nick?"

"Right before the storm."

"How do you know Nick thinks you put Dibber up to breaking in the beach house?"

"Tinker come by the house right after the law picked up Dibber." She glanced at the floor. "Nick kept a lot of stuff down there."

"You've been to the beach house?"

"I went with Tinker a couple of times." She looked up. "Before I knew Dibber. He's in a lot of trouble, ain't he?"

"Yes."

"Think you can get him off?"

"It would help if I knew what was going on. Where did they get this money? The money they gave you for the money orders?"

She gestured in protest with both hands. "I didn't ask."

"But you have an idea?"

"I could come up with one."

"Drugs?"

Her eyes darted away. "Maybe."

"How were the money orders made out?"

"Southern Nursery. Most of them."

Connolly raised an eyebrow. "Most of them?"

"At first I had them made out to Nick, but he got mad about it. Said he didn't want his name on none of them. So after that we used Southern Nursery."

"That's the name of Nick's nursery?"

She shrugged. "I guess."

"What did Nick do with them?"

"I don't know. I gave them to him. He paid me. That was all I wanted to know."

"You did this every week?"

"Every Thursday. Tinker brought me the money in the morning. I made my run that afternoon. Then I'd meet Nick that night and give him the money orders."

"Where did you meet him?"

"Winn Dixie parking lot on Ziegler Boulevard. Most of the time. Met at the beach house a few times." She shifted positions in the seat. "Think any of this will help Dibber?"

"Maybe. Who was the dead man?"

She looked away. "I don't know."

"Why was he down there?"

"I have no idea."

"Did Nick know him?"

"You need to talk to Tinker."

"I'd be glad to. How can I meet him?"

"I'll ask him." She scooted forward in the chair. "Look, I just wanted to let them know that I ain't got nothin' to do with Dibber breaking in that place." She stood to leave. Connolly came from behind the desk.

"Ask Tinker to get in touch with me." He handed her a business card. She shoved it in her pocket and started up the hall. Connolly followed her to the door and held it open as she stepped into the corridor.

When she was gone, Mrs. Gordon came from the break room. "Who was that?"

"Tiffany."

She frowned. "Tiffany?"

"Dibber's girlfriend, apparently."

"Oh."

Connolly took a seat in a chair near the door. Mrs. Gordon sat behind the desk. "Don't you have something to do?"

"I'm waiting."

"Waiting?"

"Yeah." Connolly nodded. "I'm waiting for her to get out of the building. Then I'm going up to Saraland."

"What's in Saraland?"

"The pawn shop where Dibber pawned the jet ski."

"Jet ski?"

"Yeah. According to Henry McNamara, that's how the police found him. They say he took the jet ski from the beach house. Sold it to a pawn shop. The pawn shop reported the serial numbers to the police department. A police computer matched the numbers to a stolen property report. That took them to an incident report about the dead guy from the beach house. Bada-bing! Dibber was arrested."

"Sounds a little tenuous."

"Thin."

"Paper thin."

"Ooh, Mrs. Gordon." Connolly grinned. "You're catching on."

"When does Hollis get back?" She rolled her eyes. "I can't believe I asked that question."

"Do you think I need him?"

"I never knew how much," she said in a sarcastic voice.

Connolly laughed as he rose from the chair and stepped toward the door. "Don't wait up for me."

When he reached the lobby, he could see Tiffany standing out front. As he watched, a yellow Chevrolet Caprice came to a stop on the street beside her. The windows in the car were tinted but when she opened the door to get in, he saw a man seated behind the steering wheel. She slammed the door shut and the engine made a sputtering sound as the car moved away. Blue smoke rolled from beneath it and trailed down the street. Connolly waited until the car was gone, then walked to the Chrysler.

CHAPTER 9

The Golden Nugget Pawn Shop was located on Telegraph Road in Saraland, a bedroom community on the north side of Mobile. The shop occupied a building that had once been the Grab-A-Bag convenience store. Connolly had been there before while defending Dewan Lewis. The thought of that case made him chuckle.

Lewis was a polite guy. Never much trouble. But one night, for reasons that were never quite clear, he decided to rob the Grab-A-Bag. He entered the store, walked to the cooler, took out two bottles of beer and brought them to the counter as a ruse to get the clerk to open the cash register. Because he was buying beer, the clerk asked to see Lewis' driver's license. Lewis handed the man his license and a five-dollar bill. When the clerk opened the register to give him change, Lewis pulled a pistol from the waistband of his pants and demanded the money in the drawer. The clerk backed away. Lewis grabbed the cash and the beer and ran out the door. But in the rush, he left his license on the counter.

Connolly parked in front of the building and stepped from the car, still grinning at the memory of Dewan Lewis. A man in a pickup truck beside him gave him a puzzled look. Connolly acknowledged the man with a wave and went inside.

A woman greeted him as he entered. "Good afternoon," she said.

Connolly smiled pleasantly. "Is Tommy Porter here?"

"He's in the back. Just a minute. I'll get him." She disappeared through a door behind the counter and in a few minutes, a man appeared. "You wanted to see me?"

Connolly introduced himself, then said, "I represent a man named Dibber Landry. He—"

"Dibber Landry," Porter interrupted. "Now there's a character for you." He grinned when he said it.

Connolly nodded. "He's that, alright."

"They don't make them like Dibber anymore."

"You know him?"

"Yeah," Porter said. "I know him. Been coming in here since the day I opened."

"The police say he pawned a jet ski here a few weeks ago."

The expression on Porter's face was serious. "Yeah," he said. "Surprised me. First time I've ever taken anything hot from Dibber."

"You have any paperwork on it?"

"Oh, yeah. I have paperwork." Porter moved to a computer terminal at the end of the counter. "Got lots of paperwork." He pressed a few keys on the keyboard and a printer under the counter began spitting out pages. Porter collected them and handed them to Connolly.

The first page was a bill of sale. The second was a sheet that contained information about Dibber. The third was a photograph of him standing in the store. Connolly looked over at Porter. "You took his photograph?"

"Right there," Porter said. He pointed to a small, round digital camera on top of the computer screen. "Takes a picture of every transaction. Captures it on a disk."

"How many times has Dibber sold items to you?"

Porter checked the computer again. "Let's see." He pressed a few more keys. "Looks like about a dozen …. No. Fifteen."

"Fifteen?"

"Yes, sir," Porter said. "Sold me stuff fifteen times. That jet ski was number fifteen."

"How did you find out it was stolen?"

"We run the serial numbers through the police file every time we take something in. We're wired into their system. We send them the numbers off everything we buy. Goes to them in a batch at the end of the day. Their system compares our numbers to the numbers off their police reports. I bought that jet ski on August the fourteenth. They came out here and got it August the nineteenth."

"The police took it?"

"Yeah. Loaded it on a pickup truck. I guess they took it to the impound yard. I don't know. They'd have to tell you about that."

"And you lost whatever price you paid Dibber?"

"Yeah." Porter checked the monitor. "Three hundred fifty dollars." He shrugged. "I guess I can use it as a tax write off."

Connolly glanced at the papers in his hand once more. "Did Dibber pawn anything else with it?"

"I don't think so." Porter checked the computer. "No. Before that the next time would have been in June. Sold me an outboard motor." He looked at Connolly. "I guess Dibber has a thing for water sports."

"I guess so." Connolly thought for a moment. "He didn't pawn a pistol?"

Porter glanced back at the screen, then shook his head. "No. No pistol." He pressed a key on the keyboard. "Sold me a shotgun last year. Double barrel. Stevens 311. Twelve gauge. That's the only firearm I see."

Connolly nodded. "Did you ever hear of a guy named Lutie Shaw?"

Porter gave Connolly a knowing look. Connolly grinned. "A bad guy?"

"Lutie cost me a lot of money."

"How so?"

"Too many hot items."

"What do you know about him?"

"He lives in Prichard. Used to work for the city. Lost his job or got fired. I can't remember which. But he started bringing me stuff. It was clean. Never had any problems. Then about two years ago he brought me some jewelry. Watches. Expensive stuff. Not like the things he had brought before. I asked him about it. He said it belonged to his aunt. She had died recently. He was selling it for the family."

Connolly smiled. "And it was hot?"

"Sizzling," Porter replied. "I heard that's all he does now."

"Do you know where I could find him?"

"Did he have something to do with Dibber?"

"I'm not sure. But the name came up."

"I hope Dibber's not involved with him."

"Where does he live?"

"You know where Main Street is in Prichard?"

"Yes."

"Go out Main Street towards the interstate. There's a street out there. Dobbs or Hobbs or something like that. He lives out in there somewhere. Around the old railroad tracks."

"Okay." Connolly started to leave.

Porter called to him. "Tell Dibber I hope it works out for him."

"I'll tell him."

"And tell him to stay away from Lutie."

Connolly nodded. "I don't think that's going to be a problem for quite a while." Porter grinned. Connolly gestured with the papers in his hand. "Okay if I keep these?"

"Yeah. Let me know if you need anything else."

Connolly stepped to the door and walked outside to the car.

CHAPTER 10

From the pawn shop in Saraland, Connolly drove downtown to Mobile General, the county hospital on Broad Street. He parked the car near the emergency entrance, took a notepad from the seat beside him, and went inside. A little way down the main corridor, he came to a set of double doors that separated the morgue from the rest of the hospital. He pushed open one of the doors and entered.

Directly across from the doorway was the county's single autopsy suite. From the hall, Connolly could see the stainless steel table in the middle of the room. A light above it shined down on a cadaver. The chest of the body gaped opened. The scalp had been peeled from its head. The tile floor around it was splattered with blood.

Ted Morgan, the medical examiner, stood on the far side of the table. Next to him was an assistant, a young woman whose name Connolly could never remember. Morgan was talking to her when Connolly arrived. Neither of them seemed to notice. "I'm finished here," Morgan said. He stripped the rubber gloves from his hands. "Clean this up and get those slides ready."

The assistant moved away. Morgan came around the table and finally noticed Connolly. "Counselor. What brings you here?"

"Got a minute to talk?"

"Yeah. Sure."

Morgan removed the surgical gown he'd been wearing, tossed it in a waste bin near the door, and stood in the doorway. "What can I do for you?"

"Henry McNamara said you did an autopsy on a guy they found down on Dauphin Island."

"Yeah. John Doe." Morgan pointed over his shoulder with his thumb. "He's back there in the cooler."

"What can you tell me about him?"

"Let me wash my hands and I'll see what we have." Morgan moved out of sight to the left of the door. Connolly heard the water running. Morgan called out. "Come on in. Have a look around. That guy on the table's the one they fished out of the lake at Municipal Park."

"What happened to him?"

"Not sure yet." Morgan shut off the water. He appeared in the doorway, drying his hands on a towel. "Looks like he fell in and drowned." He tossed the towel in a hamper and started through the doorway. "Come on. Let's check the file on your guy."

Connolly stepped aside to let him pass, then followed him to an office across the hall. Morgan moved behind the desk and took a seat. "John Doe from Dauphin Island." He leaned back in the chair. "Like I said, we still have the body. Nobody's come to claim it yet. I need to get it out of here. Think you can find out who it is?"

"I thought that was your job."

"Not me," Morgan replied. "Sheriff's office is supposed to take care of that. But they don't seem to be too interested."

"What happened to him?"

Morgan scooted his chair around to a filing cabinet behind the desk and opened the top drawer. Connolly stood in the doorway. Morgan glanced at him and gestured to a chair. "Have a seat."

Connolly shook his head. "Better stand. If I sit, I'll go to sleep."

Morgan chuckled. "I know the feeling." He flipped through several files and pulled one out, then moved back to the desk and laid the file in his lap. He propped his feet on an open drawer while he glanced through the file.

"There was a gunshot to the back of the head." Morgan pointed with his finger behind his head. "Bullet entered at the base of the skull right above the neck. Traveled through the center of the brain, exited the forehead."

"That's the cause of death?"

Morgan glanced up. "I'd say that did the job."

"Anything else?"

Morgan read through some more pages. "Blood gases looked okay. No alcohol or drugs."

Connolly was surprised. "No drugs?"

Morgan held the page as if Connolly could read the results of the tests. "That's what it says."

"Okay." Connolly nodded. "What else?"

"Fingernails were clean. Nothing remarkable about the body other than the entry wound and the hole in his forehead." He glanced through the last few pages of the file. "Fully clothed. Underwear. Jeans. Socks. Shoes. T-shirt with a pocket."

"No bruises?"

"I didn't find any. Were there supposed to be some?"

"I don't know. You're the expert."

Morgan grinned. "You're admitting that? Even before we get to court?"

Connolly smiled. "Anything in his pockets?"

Morgan shook his head. "Nope." He tossed the file on the desk. "Had a tattoo on his chest. A rose. Not very large. Almost missed it." He leaned forward and picked up the file again. "Wait a minute." He leafed through the pages. "Yeah. There was one thing in the little pocket on the jeans."

"The little pocket?"

"Yeah. You know. Used to call it a watch pocket. I don't know what they call it now. Nobody carries a pocket watch anymore."

"What was in it?"

"A key. A door key. Wasn't on a key ring. Just tucked in there by itself."

"A door key?"

"Yeah. I mean, I'm no locksmith but it looked like the kind of key that fits in the doorknob of an exterior door."

"Is that what it went to? An exterior door?"

Morgan shrugged. "I don't know."

"What did you do with it?"

"Gave it over to the sheriff's office. I can't remember the detective's name."

"Hodges."

Morgan nodded. "Yeah. Hodges. He came by the other day. I gave it to him. That and the clothes."

Connolly folded his arms across his chest. "What do you think happened?"

"To the dead guy?"

"Yeah."

"Somebody shot him in the head and he died."

"Not a suicide?"

"Nah. Just about impossible. Well, not impossible. But not very likely."

"Any way to tell where he was? You know, sitting, standing, that kind of thing?"

Morgan rolled his bottom lip over as he thought. "I'd say ... the dead man was standing and the shooter was sitting. But that's just my opinion."

"Why do you say that?"

"Because I like to have opinions."

"No," Connolly said. "The part about him sitting. Why do you think the shooter was sitting?"

"The location of the entry wound was low on his skull." Morgan gestured with his hand behind his head again to the spot at the back of his neck. "Bullet entered down here. Traveled up and out near the hairline in front." He pointed to his forehead with the other hand. "Either the shooter was seated, and the dead guy was standing, or the dead guy was seated and the shooter was lying on his back on the floor."

"You think ...."

"Either that," he said with a smile. "Or the shooter was very,

very short."

"So, you think the dead guy was standing."

"Yeah. I think he was standing with his back to someone he knew."

"So, it wasn't an execution."

Morgan shook his head. "No. In an execution the shooter is almost always shooting down at the victim. This wasn't an execution. Not in the classic sense."

Connolly thought for a moment, then leaned away from the door frame. "Alright. Can I get a copy of your report?"

"You ask me that every time." Morgan moved his feet from the desk and stood. "Henry goes ballistic when I do that." He stepped toward the door. "Which is a good reason to give you one. Come on. I'll get you a copy."

Connolly followed him past the autopsy suite to a photocopier that sat in the hall. Morgan opened the file and took out the report. "This is fresh stuff, you know. I haven't even sent this to Henry yet."

Connolly grinned. "They made Henry a supervisor now."

"I heard that." Morgan arranged the pages of the report in the automatic feeder for the copier, then pressed a button to start the machine. "Hard to think of Henry being in charge of anything."

Connolly grinned. "He's not too bad, really."

Morgan collected the copies from the print tray and handed them to Connolly. "He's not too bad. I've seen worse."

Connolly took the pages and slid then between the sheets of the legal pad. "Thanks."

"Sure thing," Morgan replied. "I hope it helps."

Connolly started down the corridor. Morgan stepped toward his office. At the double doors Connolly remembered one more question and called over his shoulder, "Hey, Ted." Morgan appeared from his office doorway. Connolly asked, "What about a time of death?"

Morgan disappeared inside the office. Connolly walked back to the doorway. Morgan had the file open. "By the time he got to me," Morgan explained, "he'd been dead about four days."

"When was the body discovered?"

Morgan flipped through several pages in the file. "They found him on August third. That ought to be in the detective's report. Did you get a copy of it?"

"Yeah. I have a copy. But I wanted to know what your records show. So, if he had been dead four days, then he died sometime around July thirty-one."

"Yeah."

Connolly frowned. Morgan glanced at him. "Is that a problem?"

"The hurricane hit August first." Morgan nodded. Connolly grimaced. "He was dead before the hurricane."

Morgan shrugged. "Can't really say. I'm just telling you what I know."

"And that's what you'd say in court? He died in July?"

"Time of death isn't an exact science." Morgan closed the file. "Anything else you need to know?"

"You got anything else to tell me?"

"Not really."

"I didn't think so."

CHAPTER 11

Connolly came from the hospital and walked across the parking lot toward the Chrysler. An afternoon rain had fallen while he was inside, and steam rose from the pavement. Sweat trickled down his back. He loosened his tie.

When he reached the car, he opened the door and tossed the legal pad on the seat, then slipped off his jacket. He laid it across the seat and got in behind the steering wheel. The car was like an oven. He started the engine and pressed a button to lower all four windows, then switched on the air conditioner and pointed the vents in his direction.

By the time he stopped for traffic at the street, the air conditioner was blowing cold. He raised the windows and steered the car onto Broad Street, all the while thinking about that key they found in the dead man's pocket. A door key. In the dead man's pocket. He wondered if anyone checked it against the door to the beach house.

According to McNamara, Mrs. Marchand told Hodges she didn't know the man. Had never seen him. Didn't know why he was in her beach house. Connolly found that hard to believe, but it wouldn't be the first time someone lied about a crime. "But why would anyone lie about a thing like that? It's too easy to discredit." Then he thought of Dewan Lewis and how he left his driver's license on the counter after robbing the Grab-A-Bag. Wouldn't be the first time someone did something stupid either.

The traffic light at Government Street was red. Connolly brought the Chrysler to a stop and glanced at his watch while he waited. It was four o'clock. Still time to get to the office and return a few phone calls. And phone calls made him think of Raisa. Maybe there was a call from her. Maybe she called the guesthouse and left another message on the answering machine. His heart jumped at the thought of it and his mind began to wander. Maybe she was at the guesthouse. Maybe he would give in this time. Maybe they would—

The traffic light changed. Cars started forward through the intersection. Connolly glanced to the right to check for traffic, then changed lanes and drove toward Tuttle. Five minutes later, he parked the car at the end of the driveway and went inside the guesthouse.

From the doorway, he could see the answering machine on the table at the far end of the sofa. The red light was blinking. There was a message waiting. He shoved the door closed behind him and crossed the room. His pulse quickened. He pressed the button. The machine beeped. A male voice began to speak. Connolly felt his heart sink.

A marketing firm telling him about a deal on a new swimming pool. The message ended. The machine fell silent. He lifted the cover and checked the tape to make sure that was the only message. A sense of sadness swept over him. The cover snapped closed. An image of Raisa came to his mind. He took a step back, then collapsed on the sofa and stared out the window across the room.

Time ticked by slowly and afternoon shadows crept across the floor toward him, but he didn't notice. His mind was lost in thought. Thinking about what could have been. What might have been. Maybe he'd made a mistake. Maybe he should have told her to stay. She would have stayed if he'd asked. Then the guesthouse wouldn't be empty. He wouldn't be alone. She'd be waiting for him when he came through the door.

Barbara had been the love of his life, but there was a lot of baggage with her. When they were married and he was drinking, she had to run the house. Looked after Rachel, took care of … everything. At first, she tried to cover for him. Then she tried to change him. And then she nagged. Finally, she took over. And the process changed her. Not that it was her fault, but she was different than she'd been before. More assertive. Controlling. Demanding. And always lurking in the background was the unspoken question of whether he would stay sober. Suspicion. Watching. Waiting. He couldn't live under that kind of scrutiny.

Raisa, on the other hand, didn't know about any of that. She didn't know anything about the gin bottles in the desk. Nights at the office in a drunken stupor. Marisa at the Imperial Palace. Or any of the other women he'd seen. She only knew he rescued her from a life of fear, pain, and misery. And that was all she wanted to know. She liked him and she liked him for who he was, not thinking about who he had become after being who he had been before. With her, there were no conditions. No strings. No—

Well, there was a bit of a language problem. She spoke whatever they speak in Bosnia and two or three other languages, but she didn't know much about the American version of English. Or American life. And she had all the problems one might expect after being drugged, sold into the sex trade, and forced to work as a prostitute. But the way she felt when he touched her. The way he felt. Like his entire body—

"Argh," he groaned. "Thinking like this is no good." He rubbed the palms of his hands over his face and slid his fingers through his hair, then tugged at his hair in frustration. "I need a hobby."

The sun hadn't set yet, but the angle had become more severe. The room was getting darker. Connolly leaned over the end of the sofa and switched on a lamp, then lay there, one arm dangling over the armrest, his mind again on Raisa.

After a while, he pushed himself up from the sofa and trudged down the hall to the bedroom. He hung his suit in the closet and put on a pair of jeans and a T-shirt. A pair of topsiders sat on the floor by the bed. He glanced down at them. Bending over to put them on seemed like a monumental task. Instead, he fell face first across the bed. He folded his arms for a pillow and rested his head on them.

Images of Raisa and Barbara danced through his mind.

After a few minutes he felt his stomach growl. It had been a long time since lunch. He rolled over and raised himself to a sitting position on the edge of the bed, then slipped his feet in the shoes and started toward the kitchen. Halfway there he remembered Barbara and their agreement about dinner. He called her to beg off and by the time the call ended he was in the kitchen.

In the refrigerator he found a jar of mayonnaise. He took a loaf of bread from the bread box and chose a tomato from a basket by the window. In a matter of minutes, he sliced it for a sandwich and put it on a plate. Dinner in hand, he started toward the dining room. Then he had another thought. Why not do something different? He could eat outside. He moved the plate to his left hand, took a bottle of Boylan's ginger ale from the refrigerator, and started toward the door.

A round concrete table sat in the center of the garden between the guesthouse and the main residence. In the cool of the evening, it seemed inviting, so he crossed the lawn and walked through the garden to the table. As he rounded a large azalea bush, a mosquito buzzed his ear. He tilted his head to one side and rubbed his ear against his shoulder. Ginger ale sloshed down his arm. "Maybe this wasn't such a good idea," he mumbled, and he began to second guess his decision to avoid Barbara.

In the center of the garden he set the plate and bottle on the table, then stepped over the bench and took a seat. He raised the bottle to his lips and took a drink. A mosquito buzzed his ear again. He set the bottle on the table and swatted at the mosquito to chase it away, then picked up the sandwich. As he took a bite, a fly buzzed around his head and landed on the edge of the plate. He flicked it away with the back of his hand.

A moment later, a mosquito stung him on the forearm. He smashed it against his skin leaving a red blob of blood. "Enough of this," he growled as he twisted to one side, swung his legs over the bench, and stood. He picked up the plate from the table, grabbed the bottle by the neck, and started back toward the guesthouse.

Inside the house, he set the plate and bottle on the dining room table and took a seat in a chair. He rocked the chair back on two legs and tipped up the bottle for another drink.

And thought of Raisa.

In his mind he could see her standing beside him that night when they were waiting for Hollis and the pickup truck. Her fingers were locked in his. Her head rested against his shoulder. He imagined slipping his arm around her. Pulling her close. Her head tilted back. Her dark eyes focused on his. He could feel her lips against his, moist, soft, excited.

He rocked the chair forward and set the bottle on the table. "I really need a hobby." He took a bite of the sandwich and forced his mind to think of something else.

That key. In the dead man's pocket. What if the owner…. What was her name? He tried to remember but the name wouldn't come. Frustrated with himself, he set the sandwich on the plate and walked outside to the Chrysler. The legal pad lay on the front seat. He picked it up and flipped through it as he walked back inside.

At the dining table he held the notepad with one hand and the sandwich with the other. He ate while he read. And then he saw the name. Marchand. Inez Marchand. He took another bite of the sandwich and read some more. Inez Marchand. Nick Marchand. A nursery. Southern Nursery Supply. Tinker Johnson. Tiffany Previto. A dead man in the beach house. And now he knew, with a door key in his pocket.

"A man in Inez Marchand's beach house," he said to himself. "With a key to the front door. And no one knows who he is."

The beach house was important to this case. He needed to see it, to feel it, to smell it, but the thought of going there by himself brought back memories of his friend Peyton Russo. The smell of the house when he went there that day. Blood everywhere. Footprints. The putrid odor. Even now the memory of it made his stomach churn.

He closed his eyes and tried to think of something else but all he could see were images of Raisa. Her hair. The look in her eye. Then the touch of her hand. Soft. Warm. Inviting.

"Ahh!" Connolly struck the table with his fist. "Why can't I think about … football or … flowers or anything but women?"

CHAPTER 12

Connolly awakened the next morning to find he was lying on his back in bed. He couldn't remember how he got there or what time he fell asleep. A glance toward the window told him it was still dark outside, but he was wide awake. He rolled on his side and felt along the top of the bedside table for his cell phone. The glare of the screen made his eyes squint as he pressed a button to see the time. Four in the morning. The phone slipped from his fingers and clattered onto the table. He dropped his head on the pillow and closed his eyes.

Twenty minutes later, he was still awake. Another ten passed and he stared up at the ceiling. Finally, he threw aside the covers and crawled from bed.

When he had showered and dressed, he went to the kitchen and made a cup of instant coffee in the microwave. There was a box of Krispy Kreme doughnuts in the cabinet. He took it down and ate one while standing at the sink. In between bites, he sipped from the cup of coffee.

The sun was almost up when he left the guesthouse and started toward the car. He backed it away from the house and headed toward the office. But for the street sweeper he passed near the library, the city was deserted and quiet in the gray, predawn light. He lowered the window and let the balmy, damp air blow against his face. When he reached Royal Street, he made his way behind the courthouse to St. Pachomius Church.

One of the oldest structures in the city, St. Pachomius sat behind the courthouse beneath the thick foliage of oak trees almost as old as the building itself. Steps led up from the sidewalk at the street to a portico supported by large, round columns that stood like sentries guarding access to the sanctuary inside. Beyond those columns were huge doors fifteen feet tall.

Inside, the sanctuary was cool and dark. Walls to the left and right were lined with stained glass windows depicting scenes from the life of Christ. Down front, a railing separated the nave from the marble steps that led from the sanctuary floor to the chancel. Early morning light illuminated the vivid colors in the windows, bringing the images to life and casting a rainbow of color across the dark wooden pews.

Lecterns stood on either side of the chancel, facing the nave. Behind them, pews were arranged for a split chancel choir and past the choir gallery was still another railing at the altar.

Connolly took a seat in a pew near the back of the sanctuary and let his eyes move slowly around the room. It looked old and smelled old but despite its age the building was alive with mystery and wonder.

Before long, others began to arrive for the service of morning prayer. They moved quietly down the aisle past him and in a few minutes, Father Scott entered and climbed the steps to the chancel. From the lectern he faced the pews. His voice echoed through the building. "Let us give thanks to the Lord."

In unison, those who'd gathered that morning responded. "It is right to give Him thanks and praise."

When the service concluded, Father Scott disappeared into the sacristy. Connolly waited until the others were gone, then lingered near the chancel rail. In a few minutes, Father Scott emerged in street clothes. "Have you heard anything from Hollis and Victoria?"

Connolly grinned. "Not a thing."

"I guess he has other things on his mind besides us."

"I guess so. Wish he would come on back, though."

"Miss him?"

"Not really, but I could use his help on a couple of things."

"Sorry I missed the wedding. We could have done it here."

"I told him that," Connolly replied. "But he didn't want to do it here."

"My wife and I got married at the courthouse." Father Scott's eyes danced. "She had this elaborate wedding planned. Then, at the last minute, she got fed up with the whole thing. Came and got me one night about two in the morning."

Connolly was surprised. "She came and got you?"

"Yeah." Father Scott laughed. "It was kind of strange." His laughter trailed away but his eyes still sparkled and there was a wistful tone in his voice. "Actually, it was rather exciting. A woman banging on your door in the middle of the night." He grinned again. "I opened the door. She didn't say hello or kiss me or anything. Just standing there looking at me all alive and excited and she said, 'Let's get married.' I said, 'We are. Day after tomorrow.' She said, 'No. Now.' So, we rode over to New Orleans. Got married at the courthouse. Came back the day of the wedding in time for the reception."

"How'd that go over?"

"Her mother was a little upset. Everyone else thought it was a hoot."

"I hope Hollis and Victoria have a 'hoot' at Disney World."

Father Scott looked amused. "They went to Disney World?"

Connolly grinned. "That's where Victoria wanted to go."

"Everyone has their dreams. Did Raisa get away okay?"

"Yeah."

"You know," Father Scott observed, "that woman had it bad for you."

"That's what I hear."

"She asked a lot of questions about you when we were over at

Cape San Blas."

"That's the last thing I need to hear."

"Think she'll be alright?"

"I don't know." Connolly snapped his finger. "But that reminds me. I need to call about her."

"Is something wrong?"

"We had her flight worked out so she could get to New York without much of a delay but her connection in Atlanta was late. She left a message on my answering machine. I need to check on her."

"She's a brave woman. Going back over there like that."

"Yeah. She is." Connolly started up the aisle.

Father Scott followed. "If you talk to her, tell her I said hello."

"I will."

They reached the door. Father Scott held it open and Connolly stepped outside.

When Connolly reached the office, Mrs. Gordon was busy at the copier in the break room. He stopped at the doorway. "Any calls from yesterday?"

"They're on your desk."

Connolly made his way back to his office and hung his jacket on the coat rack by the door, then moved behind the desk. A stack of phone messages lay on the chair. He picked them up, glanced through them, then took a seat and opened the bottom drawer of the desk. The sound of the drawer sliding against the desk frame caught his attention. He looked to see why he didn't hear the gin bottles clank together, then remembered he didn't drink anymore.

Mrs. Gordon spoke to him from the doorway. "Old habits die hard."

He hadn't heard her come in and the sound of her voice startled him. "Yes," he said. "I suppose they do." He took the phone book from the drawer and laid it on the desk. She glanced at it from across the room. "What are you doing with that?"

"Calling Dave Brenner."

"That book's been out of date for years. In fact, you're probably the only person in the building who still has one."

"I think Dave Brenner's number will still be the same. I just don't remember it."

"And I don't think he'll tell you anything about her."

They exchanged a knowing look. "Maybe not," Connolly said. "But I'm calling just the same."

Mrs. Gordon watched from the doorway while Connolly searched for the telephone number. "Want me to get it for you?" she asked.

"No." He ran his finger down the page. "I can still read a phone book." Three pages later he found the number and punched it into the phone.

Brenner was the agent in charge of the FBI office in Mobile. They weren't good friends, but their paths had crossed on previous cases and they maintained a cordial relationship. Brenner's office coordinated Raisa's trip. If anything was wrong, he would know it.

After several delays, Connolly reached Brenner's assistant. Brenner was out. He left a message and hung up the phone. Mrs. Gordon was still at the door. Connolly glanced up at her. "Think he's dodging me?"

"What do you think?"

Connolly shrugged. "Hard to tell."

Mrs. Gordon frowned. "Hard to tell? Did you really think he would take the call?"

"I don't know. Maybe."

"Listen, Raisa wanted to do this. You didn't make her."

"Didn't I?"

Mrs. Gordon seemed puzzled. "What do you mean?"

"What if I knew how she felt about me and pointed her toward the FBI and this trip as a way of getting her out of the way?"

Mrs. Gordon thought for a moment, then shook her head. "You aren't that clever. Or that devious." She started up the hall, then came back. "You told her what the risks were, right?"

"Yes."

"And you told her she could stay here."

"Yes. But if I had said I wanted her to stay, she would have."

"Did you really want a relationship with her?"

Connolly sighed. "No."

Mrs. Gordon pressed the issue. "That wasn't very convincing. Did you want a relationship with her?"

Connolly blushed. An embarrassed smile tugged at the corners of his mouth. "This is not something that's easy for me to talk about with you."

"Why? She was attractive. Vulnerable. Available. Experienced in making men feel wanted. Talking about that makes you uneasy?"

"It makes me uneasy to tell you that I was attracted to her in that way."

She dismissed him with the wave of a hand. "That's just hormones."

Connolly laughed. "Hormones?"

Mrs. Gordon looked serious. "Yes," she said. "Hormones. It's just physical. You know what kind of business she was in. You know all you have to do is touch her in the right places and she'll—"

"Mrs. Gordon!"

"Well it's true."

"I know it's true, but you don't have to say it."

"Might as well talk about it. Everybody knows all about it anyway."

"They know about what?"

"Do you think Barbara doesn't know how you reacted to Raisa? Or how Raisa reacted to you?"

"I hope not."

"Why?"

"Because I—"

"Because you don't want her to know what kind of things you think about when you think of Raisa?"

"Yes."

Mrs. Gordon rolled her eyes. "You men are all the same."

"What does that mean?"

"It bothers you that you look at a woman and size her up. So, you assume it bothers us that you see a pretty woman and have this idiotic reaction."

"It doesn't?"

She shook her head in a dismissive gesture. "Men understand almost nothing about women."

CHAPTER 13

That afternoon Connolly stayed at the office, sorting through files, cleaning out drawers, prowling through filing cabinets. A little after three, Mrs. Gordon appeared at his door. "What are you doing?"

Connolly glanced at her over his shoulder. "Going through old files."

"What for?"

"Taking the notes off the legal pads."

She seemed to not understand. "Taking notes off the legal pads?"

"Yeah. These files need to be closed but they have legal pads in them that only have notes on two or three pages. No sense in closing out the file and wasting the rest of the pad."

She strode across the room and snatched the files from his hand. "Move." She elbowed him aside. Connolly glared at her. "What are you doing?"

She stuffed the file in the filing cabinet and slammed the door shut, then faced him. "You've been holed up back here all day. What is going on with you?"

"First, you tell me I don't spend enough time in the office. Now you tell me I'm spending too much time."

"Whatever it is you need to do that you're avoiding, just go do it."

Connolly looked away and responded in a quiet voice. "I don't want to."

"What is it?"

"I need to go to the Marchand's beach house."

"On that Dibber Landry case?"

"Yes."

"So, go."

"I don't want to."

"Why not?"

"Last time I went to a place like that, I saw things I didn't want to see."

She frowned. "What are you talking about?"

"Peyton Russo," he said.

The drawer on the filing cabinet came open on its own. Mrs. Gordon pulled it out farther, adjusted the files to fit better and shoved it closed. The filing cabinet came open again. This time, she jerked it out even farther, grabbed a handful of files and removed them from the drawer. She shoved the drawer closed with a bang and laid the files on top of the cabinet. "I'll take care of the files," she said in a frustrated voice. "You go to the beach house."

Connolly sighed and crossed the room to the door. He took his coat from the coat rack and slipped it on, feeling the whole time like a little boy, but right then he didn't care. He didn't want to go there. And he certainly didn't want to go by himself.

From the office, Connolly walked down the corridor to the elevator and rode down to the lobby, then walked outside to the street. The Chrysler was parked in the next block. He got in behind the steering wheel and started the engine. By then, he realized Mrs. Gordon was right. He had to go to the beach house. Hollis or no Hollis. And he couldn't wait any longer to do it. But he still didn't like it.

South of town, he crossed the Dog River bridge onto Hollinger's Island and descended into the lowlands that lay along the coast. Live oaks lined the roadway, creating a moss draped canopy overhead. The road became a tunnel beneath the foliage. A tunnel through time, sending Connolly's mind back to days he remembered all too well.

When he was ten years old, his father died. His mother turned to alcohol to escape the worries of raising two children alone. Often in a drunken stupor, she frequently was gone for days at a time. Then, she met a man at a truck stop in Loxley and left altogether. Forced to fend for themselves, Connolly and his younger brother crammed what they could in a pillowcase and hitchhiked down the bay to their uncle's house in Bayou La Batre.

Uncle Guy knew everyone from Bon Secour to the mouth of Pearl River, and when he wasn't on a shrimp boat he enjoyed visiting as many of his friends as possible. He let Connolly tag along. Together they went to places along the coast that most people didn't even know existed. Places like Gasque and Delchamps and Bayou Cateau. Places that opened their arms wide for a lonely young boy and squeezed the trouble from his broken heart.

At Bailey's, Connolly crossed East Fowl River to Mon Louis Island. Just beyond the bridge he passed a sign made of plywood and nailed to a tree. The plywood was painted yellow with red letters in a simple message. "Sprinkle's Store. One Mile."

He'd been stopping at Sprinkle's since his first trip with Uncle Guy on a cool Saturday morning in October, a long time ago. They had been to see Latham Graham in Delchamps. Latham and Guy spent the morning talking about oyster beds and hurricanes. Connolly spent the morning listening. When they left, Latham gave them a gunny sack full of oysters still in the shell. Guy didn't want to spend all afternoon shucking them so when they got to Sprinkle's Store, he traded the oysters for lunch and a few groceries. They sat on the tailgate of the pickup and ate Vienna sausage from a can. Uncle Guy had a Buffalo Rock ginger ale. Connolly had a Nehi grape. A whole bottle, all to himself. The thought of it made him smile.

A few minutes later, he rounded a curve in the road. The store came into sight. Connolly lifted his foot from the gas pedal and let the Chrysler coast from the pavement onto the parking lot. The lot was paved with crushed oyster shells that crunched beneath the tires as the car came to a stop in front of the store.

Built of cypress lumber, the store had weathered to a dark gray. It had a steep roof made of tin that had rusted to a ruddy brown. Long eaves extended five or six feet past the walls on either side, the ends supported by a row of posts that were covered with mold and mildew. Near the back, Kudzu vines encroached on the building, winding their way up the posts and dangling in the sun above the roof. A porch ran across the front.

A drink machine stood near the door. Next to it was an assortment of chairs and empty bread racks. Two men sat nearby playing cards on an empty Dairy Fresh milk crate. A young man dozed in a straight back chair that was propped against the wall. His feet rested on a plastic five-gallon bucket set upside down. Connolly nodded to the men playing cards as he stepped onto the porch and opened the door.

Inside, the building was stuffy and warm. Ceiling fans stirred the air at a lazy pace but did little to relieve the heat. Near the door was a wooden counter, burnished and smoothed by the wear of countless customers. Behind it, a woman sat on a stool cooling herself with a paper fan from a funeral home in Pascagoula. She wore a sleeveless cotton dress that hung from her shoulders in a way that left the straps of her bra exposed. Her hair was bleached white and curly, and strands of it dangled near her face.

On the counter was a manual cash register. Beside it was a set of produce scales and next to it, a jar of peppermint candy. A square container filled with packages of Tom's roasted peanuts sat farther down, next to a gallon jar of pickled eggs that was tucked behind a dusty cardboard display of no-doze pills.

Connolly moved down an aisle to a cooler along the rear wall next to a display case that held packaged meats. He opened the cooler and took out a pint-sized bottle of Milo's tea. On the way to the front he picked up a bag of Golden Flake pretzels. He set them on the counter by the register and took his wallet from the inside pocket of his jacket.

The woman slid from the stool, glanced at the items, and punched some buttons on the register. "'Ats a dollar eighty-five." Her voice sounded flat and tired.

Connolly handed her two dollars and placed the wallet to his pocket. She took his money and pulled a lever. The register made a clicking noise. A bell rang. The drawer opened. She handed him the change. "You want a bag?"

"No, thank you," Connolly replied.

She shoved the drawer closed. "Kind of hot today."

"Yes, it is."

She settled onto the stool where she'd been before. "Where's that Hollis Toombs?" The words seemed to take forever to slide past her lips. "Ain't seen him in nearly two weeks." She picked up the paper fan and began fanning herself once more.

Connolly wasn't surprised she knew Hollis. Everyone knew Hollis. Or that she associated Hollis with him. They had been in the store many times and he found assurance in the fact that she had noticed. He twisted the top of the bottle of tea and took a drink. "He's on his honeymoon," he said after he swallowed.

Her mouth gaped open. "Honeymoon?!" She stopped fanning. "Hollis Toombs got married?"

"Yes."

"I wish I'd a knowed that," she cackled. "I'd a danced at his wedding."

Connolly grinned. "I don't think he wanted anyone to know."

The expression on her face clouded. "He didn't? Why not? Ain't right somebody getting married and not tell nobody."

Connolly shrugged. "I think he was worried too many people would show up."

"Huh. More likely he was worried about what we might say about him. Who'd he marry?"

"You wouldn't know her."

"You don't know who I know. What's her name?"

"Victoria Verchinko."

She frowned. "Victoria Ver-what-o?"

"Verchinko." Connolly took another drink. He glanced at her over the bottle. "I told you, you wouldn't know her."

"Where'd he find a woman with a name like that?"

"It's a long story."

"I know she ain't from around here. Ain't no Verchinkos anywhere I ever been. They gonna be livin' down there in that shack?"

"I don't think so."

"I hope he's got better sense than to do that to a woman. Even if her name is Verchinko. Garon's Bayou ain't no place for nobody to live. Not even Hollis."

"You're right about that." Connolly stepped toward the door.

The woman continued. "Off on a honeymoon." She had a twinkle in her eye and a lilt in her voice that made Connolly grin. He wasn't sure he wanted to hear anymore but she kept talking. "Where'd they go?"

He stopped at the door and took a drink from the bottle. If he told her they went to Disney World the conversation would last another hour. So, instead he said, "Down to Florida, I think."

"Hollis Toombs. Married." She shook her head. "If that don't beat all."

Connolly nodded. "It wasn't really something any of us could predict."

"I reckon not."

He opened the door and stepped outside. The woman's laughter drifted across the porch as he walked to the Chrysler.

CHAPTER 14

Conversation at the store had been a good diversion but he needed to get moving again. Otherwise, he wouldn't reach the island before sundown and he had no intention of going into the beach house at night alone.

Twenty minutes south of the Sprinkle's, he reached the Dauphin Island Bridge, a two-lane span from Cedar Point across Grant's Pass to the north side of the island. There wasn't a car in sight. He pressed the gas pedal. The Chrysler picked up speed. Expansion joints in the concrete roadway slapped against the tires. The car rocked gently in time with the sound.

At the end of the bridge he let the car coast down the grade to the road. To the left was Grant's Pass Marina. Boats of every size and shape bobbed on the water in the berths that lined the shore. Farther down on the right was the Ship-N-Shore. Since Zirlott's closed, it was the island's only grocery store. The only hardware, bait, and video rental store, too. Unlike most coastal resorts, Dauphin Island had no fast-food franchises, no amusement parks, and no gaudy souvenir shops. Just beaches, water, and sunshine.

Past the Ship-N-Shore, Connolly came to Bienville Boulevard, a broad thoroughfare lined with palm trees that ran the length of the island. He glanced around as he drove, checking to see how much damage had been inflicted by the recent hurricane. For a barrier island, things didn't look too bad. Most of the commercial buildings were open and operating. Downed trees were still piled by the road but houses near the center of the island looked to be in good shape. As he continued west, though, conditions began to change.

Beyond the public beach, the western end of the island was a flat, treeless, sandbar. Even in good weather a constant southern breeze swept unimpeded across it, blowing sand from the Gulf side and depositing it on the bay side. As a result, the western third of the island was less than three feet above sea level. But that hadn't stopped anyone from building on it. Beach houses lined both sides of the road in rows three and four deep from the pavement to the water. All of them perched atop pilings that rose ten to twelve feet above the sand.

Connolly scanned the houses as he drove past. Many were missing roofs. The decks around some were gone. And there were pilings with no houses at all. Yet, sprinkled among them was the occasional house that seemed to have escaped without even a scratch.

Near the end of the road, he noticed a house with yellow crime scene tape wrapped around the stairway that led up from the drive. "This must be the place," he muttered, and he brought the car to a stop in the driveway.

As he stepped out, a breeze tousled his hair and he paused to enjoy it. From somewhere down the beach he heard the sound of an electric saw. And across the road behind him someone was using a hammer. He glanced up at the beach house and the old reluctance emerged once more, this time stronger than ever. It looked imposing. Dark. Empty. And the storm had damaged the steps. He wasn't sure he could get up to the door. "The police must have used a ladder," he mused. He didn't have a ladder. Maybe he should come back later.

But the words of Mrs. Gordon wouldn't let him off the hook and they repeated in his mind. "You have a job to do. Just go do it." Once again, he knew she was right. He had a job to do. And he didn't know why going there seemed such a big deal. He'd been to many crime scenes by himself. But since seeing Peyton's body. Lying in all that blood…

Still, he had to do it. There was no other choice. He had to see inside that house, and it was right there, just a few feet away. So, he pushed himself away from the car and started toward the steps that led up to the entrance.

The storm had blown away the bottom rungs and washed the sand away from the pilings. What was left of the steps dangled above his head. The lowest rung was just beyond the tip of his outstretched fingers. He could jump for it, but there was no way of knowing if it would hold his weight.

The sea breeze blew harder. A loose board dangled from the eave. It creaked as it swayed from side to side in the wind and clattered against the side of the house. Connolly looked around, searching for something to stand on, but found nothing, which meant he had to jump for the bottom rung. And if that failed, maybe he could get the car close enough to use it for a step. He hated the idea of standing on the hood. Or even the trunk lid.

So, he slipped off his jacket, gripped the back of the collar between his teeth, and tossed the tail of it over his shoulder. He could make it, he told himself. The bottom step wasn't that far away. He took a deep breath, bent his legs at the knees, and jumped into the air. With his arms outstretched, his palms banged against the lowest step and his fingers locked over the edge. He had a firm grip with his hands, but his elbows banged against the runners on the sides. Pain shot through his arms. He dangled there in agony.

After a moment, he pulled himself toward the step, then reached with one hand for the next rung. Kicking and struggling, he worked his way up until his knees rested on the first step. He paused a moment to let his arms relax, then grasped the railing and stood. The stairs swayed to the left and right as he moved carefully up to the top.

When he reached the deck at the back of the house, he took the jacket from his mouth and slipped it on, then cupped his hands against the window in the door and looked inside. A large timber had smashed through the sliding glass doors on the Gulf side. Water and wind had ruined everything. But there didn't seem to be any other danger, so he reached for the doorknob to go inside and discovered the knob was missing. And that's when he noticed the frame was splintered where the bolt from the lock tore through when someone kicked open the door. It wasn't hard to figure out who. He shook his head and sighed. "Dibber, Dibber, Dibber."

Connolly pushed open the door and stepped inside to a kitchen on the front of the house, facing the road. Across the way, a countertop with a sink separated it from the living room area that once looked out on the beach through sliding glass doors. Glass from the shattered doors was strewn across the room. From the look of things, the timber had crashed through the doors, shoved a love seat across the room into the coffee table, jammed them both against a sofa, and rammed all of that against the countertop at the kitchen.

Closer at hand, the kitchen was a mess. Dirty pans and dishes filled the sink. The stove was covered with grease and splattered with something that left charred black spots all over it. The cabinets were filthy. The refrigerator door was ajar. Molded, rotten food sat on the shelves inside. Sandy grit, driven inside by the wind, covered everything.

After a moment, Connolly climbed over the sofa and made his way to a hallway that opened off the living room. A short way down the hall was a bedroom that faced the beach. Across from it was a bathroom. A door at the end of the hall led to a second bedroom. Connolly surveyed the first room from the hall.

A dresser sat along the wall to the left of the door. In the middle of the room was a bare bed frame. A pair of blue jeans lay on the floor. Beside them was a black garbage bag stuffed with clothes. Connolly stepped into the room and opened the top drawer of the dresser. It was empty. He tried the others. They were empty, too. At the end of the dresser was a closet. In it a single wire coat hanger dangled from the bar. He backed away and glanced around the room once more, then moved across the hall to the bathroom.

A washcloth lay on the sink between the faucet and the wall. Beside it was a toothbrush. Above the sink was a medicine cabinet. Connolly opened the cabinet. Inside was a wrinkled tube of toothpaste and three disposable razors. He closed the cabinet and glanced around. A tub sat along the wall opposite the door. A bottle of shampoo sat on the floor beside it. Next to shampoo was a roll of toilet paper.

In the bedroom at the end of the hall he found a dresser that looked much like the one in the other room. Unlike the other one, though, the top of it was cluttered with bits of paper, loose change, and usual things that collect on dressers over time—receipts, keys, three rusted screws, a bottle cap.

The bed sat in the middle of the room, but it had been stripped bare. A dark brown stain covered the center of the mattress. Connolly assumed the stain was blood and likely from the dead man. He scanned the room for a clue about what might have happened, even checked beneath the bed and under the dresser, but found nothing of note. Whatever hints the killer might have left, the detectives must have collected. "Or they never were here," he mumbled. He'd entertained for some time the notion that the dead man had been killed somewhere else and moved to the beach house afterward. Murder victims who bled out made a terrible mess and the room showed none of that.

Connolly moved past the bed to a closet on the far side. The door was open. Inside was a galvanized bar with a shelf above it. A pair of pants hung from a plastic hanger.

From the closet, he moved back to the dresser for a closer look. He raked through the items on top with his finger but found nothing among them that piqued his interest. There was a jewelry box at one end with a paperback novel on top. Beside it was a cobalt blue vase about twelve inches high. It had a wide mouth at the top and curved to a stem with a clear bubble in the center. Connolly recognized it only because his aunt Ruby Poiroux had collected cobalt glass. Alone on the dresser, the vase seemed out of place. He picked it up to examine it, then set it near the jewelry box.

He moved the paperback book aside and opened the box. Inside was a Casio watch and two small photos of a baby. The baby lay on a bed, wrapped in a blanket, sound asleep. Connolly closed the box and picked up the book.

Dog-eared and worn, the cover showed the sketch of a man lying on the grass beside a motorcycle. He had one arm tucked behind his head. The other held a cigarette. A thin wisp of smoke rose from it. His feet were tucked against his thighs with his knees up, stretching his black leather chaps tight against his legs. A tough guy. With a tough ride. Connolly read the title aloud. "Hotel Green."

The book fell open at a spot where a black and white photograph had been stuck between the pages. In it, a man and woman stood together beside a car. Tall and slender, the man had a solid build but nothing about him seemed athletic. The woman was much younger than he but not immature. Short and petite, she had curly hair with dark eyes. Connolly imagined she had an olive complexion, though with a black and white photo it was difficult to tell. Her arm was looped in his and her head rested just below his shoulder. The car was a 1962 Galaxie 500. Connolly knew a guy who owned one. June 1966 was stamped in the margin of the picture by the company that developed and printed it.

Connolly flipped through the pages of the book and in front he found an inscription, "To Billy and Frieda, Best regards, Harold." He read it again, then stuck the photo in the book and laid it on the dresser. There seemed nothing else to find but as he stood there, looking, a sense of fear came over him. Foreboding. Doom. Pending trouble. And the urge to be somewhere else came over him once again. This time, he'd had enough and did not resist.

From the bedroom, he retraced his steps to the living room, climbed over the love seat, and moved around the counter to the corner by the door. He intended to leave, but near the stove he noticed a plastic Dr. Pepper bottle with some sort of brown liquid in it. Connolly picked it up and swirled the bottle around, hoping for a better view. Tiny black pieces of something stuck to the sides of the bottle and a sense of realization came over him. "Skoal spit," he said in disgust. He set the bottle on the counter and brushed his hands together.

A plate sat atop the stack of dishes in the sink. Bits of food were smeared over it. Connolly found a wooden spoon that was clean enough to touch and used it to push the dishes around. A roach ran out. He jumped to one side and swatted at it with the spoon. The roach disappeared through a gap under the lip of the sink.

Beside the sink was a frying pan. Connolly nudged it with the spoon, but it didn't move. He grasped the handle and tried to lift it, but the pan was stuck to the countertop. Then he noticed it had been burned black and the handle was melted at one end. A steel fork lay in it. The handle bore the letters US Navy. The tines were corroded green.

Connolly let go of the pan and brushed his hands together again. They felt greasy and dirty. He glanced around for a final survey of the room, then started toward the door.

CHAPTER 15

The following morning Connolly arrived at the office as Mrs. Gordon unlocked the door. She gave him a questioning look as they entered. "What's wrong?"

"Nothing," he replied. "Why?"

She glanced at her watch. "You're here and it's not even eight thirty."

Connolly shrugged. "Ah, you know."

"That's the second time this week." Connolly didn't reply. Mrs. Gordon opened the door and moved to her desk. "Your messages from yesterday are on your chair."

"Do you know anything about a book called Hotel Green?"

She took a seat at her desk. "Never heard of it."

"Written around 1966."

Her face wrinkled in a scowl. "Is this a literature quiz, or do you want me to find a copy for you?"

"Just asking."

Connolly walked down the hall to his office and hung his jacket on the coat rack by the door, then moved behind the desk. The phone messages were on his chair next to a stack of mail. He moved them to the desktop and took a seat.

In a few minutes Mrs. Gordon appeared at the door, notepad in hand. She leaned against the door frame and read from her notes.

"Hotel Green. Published in 1966 by Worthen Press. New York. Written by Randy Morris. Morris was a pen name. His real name was Harold Schnadelbach. Lived in Atlanta. Taught English at Emory University."

Connolly slid the trash can from beside the desk and propped his feet on it. "Where'd you find all of this?"

"The Internet. Learn how to use a computer and you could find it for yourself. You want to hear the rest?"

"Yes."

He leaned back in his chair and closed his eyes.

Mrs. Gordon continued from her notes. "Schnadelbach wrote four books. Had some success but nothing great. Hit the big time with Hotel Green. Became a best seller. Hollywood made it into a movie." She paused again. "I saw it at The Bama Drive-In. It was pretty good. Tommy Russell played the guy with the motorcycle. If you look closely in a couple of scenes you can see a very young Megan Wicks."

Connolly opened his eyes. "You went to the Bama Drive-In?"

She gave him a sarcastic smile. "Yes."

Connolly grinned. "With who?"

"With whom," she corrected.

"Yeah. With whom?"

"With none of your business."

Connolly chuckled. "What else did you find?" She raised an eyebrow as if she thought he was making a pun. Connolly laughed. "Is this a story about some guys in high school? Spend all their time talking about leaving the little town where they live. Gonna hit the road as soon as they graduate. Then when school is over none of them does it except this one guy with the motorcycle?"

"Yes."

"I think I might have read part of the book once. Didn't know they made a movie."

"I can't imagine why."

"Neither can I. Anything else?"

"Not much. Hotel Green was a big success, but Harold never got

94

to enjoy it. He died in a plane crash that summer, not long after the book was released. Crashed in a peanut field near Sylvester, Georgia."

Connolly sat up in his chair. "That's it?"

"That's it."

"Alright." He reached for the stack of mail. "Thanks."

Mrs. Gordon lingered by the door. "Why are you interested in this book?"

"I found a copy of it in the beach house."

She frowned. "The beach house?"

"The one they say Dibber Landry looted."

Mrs. Gordon had a thoughtful expression. "It might make a good beach book."

"This one was inscribed to somebody. Bill and Frieda, I think."

"By Morris?"

Connolly shook his head. "Someone named Harold."

Mrs. Gordon's eyes opened wide. "Harold Schnadelbach."

Connolly looked up from the mail. "Yeah." He was surprised, too. "Harold Schnadelbach. I should have picked it up."

"Maybe so." Mrs. Gordon moved away from the door and disappeared up the hall.

Connolly spent the next hour or so reading through the mail and working on pleadings in some of his pending cases. As he worked, he thought about that book and the inscription in it. And the more he thought about it, the more it seemed it might have something to do with this case. But what? It seemed as out of place as the cobalt vase. And how did either of them get in the beach house?

Shortly before ten, he finished with the files on his desk. He put on his jacket, picked up the files, and started up the hall. Mrs. Gordon glanced at him from her desk. "Where are you going?"

Connolly laid the files on her desk. "To see Inez Marchand," he announced.

"Who's she?"

"She's the lady who owns that beach house."

"Are you going to give her a literary quiz, too?"

"I'm going to ask her a few questions."

"Did they ever identify the dead man?"

"Not yet."

Mrs. Gordon shook her head. "This is a really strange case. You've had some strange ones before but this one is really weird."

"Yeah," he said. "I agree."

"Dead man in a beach house," she continued. "In the middle of a hurricane. No one knows who he is. And we spend the morning talking about a novel written in 1966 by a man who died before it paid off." Her fingers began to move across the keys at her computer. "You attract an odd crowd."

"Would help if we could get some of them to pay their fee on time."

CHAPTER 16

Inez Marchand lived on Upham Street in midtown off Old Shell Road. The drive from the office took less than ten minutes. Near the middle of the block, he found her house number painted on the curb in front of an overgrown lot that covered most of the block. Large oaks and magnolias grew near the road. Farther back he could see a few pecan trees and pines. Underneath was a tangled mass of vines and bushes. A picket fence ran along the border at the street. The fence had once been painted white once but most of the paint was gone now. The boards were rotten and green with mildew. A gate drooped from rusted hinges across a narrow brick sidewalk that led into the center of the lot. The bricks in the sidewalk were covered with moss.

Past the fence with the drooping gate, Connolly came to a gravel driveway. Most of the gravel had been worn to the sides, leaving bare dirt tracks that led from the street toward a house that now was visible beyond the undergrowth. He let the Chrysler idle up the drive.

The house was a single-story cottage constructed of concrete blocks that had been painted white. It had square windows that cranked out on either side. The gabled roof was set at a steep angle and covered with slate shingles. Bushes had once ringed the house just beyond the drip line, but they had been trimmed to the ground.

Their stumps, hacked and splintered, sprouted fresh green leaves. Farther out from the house, the undergrowth had been chopped back, too, apparently to allow a paint crew access to the house. Spatters of paint dotted the ground and made a trail across the sidewalk near the front door. A wooden ladder leaned against a tree near the walk and next to it was a collection of paint cans.

At the end of the drive was a garage. Pine needles covered the roof. A 1971 Mustang sat next to it. The car, too, was covered with needles and leaves. Through the rear window, Connolly could see the back seat of the car was crammed with boxes.

Closer to the house there was a green 1989 Buick. Connolly brought the Chrysler to a stop beside it and switched off the engine. As he came from the car, he slipped on his jacket, then walked around the house to the front door. He reached to knock but before he could, the door opened with a gap of about six inches from the door frame. A woman peered out through the opening.

"May I help you?" Her voice was rough and gravely.

She was short and stocky with a full neck that made her jaw line smooth and soft but weighed against her chest to form a wrinkle in an arc along her collar bone. Her gray hair was short and curly and looked as if she'd just rolled out of bed, but her dark eyes were bright and alert. One arm held the door. The other held a heavy blue housecoat wrapped close around her. Ruffled trim from a pink nightgown poked out around the collar of the housecoat just beneath the wrinkle at the base of her neck. On her feet she wore dirty pink slippers. Something about her was familiar to Connolly but he couldn't remember why.

Cold air rushed through the open doorway. With it came the smell of cigarette smoke and fried bacon. From behind her Connolly heard the yap of a small dog. "Are you Inez Marchand?" he asked.

"Yes."

"My name is Mike Connolly. I'm an attorney. I represent—"

The dog yelped again.

"Pixie," Inez shouted. "Shut up!" The dog continued to yelp. Inez leaned away. The door opened wider. Connolly could see the

living room inside. A small table sat by the door next to a sofa with green upholstery. It was covered with a clear plastic slipcover. Inez picked up a magazine from the table and threw it across the room. Connolly heard the click of the dog's paws on the floor as it scurried away.

Inez pulled the door closer to her side. "Who did you say you are?"

"Mike Connolly. I'm an attorney. I represent Dibber Landry."

She shook her head. "Never heard of him."

"He's—"

Her eyes opened wider. "Is he that man that stole that stuff from my beach house?" Her voice was louder than before.

"Yes, ma'am," Connolly replied. "He's the one they've accused of it."

Her look went cold. "What do you want with me? I didn't do nothing."

"I was wondering if I could talk to you."

"About what?"

"About the dead man they found in the house."

She stood erect. "I'm not sure I want to talk about him. I don't know nothing about him anyway."

"Well, when was the last time you went down there?"

"I don't know."

"Have you been down since the hurricane hit?"

"I haven't been down there in years."

"It looks like someone's been living there," Connolly said. "Has anyone else been down there?"

A frown wrinkled her brow. "You've been down there?"

"Yes."

She looked angry. "What were you doing in my beach house?"

"It's a crime scene. I—"

"How'd you get in?"

"I—"

"You broke in," she said, cutting him off.

"The door was open."

"You broke into my beach house."

"No ma'am. I didn't break in. The knob's missing from the front door. There's a hole in the back big enough to drive a truck through. I didn't break into anything. Besides, it's a crime scene."

She glared at him. "And what did you find?"

"Like I said, it looks like someone's been living down there."

"I imagine it was that fella' they found. The dead guy. Or that man they arrested."

"Did anyone else have access to the house?"

"My son uses it some."

"Your son?"

"Yes."

"What's his name?" Connolly was sure his name was Nick, but he wanted her to answer.

"Nick. Why?"

"Do you think he knows anything about him?"

She frowned. "About who?"

"The dead guy."

"I don't know if he knew him or not."

"Did anyone else have access to the house?"

"No."

She was a difficult woman to talk to and Connolly struggled to think of another question. Then he remembered the key in the dead man's pocket. "The coroner said he found a key in the dead man's pocket."

Her eyes narrowed. "A what?"

"A key," Connolly said. "A door key."

She shifted her weight to the opposite leg. "So what. He had a key. That don't mean it was mine."

"Did you give him a key to the house?"

Her eyes narrowed. "I told you, I don't know anything about him. Do I have to talk to you?"

Connolly sighed. "No."

"Good." She leaned away and closed the door.

Connolly stood there a moment, trying to think of a way to

make her continue the conversation. Finally, though, he gave up and started toward the Chrysler. As he reached the car, a pickup truck appeared in the driveway. It came to a stop in front of the garage. A man got out, dressed in khaki work clothes and carrying a metal lunch box. He moved around the truck and walked toward the house. He stopped when he reached Connolly and the Chrysler. "You an insurance salesman?" he asked.

"No, sir," Connolly replied. "A lawyer."

"Huh," the man chortled. "Not much difference. What could I do for you?"

"Are you Mr. Marchand?"

"What's she done now?"

"I was trying to talk to your wife, but she closed the door on me."

"She can be ornery sometimes. What do you need?"

"I represent Dibber Landry. He's accused of killing the man they found in your beach house."

Marchand shook his head. "How do you do that?"

Connolly gave him a puzzled look, but he knew what was coming. "Do what?" he said.

"Defend those guys. How do you get up in court and say your man didn't do it, when you know he did?"

Connolly smiled. He'd heard the question a thousand times before. "That isn't exactly how it works," he responded.

"No?"

"No. When's the last time you were at the beach house?"

"I ain't never been there."

Connolly frowned. "You've never been there?"

"That beach house ain't mine. It's my wife's house." Marchand moved past Connolly and started toward the house. "And if she don't want to talk to you about it, I can't help you."

Connolly persisted. "You've never been down there?"

Marchand faced him with a defiant expression. "Mister, I ain't been in it. I ain't rode by it. I ain't never even seen that house. And I don't plan on going." He started toward the house again. "I'd be glad to tell you what I know about it, but I don't know nothing about it."

Connolly called after him once more. "The dead man had a key. Looks like it was a key to the beach house."

Marchand was at the door. He stopped with one hand on the doorknob and looked in Connolly's direction. "Do what?"

"The dead man had a key in his pocket. Looks like it fits the door at the beach house. Any idea how he came to have a key to the house?"

"Like I said, anything you want to know about that beach house you'll have to ask my wife. And if she won't help you, there ain't much I can do for you." He opened the door and disappeared inside.

Connolly made his way to the Chrysler and started down the driveway. As the car reached the street, his cell phone rang with a call from Mrs. Gordon. "Gayle Underwood wants to talk to you. I don't know her but she said she works with the D.A.'s office."

"Yeah. What did she want?"

"They've identified the dead man in Dibber Landry's case."

Connolly pressed a button to end the call, then brought the car to a stop behind a service van parked down the block from the Marchand residence. He telephoned Gayle. "You identified the body?" he asked.

"Hodges got a match back on the prints yesterday," she explained. "His name is Stephen Ellis. Last address was in Lawrenceville, Georgia. We're still trying to track down relatives."

"Anything else?"

"Born April 11, 1967. Looks like he was forty years old."

"Why was he in the system?"

"He was arrested for possession of marijuana in Valdosta, Georgia, in 1986."

Connolly switched off the phone and headed downtown. Knowing the dead man's identity opened up more possibilities that could help their case. It also raised many more questions that required answers.

CHAPTER 17

Connolly parked the car in front of St. Pachomius Church but instead of climbing the stairs to the sanctuary, he walked across the street to the sheriff's office. A receptionist greeted him as he entered. "May I help you?"

"I need to see Brian Hodges."

"Down the hall," she said, pointing. "He's the third door on the left."

Connolly found Hodges sitting at his desk in a cramped office across the hall from a row of vending machines. Hodges looked up when Connolly appeared at the door. "Mike Connolly," he said. "Let me guess. You're here about Dilbert Landry."

"You're clever," Connolly quipped.

Hodges pointed to a chair in front of his desk. "Come on in. Have a seat." He took a file from a stack on the windowsill behind him. "We just got an ID on the dead man in that case."

"So I heard. Connolly took a seat. "What did you find out?"

Hodges opened the file. "The name is Stephen Ellis from Lawrenceville, Georgia. I think Gayle already told you that."

"What else do you know about him?"

"Not much." Hodges flipped through the pages in the file. "Looks like his parents live in the same place. Lawrenceville, Georgia. Billy and Frieda Ellis."

Connolly felt his heart skip a beat at the mention of their names. "Billy and Frieda?"

"Yeah. Do you know them?"

"No. Gayle said you were still looking for them."

"Yeah." Hodges nodded. "We are. Have an address for them but we haven't been able to reach them yet."

"How'd you come up with an address for his parents?"

"He was busted for pot when he was nineteen. A student at Valdosta State. Once we got a match on the prints, we called the police over there. They gave us the information from his file. Got the parents' information from the school, I think."

Connolly nodded. "Anything else?"

"No. Other than that one charge, he was a model citizen. No warrants. No traffic citations. Nothing."

"What about the beach house?"

"What about it?"

"What did you find when you went through it?"

Hodges tossed the file on the desk. "Well, not much, really. Place was a mess. You been down there?"

"Yeah."

"With all that damage from the hurricane, it's hard to say what was there before the storm."

"You didn't find anything?"

"The tech guys found some prints."

"Whose?"

Hodges picked up the file again and leafed through it. He took out a page and glanced over it while he talked. "We found prints for Inez Marchand. Nicholas Marchand, her son. Dilbert Landry. The dead man, Stephen Ellis. Three more sets we haven't been able to identify. And some prints from Edwin Marchand, Inez's husband."

Connolly frowned. "Edwin Marchand?" That was Mrs. Marchand's husband. He insisted he'd never been to the beach house.

"Yes," Hodges replied. "Edwin. He's Inez's husband."

"And the prints were in the house?"

"Yes? Something odd about that?"

"Where were they?" Connolly asked. "Where in the house did you find his prints?"

Hodges checked the file. "They were on the frame of the front door. Countertop in the kitchen. And a door frame in the back bedroom."

"Anywhere else?"

"Not that they noted."

"Did you talk to him?"

"Yes."

"What did he say?"

"Said he hadn't been down there in years."

Years. He told Connolly he'd never been there ever, but Connolly kept quiet about that. No point in saying too much. Not until he found out more about what was really going on. Instead he asked, "Do you think he's telling you the truth?"

"I suppose." Hodges shrugged. "Prints stay around a long time. Some reason to think he's not?"

Connolly dodged the question. "I don't know. What else you got?"

"That's about it."

"That's not much," Connolly noted.

Hodges shifted positions in the chair. "It was right after a hurricane. We had several dead bodies to deal with around the county. Power was out in most places. We had to get crews with chain saws to cut our way to a couple of them. Everybody was working around the clock. We didn't have time to process every scrap of paper in the place. Had a tough time just getting down there to it."

Connolly nodded. "Did you take anything from the scene?"

"Not much." Hodges looked at the file. "I had a difficult time figuring out what was important and what wasn't. The place was a mess." He lifted a page from the file and read. "We took the sheets from the bed. A slug from the wall. Thirty-eight caliber. Got the results back on it the other day. Found some empty Sudafed boxes in the first bedroom. That's about it." He tossed the inventory list on the desk. "I mean, the sink was full of dirty dishes. Junk piled around everywhere. We could have loaded a trailer truck if we'd wanted to but none of it seemed that important to the case."

Connolly scanned the inventory document. "Sudafed?"

Hodges nodded. "From the look of the kitchen and the smell of the place, I'd say somebody was cooking up some meth in there."

Connolly hadn't noticed the odor. "You think that's what the dead guy was doing?"

"Wouldn't surprise me. Maybe your guy, too."

"Did you find any prints on the boxes?"

"One of the unidentified sets."

"Anybody else's prints on the boxes?"

"Can't say."

Connolly was puzzled. "You can't say?"

"Still investigating it," Hodges said.

Connolly was aggravated by the response. "You found somebody's prints on the boxes. You think that person was cooking meth in the house where the dead man was found. And you won't tell me who it was?"

Hodges smiled. "I'm just telling you what they told me to say. We're still investigating."

"They?"

"You know. The usual players in these cases."

Connolly bristled at the comment. He didn't like it when people tried to get cute with him. "I'm entitled to know who that person is."

"We're still investigating."

Connolly sighed. "We'll see about that."

"I'm sure you'll find someone to talk to about it."

Connolly wanted to leave right then. Track down Henry McNamara. Pin his head against a wall and make him talk. But he needed a few more things from Hodges. And he didn't want to spend the night in jail with Dibber. So, instead, he asked, "How'd you find out about the dead guy?"

"A lady from the house next door reported it." Hodges looked in the file again. "Amy Wilburn. You want the address? They live up here."

"Yeah." Connolly already had the address from McNamara, but he didn't want to tell Hodges what he knew about the case. Better to keep him wondering, especially after the way Hodges was jerking him around. "What did she say?"

Hodges scribbled the address on a legal pad and tore off the page. "The Wilburns own the house next to the Marchands." He handed the address to Connolly. "They came down to check on it after the storm. Noticed an odor. Husband went over to see about it. Called us."

"He went in the house?"

"I don't think so. Said he didn't. Said he only got as far as the steps. Or rather where the steps had been. Odor was pretty strong. I think there were flies coming from inside, too. So, he didn't want to go inside."

"The body was in bad shape?"

"Not terrible. I've seen worse. But it was smelling pretty rank by the time we got there."

Connolly nodded. "What about the son?"

"The son?"

"You said you found prints in the house for the Marchands' son."

"Yeah." Hodges glanced at the file. "Nicholas Marchand. Born August 3, 1970. Works at Southern Nursery Supply in Wilmer. I think they own it."

"Who?"

"The Marchands. I think Southern Nursery Supply is their business."

"Did you talk to him?"

"Yeah."

"What did he say?"

Hodges checked the file. "Said he didn't know the dead guy. Never seen him. Didn't know why he was in the house."

"Did you ask him about your meth theory?"

Hodges smiled. "Can't say."

"Can't say?"

Hodges leaned back in his chair and folded his arms behind his head. "Like I told you, we're still investigating this case."

"But you charged Dibber."

"That was Henry's call."

"You didn't think it was warranted?"

"We had him on possession and receipt of stolen property. The murder charge was a little much. But, you know, that wasn't up to me."

Connolly didn't like the answer, but he resisted the urge to press the issue further. "What about the key?"

Hodges looked puzzled. "What key?"

"Morgan said he found a key in the guy's pocket."

"Oh. That key." Hodges shook his head. "Haven't checked on it yet. Been trying to find out who he was."

"Don't you think that key might be important?"

Hodges shrugged. "I don't know. Might be."

"Well if it fits the front door of the beach house, wouldn't you think maybe somebody's lying about not knowing who he is? And about not giving him access to the place."

"Maybe. But he could have found it once he was inside. The door was obviously kicked open. Bolt went through the facing."

"And you think he found the key after he got in."

Hodges nodded. "Could have. Whoever went in there didn't use a key to get inside, that's for sure.

Connolly shook his head. "And I suppose the key could have fallen from the sky, too."

Hodges looked perturbed. "What are you saying with a comment like that?"

"I'm saying, nobody's going to believe he found the key."

"What are they going to believe?"

"That you're hiding something."

"Maybe I am, and maybe I'm not. But whatever else you need to know, you can get from Henry." Hodges placed the loose papers in the file and closed it. "I think I've told you all I can for now."

Hodges stood but Connolly remained seated. "Henry said you found Dibber because he pawned something from the beach house."

Hodges nodded. "A jet ski."

"How did you know it belonged to the Marchands?"

"They filed a report on it."

Connolly was taken aback. "They reported it stolen?"

"Yeah. Look, I'm not comfortable talking about—"

"Doesn't that strike you as odd?"

"What?"

"People in the house are cooking meth and they file a report with the police saying someone stole their jet ski."

Hodges smiled. "I didn't say they were smart. And I didn't say the Marchands were cooking the meth." He sat down, took a copy of the property report from the file, and handed it to Connolly. "They filed a report with the Dauphin Island police when they met with FEMA."

"FEMA?"

"After the storm," Hodges explained. "They applied for disaster relief. Look on the back." He pointed to the page in Connolly's hand. "It lists several items they say were stolen or missing from the house. They filed a report on it to back up their claim for property loss on their FEMA application."

Connolly glanced at the police report. It was signed by Inez Marchand and listed a number of items including the jet ski. Connolly pointed to the list. "Are you accusing Dibber of taking all of the things on this list?"

Hodges shook his head. "Not right now. Just the jet ski."

Connolly glanced at the report again, then handed it to Hodges. "Could I get a copy of this?"

"Sure." Hodges stood. Connolly pointed to the file that lay on the desk. "How about a copy of those other things, too. The inventory of what you took from the house. The incident report when you went out there. The report about the fingerprints you found. Whatever you have."

"You know," Hodges groused, "it would be a lot easier to cooperate with you if you were a little easier to get along with."

Connolly was astounded. He thought of himself as one of the

nicer defense lawyers. Cordial. Pleasant. Downright friendly. Most of the time. "What do you mean?" he asked.

I didn't like the way you said I did a bad job investigating this case."

"I didn't say that."

"Yeah, you did. When you were talking about that key. You said I was hiding something."

"I said that's what people would believe. If you say in court what you said to me, a jury is going to wonder why you didn't stick the key in the knob and find out if it fit the door at the beach house."

"Maybe so. And I'll get to it. But it's a long way down there and I have other things to work on besides this case. If Henry wants to know about it, I'll go find out." Hodges came from behind the desk. "Anthony Hammond was talking about you the other day."

"Yeah?" Connolly was amused to know they talked about him. "What'd he say about me?"

Hodges came from behind the desk. "He said if I didn't watch out, you'd walk off with the whole file."

Connolly grinned. "Did he also tell you I'm one of the good guys?"

Hodges had a wry smiled as he moved toward the door. "Come on," he said. "I'll get you some copies."

CHAPTER 18

The Wilburns lived in a two-story stucco house on five acres off Yorkhaven Road on the west side of town. A concrete drive ran from the road to a garage on the side of the house. A walkway curved around from the driveway to the front door. The walkway was lined with monkey grass and small accent lights with black covers. Boxwood shrubs grew beneath the windows. A wooden fence surrounded the back yard. Over the top, Connolly could see a play set. A Honda minivan was parked at the end of the drive.

Connolly brought the car to a stop behind the minivan, then stepped from the car and walked to the front door. From inside, he heard the heavy beat of music. He rang the doorbell and waited. The music continued, then stopped. Someone was talking inside, but he couldn't hear what they were saying. He pressed the doorbell once more.

In a moment, the door opened and a woman appeared. About thirty years old, she was tall and slender and dressed in a blue exercise suit. She had short brown hair cropped just below her ears in a way that made it flip toward the front. Her cheeks were red. Sweat glistened on her neck. She took a deep breath and smiled. "Hello," she said. "And what are you selling today? New windows? Lawn care?" She obviously didn't want to be bothered but she said so in a friendly way.

Connolly smiled. "I hope I didn't take you away from something important."

"No." She took another deep breath. "I needed a break."

Connolly nodded. "My name is Mike Connolly. I'm an attorney. I'm looking for Amy Wilburn."

She wiped her face with her hands. "Who's mad at me now?"

"You called the sheriff's office about a problem at a house on Dauphin Island."

"Yes."

"I was wondering if I could talk to you about that."

"Sure." She moved away from the door. "Come on inside."

Connolly stepped through the doorway. She closed the door behind him and led him to the kitchen. "Would you like something to drink? Iced tea? Water?"

"No. I'm fine."

She took a glass from the cabinet and filled it with ice. "Are you sure? I'm having tea."

"Okay," Connolly relented. "I'll have what you're having." He moved around the kitchen table and took a seat. She filled a glass and set it on the table in front of him.

"My husband is the one who thought something was wrong. He's the one who said we should call someone." She found a napkin and laid it next to Connolly's glass, then took a seat.

Connolly took a sip of tea. "What made him think something was wrong?" He expected a response about the smell. But you never knew. Witnesses had a way of saying surprising things.

"We were down there after the storm, checking on our house. He and the children were wandering around looking at the damage to the other houses. They came back and said there was a terrible smell coming from that house. We all went over and had a look. Would have gone inside but the stairs were torn up." She frowned. "It was really bad. So, finally I just called and reported it."

"You didn't go inside the house?"

"No." She shook her head. "Glad we didn't, too." She took a sip of tea. "Did they ever identify the body?"

"Yes. His name is Stephen Ellis. Does that name mean anything to you?"

"No." She shook her head. "I don't know anyone by that name."

"The sheriff's office says he was from Lawrenceville, Georgia." Connolly took another sip of tea. "Does that mean anything to you?"

"No." Amy shook her head. "I don't even know where that is. I mean, Georgia. Sure. But I've never heard of Lawrenceville."

"Have you had any trouble with people breaking into your beach house?"

"No."

"What about the neighbors?"

"Not that I know of. It's pretty quiet down there. Most people in our area know each other. Not much happens."

"Did you know the Marchands?"

"I knew that was the name of the people who owned that house, but I never met them. Mostly young guys have been in and out of there."

"That afternoon, when you noticed the smell. Did your husband go inside the house?"

"No. At least, he said he didn't. I think he climbed up to the door and looked in."

"What about your children?"

"No." She shook her head. "They're five and three."

Connolly nodded. "Did you talk to your neighbors about the smell?"

"Yeah. Sure. I mean, we all talked about it. Several of them were down there that same weekend."

"Did any of them go in the house?"

"No. This all happened in just a few hours. We talked. I made the call."

"But your neighbors noticed the smell?"

"Yes." She nodded. "There was no way to miss it. Several people were talking about it. You know, the ones who have houses around there. We were all down there after the storm, trying to see what was left."

"And you knew the name of the people who own the house, but you never met them."

"I think I might have met the woman once."

"Inez Marchand."

"Yes. Marchand. I think I met her once. She's an older woman."

"Did you see her down there much? Was she at the beach house a lot?"

"I don't think so. They've had people in and out of there most of the time when we've been down there. But most of the time it was a guy about my age. I think he's the son of the people who own it. That's what they say. And he had some young guys with him."

"They say?"

"The other owners."

"How many people did he bring with him?"

"Two or three guys." She grimaced. "A couple of them seemed rather scary to me. Not really the kind of people we hang out with."

"A rowdy group?"

"And not in a good way."

"Did you ever have any trouble with them?"

"Once or twice it got a little loud over there."

"Did you or your husband ever go over there to talk to them about it?"

"No." She shook her head. "We didn't. Some of the neighbors did."

"Have you ever been inside that house?"

"No."

"Was anyone living in it? You know, permanently?"

"I don't think so. But we're only down there on weekends, and not every weekend at that. So, I don't know what happened during the week."

"When was the last time you were down there before the storm?"

"A day or two before it hit. We went down to board up the windows."

"Was anyone in the Marchands' house then?"

"Yes." She nodded. "They were down there. Looked like they

were getting things ready. You know, preparing for the storm. Like everybody else."

"Who was there?"

"The guy who's about my age and the young guys."

"What were they doing?"

"When we drove up, they had a pickup parked at the steps and were loading things on it."

"Things?"

"A mattress. Clothes. That kind of thing."

"Did you talk to them?"

"No," she said. "We got busy doing what we were doing, and I didn't pay any attention. When we left, they were already gone."

"What time did you leave?"

"Just as it was getting dark. We got down there about two in the afternoon. Left right at dark."

"Did you ever see anyone else at the house? Other than the son and his friends?"

"Not really. I mean, there could have been other people. I wasn't watching very closely and, like I said, we weren't down there every weekend."

"Okay." Connolly took another sip of tea and set the glass on the table. He wiped his hands on the napkin and stood. "Well. I think that's about all I have for right now. I appreciate your time."

"I hope I helped."

"You did."

She came from her place at the table and led him through the house to the front door. "My husband might be able to tell you more. He'll be in this afternoon."

"Thanks," Connolly replied. "I may give him a call. And I may be back later with more questions, if that's okay."

"Sure," she said. "I'll tell you whatever I know."

CHAPTER 19

Amy Wilburn hadn't given Connolly any information he didn't already have, but she did clarify a few details about how the body was discovered. And she reinforced something he'd come to suspect—whatever was going on in that beach house, Nick Marchand was at the center of it. Nick and the group of guys who hung out with him. They were as involved as anyone.

Connolly checked his watch as he drove away from the Wilburns' home. It was almost two. Talking to Amy had taken less time than he expected. With most of the afternoon still available, he decided to look for Lutie Shaw, the man to whom Dibber had sold some of the items from the Marchands' beach house.

From the west side of town, Connolly drove across the city to Wilson Avenue in Prichard on the north side of Mobile. He knew one person in Prichard—a former client named Tyrone Jackson. If Lutie Shaw was as notorious as Tommy suggested, Tyrone would know how to find him.

As a young man, Tyrone had lived a rambunctious life. In grammar school he was in a fist fight almost every day. Midway through the eighth grade he was suspended for selling beer from his locker. In the eleventh grade he was arrested for stealing radios from automobiles in an apartment complex near the high school. Then, in his senior year he and two friends stole a beer truck. They stashed the beer in the woods behind Tyrone's house and abandoned the truck in front of the Dairy Freeze in Chickasaw. Only problem was, the Chickasaw police chief lived across the road from the Dairy Freeze. He knew about the missing truck and was on the lookout. Tyrone and his friends were arrested the next morning. The friends pled guilty and went to prison. Tyrone's mother hired Connolly.

With some hard work by Connolly and Hollis, the charges were dismissed at the preliminary hearing. It was a difficult time for Tyrone and his mother, but a critical juncture in Tyrone's life. He finished high school, attended college, and opened his own business. Mid-City Tire. In the years that followed, he married, had four children, and served as a deacon at the Eighth Street Baptist Church. Not much happened in Prichard that he didn't know about.

The drive across town took thirty minutes. A car sat on the lift. Tyrone came from beneath it with a smile. "Mr. Connolly." He wiped his hands on a rag. "Haven't seen you in a long time."

"Too long," Connolly replied.

"How's that car of yours running?"

"Doing well."

"Ready to sell it to me?"

"No. Not yet."

"Don't see many like it these days."

"No, you don't."

"What brings you up this way?"

"I'm looking for someone."

"Oh? What kind of someone?"

"Trouble."

"Trouble got a name?"

"Lutie Shaw."

"Client of yours?"

"No," Connolly replied. "He's a witness."

"Anything Lutie Shaw witnessed can't be good."

"Probably not. Do you know where he lives?"

"Yeah. I know where he lives. You got a pistol with you?" Connolly chuckled. Tyrone didn't smile. "I'm not kidding. The fire department doesn't go in there without a police escort."

"I'll be alright," Connolly assured. "Where does he live?"

"Go out Main Street to Price Avenue. There's a club on the corner. Vee-Jay's Lounge." Connolly nodded. Tyrone continued. "Take a right. Go up a couple of blocks to Lucky Street."

Connolly frowned. "Lucky Street?"

"It ain't really lucky but that's the name. Go left on Lucky. Go down Lucky about two or three blocks. Some of the blocks may be a little long in there, but two or three blocks. You'll come to Hobbs Avenue. Turn left. Lutie lives in a green house on the left. Just before you get to the railroad tracks."

"Green house on the left."

"Yeah. Green." Tyrone smiled. "Like, bright green."

"Okay. Thanks."

Tyrone smiled. "Sure is good to see you. You ought to come by here more often. I'll give you a good deal on some tires."

Connolly nodded. "Might take you up on that."

"I can get you some bias ply tires, just like the ones that came on it."

"Can you still get those?"

"I can," Tyrone said.

Connolly tossed a wave over his shoulder as he walked to the car.

Finding Lutie Shaw's house wasn't any trouble. Painted lime green—and with purple trim and a pink door—it was visible from two blocks away. A small patch of lawn separated the house from the street. The unkept grass was dotted with weeds and littered with trash.

Connolly parked the Chrysler across the street and started toward the house. As he approached the steps up to the porch, the front door opened, and a young man came out. He looked Connolly over, then said, "You lost?"

"I don't think so." Connolly was all business. "I'm looking for someone named Lutie Shaw."

"What you want with him?"

"I'm a lawyer. I would like to talk to him." Connolly reached into his pocket for a business card. The young man was suddenly alert and reached behind his back as if going for a pistol. Connolly moved his arms away from his body and held them out to either side. "It's okay," he said. He opened his jacket in both directions. "I'm just getting a business card."

The young man relaxed. Connolly took the card from his pocket and handed it to him. "I represent a man named Dibber Landry. I just want to talk to Mr. Shaw."

The young man glanced at the card, then back at Connolly. "Dibber. A white guy?"

"Yes."

"Stays down around Dauphin Island most of the time?"

"Yes."

"What's this got to do with Loo-Tay?"

"Supposedly, he bought some things from Dibber. I need to talk to him about—"

The young man shook his head and backed away. "Ain't nobody talk to Loo-Tay about no missin' property. And we sure as hell ain't talking about no Dibber. That boy's crazy. Whatever property we got here is ours. And whatever he done, he on his own."

Just then, the door opened, and an older man appeared. As tall as the door and almost as wide, he had a fat belly that bulged beneath an oversized black and white shirt that hung past the waistband of his black pants. The legs of the pants were big and floppy and so long that they piled up on top of the black canvas high-tops on his feet. The sleeves of his shirt reached past his first knuckles but beneath the cuff Connolly could see each finger bore a gold ring with a diamond in the center. Around his neck were rows and rows of gold chains. He came as far as the porch steps and paused, his eyes fixed on Connolly, sizing him up. "What you asking about Dibber?"

"Do you know him?"

"Maybe. What you want?"

"I'm looking for Lutie Shaw."

"Loo-Tay," the man corrected, placing the accent on the last syllable.

"Yes. Lutie," Connolly said. "I need to talk to him."

"Say it right."

Connolly was certain now the man before him was Lutie Shaw, but he also felt like he was being jerked around and he didn't like it. "Excuse me?"

"The name is Loo-Tay. Like it's two words. Loo. Tay. People round here respects him. You come in from the outside, people maybe don't expect you to know about all that. But you got to pronounce the name correctly if you want to do some business with us."

Connolly didn't like the tone of his voice. "Do you know him?"

The man's forehead wrinkled in a frown. "Do I know who?"

"Lutie," Connolly said. "Lutie Shaw. Do you know him?"

"Listen to me." His voice showed a hint of irritation. "I am Loo-Tay, Okay? And I want you to pronounce it the right way. Loo-Tay. Otherwise, you can get on back to wherever you came from."

Connolly realized he'd played the game far enough. "Alright. Loo-Tay." He pronounced it as instructed. "I meant no offense."

"Alright." Lutie smiled. "Now we can do some business. Come on inside."

The young man on the porch gestured toward the door. Connolly followed Lutie inside the house to a large front room. Beyond it was a dining area and kitchen. To the left was a hallway. A large-screen television hung on the wall. A rug covered the floor in front of it with oversized pillows scattered about. In the corner to the right was a leather recliner, facing the television. A woman wearing red vinyl hot pants and a yellow vinyl halter top was sprawled across the chair. Lutie strode toward her. "Woman, get out of my chair."

She smiled at him but didn't move. He slapped her on the thigh. She grimaced in pain and pouted. "That hurt!"

"Get out of my chair." She rolled off the chair and stood. Lutie put his arm around her and kissed her. His eyes followed her as she crossed the room and disappeared down the hall.

When she was gone, Lutie took a seat in the chair. The young man who had been outside stood next to him. Connolly stood facing him. A second man entered the room and took a position behind Connolly. Lutie gestured to Connolly. "Okay, ask Loo-Tay what you want to know."

"Dibber Landry sold you some jewelry a few weeks ago."

"That's what he says?"

Connolly nodded. "That's what he says."

"I don't know." Lutie shrugged. "Maybe he did. And, maybe he didn't. Hard to say. We do a lot of business up in here."

"The pieces came from a beach house on Dauphin Island."

"I wouldn't know about that. Dibber's not one of my people."

"But you know him."

"I know him. I do business with him. But he's not one of my people. Dibber's a freelancer."

Connolly frowned. "A freelancer?"

"He don't take orders. Operates strictly on spec."

Again, Connolly frowned. "Orders? Spec? I don't understand."

"Orders," Lutie said, as if explaining. "Like, somebody wants a television or a DVD player, they come to one of my people. Give them the order. They bring it to me. I look it over. If I got it, I sell it to them. We do the deal regular. If not, one of my people goes and finds it. Sell it to them at a reasonable price. They get a markup. I get a fee for my network. Everybody happy."

The man beside him snickered. Connolly ignored him. "So, Dibber doesn't do that?"

"No."

"How does it work with him?"

"Dibber on his own. Finds something he thinks we might be interested in, brings it to us. My people work on a sure thing. Dibber works on speculation."

The men around Lutie snickered again. Lutie cut them off with a glare. Connolly shifted his weight from one foot to the other. "Did Dibber sell you a pistol?"

Lutie gestured with both hands in protest. "Don't do no weapons."

"He didn't sell you a pistol?"

"I don't deal in no weapons. None of my people deals in weapons. I catch them dealing guns, they're out." His eyes bore in on Connolly. "You know what I'm saying? Out. Totally."

The look in his eye made Connolly uneasy. "I take it this wasn't the first time Dibber sold you something."

Lutie had a pleasant expression, "Dibber and me go way back. He a good guy. He just susceptible to certain things. Which we all are. But Dibber more than some."

It was a cryptic remark and Connolly wanted to delve into it but he needed to know about the details at hand so he continued, "Dibber said he tried to sell you a jet ski, but you wouldn't take it."

"That's right." Lutie nodded. "Wrong item for my business. This is where a freelancer gets hung up sometimes. Not much call for jet skis with my people. Motorcycles, yes. Jet skis, no. Not really the beach crowd, if you know what I mean."

Connolly understood exactly what Lutie was saying. He had systematized theft and sale of stolen property. Organized it. Monetized it. Incentivized it. And made it work like a retail business in both directions. It was a fascinating use of skill and acumen, and one Connolly would have loved to hear more about. But he'd stayed long enough, and it was time to go. "Well," he said finally, "I thank you for your time."

"That's all you wanted?"

"For now." Connolly took a step toward the door. Lutie stood and moved across the room with him. "Dibber's in some big trouble?"

"Capital murder."

"Woo." Lutie shook his head. "That's a heavy charge. I could have told him she wasn't right."

The remark seemed odd. "Who?"

"That skinny little thing he been hanging out with," Lutie said. "Tiffany, or whatever her name is. Some bad stuff. Girl like that get you killed quick."

"You know Tiffany?"

"No. I don't know her." Lutie shook his head. "I don't know her. And I don't want to know her. But I seen her a time or two. She was with him the last time I saw him. I seen a thousand like her. She a manipulator."

"She was with him?"

Lutie nodded. "A first-class piece of work. You ask me, she was the reason he was down there in that house in the first place."

"Why?"

"Way she acted. Trying to get something out of him. Let him take all the risk. She get all the reward. Straight up manipulator. Dibber, he's the kind don't see that kind of thing coming. Girl like that slip right up behind him, whack him in the head, he'd never know it."

"She was tough?"

Lutie shrugged. "Her type a talker. Most of my people come in here, they women don't come with them. When they do, they stand in the corner and keep quiet." He pointed toward the hall. "You see I don't put up with none of that. I pop 'em they get to acting big with me."

"She did the talking?"

Lutie nodded. "Dibber and me couldn't barely do no business with her around. Me, I would have left her ass at home." He grinned. "Well, I wouldn't never had her in the first place. But if I did, I'd leave her skinny behind at the house."

They reached the door. Connolly offered his hand to Lutie. The men around him stepped forward in a defensive gesture. Lutie waved them off. "It's alright, fellas. He just being a gentleman." They shook hands and one of the men opened the door. Lutie ushered Connolly out to the porch. "You need anything? TV? DVD player?"

The men in the room snickered and ducked down the hall. "No," Connolly said. "Not today."

"Well if you do, just let me know. I'll give you a good price on whatever you need."

"Okay."

"And tell Dibber I hope things work out for him."

"I'll tell him."

CHAPTER 20

As he drove back to midtown, Connolly thought about what Lutie had said. He was a crook, but he wasn't stupid. Men like Lutie survived by their wits. What he'd said about Tiffany was true. She was a manipulator. A gamer. Playing off other people's needs. He'd noticed that about her from their brief visit.

At the Loop, Connolly stopped at Hong Kong Buffet and picked up dinner, then called Barbara and met her at the guesthouse. Twilight faded to evening as they sat at the dining table eating.

Around seven, as they moved from the dining table to the sofa, Connolly's cell phone rang. The call was from Tiffany. "Tinker wants to talk," she said.

"Good," Connolly replied. "Put him on."

"Not now."

"When?"

"Later."

"How much later?"

"Tonight."

"Where?"

"The parking deck across from the Essex Hotel."

"How will I find him?"

"Park on the third level. He'll find you."

"Will you be there?"

"He'll find you."

"Does he know what I look like?"

"That car ain't hard to spot."

"What time?"

"Nine."

Connolly ended the call. Barbara looked over at him. "Is something up?"

"A guy I've been looking for wants to meet."

"Tonight?"

"Yes."

"We can never catch a break, can we?"

He leaned over and kissed her. "You could wait for me."

She arched an eyebrow. "Here?"

"Yes."

"I didn't bring anything to stay," she replied.

He grinned in response. She nudged him and changed the subject. "Is this about one of your cases?"

"He's supposed to know something about Dibber."

"Where are you meeting him?"

"The parking deck across from the Essex Hotel."

"Sounds like a good spy novel."

"Watergate."

"All the President's Men."

"Something like that."

"Meeting a man at night makes you look very contemporary. I'm not sure about meeting one in a parking deck."

Connolly gave her an amused look and gestured toward himself. "Me? Contemporary?"

"Yeah. You know. With it." She giggled.

"You mean like, groovy?"

"And far out, man."

They laughed. She leaned against him. "Seems like a long time ago."

"It was a long time ago," he replied.

"I know. But it seems even longer."

"Times aren't what they used to be."

"And what they used to be wasn't all that good."

"It wasn't so bad, was it?"

"Not all of it."

Connolly rested his head against the back of the sofa. "Do you ever wonder if you really know what's going on in life?"

"Wow." Barbara chuckled. "You know how to talk to a girl."

"Sorry."

"Who did you see today?"

He gave her a questioning look. "What do you mean?"

"When you first started practicing law you used to run into these strange people sometimes. I could always tell when it happened because you'd come home in a strange mood, and we'd have this conversation."

Connolly smiled. She looked at him. "So? Who was it?"

"Lutie Shaw."

Barbara had a pained expression, as if in disbelief. "Lutie Shaw? That's his real name?"

"Yes."

"What does he do?"

"Lutie Shaw is … royalty."

"Royalty?"

"Yes." Connolly nodded. "He rules a special kingdom."

She rolled her eyes. "Here we go."

"No. Really. It's a kingdom, but it's one you can't see."

"Do I need to call somebody? Have them look after you?"

"Lutie's kingdom exists just beneath the thin veneer of our everyday life."

"Seriously, are you okay?"

"He lives in a house in Prichard. Lime green with purple trim. He has courtesans who attend him. He has mistresses who cater to him. He holds power over his kingdom by keeping his subjects supplied with the things they need. And he makes a nice profit from it for himself and the members of his royal family."

Barbara frowned. "You've been smoking something."

"No." Connolly insisted. "He actually exists."

"And he's a king."

"Royalty."

"He's in jail?"

"Not yet."

"But he's a crook."

"Oh, yes." Connolly nodded. "He's a crook. But his kingdom is real. And he really rules it." His voice took a faraway sound, as if with each word he was fading into the world he saw in his mind. "There is a life out there that we know nothing about. It's hidden by what we were taught to think of as normal. But for most of the world, we are abnormal. They are normal."

"Normal?"

He cut his eyes toward her with a confident look. "There's more of them than there are of us."

"Majority rules."

"Something like that."

"Do you need me to fix some coffee before you go?"

"That would be great," he replied.

She stood and moved around to the kitchen. "I wanted to tell you something tonight."

"That doesn't sound good."

"It's sad. And it's good." She rinsed out the pot for the coffee-maker. "I've decided to sell the house."

His eyes opened wide in a look of surpise. "You're kidding."

"No. I'm very serious."

"But why? You love that house."

"And you don't."

"I love that house," he said. "But I don't want to go back to who I used to be."

She switched on the coffeemaker and came back to the sofa. "Listen to me." She took his hand in hers. "You're not the person I married. I'm not the person you married. We're not the people we were when you fell into a gin bottle. I don't want to lose you again. And if you can't go back to the house, I don't want to stay there."

Connolly tried not to cry, but it was useless to resist. Tears ran down his cheeks. She put her arms around his neck and pulled him close. He felt her crying, too. "I've been talking to a realtor," she continued. "She thinks she can sell it without any trouble."

He pulled away and wiped his cheeks with his fingers. "But it's your house. The one you wanted. Maybe I can—"

"No," she said, cutting him off. "If it's that big of a thing for you, maybe it is for me, too. Maybe I'm someone I shouldn't be."

They kissed, then kissed again. He looked her in the eye. "I don't want you to sell the house."

"And I don't want to live there if you won't come inside."

The coffeemaker finished. She nudged him. "Get a cup of coffee. You have someone to meet."

"Will you be here when I get back?"

"I don't know. But if I leave, I'll lock the door."

Connolly filled an insulated cup with coffee and kissed her goodbye, then started out to the car. As he drove away, he thought about the house. All that had happened there. And the things they'd said. That conversation was the closest they'd come to discussing whether they would get back together. He wanted them to. But he was apprehensive about how to do that. He wanted to tell her how much he loved her, but he wanted it to mean something and things weren't like when they were younger. Back then, he didn't have to prove he really meant it. He only had to muster the courage to say it. Now, after all they'd been through, it seemed he had to do something more. Something to add content—real content, meaningful content—to the words. And he wasn't sure how to do that.

But as he drove farther from the guesthouse, he thought of the meeting that lay ahead. He was apprehensive about it—meeting someone he didn't know, in a parking deck, at night, by himself, without Hollis. But it was in a prominent location. Valet drivers from the hotel were in and out of there constantly so they wouldn't be totally secluded. And the place had security cameras at every corner and support column. Still. He would rather be back at the guesthouse with Barbara.

The Essex Hotel was a downtown landmark. The main entrance opened beneath a large canopy on Royal Street. Revolving doors led to a lobby with a marble floor and a ceiling that soared four stories high. Around the corner on St. Michael Street was a second, less opulent, entrance. Across from it was the parking garage. Connolly drove up the ramp to the third floor. It wasn't as full as the lower levels and seemed emptier than he expected. He chose an open spot on the side directly opposite the hotel and checked to make sure the car doors were locked.

Nine o'clock came and went and by nine-thirty Tinker still hadn't showed. Connolly opened the car door and stepped outside. The damp night air felt cool against his face. He moved behind the car and leaned against the railing. A breeze blew in from the bay as he stared down at the cars by the hotel. Down the way to the left, a ship glided slowly up from the bay. Tugboats on either side kept it straight. In the stillness of the night, voices of the crew echoed across the water. He stood there, arms folded over his chest, listening to the sounds of the night, and waiting.

By ten, he'd had enough. He got in the Chrysler and started from the garage. As he passed the toll booth on the first floor, his cell phone rang with another call from Tiffany.

"Tinker couldn't make it," she said. "Somebody was watching us."

"I didn't see anyone."

"He really wants to talk. It's just, some people were around and it didn't look good. Tinker had a bad feeling. I don't blame him."

"Where are you?"

"At home," she said, then ended the call.

When he came from the parking deck, Connolly took the first street that headed west, away from downtown. Two blocks later, he passed a yellow Chevrolet Caprice. As he went by, the car's headlights came on and the car started toward him. At the next corner,

Connolly then made the block and doubled back. The car, though, continued west and soon disappeared from sight.

"I should have never come out here tonight," he said to himself. He hated it when people took advantage of him. And he hated it when they manipulated him. Lutie was right about Tiffany. She was a manipulator. And she had manipulated him. "But not again," he said. "I'm not chasing this."

CHAPTER 21

Connolly's first appointment the next day was in Judge Cahill's court for a preliminary hearing in a robbery case. He went by the office and collected the file, then walked over to the courthouse. He arrived early. Walter, the judge's bailiff, was busy at his desk near the bench. He glanced up as Connolly entered the courtroom. "You're here early," he said.

"Thought I'd get at the head of the line." Connolly set his leather satchel on the counsel's table. Walter caught his eye. "We got a big docket this morning. You won't be first."

Connolly shrugged. "I know." He took a seat in a chair near the rail.

Walter picked up a stack of files. "You want some coffee?"

"Sure." Connolly followed Walter through the door behind the judge's bench to the judge's chambers. Two chairs sat to the right of the door with a small table between them. Windows lined the wall opposite the door with a view of the street below. A coffee pot sat on a ledge below the windows. Judge Cahill's office was to the left. He called to Connolly as he passed the office door. "Mike, how much time do you need to get ready on that murder case? Landry."

Connolly reached the coffee pot. "I don't know, yet, Judge. I'm still asking questions. Tracking down leads."

"We need to schedule a preliminary hearing. Walter, what are we looking at?"

Walter filled a cup and handed it to Connolly. "This month is almost full, Judge."

"Give Mike a date."

Connolly stepped to the office door. "Judge, they only identified the body in that case a few days ago." He took a sip of coffee. "We haven't been able to find out much about him."

"That's alright. If you need more time, we can see about continuing it later. I don't want this case to sit around. Walter will give you a date. We can work with you if you need it."

The door behind them opened and Gayle Underwood entered. She passed Connolly and moved toward the coffee pot. "We found Billy Ellis. The dead man's father in that Landry case," she said. "He's coming in this afternoon. Are you interested in talking to him?"

"Yes," Connolly replied. "I am."

Gayle filled a cup with coffee and stood near the door to Cahill's office. "We're meeting with him around three this afternoon. You can see him after we get finished."

Judge Cahill came from his desk. "I think it would be good if you both talked to him at the same time. Save us some time."

Gayle frowned. "I don't think Henry will agree to that, Your Honor."

Cahill eyes were intense, and his jaw was set. "I'm not asking Henry to agree." The cadence of his voice was all business. "I can order him to do it. I'm just saying, we need to get this case moving. You have an out-of-state witness. I think it would help if you both talked to him at the same time. The man isn't going to be a witness to anything, is he?"

Gayle shifted the coffee cup to her right hand. "That's just it, Your Honor. We don't know what he's going to say yet."

Cahill's tone became less strident. "Well, I don't think it would hurt if the two of you talked to him together. If he has something interesting to say, you can always talk to him separately later. This way, you can both hear his story and then he can arrange to get his son's body and get out of here."

"I don't—"

Cahill's face went cold. Whatever he'd been holding inside broke free and burst from his mouth in a torrent of emotion. "The man just lost his son!" His voice was loud. The emotion, raw. "I'm not letting him hang around here two or three days while Henry tries to figure out what to ask him!"

Cahill stepped into his office and slammed the door shut. Gayle set her coffee cup on the table by the door and walked out to the courtroom. Connolly took one more sip and followed after her.

When the morning docket was finished Connolly left the courtroom and started toward the elevator. As he walked down the corridor, he felt someone tug on his elbow. He glanced to the right to see Dave Brenner. "Keep walking," Brenner said.

Connolly continued down the corridor past the elevators to a conference room near the end of the hall. Brenner guided him to the door and pushed Connolly inside. The door closed behind them. "Don't call my office any more about this," Brenner said. "In fact, don't call my office at all. About anything."

Connolly knew he was talking about Raisa. "Where is she?" he asked.

"She's in Croatia," Brenner replied.

"Croatia?"

"Bosnia."

"Which one?"

"Which ever one she's supposed to be in. She's where she's supposed to be."

"Is she alright?"

"Yes. She's fine. She's working for an American company. She's being taken care of. We have her under constant surveillance."

"You're just blowing smoke, right? You don't have a clue where she is or what she's doing."

Brenner leaned close. "Listen to me. She is fine. She's being debriefed by their people."

"Alone?"

"No. We have someone with her."

"At the meetings?"

"Yes."

"I don't know whether to believe you or not."

"I don't care," Brenner said. "I'm telling you what I know. You can believe me or not. It doesn't matter to me. The girl is safe. We're looking after her. They tell me she's adjusting. Apparently, she's telling them things they need to know."

"She'll have to testify over there?"

"Yes."

"And here?"

"Yes. But their first trial won't be for another six or eight months."

"Then what?"

"I don't know. How could I know?" Brenner asked. "The investigation has broadened since you and I talked before. They'll need her as long as they need her."

"But then she'll be able to come back here."

"Yes. If she wants to."

"Wouldn't you?"

"I wouldn't have gone in the first place." Brenner stepped toward the door as if to leave, then paused. "Don't call me anymore." He jabbed Connolly in the chest with his finger. "You keep messing with this and you'll screw up the whole deal. Leave it alone. You understand me?"

"Yeah." Connolly held his temper. "I hear you."

Brenner jerked the door open and walked out to the corridor. Connolly followed him and they went together in silence as far as the elevator. Brenner continued through a doorway that led to the judges' chambers. Connolly pressed a button for the elevator.

CHAPTER 22

At three that afternoon, Connolly arrived at the district attorney's office for his meeting with Gayle Underwood and Billy Ellis. He paused in the waiting area long enough to take a drink from the water fountain, then crossed the room to the receptionist's desk. Juanita saw him coming. "Go on back, Mr. Connolly." She pointed to the door at the end of the desk. "They're waiting for you. End of the hall. Last door on the right."

Connolly continued past Juanita's desk to the door and made his way down the hall where he found the conference room just as she said. Gayle sat on the far side of the table facing the door. Across from her was a man who looked to be in his mid-fifties, wearing a plaid shirt and blue jeans. He had a bony frame with shoulder blades and elbows that poked out against the fabric of his shirt. His thin, narrow neck seemed lost behind the collar. A crease through his hair went around his head just above his ears like he'd been wearing a hat. His legs were crossed and in the shadows under the table Connolly could see he had on a pair of black cowboy boots with brass tips on the toes.

Gayle stood as Connolly appeared at the door. The man at the table with her stood, too, and she introduced them. "This is Billy Ellis." The two men shook hands. Gayle continued. "Mike is the defense lawyer on this case."

Billy gave him a look. "You're defending the man they say killed Stephen?"

"Yes, sir."

"Well, if he's innocent I hope you can get him off. But if he's guilty, I hope they fry him."

"I'm sorry you lost your son."

"Thank you." Billy took a seat. Connolly moved to the end of the table and pulled out a chair. As he and Gayle sat down, Henry entered. "Well, I guess we can get started." Henry laid his file on the table and took a seat at the opposite end from Connolly. "Mike, I'll let you begin."

Connolly nodded. "Is this being recorded?"

Henry shrugged. "I'm not. If you want to, be my guest." He glanced at Billy. "As long as Mr. Ellis doesn't mind."

Something about Henry made Connolly laugh, and something about him made him want to slap his boyish cheeks. He took a deep breath. "It was just a thought, Henry." He looked across the table to Billy. "Mr. Ellis, have they told you what happened to your son?"

"They said somebody found Stephen in a beach house."

"His body was found in a house on Dauphin Island. That's an island south of here on the Gulf. Near the mouth of Mobile Bay. He was found in a beach house. Do you know anyone who lives on Dauphin Island?"

"No."

"Have you ever heard of Dauphin Island?"

"I don't think so. Not before this."

"Never heard anyone mention it?"

"Not that I can recall."

"Bayou La Batre? Coden? Any of those places mean anything to you?"

Billy shook his head. "No."

"Have you been over to the morgue to see the body?"

"Not yet."

Connolly thought for a moment, then continued. "I think I better back up and begin at the beginning. Do you have a son named

Stephen Ellis?"

"No. Well…" Billy had a thin-lipped smile. "He's not exactly my son."

Gayle glanced in Henry's direction. Henry stared at Billy with an odd expression. Connolly continued. "What do you mean?"

"Stephen was… Well, you might say we adopted him."

"Did you go to court and do a formal adoption?"

"No."

"What happened?"

"Stephen was… My wife—ex-wife—Frieda. We was married at the time. She had this friend named…. I can't remember her real name right now. We called her Tiny. She was from down here some-where. But she was a student back then at Emory. Emory Univer-sity. In Atlanta. Anyway, Tiny got pregnant by this fellow who was a professor. You might have heard of him. His name was Harold Schnadelbach."

Connolly felt his stomach drop. He did his best to hide his sur-prise. Billy glanced around the table, as if expecting them to acknowl-edge the name. No one responded. He continued. "He was a writer. Wrote under a different name. I can't remember it, neither. They made a movie out of one of his books." Billy paused as if expecting a response. "Tiny and Harold was seeing each other but Harold was married."

Billy's voice faded into the background. Connolly's mind was on the book. The one on the dresser at the beach house. Hotel Green. Stephen Ellis was down there looking for his mother. And whatever he found, got him killed.

Billy's voice came back into focus. "Things was alright, though, until Tiny got pregnant." Billy sounded like a man unburdening himself with something he'd held inside for a long time. "Harold wanted her to have an abortion, but she wouldn't do it. They fought about it some, but then he got killed. After that—"

"Who got killed?"

"Harold. Harold Schnadelbach." Billy's eyes brightened. He gestured with the index finger of his right hand. "Mary. That's her name. Mary. Mary Givens."

"Tiny?"

"Yeah. We all called her Tiny, but that was her name." He had a satisfied smile. "Mary Givens." He paused a moment as if remembering her, then continued. "After Harold died, Tiny wasn't the same. Things fell apart for her. She had the baby, but she didn't have no way of taking care of him. So, she decided to go home." He had a troubled expression. "But for some reason, she didn't want to take the baby with her. We tried to talk her into it, but she said she couldn't." He shook his head. "I don't know why. So, we took him." He looked over at Connolly. "Nice kid."

"And you said Tiny was from here?"

"Yeah. That's what she said. When she left, she said she was going home to Mobile."

"To her parents?"

"I guess. I mean, that's what I always assumed."

"Do you know their names?"

"No. I don't." Billy shook his head. "I don't think I ever heard her say."

"Does your wife know Stephen is dead?"

Billy's voice took a reverent tone. "She's dead."

Connolly wasn't sure he heard the response. "Excuse me?"

"She's dead." Billy cleared his throat. "Frieda's dead."

"I'm sorry."

"She died ... last year." A puzzled look came over him. "Year before last." He lifted his head and stared into space as if concentrating. "No. Last year. Right at the end of the year." He looked again to Connolly. "I guess it hasn't been a year yet. We weren't married when she died. We got a divorce about fifteen years ago."

"When's the last time you saw Stephen?"

Again Billy seemed unable to respond. "I don't remember," he said. "It's been a while. I think the last time I saw him was when he was in college. He went to Valdosta State. Got in a little trouble." Billy glanced over at Henry. "Whoever called me the other day said that's how you figured out who he was."

Henry nodded. "Sheriff's office matched his prints through the FBI."

Billy smiled. "Funny about all of that." He cocked his head to one side. "Wasn't funny then. But to think him getting in trouble solved a riddle after all these years."

Connolly continued. "Do you know when he left to come down here?"

"No."

"Any way to figure it out?"

"Well, my sister said she saw him at Frieda's funeral. She died end of last year. I think her funeral was the day before New Year's Eve."

"Where was the funeral?"

"Collier's Funeral Home."

"What town?"

"Lawrenceville. Lawrenceville, Georgia. Up there where we live."

"Was Stephen already living down here by then?"

"I don't know."

"But he was in Lawrenceville at the end of last year."

"Yes. That's what my sister says. I didn't see him then."

"Any other time between then and now when you knew where he was?"

Billy thought for a moment, then shook his head. "Nah. Me and him, we didn't get along too good."

"Any idea where Mary Givens lives?"

"No. Somewhere around here, maybe. But I don't know where."

"When's the last time you talked to her?"

"I haven't seen her since the day she left. She handed Stephen to Frieda, got in her car, and drove away. That's the last time I saw her."

"Thirty … forty years ago?"

"Yeah. Forty years ago. Something like that. Stephen was born in August of … 1967."

"Did this professor—"

"Harold?"

"Yes. Did he have any other children?"

"Oh, yeah," Billy said. "He had children. I think he had three or four."

"What happened to him?"

"He died."

"I understand. But how did he die?"

"Died in a plane crash. Down there near Albany. Right outside Sylvester."

"Was he still married, at the time he died?"

"I don't know."

"Do you know why Stephen was down here?"

Billy shook his head. "I have no idea."

"Do you think he was looking for his mother. Tiny?"

Billy shook his head once more. "He didn't know about her. Far as I know, he didn't know nothing about her."

Connolly's forehead wrinkled in a frown. "He didn't know about her?"

"As far as I know. I didn't tell him, and Frieda didn't either. At least not while I was around."

"Does the name—"

Billy interrupted. "And I doubt she ever did. Frieda didn't care too much for Tiny after that. The way she just up and left the child and all. She was glad to have him." His gaze dropped. "We couldn't have kids of our own." He glanced at Connolly. "But she didn't think it was right for her to go off and leave him like that. Told me she wasn't going to never tell him about her."

Connolly nodded. "Does the name Inez Marchand mean anything to you?"

Billy thought for a moment, then shook his head. "No. I can't say that it does."

"Edwin Marchand?"

"No."

"Nick or Nicholas Marchand?"

"Nope. Never heard of them. There's some Marchands live down at McDonough, not too far from me. But I don't know them very well."

"Alright."

Connolly nodded to Henry down the table. Henry leaned back in his chair. "Mr. Ellis, what did your son do?"

"What did he do?"

"Where did he work?"

"He worked on a road crew for the highway department. They say he's some kind of foreman."

"Did he inherit anything from Schnadelbach's estate?"

"I don't know. Never thought about it. Like I said, he didn't know about Harold and we never did nothing about that."

"But Harold could have provided for the boy on his own. Did anyone ever come around asking about him or trying to talk to you or your wife or Stephen about Harold's estate?"

"Not that I know of. I don't think Harold's wife even knew about Stephen."

"This trouble he had at Valdosta. What was that about?"

"Got caught with some marijuana."

"Did he go to jail?"

"No."

"He got probation?"

Billy smiled. "I had a friend in Lawrenceville who was a hunting buddy with the district attorney down there. They worked it out."

"Did your son have a problem with drugs?"

"Not really."

"What does that mean?"

"He was a good kid."

"Did he get arrested again, after that first time?"

"Not that I know of."

"Did he ever deal in drugs? Ever sell it?"

"Not that I know."

"Was he married?"

"No."

"Did he have a girlfriend?"

"I wouldn't know."

"Did the police or anybody ever come around investigating anything about your son?"

"What do you mean?"

"Did the police ever show up at your house asking questions about your son?"

"No. I mean, not while he was around me."

"Did you ever hear of him being in trouble or someone coming around like that?"

"No."

Henry thought for a moment, then closed his file. "I don't think I have anything else." He stood. "Thanks for your time Mr. Ellis. Your son's body is at the hospital. Ms. Underwood will take you over there. I think they're finished with it. They'll tell you when you can get it."

Henry stepped across the room to the door and disappeared down the hall. Gayle looked over at Connolly. "Do you want to join us at the hospital?"

Connolly thought for a moment. There was nothing about the autopsy that he didn't already know. And no real reason to be there when Billy identified the body, but he felt compelled to attend. And so he said, "Sure. I'll meet you out there. Are you going now?"

"We'll be out there in about an hour. Can you make it then?"

"Yes." Connolly stood and moved toward the door. "I'll be there."

As Connolly started up the hall, he thought about the things Billy had told them. Stephen Ellis was the son of the man who wrote that book Connolly found at the beach house. And he was the son of someone named Mary Givens. All he had to do was find Mary Givens before Henry found her, and the details of what happened in that beach house just might fall into place. But he had to get to her first, and that ought to be easy enough. He smiled to himself. Not much chance Henry would even look for her. This new lady, Gayle Underwood, might but not Henry.

CHAPTER 23

Gayle was already at Ted Morgan's office when Connolly arrived later that afternoon. She stood to one side of Morgan's desk. Billy Ellis was seated on a folding chair next to her. Connolly came through the doorway and glanced around. "Have you seen Morgan?"

Gayle gestured toward the doorway. "He went down the hall. Said he'd be back in a minute." As she spoke, Morgan appeared in the doorway. "I'm right here." He brushed past Connolly to the desk and picked up a file. "Everyone ready?"

Gayle spoke up. "Brian Hodges was supposed to meet us here." The double doors in the hall banged open. Gayle smiled. "Sounds like him." Hodges appeared at the office door. "Sorry I'm late."

Morgan glanced at Billy Ellis. "Mr. Ellis, do you feel up to this?"

Billy nodded. "I'm alright."

"Then let's go," Morgan said. File in hand, he started down the hall. Gayle and Billy came from the office and followed him. Connolly and Hodges tagged along behind.

They walked down the hall past the autopsy suite to the cooler where they kept the bodies. Locker doors arranged in rows lined the wall. Morgan checked the file for the number, then opened a door on the bottom row.

Through the opening, Connolly saw a body lying on a stainless steel rack. A sheet was draped over it, but the feet protruded from the end. A tag was affixed to the toe of one foot. Cold air tumbled from the cooler to the floor and with it came a stale, morbid smell. Connolly's stomach gave a visceral reaction, and he took a step back, hoping not to vomit. He hated this part. The sight, the smell of death.

Morgan grasped the end of the rack and pulled. It clattered as it slid from the cooler bringing the body with it. Morgan checked the information from the toe tag with the file, then said, "This is the body." He glanced at Billy. "Ready?" Billy nodded. Morgan moved to the other end of the rack and lifted the sheet from the head. He glanced underneath, then pulled it back and folded it across the chest.

Billy's shoulder's sagged as if the air went out of him. The corners of his mouth twitched. His lips moved in a whisper. Gayle leaned closer. "Did you say something?"

Billy cleared his throat. "That's not him." He looked at Morgan. "That's not Stephen."

Morgan frowned. Hodges moved to Billy's side. Gayle glanced at the body, then back at Billy. "Are you sure?"

"Yeah," Billy replied. "I'm sure. That's not Stephen."

She tried to prompt him. "You said you haven't seen him in fifteen years."

"I know. But that's not him." Billy pointed to the body. "That's Stephen's roommate from school. The guy he got in trouble with on that charge in Valdosta." Billy stepped away, his hand over his mouth. The look in his eye as if he struggled to recall. "What's that guy's name?" he said to himself.

Gayle looked at Connolly and shrugged. Connolly nodded to Morgan. Morgan pulled the sheet over the body and slid it back inside the cooler. The door clicked shut.

Billy wheeled around. "Bobby," he said. "That boy's name is Bobby John... No. Not John." Then his eyes brightened. "Junkins," he said. "Bobby Junkins." Billy pointed to the cooler door. "That's who that is in there. Bobby Junkins."

Gayle looked perplexed. "You're sure?"

"Sure I'm sure. Why would I lie? That's not Stephen. That's Bobby Junkins."

Hodges spoke up. "Do you know where your son is?"

"No, sir." Billy shook his head. "I have no idea."

"Do you know of any reason why this man—Bobby Junkins—would have been in the house on Dauphin Island?"

"No." Billy shook his head once more. "I have no idea."

"Do you know anything else about him? Where he lived? Maybe the name of his parents?"

"I think his father was a politician. A legislator or county commissioner or something like that. There was something about that when they got arrested."

"Where do they live? His parents."

"I don't know," Billy said. "Back then, I think they lived over around Savannah some place. Statesville, I think."

"Statesville, Georgia?"

"Yeah."

Morgan started up the hall. Hodges and Billy followed. Connolly and Gayle came behind them. Gayle spoke to him in a low voice. "You better call Henry. I think things have changed."

"Maybe now he'll be interested in making a deal."

"I think he might."

That's how most of the prosecutors thought. Better to plead a defendant to something than spend time working a case that ended in nothing. That's how Connolly approached his cases, too—most of the time. But that was because most of the time his clients were guilty. Lawyering for them came down to getting them the shortest sentence possible. Acquittal usually wasn't much of an option for the people he defended.

A week earlier he would have done the same for Dibber. He would have pushed for a plea. Fought for one. Begged for one. But this case wasn't like most. Mrs. Gordon was right. This case was strange and the more he found out about it the stranger it became, and the more confident he became that they could win. Dibber wasn't guilty. Not of murder. He was sure of that the first time they talked, but he wasn't sure they could win. Now, he was beginning to think there was reason to hope.

Connolly and Gayle walked together to the end of the hall where they parted. Gayle and Billy went to the right with Hodges following a few steps behind. Connolly went to the left and made his way to the exit that led to the parking lot in back. As he started across the lot toward the Chrysler, he slipped off his jacket and flipped it over his shoulder.

Learning that the dead man wasn't really Stephen Ellis was an interesting development. But Connolly's mind wasn't on Stephen or Billy or finding Mary Givens or wondering why Stephen Ellis' fingerprint record matched Bobby Junkins' body. His mind was on one thing. "I need that book."

The book he found at the beach house didn't get there by accident. It was a gift from Harold to Billy and Frieda. Frieda gave it to Stephen. Stephen brought it with him when he came looking for his mother. A sense of loneliness swept over Connolly at the thought of it. A young man, looking for his mother. He knew something about that. He hadn't gone looking for her, but he knew what it was like to wonder where she was and what she was doing.

That book was important, but to get it he would have to drive back to Dauphin Island. Climb in the house. Probably in the dark if he went that day. And he would have to do it by himself. But first, he needed to talk to Dibber and catch him up on what he'd learned so far.

CHAPTER 24

From the hospital, Connolly drove downtown to the jail. He was cleared through the security checkpoint in the lobby and rode the elevator to the eighth floor. Dibber was seated at the table in the interview room when Connolly arrived. "What's up?" he asked.

Connolly crossed the room toward him. "I've been over at the morgue this afternoon. Sheriff's office thought they had an ID on the dead man."

"And they don't?"

"No."

"Who did they think it was?"

Connolly took a seat facing Dibber. "Somebody named Stephen Ellis."

Dibber shook his head. "Never heard of him."

"He's from Lawrenceville, Georgia."

"So, what happened? How did they find out it wasn't him?"

"Have you ever been to Lawrenceville, Georgia?"

"No."

"Know anyone from there?"

"No," Dibber replied. "What happened with the body?"

"They got a match on the dead guy's fingerprints through the FBI. He had a record. They found his father in Georgia. Brought him here. I met with him. He doesn't know anything about the beach house. After we talked, they took him to the hospital and showed him the body."

Dibber grinned. "And that's when they found out it ain't who they thought it was?"

"Stephen Ellis' father says the dead guy is Bobby Junkins. Used to be his son's roommate in college."

"Where's the son?"

"Don't know."

"How'd they get the prints matched to him?"

"Ellis and Junkins were roommates in college. While they were in college, they got busted together. I guess things got confused. Do either of those names mean anything to you?"

Dibber had a blank look. "Stephen…"

"Ellis. Stephen Ellis."

Dibber shook his head. "Never heard of him. What was the other one?"

"Junkins. Bobby Junkins."

"Never heard of him, either. What else?"

"You're sure of it?"

"Yes."

"If these are people you know, or people you know something about, you need to tell me. Now."

"I don't know them. Honest. Never heard of them before in my life. Why?"

"I wouldn't be surprised if the DA made us an offer."

Dibber frowned. "An offer?"

"Yeah. A deal. A plea deal."

Dibber scowled. "I ain't coppin' to no plea."

"You ought to think about it."

Dibber continued to shake his head. "Ain't nothing to think about. I'm not pleading guilty."

"But you are guilty."

Dibber had an angry look. "I didn't kill nobody."

"That's true. And you're not guilty of murder. But you are guilty of trespassing. And theft."

"I didn't steal nothing." Dibber's voice was loud. "That stuff was—"

"Not yours," Connolly said, cutting him off. "It was not yours. You were in the house. You took things that belonged to someone else—"

"Not that jet ski," Dibber interrupted. "It was floating in the water."

Connolly had an amused smile. "Believe me. If you went to trial on a theft charge, you'd be convicted." Dibber sighed. Connolly changed the subject. "I talked to Tommy Porter at the pawn shop. He knows you. Has a picture of you in the store. And a copy of your driver's license. There's no way to deny you sold him the jet ski."

Dibber shrugged. "I already told you that. I sold him the jet ski." He shot a look at Connolly. "But I didn't steal it."

"I talked to the detective. Hodges. The beach house is owned by Inez Marchand. Her husband's name is Edwin Marchand. They have a son named Nick. Do those names mean anything to you?"

"No."

"You need to take a moment and think about it. Nick works at a nursery out in Wilmer. It's called Southern Nursery Supply. Do you know anyone that works out there?"

Dibber's eyes darted away. He shook his head once more. Connolly continued. "They found some prints in the house. Yours. The dead man's. Three sets they can't identify. And some from Edwin, Inez, and Nick." Connolly caught Dibber's eye. "Was there anyone with you?"

"No."

"Are you sure?"

"Yes. Are they saying I had help?"

"No."

"Will they find out who those other prints belong to?"

"I don't know. If they don't have an arrest record, they might not ever identify them."

Dibber looked away again. "Did you talk to those people? The Marchands?"

"I tried. They weren't too interested in talking. Inez closed the door in my face."

"Why did she do that?"

"I don't know. But I talked to her husband. He told me he'd never been in the beach house."

Dibber looked up, suddenly alert. "I thought you said his prints was in the house."

"They were."

Dibber smiled. "He's lying?"

Connolly nodded. "He's lying."

"Well, that helps us, don't it?"

"A little."

Wonder why he lied?"

"That's a good question."

Dibber propped his elbow on the table and rested his chin in his hand. "What about the other guy? The son? Nick?"

"I haven't talked to him yet," Connolly said.

Dibber seemed troubled and after a moment said, "Why would they lie? I mean, if they didn't know him, why lie about being in the house?"

"That's what I'm trying to find out."

"Most people lie because it helps them out somehow. I mean, some people lie all the time. Some would rather lie than tell the truth. But most people ain't like that."

"Right."

"And how did the dead guy's prints get switched with his room-mate's?"

"That's not clear."

"I bet he was relieved."

"Who?"

"The guy they brought down here. The one they thought was the father."

"Yeah," Connolly said. "He was relieved."

Dibber had a faraway look and he sat there, staring past Connolly. For a moment, neither of them said a word. Then, Connolly spoke up. "There's one more thing. Your girlfriend came to see me the other day."

"Tiffany?"

"Yes."

Dibber's countenance changed. "What's she done now?"

"Nothing. I think she's worried."

"Worried?" Dibber frowned. "About what?"

"About you. She's been talking to some guy named Tinker Johnson."

Dibber looked angry. "What did he tell her?"

"He told her Nick Marchand thinks Tiffany put you up to breaking in the house."

"That don't make no sense. Why would she do that?"

"I don't know."

"I told her she shouldn't have nothing to do with him. Nothing."

"What's going on, Dibber?" Dibber slapped the table with his hand. His face was red. Connolly insisted. "Talk to me, Dibber."

Dibber sighed. "She and Tinker had this thing. She told me it was over. Then one day I came to The Pig to see her. That idiot was there talking to her."

"Who?"

"Tinker. Had his car parked around back. They was out there talking. I knew she hadn't stopped."

"Hadn't stopped what?"

Dibber hesitated, as if thinking. Then, he slapped the table once more. "Damn, I hate them both."

"Tell me what's going on."

"Tinker works for that guy you mentioned. Nick. I don't know him. I ain't never talked to him. But Tinker works for him. They're into all kinds of stuff. And they use that nursery for a cover. Tinker set her up with Nick to buy money orders."

"Money orders?" Connolly said it as a question, but from his conversation with Tiffany he knew what it meant.

"Yeah," Dibber said. "He gave her money every week. She'd go to convenience stores and buy money orders."

"Laundering money."

"I reckon that's what you call it. Once he got them money orders, then he could put them in the bank. It would be in the system. Nobody would ask any questions."

"So, you knew whose beach house it was."

"Yeah." Dibber sighed. "I knew. But I didn't kill nobody."

Connolly was aggravated that Dibber had denied it for this long. But he was no different from any other client. They all thought they could finesse their way past a charge. "What else have you not told me?"

"Nothing. Honest. I've told you all I know about this."

"Really?"

"Really."

Connolly did not believe him. "When you went in that house, what were you looking for?"

"Whatever I could find. Something I could use." Dibber smiled. "Hit the jackpot, too."

"What did you find?"

"Money." He looked at Connolly. "And receipts."

Connolly frowned. "Receipts?"

Dibber nodded. "I found a cigar box in the closet. Had a bunch of cash in it. Underneath the cash was a stack of receipts for all them money orders. One of them had her name on it."

Connolly smiled. "What did you do with the box?"

Dibber grinned. "It's at the house."

"The beach house?"

"No." Dibber shook his head. "My house."

"Where?"

"You want it?"

"Yes."

"Okay. It's in the closet in the back bedroom. Think it'll help?"

"It might. How can I get it?"

"If you go in the front door, there's a hall down both sides of the stairs. Take the one on the right. All the way to the back of the house. The bedroom is on the right, across from the bathroom. Box is up in the top of the closet. Under a bunch of old clothes."

"How do I get inside? Does Carl have a key?"

"No." Dibber scowled and shook his head. "Don't ask him. Just go down there yourself. There's a key hanging on a nail behind the water heater."

"Where's the water heater?"

"Back porch." Dibber fell silent a moment, as if thinking. Then he slapped the table again. "I told her not to have nothing to do with him. Nothing."

Connolly leaned away. "Tiffany said she would ask Tinker about talking to me."

"Huh." Dibber snorted. "I wouldn't believe nothing he says. Nothing."

"I need to talk to him."

"Better watch your back."

CHAPTER 25

Afternoon was almost gone by the time Connolly left the jail. He drove across town to Tuttle Street and The Pleiades, the estate where he lived. Cool shade from the oaks that surrounded the mansion engulfed him as the car idled to a stop near the guesthouse. Connolly switched off the engine and stared out the windshield, lost in thought.

If what Dibber said was true, if he had those receipts, they might have a chance at winning this case. At least they would have something besides the dead man to talk about at the preliminary hearing. Connolly thought about it a moment longer, then shook his head. "Doesn't prove a thing."

And Judge Cahill would see right through it. Might help with a jury if the case went to trial, but it wouldn't do much good in a preliminary hearing. They could have all the receipts they wanted, talk about Nick Marchand and drugs and money orders and Tinker, and it still wouldn't make any difference. Dibber was charged with murder. They had a body. They had Dibber's fingerprints.

He took the key from the ignition and opened the car door. "But it makes more sense that someone killed the guy over a drug deal than Dibber killing him for a jet ski."

Connolly's legs felt like lead as he stepped from the car and started toward the guesthouse. The thought of driving all the way to

Dauphin Island left him feeling weary. For a moment he considered not going. But he had to. He needed Dibber's receipts. And, besides that, he needed that book from the beach house.

He looked up through the branches of the trees toward the sky. It was getting late. Darkness was coming fast. The thought of going in that beach house after dark sent a chill up his spine.

From the door by the kitchen Connolly glanced across the living room to the table at the end of the sofa. The light on the answering machine was out. He crossed the room and pressed the button to play the messages anyway, just to make sure. The machine was silent.

In the bedroom, he put on a pair of jeans and a T-shirt. He set his black winged tips on a rack in the closet and slipped on a pair of worn leather topsiders. The shoes felt soft and comfortable against the balls of his feet.

Dressed and ready, he went to the kitchen. He stood at the sink and ate a piece of cold pizza leftover from a few nights before, washed down with a bottle of Boylan ginger ale. As he took the last drink from the bottle, he checked his watch. It was six o'clock. He had stalled as long as he could. He set the empty bottle on the counter, phoned Barbara to beg off on dinner once again, and walked out the door to the car.

When Connolly crossed the bridge at Cedar Point, the sun was an orange glow behind a towering bank of dark clouds on the western horizon. Billowing high above the water, the clouds formed ominous shapes outlined in red and gold as the fading sun sent streaks of purple and amber across the evening sky. Connolly took in the scene with quick glances out the window as the car rolled across the bridge.

Lights were on at the Ship-N-Shore near the center of the island. Connolly slowed as he passed it, then turned onto DeSoto Avenue. The car crept along as he checked the house numbers. Three blocks later, the paved street came to an end in front of a two-story house that faced the sound on the leeward side of the island. A lush green lawn ran from the house down to the water. Connolly parked the car on the grass at the end of the pavement.

The house had a porch that ran all the way around. In front, there was a swing and three rocking chairs. Around back, the porch was cluttered with an assortment of buckets and pails and three ice chests. Near the corner was a door. A washing machine and dryer stood to one side of it. The hot water heater sat on the other. Connolly stepped onto the porch and slid his hand behind the heater. A door key was hanging on a nail beneath a water pipe. He slipped it off the nail and shoved it in the lock above the doorknob.

The door opened to a kitchen that seemed as large as Connolly's house. Cabinets and counters lined the walls all the way around to a door on the opposite side of the room that led to a hall. A white porcelain sink sat beneath a window on the wall to the right. A stove stood along the far wall. A table sat in the center of the room.

Connolly moved across the kitchen to the hall and located the downstairs bedroom. To his surprise, the bedroom was neat and clean. In fact, the whole house was clean and straight. Then he noticed a scent in the air. "Pine cleaner," he mumbled. Someone had cleaned the place. Dibber wasn't the kind to clean anything. Tiffany? He shook his head. No way. She wasn't the kind, either. More likely Carl Landry hired someone.

He crossed the room to the closet and opened the door. Clothes on hangers were arranged neatly across a galvanized bar. Faded blue jeans and four flannel shirts were folded and stacked on the shelf above. Connolly slid his hand under the stack. Nothing. He moved the clothes aside and stood on his toes, reaching as far back as possible. Near the corner, his fingers struck something. He worked it forward with his fingertips until he could see it was a cigar box. He took it from the shelf and opened it while seated on the bed.

Inside the box he found a small velvet sack with a gold drawstring. Bon Ton's Jewelry was emblazoned on the front in gold letters. The money order receipts lay beneath the sack. Connolly set the sack aside and looked through the receipts. All of them carbon copies from the back of money order forms. The ones near the top were made out to Southern Nursery Supply but near the bottom of the box he found several made to Nick Marchand, one of which bore Tiffany's name on the memo line in the lower left corner. Each of the money orders were for one thousand dollars.

Connolly stared at them a moment, thinking. Only one business generated both large amounts of cash and an accounting problem. The drug business. "Nick was using his mama's beach house as a meth lab."

After a moment, he set the box on the bed and picked up the velvet sack from the jewelry store. He loosened the drawstring and emptied the contents into the palm of his hand. Two silver earrings. A cheap bracelet. And a man's class ring with a blue stone. He held the ring between his fingers and read the words inscribed around the stone. His heart skipped a beat. "Lawrenceville High School. Class of 1985." Connolly dropped the ring into the bag and pulled the top closed. "I really need that book now."

CHAPTER 26

Darkness had fallen by the time Connolly left Dibber's house. In the distance, a large, red moon rose over the Gulf. He walked across the grass to the car and started up the street.

From Dibber's, he made his way to Bienville Boulevard, then drove past the dunes to the sandy flats at the western end of the island. Ten minutes later he came to the berm at the end of the road. The car coasted to a stop across from the Marchands' beach house.

Connolly felt beneath the seat of the car and took out a flashlight. He pushed the switch to make sure it worked, then opened the door and stepped out. In the distance he heard the waves crashing on the shore beyond the house. In the distance, between the houses, he saw the churning surf shimmering in the moonlight. He would have enjoyed a stroll on the beach, and a moment considered doing just that, but there was no point in avoiding the task at hand. He closed the car door, then started across the street.

When he reached the house, he paused beneath the broken stairs and stared up at the bottom rung. Somehow it seemed farther out of reach than before. He stretched one arm above his head as far as it would go and tried to judge the distance, but with little success.

Having no other options, he shoved the flashlight in his hip pocket and backed off a little way, then took three steps forward and sprang into the air like a basketball player. His fingers slapped against the ends of the runners as he sailed past. A splinter jammed beneath the fingernail of his right hand and he clutched it in pain. "This didn't used to be so hard," he growled.

He took the flashlight from his pocket and flipped it on. In the shadows near the pilings on the far side of the house, he saw a red and white ice chest protruding from the sand. He hadn't noticed it before. Maybe he could use it for a step, and he started toward it.

Two-thirds of the chest was buried beneath the surface, but he decided to give it a try anyway. He knelt beside it, dug around the edges with his hands, and in a few minutes worked it free. He pulled it to the front of the house and placed it beneath the steps, then flipped on the flashlight again and glanced up to make sure the chest was aligned with the stairs. That's when he saw the fresh breaks at the ends of the runners.

In the glare of the light, fresh wood shone from the boards at the end of the steps where they had broken off. "Someone else has been down here, too." He shined the beam of light across the sand, searching for other signs of their presence. Pieces of the steps lay in a clump of sea oats a few feet away. He switched off the flashlight, shoved it back in his hip pocket, then stood atop the ice chest.

With his knees bent, he sagged as low as possible and pushed off with all his might. His body sailed upward and seconds later, his outstretched arms banged against the runners on either side. He dug in with his fingers and held on, then worked his hands around the bottom step. Muscles in his forearms ached but he hauled himself up, hand over hand, to the second step and made it far enough to stand. When he reached the top step by the door, he shoved open the door and went inside.

In the beam of the flashlight, he saw the timber that had been lying in the living room now lay to one side, away from the kitchen counter. The sofa and love seat that had been piled against the wall by the counter now sat in the center of the room. He flicked the light around the kitchen. Dishes and pans still filled the sink. The stove was still covered with grease.

From the opening to the hallway, he saw the door to the bedroom at the end of the hall. Across the room, the floor creaked. He glanced in that direction but saw nothing and continued into the hallway.

Midway down the hall, he passed the door to the first bedroom. Moonlight streaming through a window caught his eye. Shadows danced on the wall and played across the open closet door in the corner. He was tense now with fear, but he kept walking, moving closer and closer to the door at the end of the hall.

By then he was convinced someone was in the bedroom. Waiting for him to enter. They knew he was coming. They'd been watching out the window. Someone. In the bedroom. With a knife. Ready to stab him the moment he opened the door. Hair on the back of his neck stood up. His skin tingled. He stole a quick glance over his shoulder, checking to see, but finally he could stand it no more.

Shouting at the top of his voice, he charged to the end of the hall and jumped through the doorway. One arm protecting his face, the other ready with the flashlight raised over his head ready to strike whatever awaited him. But no one was there. An embarrassed grin spread over his face. He stood listening to the sound of the waves crashing on the beach outside. Finally, he lowered the flashlight and shined it across the room.

The mattress and box springs had been moved from the bed frame. They lay to the side, one corner resting on the floor, another propped in the air at an angle. The dresser still sat along the wall but the things on top had been moved. Some of them lay in the floor. The blue vase was on its side. And the book was missing.

Connolly came from the door to the dresser and the light flashed across the top. Next to the vase there was a gap in the clutter where the jewelry box had been. He was about to give up but as he reached the far end of the dresser, the beam from the flashlight fell on the carpet below. And there it was. The book. Laying face-up. He knelt on one knee and picked it up, then checked the front for the inscription. It was just as he remembered. He flipped through the pages with his thumb until he reached the picture that was stuck inside, then held it beneath the light.

The woman in the photograph was much younger. But her hair was still curly. And those dark eyes gave her away. "Inez Marchand," he whispered. "And I'd bet a lot of money that's good ol' Harold Schnadelbach standing beside her." He stuck the photo in the book and closed it.

The night sky was ablaze with stars as Connolly crossed the bridge from Dauphin Island back to Cedar Point. He lowered the window and let the night air blow through the car. His skin grew tacky and moist from the humidity, but he didn't mind. And, in fact, found it refreshing. He propped his elbow on the window ledge and pointed the car toward Mobile.

As he drove, he thought of Barbara and the house. He didn't want her to sell it. In spite of all that had happened, they had made good memories in that place. He didn't want to go back to them. Didn't want to be trapped by them. But he didn't want to lose them, either. Surely, there was a way to work that out. To enjoy the memories without being victimized by past behavior. To enjoy the place without being forced to repeat the mistakes he'd made.

Forty minutes after leaving the beach house, he was back in town. He glanced at his watch to check the time and saw it was after midnight. He'd been tired earlier when he left for the trip. And worn out by the time he reached the coast. But now, after climbing inside, finding the book, and surviving despite being afraid, he was wide awake.

Instead of driving home to the guesthouse, he continued a few blocks farther to Ann Street. And that's when he saw it. A white sign with neat black letters and the realtor's logo. For Sale. He had tried to imagine what it would look like, seeing the sign in the yard and knowing the house was for sale. But nothing prepared him for the sense of sadness, the sense of loss.

Connolly slowed the car to an idle and brought it to a stop at the curb. He switched off the engine, and the headlights, and stared out the window. The house was dark but in the glow of the streetlight he saw Barbara's car parked at the end of the drive. Limbs from an overgrown wisteria bush sprawled above the hood. And then his mind began to wander. To a different time. Rachel on a tricycle, pedaling up the sidewalk. A child's swimming pool in the back yard. Toys strewn everywhere. A child giggling. Laughing. Splashing in the water.

It was two in the morning when Connolly finally came back to the guesthouse. He collapsed across the bed and fell asleep, fully clothed, with his shoes still on his feet.

CHAPTER 27

Sometime the next day, Connolly was awakened by the ring of his cell phone. Groggy and disoriented, he squinted against the glare of sunlight through the bedroom window as he tried to remember where he was. By the time he found the phone, the call had ended. He dropped the cell phone on the bed and buried his face in the pillow.

A few minutes later, he opened his eyes wide enough to check the phone for the time. It was ten. In the morning. He rolled to a sitting position at the edge of the bed and rubbed his eyes. The screen on the cell phone blinked with a message telling him he'd missed a call. He pressed a button to check the number. The digits appeared on the screen. It was a local number, but he didn't recognize it.

"Probably a wrong number," he groaned. He tossed the phone on the bed and kicked off his shoes, then started toward the bathroom. After ten minutes in the shower, he remembered the events of the previous day. Viewing the body at the morgue. His conversation with Dibber. Driving down to the beach house to get the book.

Edwin Marchand was lying. Inez was, too. And the dead man in the house wasn't who his fingerprint records said he was. Bobby Junkins was dead, whoever he was, and Stephen Ellis was Inez Marchand's son. Connolly dried himself with a towel and walked into the bedroom.

"But for some reason, Henry thinks it's a good idea to charge Dibber with murder." He stared at himself in the mirror as he knotted his tie. "I don't like it when people lie to me."

From the bedroom, he walked to the kitchen and heated a cup of instant coffee in the microwave. While he waited for it, he checked the bread box and found a bran muffin. There was a spot of mold on top, but he pinched it off and took a bite. It was a little dry but not that bad.

Yet, all the while, his mind was on the events of the previous day, the things he'd learned about Dibber's case—and the lies. Inez lied. Edwin lied. Somebody lied about that dead body in the morgue, too. "The whole thing is built on a lie," he said, between sips of coffee. "Dibber's just the one who got caught."

By the time he'd finished eating, he was determined to get to the truth of the matter. Not just for the sake of Dibber's defense, but for his own. His own interest. His own vindication. A little too personal, maybe, but that's the way it was for him. And so there was nothing else to do but go back to the Marchands and confront them.

Ten minutes after leaving the guesthouse, Connolly arrived on the street where the Marchands lived. He slowed the car as he approached the house and checked for signs that someone was present. A pickup truck was parked near the garage. It looked like the truck he'd seen Edwin in before. Connolly started up the driveway toward the house. Gravel crunched beneath the tires as he came to a stop between the garage and the house.

Through a window near the door he saw Inez in the kitchen. He tapped on the glass and the sound of it startled her. She looked up from the sink, her eyes alert, but when she saw him they clouded with anger.

"I need to talk to your husband," Connolly said. He spoke in a voice loud enough to be heard inside.

She glared at him with her arms folded across her chest and an angry look on her face. "We ain't got nothing to say to you."

"Your husband," Connolly repeated. "I want to talk to Edwin."

Just then, someone tapped Connolly on the shoulder. He was surprised to find Edwin Marchand standing behind him. Marchand had a serious look on his face but did not appear angry. "What you want with me?"

Connolly was startled but gathered his composure. "I talked to Hodges," he said.

"Who's he?"

"The detective on your case."

Edwin frowned. "What case?"

"The one about the jet ski and the dead man they found at the beach house."

Edwin stepped toward the garage. He gestured over his shoulder toward the house as he walked away. "That beach house is hers. You'll have to talk to her about it."

Connolly called after him. "Hodges found your prints in the house."

Edwin faced him with a look of consternation. "My prints?" He seemed genuinely puzzled. "Where?"

"In the beach house."

Edwin shook his head. "That's a lie. I ain't never been in that beach house. I haven't seen that beach house. I don't even know where it is. If my life depended on it, I couldn't take you to it."

"The FBI matched the prints."

Edwin had a blank look. "Prints?"

"Fingerprints."

Edwin's mouth formed a sarcastic smirk. "Now how's the FBI gonna have my fingerprints?"

Connolly shrugged. "I don't know. Were you ever arrested?"

"No."

"Ever been in the Army?"

Edwin shook his head.

"Do you have a pistol permit? Ever apply for one?"

"Mister, I'm telling you. I ain't never been checked for nothing."

"A background check maybe?"

Edwin was adamant. "I ain't never been arrested for nothing. I ain't been checked for nothing. I ain't never had nobody take my fingerprints for nothing. Who did you say told you this?"

"Brian Hodges."

"And he's—"

"A detective," Connolly interrupted. "With the sheriff's department."

Edwin looked alert, as if he'd thought of something. Connolly kept talking, repeating the thing he'd already said, hoping to jostle his memory. "He's handling the case about the dead man they found at the beach house. I talked to him the other day. They checked the house for prints. They found yours inside the house. He has a report."

Before Connolly finished, Edwin started toward him. Connolly stepped to one side, as if to let him pass, unsure what was about to happen next, but Edwin moved around him and kept going toward the house. Connolly watched as he reached the door, jerked it open and went inside. The door slammed shut behind him.

Through the window Connolly saw Edwin standing in the kitchen, facing Inez. He shouted at her, flaying the air with his arms as he spoke. From the look on Inez's face, she was shouting back. The sound of their voices drifted across the yard, but Connolly couldn't understand what they were saying.

After a moment, Edwin left the room and disappeared from sight. Inez moved to the sink. Connolly could see her lips moving as she washed a plate, then rinsed it under the faucet. As she moved the plate to the drain board, she glanced out the window. Her eyes met Connolly's. An angry scowl came over her. She set the plate aside, reached to the edge of the window, and lowered the blinds.

Connolly waited a moment, but when Edwin did not come back, he walked to the Chrysler and got in behind the steering wheel. He was frustrated that the conversation had simply ended. No resolution. No great revealing truth. Only a complete disregard for his presence. And for his questions. Yet, he felt an odd sense of satisfaction, too. Seeing Inez confronted by her husband. Hearing them shouting at each other. His questions had struck home. The revelation about the fingerprints hit a nerve with Edwin. Connolly was certain more would come of it. He just didn't know what or how.

With a twist of the key, the car started and drove toward the street. As he did, he thought about what he could do next. And then he remembered Nick Marchand.

Connolly didn't know Nick Marchand. Had never seen Nick Marchand. Never heard his voice or even viewed him from a distance. And there was a reason for that. Something about him—about the idea of him—made Connolly want to delay meeting him. Now, however, Nick was the final man on the list. The only person associated with Dibber's case that he hadn't interviewed. Now there was no choice but to find him and put the same questions to him that he'd asked Edwin.

CHAPTER 28

From the Marchands' house, Connolly drove west and twenty minutes later came to Wilmer, a rural community in the northwest corner of the county. Downtown Wilmer consisted of West End Market which was a convenience store, a post office, and an automotive repair shop.

About a mile past the store, Connolly rounded a curve in the road and came to a large wooden building designed like a traditional barn with canvas awnings all the way around. Beneath the awnings were potted flowers and garden plants. Sacks of fertilizer and topsoil were stacked on pallets to one side. A yellow sign out front had blinking lights that spelled the name, "Southern Nursery Supply."

Connolly steered the Chrysler from the road and brought it to a stop in front of the building. As he stepped from the car a woman came toward him. "May I help you?" She was young and had a friendly smile.

"I'm looking for Nick Marchand."

"Oh." Her countenance dropped. "He's probably in the barn."

Connolly gave her a puzzled look. "The barn?"

She gestured over her shoulder. "It's in back." She pointed. "Go through the gate over yonder. Follow the road. You'll see it." The woman moved past a table of plants and disappeared inside the building.

Behind the flower shop, a hundred acres spilled over rolling hills lined with rows and rows of trees and shrubs, most of them growing in black plastic pots. From the parking lot Connolly saw the gate fifty yards down. He walked to the car and drove in that direction.

A sign on a fence post said "Private," but the gate was open. Connolly let the car roll through and continued down a farm road that cut across the property. On either side, sprinklers sprayed water in lazy circles that kept the plants moist and the road muddy.

Not far from the gate, the road descended a low hill. Farther on, it rose up another to a barn perched atop the rise. Connolly made his way in that direction, past the rows of shrubs and trees, and brought the car to a stop near a blue and white Ford tractor. He got out of the car and walked around the corner of the barn.

Twenty yards away, a pile of empty plastic sacks and cardboard boxes towered above a circle of steel drums. Charred and rusted, the drums looked as though they'd witnessed several years of trash fires. A young man was at the pile, trampling over the refuse, compressing and tamping it down. Dressed in blue jeans and a white T-shirt, his skin was pale. Almost translucent. His eyes were hollow and lifeless. A three-day growth on his face left him looking scruffy and unkempt. He glanced up as Connolly came toward him, startled by his sudden appearance. "Who are you?" the young man asked.

Connolly moved closer. "Mike Connolly. I'm looking for—"

The young man ignored him and climbed from the trash pile. When he reached the ground, he took a cigarette lighter from his pants pocket, then flicked a button on the side. A flame appeared at the end of the lighter. He leaned over a barrel and touched the flame to one of the boxes. When the box caught fire, he grasped it by the corner and used it as a torch to spread flames all the way around. The plastic sacks caught fire first and black smoke from them billowed into the air. Soon the entire pile was ablaze.

The young man finally said, "You're looking for something?"

"I'm trying to find Nicholas Marchand."

The young man yelled, "Hey, Nick!"

A door along the back wall of the barn slid open and a man

appeared. In his mid-thirties, he wore blue jeans and a work shirt with tan boots and a baseball cap. He glanced at the fire as he started from the barn. The young man caught his eye. "This guy wants to talk to you."

The young man picked up a cardboard box that had fallen off the pile and threw it in the fire, then moved away. Nick stood near Connolly. He shoved his hands in his pockets and waited. Connolly gave him a polite smile. "You're Nick Marchand?"

"Yeah." He had a sullen look in his eye and an arrogant tone in his voice.

Impulsively, Connolly moved to shake hands with him, then thought better of it. "My name is Mike Connolly. I represent a man who's accused of stealing a jet ski from your mother's beach house." Nick nodded. Connolly continued. "When's the last time you were down there at the beach house?"

"I don't know." Nick shrugged. "Probably two or three weeks before the storm."

"Did you see anyone down there then?"

"Nope."

"It looks like someone has been living down there. Is that where you live?"

"I stayed down there some."

"Did anyone else stay down there with you?"

"A few friends. Off and on. Over the years."

"Was anyone with you the last time you were there?"

"I don't remember."

"Look, I'm not trying to make trouble for anyone. I'm just trying to defend my client."

An acrid odor wafted through the air. Connolly's nose wrinkled. He glanced around. "What's that smell?"

Nick glanced over his shoulder toward the barn. The door slid shut. "Just stuff we put on some of the bushes. Helps them grow. Makes them tolerate the weather a little better."

Connolly wiped his hand over his face. "What a smell."

"Yeah." Nick grinned. "Smells like money to me."

"They found a dead man in the beach house. Did you know him?"

"Nope."

"Ever seen him before?"

"Nope."

"They say his name is Bobby Junkins. Does that name mean anything to you?"

"Nope." Nick shook his head. "Don't mean nothing to me."

"What about Stephen Ellis?"

Nick's eyes darted away. He twitched his head to one side and shrugged. Connolly pressed the question. "Do you know anyone by that name?"

"No." Nick's eyes went cold. "Never heard of him. Got no idea why he'd be in that house."

Connolly struggled to keep the conversation going. "Was anything else missing from the house besides the jet ski?"

Nick took a deep breath. "I don't know. Hard to tell. The place was so broke up by the storm."

"You filed a report with the Dauphin Island police department."

"That was Mama's idea."

"You didn't file the report?"

"Nah."

"Have you been down there since the storm?"

"Rode by it once."

"You didn't go in?"

"Nah."

Connolly was certain Nick was lying. How else would he know the house was too damaged to determine what else was missing? Still, he kept going. "Does the name Harold Schnadelbach mean anything to you?"

Nick's eyes darted away again. "Nope." He looked over at Connolly. "How many more of these questions do you have?"

Connolly ignored him. "Have you ever heard of Billy and Frieda Ellis?"

"No."

"Do you know anyone in Lawrenceville, Georgia?"

"Nope."

"Is there anything at all that you've thought of that might explain why the dead man was in your mother's beach house?"

"No."

"Your father says he never went to the beach house."

"I don't think he did."

"Your mother?"

"She went down there a time or two."

"Why did they buy the house?"

Nick shrugged again. "I don't know. You'd have to ask them."

"When did they buy it?"

"I don't know. You'd have to ask them that, too. They've had it since I was a kid."

"Did they ever rent it out?"

"I don't think so." Nick glanced over at Connolly again. "You about through with this? I got things I need to do."

"I guess." Connolly sighed. "This is hard to get a handle on."

"Yeah," Nick said. "Tell me about it." He started toward the barn. Connolly walked to the car. He lingered a moment, though, watching Nick as he slid open the barn door just wide enough to squeeze through, then quickly shoved it closed once he was inside. And then that same acrid odor he'd smelled before wafted through the air.

CHAPTER 29

As Connolly drove back through the nursery toward the highway, he glanced in the mirror. Behind him, someone came from the barn and threw two more boxes on the fire. Smoke billowed into the sky.

Not far from up the road from the nursery, the West End Market came into view. He glanced at his watch. It was one o'clock. "No wonder I'm hungry." The Market had a lunch counter. He had eaten there before. Fried food. Hot and greasy. He let the car coast past the gas pumps and brought it to a stop under an oak tree on the far side of the building. He stepped from the car and went inside.

To the right of the door was a counter. Windows behind it gave the clerks a view of the gas pumps and the parking lot outside. A few feet down the counter was an ice cream freezer. Past it was the lunch counter. The smell of cigarette smoke and hot grease filled the air. A line of customers stood at the cash register by the door waiting to pay. Connolly moved past them and made his way to the lunch counter.

A warmer with a glass front sat atop a waist-high stainless steel counter. Inside, a lamp cast a red glare across metal trays filled with fried potatoes, fried catfish, fried chicken, and fried pickles. Grease and condensation fogged the corners of the glass.

Behind the counter was a deep fat fryer. A woman stood at the fryer, her back to Connolly. Dressed in blue jeans and a green T-shirt, she seemed oblivious to all but the sound of something sizzling in the oil. After a moment, she lifted a basket from the fryer, let the oil drip for only a second, then dumped the contents onto a tray. Connolly wasn't sure but it looked like fried potatoes. She sprinkled salt and seasoning over it and shoved the tray into the warmer. Their eyes met. She acknowledged him with an arched eyebrow. "What'll you have?"

Connolly pointed to the warmer. "Is that catfish?"

"Snack or meal?"

"Catfish," he said.

She sighed and rolled her eyes. "You want the snack box or the meal?"

"Meal."

She took a waxed cardboard box from beneath the counter. "Drinking anything?"

"Coca-Cola."

She used metal tongs to fill the box with fish, fried potatoes, and a fried pickle, then handed him the box and moved to the dispenser to get the Coke.

Food in hand, Connolly joined the line at the cash register and paid, then took a seat at a table as far from the door as possible. He pulled a stack of paper napkins from the dispenser on the table and laid them to one side, then opened the box and began to eat. The store was busy. People moved in and out. Connolly was hungry. He concentrated on eating.

A few minutes later, he heard a familiar voice and glanced up to see Toby LeMoyne standing at the lunch counter. Toby was a deputy sheriff. Tall and athletic, he had broad shoulders and muscular arms that bulged beneath the sleeves of his shirt. His size and physique were intimidating but he had a kind face and a smile that lit up the room. Connolly had known Toby since he first became a deputy.

The clerk handed Toby a brown paper sack. He took it from her and crossed the room toward a cooler along the wall. A moment later, he slid onto the seat across from Connolly. He set the sack on the table and twisted the top off a bottle of Milo's tea.

Connolly wiped his fingers on a napkin. "Did you come for the grease or the calories?" They'd known each other too long to bother with pleasant greetings.

Toby opened the sack. "This place has the best hamburger in the county. What brings you out here?"

Connolly took a bite of fish. "Witnesses."

Toby smiled. "What poor, misunderstood crook are you trying to set free on society today?"

"Dibber Landry."

Toby nodded. "I heard about that. Looting houses on Dauphin Island?"

"That's what they say."

Toby chuckled. "Looting during a hurricane. Couldn't wait for it to blow over." He shook his head. "Some people will do anything."

"Yeah." Connolly took another bite of fish.

Toby took a drink of tea. "I saw you coming out of that nursery down there. Are they involved in your case?"

"Sort of," Connolly said. "I was talking to Nick Marchand. It was his mother's house they think Dibber broke into."

Toby shook his head again. "Those Marchands are some strange people."

"You're right about that."

"All those trees and bushes, and you never see anybody around there."

"Is it like that all the time?"

"Yeah." Toby took another bite of hamburger. "First big case I ever worked on was out there. Old man that owned the place got shot. Just about the time I came on the force. Everybody seemed to know who he was. I'd never heard of him."

"What was his name?"

"Givens. Earl Givens."

A bite of fish stuck in Connolly's throat. He tried to breath but couldn't and clutched at his neck as if squeezing it could make things better.

Toby's eyes were wide. "Mike? What's the matter?" Connolly could only gasp in response.

Without waiting, Toby slid off the bench and jumped to his feet. In one quick motion he slipped his arms around Connolly's chest and lifted him from behind the table. He placed his fist just below Connolly's ribs and gave a sharp squeeze. A clump of fish shot from Connolly's mouth and splattered on the floor. Connolly took a deep breath. Then another. Toby eased him down to the bench. "Are you alright?"

"Yeah." Connolly wiped his mouth on a napkin and took another deep breath. "Thanks."

"Are you sure?" Toby took a seat. "Take a drink. Make sure your throat is clear. You were blue."

"I felt blue."

"Man, that's scary." Toby pointed to the Coca-Cola. "No kidding. Take a drink." Connolly sipped from the drink. Toby looked concerned. "Maybe you shouldn't eat any more of that fish."

"Maybe so."

Connolly was scared and nervous but didn't want to show it. Instead, he took a napkin from the table and stooped to wipe the fish from the floor. A boy with a broom and a dustpan appeared and nudged him aside. "I got it," he said as he scooped up the fish, wiped the spot on the floor with a damp cloth, and walked away.

Connolly took another sip of Coca-Cola, then tried to resume their conversation. "What was the old man's name?"

"Givens." Toby wiped his mouth. "Earl Givens."

"How long ago was that?"

"Early '80s. About the time I came on the force."

Connolly kept talking as he pushed the thought of choking aside. "And you said someone shot him?"

"Yeah."

"Who did it?"

Toby shook his head. "Never found out. I think it's still an open case. Everybody had their theories, but we never found enough to charge anybody with it."

"Who was the detective?"

"Clyde Ramsey."

"Clyde Ramsey," Connolly repeated. "That name sounds familiar."

"He's retired now. Lives in midtown. Not too far from you."

"Yeah? Where?"

"Crenshaw Street, I think. Up there by the Loop." Toby took a drink of tea. "Hodges is working your case, isn't he?"

"Yeah." Connolly nodded. "Why?"

"He's married to Clyde's daughter."

Connolly's eyes opened wide in a look of surprise. "You're kidding."

"No, I'm not." Toby laughed. "It's not that uncommon. Lots of us are married to officers' children."

"Lots of us?"

"Yeah. Merris' father was with the Prichard police. The guy who relieves me is married to a girl whose father is with Mobile. We're all pretty tight."

"You've been patrolling out here a long time," Connolly observed.

"They try to rotate us around the county, but I get sent out here every few months."

Connolly grinned. "Are they still mad about that Agostino thing?" That case seemed like a long time ago, but he remembered the details vividly.

Toby smiled. "I don't think so. At least, they don't mention it anymore."

"So, what goes on out there at that nursery?"

"Hard to say."

Connolly gave him a questioning look. "Hard to say?"

"We hear rumors about a super meth lab, but nobody's been able to find it, yet. If that's what they're doing at that nursery, you better watch out."

"It stinks out there."

Toby seemed curious. "I would love to get a look inside that barn. Haven't found a reason for a warrant. But I'm looking."

"Yeah?"

"Yeah. Toby grinned. "They don't keep sending me out here because they're mad at me. I know this place."

"What if I could help?"

Toby shook his head. "I don't think so. They don't like us using civilians like that."

"I'm not exactly a civilian."

Toby sighed. "I can't tell you not to poke around out there, but you better be careful. If they're into things people around here think they're into, you could get yourself in a bad situation right quick."

CHAPTER 30

When Connolly finished lunch, he said goodbye to Toby then walked outside. It felt good to be outside, and for the first time he realized how deeply scared he had been when he choked on the food earlier. The air. The sunlight. The sounds. They seemed fresh and new, and he paused a moment to bask in the sunlight, even though the day was quite warm. Hot even.

After a moment though, his thoughts came again to the case at hand. Dibber. The Marchands. And the nursery just up the road. Despite the interruption at the table, the conversation with Toby had been intriguing. Especially the part about Clyde Ramsey and the earlier case Toby had worked on. Perhaps Ramsey could fill in a few of the details.

As he made his way across the parking lot toward the car, Connolly used his phone to check for Ramsey's address and found he lived on Crenshaw Street. Connolly knew about Crenshaw Street. His childhood home was on Crenshaw Street. His mother had abandoned them on Crenshaw Street. He had lots of memories from there, but none he cared to recall.

Yet, as Connolly drove back to town, thoughts of his childhood kept pressing in and he found them harder and harder to resist. Even now, years later, they still were painful and recalling them only made him angry. His mother abandoning them. First emotionally, then physically. The fear. The loneliness. The despair. And though he struggled against the memories, this time they wouldn't go away.

In an effort to pry his mind away from the past, Connolly recounted the conversation with Toby. And the moment when he chocked. The fear. The panic. And the reassurance he'd sensed when Toby grabbed him to pop the fish from his throat. He liked Toby and even more than that, he trusted Toby. Not in the glib way people often used that term but in the deeper sense of knowing. That was it. Knowing. He knew from the moment he felt Toby's arms against him that he would be alright. And he was.

Toby was an easy guy to like. Tall. Broad shouldered. Looked like a football player, which he had been, and he had a winsome personality. The kind of person you wanted to know and be known by. But the conversation. The details. Some of it had been disturbing. And some of it confirmed what he'd already suspected.

Toby said Earl Givens was Nick Marchand's grandfather. Which meant Inez was Inez Givens Marchand. Two Givens on the same case? Not likely. Inez Givens Marchand was Mary Inez Givens Marchand. "I'd bet all the money in my pocket on it," Connolly mumbled. Which meant she was the same Mary Givens that Billy Ellis told them about. "Has to be," he said to himself. "She has to be Mary Inez Givens Marchand."

Mentally, he made a note to check with the DA's office about the name. If they didn't know, he could always check the records at the courthouse. Or get Mrs. Gordon to search for it online. She was good at that sort of thing.

But if she was Mary Givens, that meant Stephen Ellis—the boy whose body they found in the beach house—was her son. Why would she deny it? "What could possibly make a mother abandon her son like that?" No sooner had he said it than memories of his own mother came rushing back. He shouted in the air as if shouting at her. "Go away! I don't want to think about you today." When that seemed futile, he switched on the radio and cranked up the volume.

❖ ❖ ❖

Crenshaw Street intersected Airline Highway near the Loop, a few blocks from Government Street. Connolly steered the Chrysler down the street and checked the house numbers. The address he had for Clyde Ramsey was in the middle of the third block.

Like all the other houses in that part of town, Clyde's was a 1920s bungalow with white siding and metal awnings over the windows. Leftovers from a bygone era. Untouched by gentrification. A small patch of grass separated the house from the sidewalk by the street. Beside the house was a driveway that led to a detached garage in back.

Connolly parked at the curb in front and walked to the door, then pressed the doorbell and waited. After a moment the door opened part way. A man dressed in khaki pants and a wrinkled white shirt appeared. He appeared to be about seventy, with short gray hair cut in a flat top and a two-day growth of stubble on his face. "Yes?" he asked as he peered out through the opening.

"I'm looking for Clyde Ramsey."

"You've found him."

"My name is Mike Connolly. I'm an attorney. I was wondering if I could talk to you a minute."

"What about?"

"A case you worked on."

"Been a long time since I worked on a case," Ramsey replied. "I don't remember much of that stuff anymore."

"If Toby LeMoyne is right, you'll remember this one."

A smile came to Ramsey's face and he seemed to relax. "Toby LeMoyne. Haven't heard that name in years. You know Toby?"

"Yes. Had lunch with about an hour ago."

Ramsey pushed the door open and gestured to Connolly. "Come on in," he said. "Have a seat. If you know Toby, you must not be too bad. Who knows, maybe I'll think of something that can help you."

The door opened to a living room that was dark and cool. It was pleasant in appearance, but the air was stale and heavy and the smell of it tickled Connolly's nose. Ramsey closed the door behind them and switched on a lamp.

A sofa sat beneath a window along the wall by the door. Two chairs faced it across a cluttered coffee table. At the far end of the room was a spinet piano that stood to the left of a brick fireplace. The morning newspaper lay on the sofa. Magazines cluttered the floor nearby. Ramsey scooped up the paper. "Have a seat." He dropped the papers on the floor by the piano bench. "Sorry about the mess. I'm here by myself. Not much reason to clean the place up."

Connolly took a seat on the sofa. Ramsey sat in a chair opposite him. "So, how's Toby doing?" he asked.

"He seems to be doing well," Connolly said.

Ramsey crossed his legs. "I haven't seen him in years."

"He said he worked with you when he first came on the force."

"He was a young recruit when they sent him to me." Ramsey chuckled. "Didn't know much about anything. But he was a good guy. Smart. Caught on pretty quick."

"I was wondering if you could tell me something about a man named Earl Givens. He used to own a nursery out at Wilmer."

A somber expression came over Ramsey. Not exactly defensive, but on guard. He propped his elbows on the arms of the chair and looked away. "That was a tough case."

"Toby said it was his first."

"Yeah." Ramsey smiled. "Probably was."

"What do you remember about that case?"

"Not much." Ramsey seemed uncomfortable and shifted positions in the chair. "Dispatcher called me one morning. Said the hired help found the old man's body in a barn at the nursery. Deputies secured the scene. I went out. Got there around the middle of the morning. Something like that. The body was lying on the ground. Best I can remember, the coroner said he had been dead since sometime the day before."

"What happened to him?"

"Somebody shot him in the head. Never could figure out who—"

The phone rang, interrupting their conversation. Ramsey stepped out to answer it. While he was gone, Connolly glanced around the room. The mantle above the fireplace was lined with vases and bowls. Some were cobalt blue and caught his eye. Connolly stood and crossed the room for a closer look.

As he approached the mantle, he noticed a row of framed photographs on the piano. He picked up one and saw it was of a woman sitting at a table. She wore a blue suit with a corsage pinned near her lapel.

Ramsey came back to the room. "That's my wife, Eva," he said, pointing to the picture.

"She's a pretty lady," Connolly replied.

"Yes. She was."

"Is she deceased?"

"Yes." Ramsey took the picture. "She died year before last." He set the photo in its assigned place on the piano. As he set it there Connolly's eyes fell on a cobalt vase. It had been behind the picture and he hadn't noticed it before. This one had a wide mouth at the top and curved to a stem that had a clear bubble in the middle, just like the one he'd seen in the beach house.

Ramsey seemed not to notice Connolly's fascination but took a seat and continued to talk about his wife. "It was for the better," he said. "My wife. It was for the better that she's gone."

"She was not well?"

"Alzheimer's," Ramsey explained. "She couldn't remember a thing."

"I'm sorry." Connolly sat on the sofa. "That must have been tough for you."

"Yes." Ramsey nodded slowly. "Very tough." They sat in silence a moment, then he sighed and said, "But you didn't come here to talk about that. You were asking about Givens."

"Do you have any notes on the case?"

Ramsey shook his head. "All that stuff is downtown somewhere. I guess. They might not even have a file on it anymore. That was a long time ago. Some of the old files get thrown out, I think."

"Mr. Givens had a grandson. Nick."

Ramsey's eyes narrowed and he seemed to look right through Connolly. "What about him?"

"His mother is Inez Marchand."

"Yeah."

"Was she also known as Mary?"

"Yeah." Ramsey's eyes focused on Connolly's. "Why do you ask?"

"Just curious."

"About what?"

"About everything."

"What kind of case are you working on?"

"Murder."

"You're defending someone?"

"Yes."

"What's your client's name?"

"Dilbert Landry."

Ramsey chuckled. "Funny name."

Connolly ignored the comment. "In that case you worked on back then, how many times was Givens shot?"

"Twice."

"Where? In the head? The body?"

"Once in the stomach and once in the head."

"What did they shoot him with?"

"Thirty-eight, I think. As I recall, the coroner said they shot him in the stomach first. Then the head."

"How did he know that?"

"Shot to the head hit him right between the eyes. No need to shoot him anywhere else after that."

"And that's how you knew the shot to the head was the second shot?"

"Average person couldn't hit a man between the eyes like that with a pistol. And, like I said, why shoot him in the stomach if you've already shot him in the head?"

Connolly nodded. "Any idea who killed him?"

Ramsey shifted in the chair again. "Not really. Like I said, we never figured that part out."

"But you had a theory."

"This is an old case." Ramsey gave him a look. "Why are you so interested in it?"

"Inez Marchand owns a beach house on Dauphin Island. After the hurricane, some of the neighbors down there found a dead man in that house. My client is accused of killing him."

"And you think this old case has something to do with that one?"

"I don't know." Connolly shrugged. "Right now, I'm looking for anything I can find."

The comment didn't set well with Ramsey. "So, you're just out here stirring up anything you can find. Looking for something to talk about in court besides the truth. Like every other defense lawyer I've ever known." He stood. "I think I've said about all I want to say about this." He moved across the room toward the door.

Connolly hesitated a moment, wondering if he could convince Ramsey to talk a little longer, but by then, Ramsey had reached the door and was holding it open. The look on his face said their conversation was finished and when Ramsey gave a quick gesture toward the door, Connolly knew it was time to leave. Reluctantly, he rose from his place on the sofa, crossed the room, and stepped outside to the porch. He heard the door close behind him as he started down the steps.

Obviously, Ramsey knew more than he was willing to say and at least one of the questions Connolly had asked touched a nerve. He just didn't know which one. Or why. When he reached the car, Connolly glanced back at the house and saw Ramsey glaring at him through the front window. Yep. Something about Givens' murder connected to Dibber's case. But what?

As he started the car and pointed it down the street, Connolly thought again of the things he knew, and didn't know, about Dibber's case. He'd pieced together a number of facts about the relevant participants, but none of them would talk to him. And now even a retired deputy wouldn't talk to him, either. He'd had cases in the past with a witness that refused to talk, but not every witness. Inez. Edwin. Nick. None of them wanted to talk about the dead man in the beach house. And now a seventy-something retired detective wouldn't talk about a ten-year-old unsolved case.

Connolly shook his head. "Mrs. Gordon is right. This is a strange case. It's like every secret in the world has converged in one spot."

CHAPTER 31

From Ramsey's house, Connolly continued down Crenshaw Street through the old neighborhood. Seeing the houses again took him back to the memories he'd avoided earlier in the day. He knew it would, but this time the tug was too strong to resist.

The house on the left was where Jeff Berry had lived. And next to him was Russell Gray. Down the street on the right, Scott Darnell. Memories flooded his mind. Baseball games in the street. Secrets shared in the quiet of a hot summer night. Memories made bittersweet by the direction his life took that day his father died on the back porch. A tragedy compounded by the things that had happened since.

When he and his brother walked away, Connolly had vowed never to go back to their old house, or the neighborhood, or even that part of town, but it was a vow his heart wouldn't let him keep. Over the years, he'd driven down the street many times, looking at the houses, remembering the people he'd known, and thinking of what might have been. After he and Barbara married and moved to the house on Ann Street, he drove that way every morning to the office, just to go past the house. Hoping with some childlike hope that his mother might be there. That he might catch a glimpse of her. That everything might suddenly be back to what it was before his father died. But those daily drives past the house were a long time ago. It had been years since he was last there.

At the next corner he slowed the car almost to a stop. There was no traffic on the cross street. He stared down the street, his eyes scanning the houses on the right. He let the car roll through the intersection. And then he saw it. His heart skipped a beat.

A little cottage like all the others with white clapboard siding and a patch of lawn in front. An oak tree grew near the corner by a driveway that led to a garage in back. When he was squarely in front of it, he brought the car to a stop and stared at the house.

The lawn had seemed as big as the world when it was his turn to mow it. Now, it was not even the size of the waiting area in front of Mrs. Gordon's desk. To the left of the house, vines and thorns wound around the trunk of the oak tree, reaching almost to the top. A dead limb from the tree lay on the roof. Another lay near the porch. Trash littered the steps.

He should have kept going. There was no reason to stop. No reason at all. Just an ache from somewhere deep inside that needed relief. Instead of continuing on, he switched off the engine and stepped from the car.

A warm breeze tousled Connolly's hair as he came from the street and walked up the driveway toward the garage. At the end of the house, he glanced through a window to the room that had been their dining room when he was a boy. The walls were bare. A water stain marred the wall to the left. A table sat in the center of the room. It looked like the one they had used but it was covered with boxes and papers. He stared through the window a moment, studying the scene, wondering who had lived there last. Whether they had fond memories, too. Or only the pain. After a moment, Connolly continued past the house to the garage.

Like the house, the garage had wooden siding that once had been painted white, but years of neglect had taken a toll. Mildew coated the boards along the side with a green film and the doors sagged in the middle. A tree limb had punched a hole in the roof and decaying leaves were everywhere.

After a moment to gather himself, Connolly grasped the handle on one of the doors and pulled. The bottom of the door scraped across the concrete, but he pulled harder and forced it open. As he moved the door aside, light streamed into the garage and Connolly's mouth fell open in a look of disbelief.

Parked in the garage was a black 1941 Ford, exactly like the car his father drove. Chrome trim. Chrome hub caps. Everything. And then reality settled on him with a weight almost too heavy to bear. "This is not possible," he whispered. The car was covered in dust and grime but the longer he stared at it, the more he was convinced this really was his father's car.

Connolly moved slowly forward, inching along. His hand lightly on the metal. Fingertips just touching it. Wondering, dreaming, remembering. When he was near the rear door, he used his fingers and wiped away the grime from a spot on the rear window. Through the smudges, he peered inside and thought of the last time he'd ridden in the car. They went to the drugstore. He and Rick and their mother. The afternoon before she left. He hadn't known what was coming. Not even a hint. A day just like any other. Mother attending to business. Brothers arguing in the backseat. And then, she was gone.

Unable to resist the moment, he leaned forward even closer and cupped his hand against the glass to shield his eyes from the glare. Inside he saw a candy wrapper tucked in the crease of the seat, right where he'd left it. Tears filled his eyes. "This really is the car," he whispered.

Connolly opened the front door of the car. Mold covered the interior, but he saw a key dangling from the ignition. He removed it and found a metal tag at the end of the key chain. He rubbed it clean with his thumb until the letters on it were legible. "Service Cleaners and Laundry," he mumbled. They had driven there many times when he was a boy.

By then, spores from the mold and mildew had become overpowering and his nose began to drip. Reluctantly, he pushed the door closed, wiped his nose on the back of his hand, and glanced around the garage once more, wondering what else he could find of his past in there. He was about to leave when he noticed a baseball glove on a shelf to the right. A ball was stuck in the web. The glove was mildewed and stiff, but he could read the initials scrawled on the heel of the palm. "MC." Tears welled in his eyes again and this time he did nothing to stop them as they rolled down his cheeks.

Before his father collapsed that day, they had been tossing the ball in the backyard. When the ambulance finally arrived, the driver pushed Connolly aside. The radio on the porch was still playing the game they'd been listening to—the Mobile As were playing the Birmingham Barons at Hartwell Field. Connolly clutched the glove against his chest with both hands, as if embracing his father, holding onto him, trying to will him not to die. He was holding the glove and ball as they loaded his father into the ambulance but even then, at that age, without a word or look from an adult, he knew his father already was dead. To escape the pain of the moment, he ran into the garage and hid behind the car. As he stumbled past the rear bumper, he threw the glove on the shelf. That was the last time he'd touched it. And that's where he—

A voice from behind interrupted his thoughts. "What are you doing out here?" Startled by the sound of it, Connolly wheeled around to see a frail, elderly woman standing in the doorway. Their eyes met and she glared at him "What are you doing in my garage?" she demanded. "I oughta call the law."

She sounded angry but something about her was familiar and Connolly didn't feel threatened at all. "I'm sorry," he said as he laid the glove on the shelf. "I used to live here, and I was just—"

"Lies," she snapped, cutting him off. "Ain't nobody ever lived here but me." She gestured toward the street with a jab of her finger. "Now you get outta here right this minute. This here's my garage. And I don't allow nobody in here but me."

Barely five feet tall, she was thin and when she pointed with her finger, Connolly could count the bones pressing against the skin on the back of her hand. Her hair was gray and pulled in a bun that was tight against her scalp. And even though it was hot that day, she wore a black long-sleeved dress with a hem that fell below her knees. The dress was buttoned up the front and she had it fastened all the way to the top. Deep lines creased her face and her skin looked tough and leathery. She smelled like alcohol, too. Cheap liquor. Connolly had recognized it before he noticed anything else.

But her eyes were the thing that gave her away. And that look. He'd seen it many times, though years had passed since then. Still, not so many that he didn't recognize her. Tears filled his eyes once again. "Mama," he said softly.

The scowl on her face changed to a puzzled frown. "Mama?" she chortled. Then the expression vanished, leaving only a cold and aloof emptiness. "I ain't got no children," she growled.

Without saying more, she started toward the house. Connolly wanted to call after her. To grab her and make her stay. Make her talk to him. Explain why she left. Explain where she'd been. Explain why she hadn't come for them. Instead, he watched as she climbed the steps to the back door, took hold of the doorknob, and gave it a defiant twist. Just before disappearing inside, she glanced over her shoulder in his direction and said, "Close them doors when you leave."

Connolly waited while the door to the house banged shut, and he waited a moment longer hoping she would come out again. Hoping she would talk to him. Explain things to him. Fill in the blank spaces of the last forty years. Ease the aching loneliness that plagued his every moment. But when ten minutes passed and there was no sign of her, he knew she wasn't coming out. So, he did as she said and closed the garage doors, then started up the driveway toward the street.

As he passed the window at the end of the house, he paused a moment and stared into the dining room again. It was just as he had seen it when he arrived a few minutes earlier but this time, instead of studying the items in the room he kept his eyes on the doorway. Through it, he had a glimpse of the hall and he could see from the reflections in the shadows that she was moving about inside. Probably in the kitchen.

Connolly waited a moment longer, but when she did not appear, he continued toward the Chrysler. He glanced again toward the house as he placed the key in the ignition and saw his mother standing at the front window, staring at him. Their eyes met, but only briefly, then she was gone.

CHAPTER 32

From the house on Crenshaw Street, Connolly drove downtown toward the office. Buildings and houses passed him on either side, but he paid them no attention. His mind was lost in memories of the past and the emotion of seeing his mother again. Seeing her, only to hear her deny he even existed. Denied him when she left. Denied him by not coming back. "She knows who I am," he mumbled to himself. But how was it possible? Her, alive after so long. And right there in that house.

In the years since she left, he had passed that house many times and never once thought she might be living there. If he had thought about it—if he had even considered the possibility for a moment— he would have stopped to see for himself. He would have banged on the front door. Would have charged in and demanded answers. Yet just then, when she was right there in front of him, he couldn't think of a thing to say. And when she walked back to the house, he didn't go after her. Just stood there in the garage, dumbfounded.

A car horn blared behind him. Startled by the sound of it, Connolly glanced up to find he was stopped at the traffic light at Water Street. The car horn blared again. Connolly pulled on the steering wheel hard to the left, made a U-turn in the intersection, and started up Government Street in the same direction he'd just come. He intended to drive to the guesthouse and collapse on the sofa in the living room, but by the time he reached Tuttle Street he knew that was a bad idea. He would sit there until the sun went down and as the house grew darker, he would become depressed and feel sorry for himself and the darkness around him would descend into his soul. After that, anything could happen. Better to avoid that situation altogether. But where could he go. He wasn't hungry. He wasn't thirsty. Not for food or drink. What he needed was answers and there was one person left alive who could tell him what he wanted to know. One person. Uncle Guy. And he knew precisely where to find him.

A thirty-minute drive south from town brought Connolly to Bayou La Batre, a fishing village on the coast. Nestled along a broad, meandering bayou, the town lay hidden beneath towering cypress trees and sprawling oaks. Shielded against popular culture and the outside world, life there was a microcosm of the past. An odd and intriguing mixture of ritual, superstition, and dissipation. A fun place for a kid to grow up, but a place many wanted to escape as adults.

At the draw bridge near the center of the village, Connolly headed south onto a road that followed the bayou. Two miles later, he came to a large mailbox that dangled from a rotting wooden post at the side of the road. A driveway ran from the road at the box to a house that sat in the midst of a pecan grove. The house was made of concrete blocks and had jalousie windows that were shaded by oversized aluminum awnings once painted green and white. Beneath the windows, unkept azalea bushes grew near the side of the house.

The driveway was paved with oyster shells that crunched beneath the tires as the car approached the house. Connolly liked the sound of it and listened with his head cocked to one side until the car came to a stop a few feet from the kitchen door.

Through the screen door at the kitchen, Connolly saw a table with a red Naugahyde top and four matching chairs. They'd been in that same spot all his life. Beyond the table was a gas stove that stood against the far wall. A new one, not the one Ruby had used when she was alive. A skillet sat atop the front burner. Behind it was a pot with steam wafting from it. Farther to the right, Uncle Guy was at the sink, his back to the door.

Almost eighty-five now, Guy spent most of the day in the living room, napping in a recliner, a luxury he had only recently allowed himself. For most of his life, he'd done nothing but work. Dropped out of school in the sixth grade to work an oyster skiff. Did that until he was fifteen when he took a job as a deck hand on a shrimp boat. By twenty-one he was a boat captain and spent the next fifty years piloting shrimp boats, first on week-long runs south of town, then on trips far out in the Gulf lasting months at a time. It was a hard life, but one that favored him.

When Connolly's mother disappeared, he and his younger brother crammed what they could in a pillowcase and hitchhiked to Bayou La Batre. Guy and his wife, Ruby, raised them as their own. It was Guy who paid for Connolly to attend college and Guy who pointed him toward law school.

Connolly opened the screen door. As he stepped inside, Uncle Guy wheeled around to face him, startled by the intrusion. Alert at first, he smiled when he saw who it was. "Didn't expect to see you today." His smile became a grin. "You're just in time for supper."

"Great." Connolly closed the door. "I'm hungry enough to eat most anything."

Guy wiped his hands on a dish towel and threw his arms around Connolly in a bear hug. Connolly slipped an arm around the old man's waist and rested his head on his shoulder. The feel of that shoulder, the smell of sweat and aftershave lotion. Like a thousand times before, the world seemed to melt away.

After a moment, Guy eased his grip and pulled away. "You don't come down here often enough anymore."

"I know, "Connolly said as he took a seat at the table. "I've been busy lately."

Guy opened the refrigerator and stooped to look inside. "A man needs to be busy." He took a pan of fish from the shelf. "Is mullet alright with you?"

Connolly smiled. Mullet was his favorite fish. "Where'd you get them?"

"Caught them last night."

Connolly raised an eyebrow. "You caught them?"

Guy cut his eyes at him. "I ain't that old."

Connolly chuckled. "Where'd you go?"

"Little River." Guy closed the refrigerator and set the pan on the counter. "Poled the boat down to the mouth. They were jumpin' everywhere. Could have had a boatload but I didn't feel like cleaning that many."

The thought of Guy standing in a boat, throwing a cast net, made Connolly smile. An old man, still enjoying the things that had occupied his entire life.

Guy dipped the pieces of fish in a mixture of egg and buttermilk, then covered them with corn meal and laid them gently in the skillet on the stove. The fish sizzled in the pan. Steam from the pot on the back burner caught Connolly's attention. "What's in that other pot?"

"Grits," Guy replied. They always ate grits with mullet. Connolly loosened his tie and opened the collar of his shirt.

In a few minutes the fish were done, and they sat down to eat. Fish and grits with iced tea. One of Connolly's favorite meals. They sat across from each other and ate in silence. Connolly was on his third piece of fish before he realized he'd had fish for lunch that same day.

Guy paused to take a sip of tea. "So," he began. "Did you come down here for something, or just to see me?"

Connolly wasn't sure where to begin so he had another bite of fish, then a long drink of tea. Guy stared at him from across the table. "Well," he insisted. "What's the matter?"

Connolly took another sip of tea. Guy grew impatient. "Set that glass down and talk to me."

Reluctantly, Connolly said, "I went by the house on Crenshaw Street today."

"Oh." Guy leaned back in his chair. "And you stopped."

"Yeah."

"And she was there."

The comment caught Connolly by surprise. "How did you know she was there?"

"It's her house."

Connolly frowned. "You knew she was there?"

"Yeah."

"Has she been there all this time?"

"Not all of it."

"How long?"

Guy shrugged. "I don't know."

Connolly knew that wasn't a forthcoming answer but, in spite of what he had experienced that day, he didn't want to be rude to his uncle. Instead, he asked, "When was the last time you talked to her?"

"Ahh … she called me from a pay phone in Chiefland, Florida, about two weeks after you and Rick came down here."

Connolly frowned. "That's the last time you talked to her?"

Guy nodded. "She called here one other time. Ruby talked to her. I didn't."

"When was that?"

"About the time you were taking the bar exam."

"And that's it? That's the only time you talked to her?"

Guy gave him a stern look. "You think I been keeping something from you?"

"I don't know what to think. How she could be living in that house all this time and me not know it. Has she been there all this time?"

Guy sighed. "Maybe not all the time. Off and on, I think." Connolly gave him a skeptical look. Guy shrugged again. "I rode by there a time or two. Didn't stop but even from the street I could see the place was in bad shape. At first I thought it was empty but then I noticed a light and one other time I saw her out there by the garage." Guy wiped his chin with a napkin. "I know this is tough for you, but…."

"Why?" Connolly shouted and he struck the table with his fist as fifty years of emotion boiled to the surface. "Why did she leave us like that? Why didn't she come looking for us?"

"I don't know."

"Daddy left us. She left us."

Guy stood and took his plate to the sink. "There's a little more to the story than that," he said.

Connolly was perplexed. "More than what?"

Guy leaned against the kitchen counter with his arms folded across his chest. "For one thing, John didn't leave. He had a heart attack."

Connolly gave a dismissive gesture. "I know."

Guy shook his head. "No, you don't. Not all of it."

Connolly frowned. "What do you mean?"

"I mean … the man you know as your father—John Connolly. He isn't your father. Not biologically."

Connolly felt confused. "What are you talking about?"

"When your mother married John, they moved up to Mobile, met new people, found a life she hadn't known before. She and John got to running with folks who liked to go out at night. Started going to places. Radio Ranch. Ivey's Supper Club. Bunch of places I don't even know about."

Connolly frowned. "Radio Ranch?"

"It was a nightclub on Dauphin Island Parkway. Nice enough place. I mean, you didn't have to worry about a fight breaking out or anything. But it was a place where all kinds of people went to eat and drink and party." Guy shifted positions. "Your mother met this guy there. A surveyor. Worked for the railroad. They met, then first one thing and another happened and then…."

"I appeared."

Guy nodded. "She got pregnant with you."

"Who was he?"

"I don't know."

Connolly gave him a skeptical look. "Really?"

"I would tell you if I knew."

"Did she tell Dad?"

"Eventually."

"What did he say?"

"He moved out. Elizabeth moved in with us down here. Stayed a few months. John came and got her right before you were born."

Connolly shook his head slowly. "The things you don't know."

"Your mother was a mixed-up woman. Been that way all her life. I mean, she's my sister and I love her, but she has a strange way."

Connolly stared at the floor. "She smelled like liquor. Night Train, I think."

Guy nodded. "Fortified wine. That sounds like her. She always liked to drink. Used to sneak around and drink when we were in school. Then it got a hold of her and she couldn't get rid of it."

"Sounds familiar."

"Runs in the family," Guy said. "Did you actually talk to her?"

"I tried to. Walked down to the garage. Found the car. And then she was there. I was surprised that anyone was there and then I realized it was her. All I could say was 'Mama?'"

"What did she say about that?"

"I said I used to live there. She said nobody ever lived there but her. I told her she was my mother. She said she didn't have any children. Then she just walked away. Went inside the house. Never said another word."

Guy wiped his hands on the dish towel again and tossed it onto the counter. "Well, there's one more thing."

Connolly wasn't sure he wanted to hear anymore but he said, "What's that?"

"After you and Rick had been down here a while, I went to court in Mobile and got custody of you. She found out about it and from what I hear she didn't like it." He looked away. "Wasn't much she could do about it, but that's probably what she was talking about when she said she didn't have any children."

Connolly frowned. "You took us from her?"

Guy was uncompromising. "I wasn't about to let her take you. She was riding from truck stop to truck stop. Hopping around from man to man. Living in the cab of a truck. You can hate me for it if you want to, but I did what had to be done and I would do it again."

Guy pushed away from the counter, crossed the room, and walked up the hall. Connolly heard the recliner open in the living room. He took one more sip of tea, then rose from the table and put his plate in the sink.

What a day, he thought to himself. First Nick Marchand. Then nearly choked at lunch. Clyde Ramsey. His mother. Now this. He wiped his hands on the towel and walked to the living room. Guy was in the recliner with his eyes closed. Connolly took a seat on the sofa. "I don't hate you," he said. "I owe you everything."

"You don't owe me anything. Whatever we did for you and Rick, we did it as if you were our own children. And you were. It was a tough time. I didn't know what else to do. You and Rick were just kids. She left you in that house all alone—no food or anything—and ran off with that truck driver...."

"Who was he?"

"The first one was a guy named Harley Mullins. I never heard a name for any of the others."

"You knew Mullins?"

"No. She told me who he was when she called that time from Chiefland. Harley Mullins from Okahumpka, Florida. Met him at a truck stop in Loxley."

"What was she doing there?"

"Where?"

"The truck stop. In Loxley."

"I don't know. I imagine she'd been off with that bunch she used to hang around with. They liked to go to the speedway over in Pensacola. Probably coming back from there and stopped to eat." Guy sighed. "I don't know. That's what I figure happened."

Connolly rested his head against the back of the sofa. "We got hungry."

"I know you did. I was worried. I didn't know she was gone but I knew what she was like and when John died, I was worried something would happen."

"Rick cried himself to sleep that first night."

Guy took a deep breath. Connolly glanced at him. The old man's eyes were open now, and moist. "You did the right thing. Coming down here." A tear trickled from the corner of one eye. "I was proud when I saw y'all coming up the driveway. I knew it was your idea."

Connolly reached over and rubbed the back of Guy's hand. They sat in silence again and after a moment Connolly said, "So, what about Rick? Who was his dad?"

"John was. But he gave you his name."

A frown wrinkled Connolly's forehead. "His name?"

"John Michael Connolly," Guy explained. "That was his name. And he gave it to you."

Connolly grinned at the thought of it. No one ever called him by his full name. He never even used it himself. Sometimes he even forgot about the John part. All his life he'd thought of himself as Mike. But his full name was John Michael Connolly, Jr. "That was a good thing," he said finally.

"Yes, it was." Guy reached behind him and switched off the lamp. "Name's all that matters." He settled back in the chair. "A good name gives a man a good start in life."

CHAPTER 33

The following morning, Connolly was awakened by the pre-dawn light glowing through the front window. Somewhere in the east, the sun was about to rise above the trees, but right then, it cast only a gray hue across the living room. It was a familiar sight. He had seen that look many times. It was the way the morning appeared when he finally arrived back at home after an all-night binge. That life was behind him now and he pushed the thought of it away, focusing instead on the things he had learned from Guy.

What he learned about his father didn't bother him. Not really. John Connolly was his dad, and nothing could change that. But the things about his mother … that part was painful. She had been alive all this time and never once tried to find him. Not at Christmas. Not on his birthday. Not at all. It was as if he and Rick didn't even exist. And then he remembered what Guy had said about going to court to get custody of them.

Guy lay snoring in the recliner. Had looked after him as much as John Connolly. More, in fact. And he had been willing to do the difficult things. Work when he didn't feel like it. Go to court against his own sister. Take on the responsibility of two young boys. Connolly smiled at the thought of it. Two men had gone out of their way to see that he had a life. Then he thought of how little he made of it. And that was as painful as thinking about his mother.

Across the room beneath the window was a table with pictures of Ruby, Connolly, and Rick, all of them taken years ago. The one of Connolly was made when he graduated from college. The one of Rick was taken when he was still in high school. The night before a dance. Wearing a leisure suit with a paisley shirt. Connolly chuckled. The past really was a foreign territory.

Sleeping on the sofa left his neck stiff. He stood and rubbed it, then leaned over and kissed Guy on the forehead. The old man responded with a faint smile. Connolly crossed the room to the hall. As he reached the doorway, Guy said, "Whatever she did, she did because of her. Not because of you."

"Sometimes that's not easy to remember."

"I know. But it's true. She was like she was before you ever came along." Guy sat up straight. "And there's something else you should remember."

"What's that?"

"She's still your mother."

"I know."

Guy closed his eyes. Connolly crossed the kitchen and stepped outside.

By seven that morning Connolly was at the guesthouse. He showered, changed clothes, and headed downtown. It seemed like years since he had been to the office but instead of going straight there, he went to St. Pachomius Church. He parked the Chrysler in a space in front and made his way up the steps to the sanctuary.

Inside, the air was cool and refreshing. Morning Prayers had ended. The sanctuary was empty and quiet. He took a seat on a pew near the front and lowered a kneeler, then placed his knees on it and leaned forward, resting his head against the back of the next pew. With his eyes closed, he could see in his mind his mother standing in the doorway at the garage. He could hear her voice. "Nobody ever lived here but me," she said. The sound of those words made his soul bristle.

The pew beside him creaked. He opened his eyes and glanced to the right. Father Scott sat next to him. "We missed you this morning." Connolly slid back in the seat. Father Scott smiled at him. "You look tired."

Connolly nodded. "Feels like I've been away. On a long trip."

"What's up?"

"You ever feel like sometimes the world just turns inside out? Like you go around a corner thinking everything is one way. Then, wham! Nothing's really what you thought it was."

Father Scott grinned. "Did Raisa call you?"

Connolly frowned. Raisa? Oh. The girl from the warehouse. Connolly shook his head. He hadn't thought about her in … at least a day or two. That whole thing seemed a distant memory. "No," Connolly replied. "Not that."

"Are you still working on that case about that dead body in the beach house?"

"Yeah." Connolly nodded.

Father Scott crossed his legs and seemed to relax. "I read about it in the paper. The article mentioned you."

That case wasn't what he'd come there to think about and pray about. And it wasn't what he had hoped to talk about when he noticed Father Scott beside him on the pew. But it was more comfortable to talk about it than about the situation with his mother, so he said, "It's a strange case. It's like all the secrets in the world converged in that one case."

"Did they ever figure out who he was?"

"Yeah." Connolly nodded. "Sort of."

Father Scott frowned. "Sort of?"

Connolly grinned. "They matched his fingerprints to an arrest record from Georgia that says he is Stephen Ellis and used that to find his parents. The DA brought his father down here to see the body. But when we went to the morgue and the father looked at the body, he told us the body isn't Stephen's."

"That's interesting."

"Yeah. The records are all confused. Turns out, the dead guy was Stephen's best friend."

"I guess the father was relieved."

"Yeah, but that's a strange thing, too, because Stephen's father isn't really his father. He's just the husband of the woman who raised him. She's not his mother, either." Connolly glanced over at Father Scott. "Is this making any sense?"

"Actually, yes." Father Scott chuckled. "So where is the son?"

"Stephen?"

"Yeah."

Connolly shrugged. "No one knows. Or, at least, no one's talking about it—which isn't anything new for this case. But that's not the end of it."

"There's more?"

"Oh yeah. There's more."

"Is that why you came in here?"

Connolly looked away. "I was talking to Toby LeMoyne yesterday. Do you know Toby?"

"We met once."

"There's this old case. Might have something to do with this one. We were talking about it. He gave me the name of a guy who knew something about it. The man lives on Crenshaw Street. I went to see him yesterday." Connolly looked over at Father Scott. "I used to live on Crenshaw Street."

"When you were married?"

"No." Connolly shook his head. "When I was a boy."

Father Scott nodded.

Connolly took another deep breath and continued. "So, I went to see this guy. After I talked to him, I drove down the street. It's the old neighborhood. I hadn't seen it in awhile. Not too far from his house, I came to the house where we used to live. Looked like nobody lived there. Grass was all grown up. Place hadn't been painted. So, I stopped and walked down to the garage." Tears welled in his eyes. He glanced over at Father Scott. "His car is still in the garage."

Father Scott looked puzzled. "Whose car?"

"My dad's." Connolly cleared his throat. "Well …." He shrugged. "Not exactly my dad."

Father Scott shook his head. "I'm not following what you mean."

Connolly wiped his eyes. "While I was in the garage looking at the car and trying to figure out why it was still there, this woman came out there and told me to get out." Tears ran down Connolly's cheeks. His voice was a whisper. "She was my mother."

Father Scott looked surprised. "Your mother?"

"Yeah." Connolly's voice was little more than a breath.

"I thought she was dead."

"I did, too." They sat in silence a moment, then Connolly began again. "So, after I left there, I went down to see my uncle. And I asked him about her. He knew she wasn't dead. Hadn't seen her in a while but knew she was alive. Then he told me the man I knew as my father wasn't really my father. My mother had an affair." Father Scott acknowledge the pain in his voice with a hand on his shoulder. Connolly wiped his eyes again. "I don't know what's going on."

"Did your uncle tell you anything about him. About your biological father?"

"Not really. I mean, he doesn't know much about him."

"Did he give you a name?"

"No." Connolly shook his head. "He doesn't know what it is. Just that he worked for the railroad. A surveyor, I think. Why wouldn't she talk to me?"

"Did she say anything?"

"Told me to get out of the garage. When I said she was my mother, she said she didn't have any children."

"What did you say?"

"I couldn't say much of anything." An angry scowl came over Connolly's face. "I hate that woman."

"I know."

Connolly leaned forward, his hand balled in a fist. "She left us there." He pounded his fist into the palm of his other hand. "She didn't care whether we lived or died."

Father Scott leaned closer. "That's the part you need to get rid of."

Connolly glared at him. "What part?"

"The bitterness."

"Bitterness?" Connolly's forehead wrinkled in a frown. "She was wrong." His voice grew loud. "I wouldn't treat anybody like that. We could have died, and she wouldn't have cared."

"She was wrong. But this isn't about her." Father Scott pointed at Connolly. "It's about you."

"Me?"

"You can't change her. You can't change the past. And you can't stay there, either."

"Can't stay where? What are you talking about?"

"You're still right there at that same spot."

"What spot?"

"That night," Father Scott said. "When you realized she wasn't coming back. That next morning, when you had to get up and take care of your brother. You're still right there at that moment and you need to get free from it." Connolly looked away. Father Scott leaned toward him. "You can't stay there. You've got to move on."

"I want her to talk to me."

"I know. But this isn't about her."

Connolly's voice took a sarcastic tone. "You mean it's about me learning to forgive?"

"That might be part of it. But listen to me. You are at a critical point. This is an opportunity to close the door on who you used to be."

Connolly felt puzzled. "I don't know what you mean."

"You've held on to what your mother did to you and what she did to your brother. In many ways you moved on. Went to school. All of that. But emotionally, you held on to what she did, and you've been waiting for her to come make it right. And you've been waiting for a chance to bust her with it. To show her how wrong she was."

Connolly had a determined look. "And now I can do just that." He jabbed the air with his finger for emphasis.

Father Scott's voice softened. "And now you must let it go. That thing you've been holding onto. That thing she did, is an open door. It's an open door to the past that has tied you to her."

"Tied me to her?"

Father Scott nodded. "It's a door, and it goes both ways. You could always get back to that moment. And she could always get to you."

Connolly gave him a sullen look. "She doesn't want anything to do with me."

"You became like her."

Connolly thought a moment, then leaned back. A whisper slipped from his lips. "Alcohol."

Father Scott nodded. "If you can get this resolved, you can move on from being a sober alcoholic to a man who used to have a drinking problem."

"You may be right. But what about all this other stuff? The stuff with the people in this murder case? The secrets and all that?"

"I don't know. Maybe that's part of the bigger picture. I don't know about all that. But this business with your mother has brought you to a crucial point in your life."

Connolly stared ahead, thinking. Father Scott sat there a moment, then slipped from the pew. "Sit there and think about that a while."

CHAPTER 34

By the time Connolly left the church, the morning was already hot and humid. Sweat trickled down his back as he walked down the steps toward the car. He thought of what Father Scott had said. It had been a long trek from the gin bottle and Marisa. Living from drink to drink. Then living from no to no. Most days had been a battle. Often, he could only say to himself, "Not today." Maybe it was time. Maybe he could finally get free from the past, once and for all.

At the sidewalk, he slipped off his jacket and opened the car door. He dropped onto the front seat and sat sideways with his feet outside the car, resting on the pavement. The past two days had been rough. Going to the office was the last thing he felt like doing. Maybe he should call Rick and ask him about their mother. Or talk to Barbara.

Across the street, an inmate from the jail washed the sidewalk outside the sheriff's office. Connolly stared at him and thought of Dibber. A dead body in Inez Marchand's beach house. Inez. Mary Inez Givens Marchand.

The conversation with Clyde Ramsey drifted through his mind. Earl Givens, murdered. Shot in the head with a thirty-eight. Connolly perked up. Earl Givens. Murdered. They did an autopsy. Morgan would have a report. He swung his feet inside the car, started the engine, and drove up Church Street.

Traffic was heavy by the time Connolly arrived at Mobile General. All of the spaces near the building were taken. He parked on the far side of the lot and started toward the emergency room entrance. As he stepped away from the car his cell phone rang. He took it from his pocket and checked the number on the screen. The call was from Mrs. Gordon.

"Are you coming to the office anytime this week?" she asked.

"What's up?"

"I'm working," she replied. "What are you doing?"

"I'm at the hospital."

The tone in her voice changed. "What happened?"

"Nothing. I'm at the morgue. I need to talk to Ted Morgan."

"Oh."

"Any calls for me?"

"Several."

"Any of them important?"

"They seem to think so."

"I'll call them when I get to the office. I'll be down there in a little while."

Connolly switched off the cell phone and entered the building. He crossed the waiting room, past the receptionist's desk, and made his way down the corridor to the morgue. Ted Morgan was seated at the desk in his office. He glanced up as Connolly appeared. "Back again?"

"Yeah."

"Did the DA's office call you?"

"About what?"

"Junkins' family will be in tomorrow."

Connolly frowned. "Junkins family? What's that about?"

"That dead guy they thought was somebody and turned out to be someone else."

"Stephen Ellis," Connolly offered.

"Yeah," Morgan replied. "But he was really Bobby Junkins."

"Oh. Yeah. Sorry. A lot has happened since then."

"So, what brings you in today?"

Connolly took a seat near the desk. "I wanted to ask you about an old case."

"How old?"

"Fifteen or twenty years ago."

"Got a name?"

"Earl Givens."

Morgan frowned. "Name sounds familiar. One of your clients in prison trying to find a way out?"

Connolly shook his head. "Givens was a victim."

"Who killed him?"

"I'm not sure. Nobody wants to talk about it. Clyde Ramsey was the detective. Do you know him?"

"Yeah. I know him. But he's retired."

"I know."

"I always liked him. You talked to him?"

"Yeah."

"How's he doing? I heard his wife died not too long ago."

"Yeah. Alzheimer's. He's alright. Do you remember the case?"

"Maybe."

"Got a file on it?"

"Files that old would have been closed a long time ago."

"They never solved it. Ramsey says it's still open."

Morgan rolled his chair around to a row of file cabinets along the wall behind the desk. The latch on the bottom drawer clicked as he pulled it open. "If it's still active, it might be in here. Got a few old ones down here." He leaned over the drawer and thumbed through a row of manila folders. "Earl Givens." He took the file from the drawer. "April 23, 1985." Morgan glanced through the file as he scooted the chair back to the desk. He looked up at Connolly. "I remember this guy." He glanced back at the file. "The underwear robbery."

A frown wrinkled Connolly's forehead. "The what?"

Morgan cackled. "Somebody killed him and left everything except his underwear."

"What are you talking about?"

"I went to the scene." Morgan laid the file on the desk. "A farm.... No. A nursery. Out near Wilmer or someplace like that. He was lying face down in this old barn. Fully clothed. Had his wallet in his hip pocket. Some change in a front pocket. Keys. Watch was still on his wrist. Nothing missing. Even found his cap right there by the body. Brought him down here to do the autopsy and found out he didn't have on any underwear." Morgan chuckled. "I called it the underwear robbery."

Connolly scowled. "You're sick."

Morgan shrugged. "Clyde didn't think it was funny either. But an old guy going without underwear."

"Commando."

"Yeah. Commando. It seemed funny to me."

"Anything interesting besides the underwear he wasn't wearing?"

Morgan picked up the file. "Not that I recall." He glanced over the pages in the file as he flipped through. "Looks like everything else was normal." A few pages farther he paused and scanned down the sheet. "Adrenaline was high. Nothing too special about that." He glanced at Connolly. "Yours would be elevated if someone was pointing a gun at you." Morgan looked at the next page. His eyes brightened. He tapped the file with his finger. "Now, this was something I was never quite sure of."

"What's that?"

"There were traces of prolactin in his blood. And the lab found phenylethylamine."

"What does that mean?"

"He was excited."

"I thought you said that was normal."

"I said the elevated adrenaline was explainable."

"And this isn't?"

Morgan shifted positions in the chair. "No. It's explainable. It's just unusual in this kind of case."

Connolly waited a moment but when Morgan didn't continue, he said, "Well? What's the explanation?"

Morgan looked uncomfortable. "Both of these chemicals are present during … arousal."

Connolly felt his forehead wrinkle in a frown again. "Arousal? You mean sexual arousal?"

"Yes." Morgan nodded. "That's exactly what I mean."

"He was having sex when he was shot?"

"Maybe. He might just have been aroused."

"Did you…?"

"Yes," Morgan said, interrupting. "I checked. No traces of semen on his clothes. No traces of—"

"But his underwear was missing."

"Yes."

Connolly gave him a sarcastic look. "Doesn't that strike you as odd?"

"Well, despite my attempts at humor about it, not really. You'd be surprised what people wear under their clothes. And what they don't. But that doesn't matter. We would have known if he had engaged in that kind of activity."

"Twenty-five years ago?"

Morgan gave him a look. "It was the '80s. Not the dark ages. We didn't have all the DNA tests we have now, but we could detect the presence of semen on his clothing or skin. Believe me. It's not that difficult to find."

"Did you check his clothing?"

Morgan glanced at the file. "I'm sure we did. That would have been standard." He fell silent as he scanned through the last pages of the file. Then, something caught his eye. Connolly noticed the look. "What?" he asked.

"Nothing." Morgan slapped the file closed. "Nothing at all," he said as he scooted to the file cabinet and opened the drawer. He slipped the file in place and shoved the drawer closed with a bang.

Connolly caught his eye. "I saw the look on your face. What's in the file?"

Morgan rolled the chair back to the desk. He swiveled around to face Connolly and folded his hands in his lap. "Not everything in that file pertains to the dead man."

"What do you mean?"

"I mean, there are things in our files that aren't open to the public."

"There was someone else present?"

"Maybe."

"Who?"

"I can't say."

"Can't say, or won't say?"

"Can't."

Connolly thought for a moment. "A minor?"

Morgan smiled. Connolly stared at him. Morgan lifted an eyebrow. "Can't say."

"They wouldn't be a minor now."

"No. But I can't tell you about him without a judge's order."

Their eyes met and Morgan gave him a knowing look. Connolly understood. "Thanks," he said, and he started toward the door.

Without saying so explicitly, Morgan had confirmed for Connolly that the minor present when Earl Givens' body was found was a young male. Proving that in court would require direct evidence. If he used the information from Morgan's file, he would have to file a motion with Judge Cahill and argue the grounds in court. Doing that would alert everyone to the matter he wished to explore. That might become necessary, but right now he didn't need to get into all of that. He knew enough to be able to ask the right questions of the right people. And the first of those was Clyde Ramsey.

CHAPTER 35

From the hospital, Connolly drove back to Clyde Ramsey's house on Crenshaw Street. As he reached to ring the doorbell, a gray Buick appeared in the driveway, emerging from behind the house, backing toward the street. Clyde Ramsey was seated behind the steering wheel. Their eyes met and the car came to a stop. Ramsey glared at him through the car window. "I've got nothing else to say to you."

The car started down the driveway. Connolly stepped from the porch. "I know about the boy." The car came to a stop again. Connolly came from the front porch. "I know you interviewed him." Ramsey scowled at him angrily. Connolly was even closer by then. "I know he was there when the old man was killed."

Ramsey snarled. "You just won't leave well enough alone, will you."

Connolly came around to the driver's door. "We need to talk about this case. I know he was there. I know you interviewed him. I just want to talk about it."

Ramsey shut off the engine and gave a heavy sigh. His shoulders slumped and the anger he'd shown before seemed to evaporate. A faraway look came in his eyes. "He needed killing." Connolly was unsure what to say next and didn't want to say anything that might stop him from talking.

Ramsey opened the door and stepped from the car. "Every day." He slammed the car door shut. Connolly jumped. Ramsey's eyes were on fire. "Every day! That kid went out there after school. Every day." He took a deep breath and lowered his voice. "Do you know what I'm saying?" Connolly nodded. Ramsey banged his fist against the car door. "The old man was there. Every day." Ramsey looked Connolly in the eye. "When he told me. The boy. When he told me what that old man did to him." Ramsey clinched his teeth. He seemed to force himself to take another deep breath. This time, he let it out slowly and seemed to gather himself. "If the old man hadn't been dead already, I would've killed him myself." He gave Connolly a look. "I promise you. I would have killed him myself."

"Nobody knew what was going on?"

Ramsey looked disgusted. "His mother knew."

"Inez Marchand?"

"Yeah." Ramsey nodded. "He'd done the same thing to her when she was a girl." Connolly felt sick to his stomach. Ramsey continued. "Nick tried to tell her, but she wouldn't listen to him. Then I think one day she saw something in his clothes." Ramsey sighed again. "It was—" He grimaced. Gathered himself yet again. Forced the words from his mouth. "The man needed killing."

"So, Inez killed her own father?" Ramsey didn't respond. Connolly tried again. "You interviewed Nick." Ramsey still didn't respond. Connolly tried another question. "No one was ever prosecuted?" Ramsey just looked at him. The muscles along his jaw flexed.

"A boy is not supposed to be treated like that," Ramsey said. "That old man was supposed to protect him from shit like this." He leaned against the car. "And he was dead. I wasn't going to let them put the kid through a trial. He already had the pain of what the old man did to him. If the case went to trial, he'd have to tell a courtroom full of people about it. And he'd have to live all his life with that memory." Ramsey folded his arms across his chest in a defiant pose. "I wasn't gonna let that happen."

"So, you convinced them to let it go."

Ramsey's eyes brightened. A grin lifted the corners of his mouth.

"The district attorney and I went back a long way. He didn't have much choice."

"You and the DA?"

Ramsey nodded. Connolly frowned. "Is this something I want to know about?"

"I don't know that it matters now," Ramsey replied. "It's been a long time. The DA from back then is dead now. I don't think this part of the story matters much. But I'll tell you if you want to know."

"Okay."

Ramsey shifted positions against the car and seemed to get comfortable. "The DA back then was a guy named Lem Covan. You remember him?"

"I actually tried a case or two against him before he retired."

"Right. Well, his daddy was Harley Covan."

Connolly nodded. "Harley E. Covan. They say when he was DA, he would just tell the judge which ones were guilty, and the judge would send them to prison."

Ramsey chuckled. "That's not far from the truth." He moved his hands to his side. "Harley was a decent enough guy, but he loved to gamble. Poker. Craps. Roulette. Only thing was, he was afraid to fly. He'd get in a boat and ride fifty miles into the Gulf to fish, but he wouldn't get near an airplane. Which meant he'd never go to Las Vegas or any of the usual places where that kind of thing was legal. Instead, he would drive to some rug joint in Biloxi or Panama City or someplace like that."

Connolly shook his head and smiled. "All of them illegal."

"Yeah." Ramsey paused for a moment as if thinking, then continued. "So good ol' Harley was over in Biloxi one night in the back room at this club when the sheriff raided the place. New guy. Hadn't been sheriff very long." Ramsey chuckled. "Didn't stay sheriff very long either. Not after he did that raid. They came in, scooped up everybody. Took them off to jail. Seized a truckload of machines, tables, money. Everything."

Connolly finished for him. "Including Harley E. Covan."

Ramsey grinned. "Including Harley Covan. The District Attorney from Mobile."

"What happened?"

"I got a call from my brother about three o'clock that morning. He was a deputy over there. Told me they had Harley in one of their interview rooms. Said they'd let him go and forget the whole thing if I came and got him." Ramsey's eyes sparkled. "I went over there and got him. Drove him back to Mobile. Far as I know, no one else ever found out about it." He gave Connolly a knowing look. "Except for me and Harley."

"Did you have to explain all this to Lem?"

"About the raid?"

"No. About the kid—Nick—and not prosecuting his mother."

Ramsey shook his head. "I just told him to tell Harley I was cashing in my Edgewater chit."

Connolly was puzzled. "Edgewater?"

"That was the name of the place in Biloxi. The Edgewater Club."

"And they decided not to prosecute Inez."

Ramsey looked down at the grass. "The case just … faded away."

"Well," Connolly said. "It might be making a comeback."

Ramsey was alert. "What do you mean?"

"You remember I told you I was working on a murder case?"

"Not this one."

"No. But it involves Inez's son."

"Her son? What are you talking about?" A frown wrinkled Ramsey's forehead. "Nobody said Nick was charged with anything. I just saw him the other day. He didn't say anything about—"

"She had another son."

"Another one?"

"Before Nick was born, she went off to Atlanta. Met a guy. Got pregnant. Had a little boy." Ramsey looked away. Connolly continued. "Father was a guy from Atlanta. A writer. Had a couple of books. It was the '60s. She got swept up in it. Got pregnant. Not long after that, the writer was killed in a plane crash. She was alone. Didn't really know what to do. Left the baby with some friends and moved back to Mobile."

"I thought you were defending somebody over that body they found in her beach house."

"I am," Connolly said.

"I don't know anything about all that."

"When's the last time you saw Nick Marchand?"

"Uh. It's been a while."

"When?"

"I can't remember."

"A moment ago, you said you'd just seen him and he—"

Ramsey cut him off. "I said I can't remember." He opened the car door and got in behind the steering wheel. "I have to go. I was on my way to the bank." He started the engine. "I'll see you later." He backed the car down the driveway to the street.

Connolly watched as Ramsey drove away. At first his eyes were focused on the car but then he saw the corner of the front porch at his mother's house, two blocks away. Thoughts of her rushed in. Part of him wanted to drive by the house one more time, to see if she was there, to see if she would talk. And part of him wanted to drive in the opposite direction and never think of her again.

A check of his watch showed it was already past noon. He needed to get to the office. Issues with his mother would have to wait.

CHAPTER 36

A parking place was open on Dauphin Street near the office building. Connolly parked the car and rode the elevator to the third
floor. Mrs. Gordon came from the copier room as he started down
the hall. "You finally decide to come to work?"

Connolly ignored her question. "Where are those messages you
mentioned?"

"On your desk."

He brushed past her and continued down the hall. She called to
him as he walked away. "What's got you so aggravated?"

He stopped and faced her. "There are maybe three or four people who could bust this case wide open. And not one of them wants
to talk about what they know."

"The one with Dibber?"

"Yeah."

"Relax." Mrs. Gordon dismissed him with the wave of a hand.
"Carl sent us another payment on the fee."

"I'm not sure it's worth it at any price." Connolly hung his jacket
on the coat rack by the door in his office and took a seat behind the
desk. A stack of phone messages awaited him. He sorted through
them and began returning calls. As he finished his third, Mrs. Gordon appeared at the door. "There's a call for you on line two. Somebody named Tiffany. I think it's that girl you saw a few days ago."

Connolly took the call. Tiffany wasted little time with formalities. "Tinker wants to see you. Come to the Pig tonight around eight."

"Is he gonna show this time?"

"Come around eight." The call ended abruptly.

Mrs. Gordon was still in the doorway. She gave him a puzzled look. "What was that about?"

"One of her friends wants to talk."

"And you're going to meet them?"

"Yeah."

"Maybe it wouldn't be so bad to have Hollis around after all."

Connolly leaned back in his chair, rested his head against the wall, and closed his eyes. He heard Mrs. Gordon scoot her chair across the floor, then heard the click of her fingers on the keyboard. And then he was asleep.

Late that afternoon, Connolly walked over to the district attorney's office. Juanita was seated at her desk as he stepped from the elevator. "Yes?" she asked in an imperious tone.

"I was wondering if Gayle Underwood could see me."

"I'll check." She pressed a number on the telephone keypad and stared at him while she waited for an answer. Connolly backed away from her desk and tried not to look intimidated. In a moment she called to him. "Ms. Underwood will be right—" Before she could finish, the door near her desk opened. Gayle Underwood appeared.

"Mr. Connolly. Come on back." Gayle held the door for him, then led the way down the hall. "You caught me at a good time. Judge Cahill had something going on this afternoon and canceled the docket." She guided him to a small conference room a little way down the hall. "What's on your mind?"

"I hear Mr. and Mrs. Junkins are coming to town."

"Yes. Did we call you about that?"

"I don't know. I haven't gotten that far in my phone messages. Ted Morgan told me they were coming."

"We're meeting with them tomorrow around two. I think Judge Cahill will be upset if you don't join us."

Connolly chuckled. "Judge Cahill wants you to think he'll be mad."

Gayle frowned. "I don't like it when he shouts." She pointed to a chair. "Have a seat."

Connolly sat across from her at the table. "I was in Cahill's court one day," he said. "And he had a man in there on a domestic abuse case. Got in a fight with his wife. Hit her, I think. It was a serious situation but not as bad as some, but Cahill doesn't like those cases at all. The guy didn't really understand what was going on, though. He made some offhand remark and Cahill exploded. Gave him sixty days in jail. Plus, a huge fine. Came up out of his chair, shouting and ranting. Walter cuffed him and took him out right then. As soon as they were gone Cahill settled down and called the next case."

"He's out of control sometimes."

"No." Connolly shook his head. "Not really. I asked him if he was going to leave the guy in there for sixty days. He laughed and said he'd give him a week to cool off and see what they could work out."

"You seem to get along with him."

"I like him. He tells me what he thinks about my cases. I tell him back."

Gayle nodded. "What did you want to see me about?"

"I was wondering if we could talk about a case. An old one."

She looked puzzled. "What case is that?"

"Earl Givens."

"I don't think that's one of mine. Do you represent Mr. Givens?"

"Mr. Givens is dead."

Gayle looked confused. "What kind of case is this?"

"Murder."

"Murder?"

"Yeah."

"Well, if he's dead, doesn't that resolve the case?"

"He was the victim."

"Oh." She frowned. "Well, someone else must have it. I don't think I can talk about someone else's case."

"This case was never really solved. I know there was an investigation but I'm not sure it resulted in a prosecution."

"And you think we have a file on it?"

"I'm sure you do."

"Earl Givens?"

"Earl Givens." Connolly grinned. "You know his daughter."

"I do?"

"Yes."

"Who is she?"

"Inez Marchand."

Gayle's eyes opened wider. "Interesting. And you think the two cases are related."

"They might be. Think you could find the file?"

"I don't know. It might take a while. They keep some old files up here but to tell you the truth, I'm not sure where they are."

"Maybe you could take a look? Call me and let me know what you find?"

She shrugged. "Maybe."

"I can go to Judge Cahill and ask him for it."

"Think he'll give it to you?"

"I'm entitled to any information that tends to exonerate my client. He'll make you look for it."

"And you think this old case will exonerate your client?"

Connolly gave her a look. "I think it might."

"Is this just a hunch, or do you have something specific in mind?"

Connolly stood. "Find that file and we can talk about it."

Gayle stood and waited while Connolly stepped into the hall. She followed him out to the hall. "What if Henry decided to charge your client with the old case?"

Connolly chuckled. "Not even Henry is that crazy."

She smiled. "Really?"

"Givens was killed in 1985. My client would have been ... about fifteen at the time."

"I'm not so sure Henry would see that as a problem."

Connolly laughed. "You're learning fast, Ms. Underwood."

Juanita was gathering her purse to leave when Connolly stepped from the hallway to the lobby. He avoided eye contact with her and walked to the elevator. As he waited for it, Henry McNamara appeared at his side. "Mr. Connolly, what brings you down here?"

"Just checking on a few details. Are you leaving for the day?"

"It's after five."

Connolly glanced at his watch. He didn't realize it was that late. McNamara looked over at him. "How's Mr. Landry?"

"Fine."

"There's a tropical storm out in the Gulf." McNamara had a cheesy grin. "Too bad he won't be out of jail in time to loot some more houses when it makes landfall."

Connolly smiled. "That depends on how fast Cahill can get us a preliminary hearing."

"In your dreams."

"We'll see."

The elevator doors opened. They stepped inside. McNamara pressed the button for the lobby. "You don't really think you can get him off, do you?"

Connolly stared ahead, avoiding eye contact. "I've got as much in my favor as you have in yours. And that's enough to negate probable cause right there."

"Not in this county."

"Maybe."

"Not in this state."

"You may be right."

The elevator reached the lobby and Connolly walked toward the exit. McNamara went in the opposite direction.

CHAPTER 37

From the courthouse, Connolly drove to Ann Street. As he made the corner, he saw the black and white 'For Sale' sign in the yard at Barbara's house. He brought the Chrysler to a stop at the curb and got out. At first, anger rose inside him but it was quickly replaced by an overwhelming sense of sadness. He wanted to pull the sign up and fling it across the street. He wanted to shout and cuss and scream. Instead, he pushed the car door closed and walked up the walkway to the front door.

Barbara answered the doorbell with a smile. She seemed glad to see him. "Are you coming inside this time, or just standing on my porch?"

He liked the way she looked at him and the anger he'd felt before melted away. A grin broke across his face. "Want to have dinner?"

"I thought we already were."

"Isn't it nice to be asked, though?"

"You're in a mood. Has something happened?"

"Yeah."

She looked concerned. "Something bad?"

"Nothing like that."

"Well." She glanced at the jeans and shirt she was wearing. "I need to shower and change."

Connolly shook his head. "Not for this place."

Barbara gave him a playful look. "Where'd you have in mind?"

"The Whistlin' Pig."

The playfulness left her face. Her eyebrows curled in toward each other in a frown. "The Whistlin' Pig?"

Connolly shrugged. "Seems like a good night for barbeque."

"I haven't been to that place in—"

"Never," Connolly said, interrupting her. "We've never been there."

"Actually," she said, "I think I went there once."

"Yeah?"

She gave him a sly grin. "Bobby Patrino took me there."

The smile left Connolly's face. He felt his body tense. "Bobby Patrino?"

"Yeah."

"When did you go out with Bobby Patrino?"

"In high school."

Connolly relaxed. "Do you want to go there with me?"

"Sure." She closed the door and stepped outside. "Ready?"

Connolly glanced at his watch. "We don't have to be there 'til eight."

"You have a reservation at The Pig?"

"No. I have to meet somebody there."

Barbara's smile lost some of its luster. "This is about a case, isn't it?"

"Yes."

"And I thought you wanted to see me."

"I do. It's just, I had to go there anyway, and I thought—"

"Relax." She took his arm. "I'm not upset."

They started down the steps and up the walkway toward the street. Halfway to the car, Connolly stopped. "I'm sorry. If you don't want to go—"

"Don't be silly. I never should have said anything. I'd love to go." She tugged on his arm. He resisted. She nudged him. "Mike. Get in the car."

They passed the 'For Sale' sign without mention of it. Connolly opened the door for her. When she was seated, he moved around the car and got in behind the steering wheel. She caught his eye with a wry smile. "So, what do we do 'til eight?"

"We could cruise around town."

Her smile grew more playful. "And then what?"

"Park in the shadows some place."

She propped against the door and crossed her legs. "We wouldn't have to go to some side street for that."

Connolly started the car. "Let's go to a movie."

"A movie?"

"Yeah. It's six now. We could find one at The Roxy. It'll get out around eight."

Barbara laughed. "The Roxy is closed."

"Closed?"

"Been closed for years."

"Well, we could—"

"Let's go to your place," she said.

"My place?"

"Yes. Your place. Why not?"

"Are you sure?"

"Sure I'm sure. Let's go to your place."

"Okay."

The guesthouse where Connolly lived was only a few blocks away. They reached it in less than five minutes. He ushered her inside and closed the door. "You want something to drink?"

She wandered toward the living room. "What do you have?"

He opened the refrigerator and looked inside.

"Looks like there's water, some soured milk. A little orange juice." He opened the carton and smelled inside. "Been in here a while." He closed the refrigerator and moved to the cabinet by the sink. "There's Coca-Cola. And a few bottles of ginger ale." He took a bottle from the cabinet. "I'm having ginger ale."

"Okay." Barbara called to him from the sofa. "I'll have some, too."

Connolly filled two glasses with ice and ginger ale and brought them to the sofa. They sat together in silence a moment, then a puzzled look came over her. She held the glass at arm's length and stared at it. "What is this?"

"Ginger ale."

"I know. But what kind?"

"You like it?"

"This is better than I remember ginger ale being."

"It's Boylan ginger ale."

"Never heard of it."

"Bottled in New Jersey."

"How'd you hear about it?"

"Buie Hayford."

She frowned. "Buie?"

"Yeah."

"What's Buie doing now? I haven't heard about him in years."

"Right now, I imagine he's doing his best to explain his way out of some criminal charges."

"Oh?"

Connolly took a sip. "He was up to his neck in that stuff with Raisa and those women."

"He was involved in that?"

Connolly nodded. "He and Perry Braxton."

"I think I knew that and tried to forget about it."

"Me too."

Barbara took another sip from her glass. "How's Dibber?"

"Still in jail, but Dibber's situation is looking a little better."

"Think he can get out of it?"

"Maybe." Connolly shifted positions on the sofa and changed the subject. "Are you really going to sell the house?"

Barbara sighed. "I was hoping we could get through the evening without talking about that."

"Are you?"

"A young couple looked at it today."

"Were they interested?"

"I think so."

"I don't like it."

"You don't have to like it. It's my house."

"I know it's your house but it's my memories."

She gave him a kind look. "Is that what you're running from?"

"I'm not running from anything."

"Then why won't you come past the porch?"

"If I go in there, I might not come out."

She grinned. "That would be so bad? Trapped in the house with me?"

"With you would be fun. But with the who I used to be would be terrible."

"I don't think it works that way."

"I don't want to risk finding out."

"Well, I know it's hard to part with the place, but I think it's the right thing to do."

Connolly sighed. "Maybe so."

They sipped in silence again. A moment or two passed, then she said, "You mentioned something else happened."

"Yeah."

"What was that about?"

"I had to go over to Crenshaw Street to see a man about Dibber's case. A retired detective. He lives over there."

The expression on Barbara's face was serious. "And you drove by your old house."

"I stopped," Connolly replied.

She looked surprised. "You stopped?"

"Yeah."

"Stopped on the street, or stopped and got out?"

"I got out."

"Is anyone living there now?"

Connolly nodded. He took a sip of ginger ale. "The car was in the garage."

"Their car?"

"No. Our old car."

Barbara frowned. "Your father's car?"

"Yes."

"Did you know it was still there?"

"No. And that's not all. My baseball glove. Rick's old bicycle. All of it was just like we left it."

"Who's living there?"

Tears filled Connolly's eyes. He took another sip. Barbara's face softened. Her voice became a whisper. "Your mother was there."

Connolly nodded. The tears rolled down his cheeks. Barbara set the glass on the coffee table and moved closer to him. "I had no idea she was alive."

"Neither did I." He took a deep breath. "And when I saw her, I thought I was losing my mind."

"Did you ask anyone about her? Rick? Uncle Guy?"

Connolly nodded again. "I saw Guy last night. Spent the night down there at his place."

"What did he say?"

"He wasn't surprised. Said he had driven by there a time or two. Thought she might be there."

"Has he talked to her?"

"I don't think so."

"Did you?"

"I tried."

"What happened? What did she say?"

"She said I couldn't be her son. She never had any children."

Barbara leaned against him. She gripped his thigh with her hand and gave him a squeeze. "You're sure it was her?"

Connolly set the glass of ginger ale on the end table by the answering machine. He slipped his arm around her shoulder and pulled her closer. Her hair brushed against his cheek. The smell brought back memories. Good memories and he buried his face in her hair. She pulled away. "What are you doing?"

"Smelling your hair."

"Smelling my hair?"

"Yes."

"Why?"

"Because I like the way it smells."

"I thought we were talking."

"We are. I was just smelling your hair."

She stared at him a moment. "You're strange sometimes, you know."

"You've told me that before."

She leaned against him once more. "Are you sure it was her?"

"I'm sure."

"What are you going to do?"

"I don't know. I'm thinking about going back over there."

"Want me to go with you?"

"Not yet."

CHAPTER 38

A little before eight, Connolly and Barbara left the guesthouse and drove to the Whistlin' Pig. Located three blocks off Government Street, it was housed in a 1940s era art deco style building that had curved walls and glass blocks. The exterior was painted gray with molded aluminum trim that gave it the look and feel of a diner, which it once had been.

Above the building was a sculpted pig about the size of a Volkswagen. Painted pink, it had a curly tail that slowly spun round and round. Its mouth was puckered as if whistling and smoke drifted from its nostrils. Standing atop the pig were large neon letters that spelled out the name—The Whistlin' Pig.

Connolly brought the Chrysler to a stop in a parking space in front, then came from the car and opened the passenger door for Barbara. She sniffed the air as she came from the car. "Smells like a barbeque place."

Connolly grinned. "I wonder why." She took his arm as they went inside the building.

Along the wall opposite the entrance was a counter with stools that ran the length of the building. The front wall was lined with booths. Tables were arranged in the space between. Connolly guided Barbara to an open booth. They sat across from each other. He took a menu from behind the napkin holder and handed it to her. "Do you need one of these?"

"Might be interesting reading."

In a few minutes, Tiffany appeared. She glanced at Barbara, then over to Connolly. "Who's she?"

"Don't worry about it. Is he here?"

"Yeah. But we thought you was coming by yourself."

"Is he coming to the table?"

"No." She gestured over her shoulder. "He's in the bathroom."

"Okay." Connolly said. "Let me know when he comes out."

"He wants you to come in there."

Connolly gave her a look. "He wants to meet in the bathroom?"

"I put a sign on the door. People will think it's out of order. He just went in there when you drove up."

Connolly glanced over at Barbara. "I'll be back." He slid from the booth and crossed the room to a hallway near the end of the counter. The men's room was on the left. A plain sheet of paper was taped to the door with the words "Out Of Order" scrawled across it. Connolly pushed the door open and stepped inside.

Three toilet stalls were situated along the wall to the right. Doors on the stalls were closed but from what he could see beneath them, there was no one in the room. He walked to the sink and washed his hands. Behind him, he heard a toilet seat rattle. Connolly dried his hands. "Tinker? Are you in there?"

A voice replied from the stall on the end. "Yeah. I'm here."

Connolly faced the stalls and leaned against the sink. "Tiffany said you wanted to talk."

"Yeah."

"Well come on out."

"No way. We'll do our talking like this."

"Be easier if I could see you."

"It's better for both of us if you don't."

"Okay…. What did you want to talk about?"

"You was out at the nursery yesterday. Asking a bunch of questions."

"Yes."

"Tiff says they got Dibber charged with killing that man."

"Do you know something about it?"

"I know a lot about it."

"Where's Stephen Ellis?"

"You was real close to him when you was out there."

"He's alive?"

"No. That boy's dead and gone. But you was real close to him."

"Come on out. Let's do this face to face."

"I told you, I ain't doin' it like that. Look, here's the deal. Nick has this meth lab. He and a bunch of guys are in it in a big way. That guy you're looking for showed up. Nick was worried he was gonna blow everything. And then his friend started mouthin' off. He got on everybody's nerves. So, after they done Stephen...." Tinker paused. Connolly heard him take a draw on a cigarette, then he continued. "After they done him, they did the other guy, too."

"Why did they leave one of them at the beach house?"

"Wasn't goin' to. But some of them neighbors came around while we—they was loading up and everybody got scared. So, they just left him in there. Storm was comin'. Nick figured the whole place would get washed away. Even if it didn't, he didn't think nobody'd be able to pin it on him."

"Even though it was his mother's beach house."

"Nick never was too bright when it come to stuff like that."

"So, Nick shot Steve?"

Just then, the door to the hallway opened. A man appeared. Connolly jerked around, startled. "Sign says this thing's out of order," the man said. "Does it work?"

"I don't know about the toilets. I just washed my hands." Connolly heard Tinker latch the door to the stall. He cleared his throat to cover the sound and moved around the man. "I guess if it doesn't work, you'll find out pretty soon."

The man chuckled. "I reckon so."

Connolly went back to the dining room and slid into the booth across from Barbara. Two glasses of iced tea sat on the table. He picked up the one on his side and took a drink. Barbara took a sip from her glass and smiled at him. "Is everything okay?"

"I guess."

"Was he in there?"

"Someone was."

"Someone?"

"He wouldn't come out so I could see him."

"Did he tell you anything?"

"A little. We got interrupted."

"I saw that guy go in there." She looked over at him. "Was there trouble?"

"I don't know."

Before long the man appeared in the dining room. He made his way to a table and took a seat with a woman and two children. Barbara noticed Connolly was watching them. "Is this a problem?"

He took another sip of tea. "I think it's alright."

"Are you going back in there?"

"No."

A waitress appeared at their table, an older woman with jet black hair and heavy makeup. "Ready to order?"

Connolly looked up at her. "Where's Tiffany?"

"She's not working tonight. I saw her in here a while ago, but this is her night off. What'll you have?"

Connolly looked across the table to Barbara. "Pork sandwich," she said.

The waitress scribbled the order on her pad and nodded to Connolly. "And you?"

"I'll have the same."

The waitress stepped away. Connolly glanced out the window. Across the parking lot he saw the yellow Caprice he'd seen before. Two people were seated inside but he couldn't see their faces. While he watched, the car drove from the lot and disappeared from sight.

CHAPTER 39

After dinner, Connolly and Barbara left the café and walked out-side to the Chrysler. He opened the passenger door for her. She glanced at him as she slid onto the seat. "What do you think?"

Connolly was puzzled. "About what?"

There was a twinkle in her eye. "Think she's home?"

Connolly grimaced but didn't respond. Instead, he closed the passenger door and walked around to the driver's side. The car keys jingled in his hand as he reached for the door, pulled it open, and dropped onto the seat.

Barbara glanced at him. "We could ride by and see."

Connolly put the key in the ignition and the car came to life. He laid his arm along the top of the seat and twisted around to look out the rear window. A pickup truck came from the street into the park-ing lot behind them. Connolly waited for it to pass, then backed the Chrysler away from the building.

Barbara gestured with a nod. "Let's go see."

Connolly shook his head. "Not tonight."

A block beyond the Loop, Connolly cut over to Airline Highway. In the glow of the lights from the dash he saw Barbara smile. A little way down Airline, they came to Crenshaw Street. Beyond Ramsey's house, Connolly slowed the car. "Okay. You wanted to see it." He pointed to a house in the middle of the block. "There it is."

Shadows from the streetlight played across the lawn, then disappeared only to appear again on the side of the house. Barbara leaned close to Connolly and looked out the window on his side of the car. "Oh, Mike," she whispered. "Are you sure she's living there? It looks abandoned."

"Yeah." Connolly nodded. "I'm sure."

Barbara stared past him at the house.   "And you're sure the woman you saw was your mother?"

"Yeah." He mumbled. "It's her."

Through the front window by the porch Connolly saw a light in a room at the back of the house. "There." He pointed. His voice was tense and quick. "See that light."

"Where?"

"In the—"

"I see it," Barbara sounded surprised at first, then her voice dropped off. "Or is that a reflection from the light at the neighbors?" In the house, someone moved past the light and a moment later it went out. "Oh," Barbara said. "I guess you were right."

Connolly took his foot from the brake. The car started forward. "Well," Barbara said. "You can't let her live like that."

He gave her an angry scowl. "What do you mean?"

"She's your mother, Mike."

"She didn't worry about that with me and Rick."

"Mike."

His voice grew louder. "We ate out of a can for two days."

"But—"

"No!" he exclaimed, and he slapped the steering wheel in frustration. "I listened to Rick cry himself to sleep. I had to...." His mouth quivered and his voice broke. He swallowed and tried again. "I had to get him up for school." Tears in his eyes made it difficult to see. "We ate sardines for breakfast." Tears rolled down his cheeks. "You're supposed to have pancakes or eggs or something." His voice became a whisper. "We had sardines and pimento cheese. On stale Graham Crackers." He wiped his eyes and took a deep breath. His voice took a resolute tone. "She didn't care about us. Why should we care about her?"

The car crept through the intersection at the next block. Barbara put her arm across his shoulder. "Pull over." Connolly shook his head. Barbara insisted. "Pull over." She pointed with her free hand. "There's a spot. Pull over. Right here."

Connolly guided the car to the curb and took it out of gear. He leaned his head against the seat and sobbed. Barbara squeezed him closer and ran her arm around his waist. "You can't keep hating her." She rested her head on his chest. "Whatever she did, it wasn't because of you."

"It was us she went off and left."

"That was because of who she was. Not you. Not Rick. I never met her but I'm sure she was that way before you came along."

Connolly sighed. "Came along is right."

Barbara lifted her head to look at him. "What do you mean by that?"

"John Connolly isn't my father."

Her eyes were wide. "What are you talking about? Who told you that?"

"Uncle Guy."

"When did he tell you that?"

"Yesterday. Day before. Whatever day it was I was down there at his house."

"Who did he say is your father?"

"A surveyor for the railroad. My mother met him at a club. Had an affair with him. Not long after she married John." His eyes met hers. "What do you call the man you've thought of as your father all your life, and then after all these years you find out you aren't his son?"

Barbara smiled. "How about 'Daddy'?" She stared at him a moment. "How did Guy know all this?"

Connolly slid lower in the seat. "Daddy found out about the affair and left. Mama was pregnant with me. She moved in with Uncle Guy. Daddy came back right before I was born."

"He came back."

"Yeah."

"He was a good father."

"Yeah." Connolly took a breath. "I think I miss him more than I miss her."

They sat there a while. Neither one said a word. Finally, Connolly glanced at Barbara. "We stopped on a dark street after all."

"I know. But I didn't get a kiss."

"We can fix that." He pulled her close and pressed his lips to hers.

CHAPTER 40

At two the following afternoon, Connolly went to the district attorney's office to meet with the Junkins family. Gayle Underwood met him in the office lobby and led the way to a conference room, the same one where they had met with Billy Ellis the week before.

From the hall, Connolly saw Hadley and Flora Junkins standing between the conference table and the wall opposite the door. Hadley was dressed in a dark gray business suit. Flora wore a navy-blue dress and three-inch pumps with a string of pearls around her neck. Gayle introduced them. "I'm sorry we have to meet under these circumstances," Connolly said politely.

Flora's eyes were cold. "You represent the man who killed our son?"

Connolly nodded. "I represent the man they've accused of it."

Gayle gestured to the chairs around the table. "Why don't we have a seat?" She pulled a chair away from the table and offered it to Flora. "Here. Have a seat."

The Junkins sat next to each other on the far side of the table. Connolly sat opposite them with his back to the door. Gayle moved to the end of the table. "Henry will be here in a minute." She pulled out a chair and took a seat.

Flora looked over at Connolly. "How do you do it?"

"Do what?" He knew what was coming next.

"How do you defend those people?"

He knew what she meant but he didn't like the implication. "What people?" he asked.

"People who kill boys like our son."

For some reason, the look in her eye made him suddenly self-conscious. "Well … for one thing, there's usually a question as to whether the person the police arrested actually committed the crime they've charged them with."

"You think that's the case with our son?"

"There's little doubt the man in the beach house was murdered. But the only connection between the body and my client is that they were both supposedly in the beach house."

"And that isn't enough?"

"Not to prove murder."

Hadley cleared his throat. "They don't have the weapon?"

"No."

"But they have prints."

"Yes. They have prints. But that only shows he was present. He and several others."

"Other people were in the house?"

"Yes."

Henry entered the room. "I see you all are getting acquainted." He glanced at Connolly as he took a seat. "Don't let me stop you."

Connolly looked to Hadley. "Mr. Junkins, where do you live?"

"Savannah, Georgia."

Connolly pointed to Flora. "The two of you are married?"

"Yes," Hadley replied. Flora sighed and leaned away.

"How many children do you have?"

"Three."

"And one of them is named Bobby?"

"Yes."

"Do you know a man named Stephen Ellis?"

"Yes."

"How do you know him?"

"He and my son are friends. They met in college."

"Met in college and remained friends after they finished?"

"Yes."

"When was the last time you saw your son?"

"About three weeks ago."

"Where was he?"

"At our house. In Savannah."

"Was he living with you?"

"No. He lives in Atlanta."

"When was the last time you saw Stephen Ellis?"

"I don't know …."

Flora spoke up. "It's been years."

"He didn't come around regularly?" Connolly asked.

"He was our son's friend. Not ours."

Hadley spoke up again. "He and Bobby got into some trouble in college. We tried to tell Bobby to stay away from him."

"But that was some time ago?"

"Yes. Fifteen or twenty years ago, I suppose."

"Did they get into any trouble since then?"

"Not that I'm aware of."

"What does your son do in Atlanta?"

"He works for a freight forwarding company. They have a warehouse near the airport."

"Did he come down here with Stephen?"

"I don't think I can say."

Flora spoke up. "Yes," she said. "They came down here together."

"You're certain of that?" Connolly asked.

"Yes."

"How do you know?"

"He told me."

"Stephen told you?"

"No. Bobby told me."

"Did he say why they were coming?"

"Stephen wanted to find his mother, but he didn't want to make the trip alone. Bobby agreed to come with him."

"He knew who she was?"

"I guess so. You could never tell. Stephen always had a story about—"

Hadley interrupted. "He said his father was a writer. Said they made one of his books into a movie."

"When did he tell you this?"

Flora smiled. "He's been telling us that tale as long as we've known him. Talked about it all the time. I think he told us about it the first time we met him." She glanced at Hadley. "You remember that?"

"Yes. At the Pitty Patt, in Quitman."

"The Pitty Patt?"

"A restaurant. Just outside Valdosta. We all went there to eat."

"All of you?"

"Bobby, Flora. Me. Billy."

"And Frieda," Flora added with a roll of her eyes. "Don't forget Frieda."

"Yes." Hadley smiled. "Frieda."

Connolly looked at Hadley. "Frieda and Billy Ellis were both there?"

"Yes."

"And you're sure Stephen told you about his father. His biological father. With both of them present?"

"Yes."

"Any idea how he found out about his father?"

Flora frowned. "Is it true?"

"Yes." Connolly nodded. "I think so. Do you know when Stephen and Bobby came down here?"

Hadley answered. "About three weeks ago."

"I thought you didn't know?"

"I didn't say I didn't know. I said I couldn't answer." Hadley sighed. "I guess it doesn't matter now. Bobby was in Savannah for the weekend and told us they were coming here. They left that following Monday. We weren't supposed to tell anyone about it."

"They were traveling together?"

"Yes."

"Did Bobby call you at any time during the trip?"

"No.

Flora interrupted. "Yes."

Hadley looked surprised. "He did?"

"Yes."

Hadley frowned. "You didn't tell me."

Flora shrugged him off. "I forgot." She looked over at Connolly. "They were supposed to be down here a week. Bobby should have been back by the following Sunday. Only had that one week off from his job. Was supposed to be back at work that next Monday. He called me Saturday afternoon. Said they found Steve's mother and they were staying over. Something about the beach being nice and Stephen wanted a few more days with her."

"Was that it?"

"I think so."

"So, Stephen was just trying to find his mother. His biological mother?"

"Yes."

Hadley interrupted. "No."

Flora looked at him. Connolly glanced in his direction. "No?"

"There was a little more to it."

"Okay."

Hadley took a deep breath. "The woman who raised him. I can't ... Frieda. She told him about the books and the movie and his father. The man he knew as his father ... Mr. Ellis—"

"Billy," Flora said, interrupting.

"Yes. Billy. He didn't want Stephen to know the story, but Frieda told him. And, before she died. She died last year some time, I think. Anyway, before she died, she started talking to Stephen about the father's estate. Told him about all the money he made. Told him he was entitled to part of the guy's estate. The father. The biological father. The writer."

"Frieda told Stephen that he was entitled to his father's estate?"

"Yes."

"What happened to the estate?"

"From what I understand, most of it went to the man's wife."

"The writer's wife?"

"Yes. But his mother—Stephen's biological mother—received a percentage. A small percentage. I think she received this while he was still alive."

"While Stephen was alive?"

"No. The writer. While the writer was still alive. I think he gave her an interest in the royalties from his works. Sounded like a way to give her some support. I don't know."

Connolly had a questioning expression. "How do you know this?"

"Stephen asked me about it." Hadley glanced around the table. "I'm a lawyer. He called me at my office. Asked me if there was any way to get part of it."

"And what did you tell him?"

"Whatever I said to him would be protected by attorney-client privilege." Hadley sighed. "But it would be my opinion that under Georgia law he could probably find a way to have his claim heard in court."

Connolly leaned away from the table. He stroked his chin with his fingers and smiled. At last, the case was beginning to make sense.

CHAPTER 41

Later that afternoon, Connolly drove to Mobile General and once again made his way to Ted Morgan's office. Brian Hodges stood in the hall near the office door. Connolly glanced inside the office and saw Gayle Underwood seated with Hadley and Flora near Morgan's desk, but Morgan was not there. He glanced at Hodges. "Is Ted around?"

"I don't know." Hodges shrugged. "We haven't seen him."

Connolly started toward the autopsy suite. "I'll check down here."

Just then, Morgan came from around the corner. "I'm right here," he said. "Everybody ready?"

"Waiting on you," Connolly replied.

Morgan entered the office. Connolly followed and stood near the doorway with Hodges. Morgan glanced at Hadley and Flora. "You are Mr. and Mrs. Junkins?"

"Yes."

"I'm Ted Morgan. The county coroner." He acknowledged Flora with a nod and shook Hadley's hand. "Are you ready for this?"

"Yes," Hadley said as he rose from his chair. "If we must."

Flora, however, didn't budge. Her eyes filled with tears. Connolly caught Morgan's attention. "You don't need her, do you?"

"No." Morgan shook his head. "Not at all. Mrs. Junkins, you

can wait here if you like." He came from behind his desk. Hadley followed him out. Gayle came behind. Hodges and Connolly joined them. As they started up the hallway, Flora bolted from the office. "Wait," she said. "I want to come with you." Connolly and Hodges stepped aside to let her pass. She caught up with Hadley and took his arm.

Gayle moved alongside Connolly. "See me before you leave," she said, quietly.

They followed Morgan to the refrigerated lockers at the end of the hall where the bodies were kept. As before, Morgan checked his notes for the locker number, opened one of the doors, and pulled out a table bearing a corpse. When he was certain he had the correct body, he glanced over at Hadley. "Ready?"

Hadley nodded. Morgan lifted the sheet from the face. Hadley gasped at the sight of it. Flora placed her hand to her mouth and sobbed. Their reaction left little doubt the body was that of their son, Bobby Junkins.

Morgan replaced the sheet over the body and placed it in the locker, then took Hadley and Flora back to his office. Gayle went with them. Hodges and Connolly walked outside and stood in the shade of the building near the entrance to the emergency room. Connolly slipped off his jacket. "I talked to Edwin Marchand," he said.

Hodges seemed puzzled look. "Who?"

"Edwin Marchand."

"Oh." Hodges smiled. "Not much of a talker, is he?"

"He had a lot to say about one subject."

"What was that?"

"His fingerprints in the beach house."

A cold look came over Hodges. "That client of yours is guilty and you know it. He needs to take a plea and put an end to all this." He gestured over his shoulder. "You saw those people in there. Haven't you drawn this out long enough already?"

Connolly ignored him and continued. "Edwin is rather adamant about those prints you say you found."

A frown wrinkled Hodges' forehead. "What do you mean?"

"He says he has never been in that beach house."

"And you believe him?"

"Says he's never even seen the house. Where'd those prints come from?"

"The FBI."

"But how did the FBI come to have his prints on file?"

"I don't know. Military records, I imagine."

"Edwin says he's never been in the military."

Hodges shrugged. "Then I don't know."

Gayle came from the building. Connolly continued talking as she approached. "He says he's never been fingerprinted by anybody."

Hodges' face was flush. "Look, all I know is we lifted some prints. Sent them to the FBI. They came back with a match."

Connolly noticed Gayle was staring at Hodges with a quizzical look. "Whose prints?" she finally asked. "What are y'all talking about?"

Hodges turned away. "I gotta go." He stepped off the sidewalk to the parking lot pavement.

Connolly spoke up. "Edwin Marchand," he said, answering the question.

Gayle frowned. "Edwin Marchand?"

Connolly nodded in Hodges' direction. "He says the FBI matched a set of prints from the beach house to Edwin Marchand."

Hodges came back to face them. Gayle looked over at him. "This is the first I've heard of this, Brian. What's this about?"

Hodges looked away. "It's nothing."

Gayle pressed the point. "The report you sent me didn't say anything about Edwin Marchand."

Hodges sighed. "It's nothing. I talked to him about it."

"What did he say?"

Connolly answered for him. "Edwin Marchand insists he has never been in the beach house. Says he's never even seen the house."

"None of this is in the file." Gayle's eyes were fixed on Hodges. "Can he account for his time?"

"I don't know."

"What do you mean you don't know?"

Hodges' voice took a sharp tone. "I mean, I don't know."

"Don't you think you better find out?"

Hodges gave her a sullen look. "Maybe you better talk to Henry."

Gayle stared after him as he walked away, then glanced at Connolly. "Walk me to my car."

They crossed the parking lot together. Gayle looked grim. "That was rather unpleasant."

"Hodges isn't really acting himself today. But I don't think Edwin Marchand was involved in this."

"Perhaps not. But that's not the unpleasantness I was talking about."

"Oh?"

"I meant about what happened in there just now with the Junkins. They seemed so distraught."

"I guess that's why Henry stayed at the office and sent you. Was this your first?"

"With a victim's family?"

"Yes."

"Not really. But it doesn't get any easier."

They walked a little farther in silence, then Connolly said, "You wanted to talk?"

"Yes," she said.

Connolly waited for her to continue but when she didn't, he said, "We could talk later if you rather."

"I took a look at that file you mentioned," she replied. "The old one."

"Find anything?"

"There are one or two things you might be entitled to know about."

Connolly chuckled. "Henry actually wants to follow the rules?"

By then they had reached a dark blue sedan. "I didn't ask Henry," Gayle said. She opened the trunk of the car. A briefcase sat inside, and she took a file from it, then closed the lid. The file made a slapping noise as she dropped it on the fender. "There it is," she said.

Connolly looked at the file, then back at her. "That's Earl Givens' file?"

"Yes."

"The D.A.'s file?"

"Yes."

"For me?"

"It's right there. On the car."

"You would let me see the file?"

A sly expression lifted the corner of her mouth. "It's lying right there." She took a cell phone from her pocket. "I'm going to step over here and make a phone call."

Gayle walked to the front of the car and leaned against the front fender. Connolly heard her phone beep as she pressed some numbers and placed a call. He opened the file and began to read.

The file contained the usual documents: an incident report from the officers who responded, Toby had signed it; Statements from several of Givens' employees; a diagram showing the location of the body. Near the back of the file was a copy of the coroner's report. Connolly flipped through it. There was nothing in it that Morgan hadn't told him already, until he came to the last page. And then he saw the thing that had caught Morgan's eye when they were talking in the office earlier. On the last line of the report was a note indicating a copy had been sent to Amelia's House, a center that specialized in counseling minors who had been sexually abused.

"I was right," Connolly whispered. "A minor was involved."

Connolly closed the file. Gayle glanced in his direction, then slipped her cell phone into her pocket. "See enough?"

"Yeah."

"Anything in there you want?"

"The coroner's report, including the final page."

"Okay. Anything else?"

"Do you have the pistol?"

"The inventory says we have it and the bullets they took out of the victim. I went over there to look. The bullets are there, but I couldn't find the pistol."

Connolly gestured with the file. "Think you could get someone to compare the bullets from this old case to the ones in Dibber's?"

"Not without asking Henry." Gayle picked up the file and put it in the briefcase. "Do you want me to ask him?"

Connolly shook his head. "Not yet."

She opened the trunk, placed the briefcase inside, then closed the lid. "Well, just let me know. I think it might be a good idea to do it anyway." She walked around to the driver's door and opened it. Connolly was still standing by the rear bumper. She looked in his direction. "Are you alright?"

Connolly smiled. "Yeah," he said. "I'm fine."

CHAPTER 42

The information in the DA's file on Earl Givens confirmed what Connolly already knew. Clyde Ramsey talked to Nick about what happened at the barn the day Givens was shot, and that conversation uncovered a family secret. But what stuck in Connolly's mind that afternoon had nothing to do with Ramsey or Givens or any of that. What stuck in his mind was the exchange he heard between Gayle and Hodges about Edwin's fingerprints. She didn't know Edwin had denied being there.

Hodges' response continued to play through Connolly's memory as he drove away from the hospital. *Maybe you better talk to Henry.* Hodges had given him a copy of a report on the fingerprints from the house. He said it came from the FBI. Connolly had glanced at it the day Hodges gave it to him, but he hadn't given it much of a look. Gayle gave him one also, but he hadn't done anything with it, either. Maybe he should take a closer look.

As he drove past the Port City Diner, he began looking for a parking space. He found one on Royal Street and parked the car, then walked back to the building. Mrs. Gordon came from the hallway as he entered the office. She glanced at him as she took a seat at her desk. "Who are you?"

Connolly ignored her sarcasm. "Hello, Mrs. Gordon. Any messages for me?"

"They're on your desk. Are you keeping up with your time in this case?"

"My time?"

She scooted her chair away from the desk to see down the hall. "I assume you've been off searching yet again for a sliver of hope for Mr. Landry?"

"Yes," he said. "And I might have found some."

"Give me your time so far. We need to update his bill before the preliminary hearing."

Panic swept over him. Hearing? What hearing? Had he forgotten? How could he have forgotten? "Have they set a date for it?" he asked.

"Not that I know of. But we need to bill them before that happens."

A sense of relief came over him. They weren't ready for a hearing. Not yet. Maybe in a week or two, but not now. "Okay," he said.

"Do you want me to call and see if they'll give us a hearing date?"

"No," he said in an authoritative tone. "We need more time."

"That's what I'm talking about. Time. Give me your time so I can add it to the bill. I'm sure you've done more than you'll ever get paid for."

"I thought you said we were making money on this case."

"Give me your time."

"Okay," Connolly chuckled.

In the office, Connolly laid his jacket across a chair near the door and made his way to the filing cabinets on the far side of the room. He located the files for Dibber's case and found the one that held the documents he had collected so far. From it he retrieved the reports Hodges had given him and flipped through the pages.

The first document was an incident report created when the police responded to the call from neighbors about the beach house. With it was a diagram of the bedroom indicating the location of the body and other items in the room.

The third page was a memo from Hodges to the file that summarized information he had received regarding fingerprints collected at the house. That memo indicated the same thing Hodges told him—the FBI had matched prints from the house with prints from Dibber, Stephen Ellis, Inez, Nick, and Edwin. Three other prints were also found but they were unidentified.

Connolly laid the memo on his desk and found a second file. In it were the reports he had received from Gayle, most of them duplicates of things Hodges had supplied. He leafed through those and found her copy of Hodges' memo. Her copy indicated the FBI had matched only prints for Dibber and Nick. Six others were unidentified. Obviously, the two reports were not the same. Connolly stared at the pages as he considered why that might have happened.

Preliminary reports were common. One copy of the memo could have reflected a preliminary report. The other, final results. And locating a match for Stephen Ellis' prints had taken a while. Nothing unusual about that, either. All Hodges had to do was prepare a memo to update the file once confirmed information arrived. But that's not what happened. Hodges gave Connolly one report and Gayle another. And when Gayle confronted him about the discrepancy, Hodges had done nothing to correct or explain the situation, other than to refer her to McNamara.

Why would he do that? Had Hodges not talked to Edwin? It didn't seem that was the case. Connolly remembered Hodges' comment outside the hospital. "Doesn't say much, does he?" Hodges was right, Edwin didn't have much to say. Which meant they had talked. And if he talked to Edwin, he knew Edwin denied being in the house. So, why not correct the matter when Gayle asked about it? And why had he referred her to McNamara?

Connolly took a seat at the desk and propped his head against the wall. He closed his eyes and played a mental game with himself to consider the possibilities.

Suppose Edwin was telling the truth. Suppose he had never been inside the beach house. That would mean Hodges was lying or the FBI made a mistake. The FBI had been known to make mistakes. Plenty of news reports about that. But if that was the case, then why not say so? And why would he let Gayle go to court with something as crucial as fingerprint identity unresolved?

Maybe Hodges was simply lying. And over-zealous detective determined to get a conviction. But why would Hodges lie? Why would anyone lie? The typical reasons came to mind quickly. To cover up the truth. To keep someone from knowing what really happened. To protect someone. Protect someone. That was a possibility.

If Hodges was unwilling to address the matter, then the prints must have belonged to someone else. Someone Hodges didn't want to make known. Someone who didn't want anyone to know. Someone who wasn't supposed to be in that beach house. But who could that be? Connolly had talked to everyone who knew anything about the case, and none of them told him about anyone who would have meant anything to Hodges. Hodges didn't know the Marchands. They weren't his friends. Tinker and the men who worked for Nick spent most of their day strung out on meth. They would have meant nothing to Hodges.

Maybe Hodges was like all other detectives Connolly had ever known. He arrested the first person who seemed obvious and wasn't interested in entertaining any other theories about the case. But what about McNamara? He dreamed of being an FBI agent, or district attorney, or even more. As a prosecutor, McNamara wasn't very creative, but he wasn't corrupt and even if he might like to shape a case to suit himself, he wouldn't risk his reputation on something like this. Whatever it was Hodges found in that house had to be something McNamara would go for. Something that would pique his interest. Something that McNamara needed to protect, too.

Suddenly Connolly's eyes popped open in a moment of realization. "An informant." He rocked forward in the chair. "Someone in that house was working for the sheriff's department." He stood and started around the desk. "And I know who it was."

Connolly came from behind the desk, grabbed his jacket from the chair by the door, and started up the hallway.

CHAPTER 43

The drive from downtown to The Whistlin' Pig took ten minutes. Connolly parked the car in back near a dumpster and entered through the kitchen door. To the left was a large stainless steel sink. An older man was at it, scrubbing pots and pans. Beyond the sink was a dish machine. It made a swishing sound as water circulated through it. Racks of clean dishes sat at the end of the machine.

Across the room, opposite the door where Connolly entered, a waitress stood at the pickup window waiting impatiently for an order. Their eyes met and she smiled at Connolly as he entered the kitchen. Another waitress at a drink machine glanced in his direction, but quickly moved away and paid him no attention.

Between the door where Connolly entered and the pickup window was another stainless steel table. Two plastic ice chests sat near the center. Splotches of barbeque sauce covered the lids but beneath the greasy red smears was the word "chicken" written in black letters on the first one. The second chest was labeled "pig." Near them were pans that contained side dishes—potato salad, baked beans, fried potatoes, pickles.

Women with sauce-stained aprons stood at both sides of the table arranging food on plates. One side worked the pork container. The other side worked the chicken. Another woman stood near them. Younger, slimmer. A brunette with her hair pulled behind her head. She wore a pink T-shirt with blue jeans and from the way she shouted at the others, Connolly assumed she was in charge. Her voice had a grating tone that cut like a knife through the chatter of the workers and the clatter of pots and pans. She glanced in Connolly's direction as he crossed the room toward her. "You'll have to come back tomorrow," she said. "We only take sales calls in the mornings." He was beside her by then had to move quickly to get out of the way as she reached past him to take a plate of food from the table.

"I'm not a salesman," he replied.

The woman set the plate on the ledge by the pickup window, then shouted toward the pass-through, "Order up!" She brushed past Connolly again and slapped an order ticket on the table. "Two chicks, off the bone! One pig and a fry!" She glanced over at Connolly. "Well, what do you want? I don't really have time for this right now." Her voice was authoritative and demanding. "If the health department finds out you're back here we'll be in big trouble."

"I'm looking for Tiffany. Is she here?"

"Not yet."

"Know where I could find her?"

"Who wants to know?"

"I'm Mike Connolly. I just—"

"The lawyer?"

He was surprised she recognized his name and wondered if Tiffany had been talking about him. "Yes," he said. "I just need to ask her a few questions."

The woman nodded toward the far side of the room. "Ask Eric. And then get out of my kitchen." She nudged her way past him yet again, this time with another plate. "Order up," she shouted. She snatched another ticket from the pickup window. "Three pigs on a bun. Two fries!"

Across the room, a young man tended a fire at a grill that was placed inside the firebox of an enormous fireplace. Thin, but with a wiry build, he seemed to be about Tiffany's age. He wore white workpants with a white t-shirt and over it was a white apron stained with grease and smut where he'd wiped his hands. A chord dangled from earbuds in each ear and dangled down his back to a device that was shoved in his hip pocket.

Chickens cut in quarters lay on the grill, arranged neatly in rows from one side to the other. Flames crackled beneath them. Smoke rose up the chimney above. With a long-handled meat fork and the flick of his wrist, the young man worked his way across the grill flipping the meat. As he did, grease dripped onto the fire below. Flames leapt around the meat. He shifted the fork to his left hand, took a garden hose from a hook at the corner of the fireplace, and sprayed the grill with a fine mist. Steam filled the air. The fire died away.

Connolly tapped him on the shoulder and took one of the earphones loose. "Are you Eric?"

"Yeah."

"I'm looking for Tiffany. Have you seen her?"

Eric shook his head. "Ain't seen her all week."

"Do you know where she lives?"

He gave Connolly a closer look. "You the law?"

"No. Just a lawyer."

"Not much difference, is there?"

"Do you know where I could find her?"

"Is she in trouble?"

"No. I just need to ask her a few questions."

"Are you that guy she went to see?"

Connolly had no idea what he was talking about. "Yeah," he said anyway. "We've had a couple of meetings. Where does she live?"

"Staples Road."

"Do you know the house number?"

"Nah." Eric shook his head. "But you can't miss it. 'Bout the third house on the right. It's in bad shape, but it's got a yellow door. You'll know it when you see it."

Connolly stood. "Thanks," he said.

"No problem."

❖ ❖ ❖

Staples Road intersected Dauphin Island Parkway at the Food World shopping center about ten miles south of town in an area that once had been a middle-class neighborhood. Back then, most of the residents worked at Brookley Air Force Base, a defense complex on the southern edge of Mobile built during World War II. When the base closed, workers lost their jobs, businesses closed, most of the houses fell into disrepair.

Connolly found Tiffany's house without any trouble. A wooden frame structure with asbestos siding. A window on one end was broken, the missing pane replaced with unpainted plywood. In front, a stoop sagged over a faded yellow door that was rotten and crumbling along the bottom. On the wall next to the door was a large picture window with a crack down the middle. In the yard, a bulldog strained at the end of a chain that was fastened to the base of a pine sapling.

Connolly parked in the driveway, came from the car, and walked to the front door. There was no doorbell, so he rapped on the side of the house with his knuckles. In a moment the door opened, and Tiffany appeared. She wore blue jeans and a green T-shirt with stains on the front and a rip at the shoulder seam of her left arm. She stared at him blankly. "You got Dibber out of jail yet?"

"We need to talk," Connolly replied. Tiffany moved aside. Connolly stepped past her through the doorway to the living room.

A sofa sat beneath the window in front. At the far end of the room was a television and a recliner with torn upholstery. Opposite the door was a dining area. To the left of it was a kitchen. A hall opened to the right.

Tiffany closed the door and shuffled across the room to the recliner. Connolly took a seat on the sofa. "So," she said. "What do you want to talk about?"

"Dibber said you told him Nick Marchand kept his money in the beach house and that's why he was down there during that storm."

Her vacant expression became sullen. "What if it was?"

"Is that why he was there?"

"Like I said, what if it was?"

"He said you were working for Nick. Buying money orders for him."

"Maybe."

"Did you send Dibber into that house?" She stared at him but didn't respond. Connolly kept going. "He said he went there because you told him there was money in there."

"He didn't find no money."

"How do you know that?"

"He told me."

"So, you've been back to that house since all this started. To see for yourself."

She stared at him a moment. "Dibber didn't know where to look."

"But you did."

She smiled. "Maybe."

Something about her expression made Connolly uncomfortable. He glanced through the doorway to the dining area, wondering if anyone else was present, and saw an assortment of bottles and containers on the dining room table. An acrid odor drifted through the house. "What were you doing when I drove up?"

"Huh?"

"What were you doing when I drove up?"

"Cooking."

"Cooking?"

"Yeah."

Connolly was puzzled. "Supper?"

"Yeah." She had an odd smile. "Supper. That's a good word for it."

He realized she meant meth, so he changed the subject. "Did you know the dead man?"

"Seen him a time or two."

"What's his name?"

She shrugged. "I don't know."

"See anybody else?"

"Lots of people."

"I meant at the beach house," Connolly said.

"I know," she replied. "Lot of people at the beach house."

"Ever see anyone named Steve."

"Yeah."

"What about somebody else. Somebody—"

Just then the front door opened, and a man entered. He glanced across the room at Tiffany. "Whose car is that—" Then he noticed Connolly sitting on the sofa. "Who are you?"

Connolly recognized the voice and smiled. "Hello, Tinker. I'm Mike Connolly."

Tinker had a nervous grin. "What are you doing here?"

"Talking. Have a seat. You can join us."

Tinker glanced at Tiffany, then back to Connolly. "I don't think she'll be with us much longer."

Tiffany's eyelids fluttered, then closed, popped open, then closed again. Her neck relaxed and her head flopped against the back of the chair. Connolly was concerned. Tinker seemed to notice. "It's alright," he said. "She does this all the time."

"Nods off?"

"Yeah. She'll be awake in a little while." Tinker brought a chair from the dining table and sat facing Connolly. "What did you want to talk about?"

"The other night at the café, before we were interrupted, you were talking about Stephen Ellis." Tinker nodded. Connolly continued. "What happened to him?"

"Wait right here." Tinker slipped from the chair and walked quietly into the hall. Connolly could see him checking the first room, then he disappeared from sight. He came back a moment later and took a seat again. "Sorry," he explained. "Had to check. Make sure nobody was listening."

"Where is Stephen Ellis?" Connolly asked.

Tinker shook his head. "If I tell you that, they'll know where it came from." He took a pack of Camel cigarettes from his pocket, tapped one from the pack, and stuck it in the corner of his mouth. "Actually." He paused to light the cigarette and take a long drag from it. "He's not there no more. Not all of him, anyway."

Connolly swallowed hard to keep from vomiting. "What did they do with his body?"

Tinker grinned and shook his head again. "I'd love to tell you, but I can't."

"Why not?"

"Because I'm not ready to die yet."

Connolly thought for a moment, then tried a different approach. "You were telling me the other night about what happened. Start from the beginning."

Tinker took another drag off the cigarette. "We—" He corrected himself. "They was all down at Dauphin Island. Nick, Pete, Tony—"

"Pete?"

Tinker nodded. "A guy who works for Nick." He took another drag from the cigarette. "They was down there at that beach house. Nick and Steve got to arguing. Something about some guy that died and how much money he had made off a movie. I'm not sure. I was a little tight, if you know what I mean. But I know they was arguing and then Nick pulled out a pistol and shot the guy in the head."

"He shot Stephen?"

"Yeah." Tinker nodded. "Just like that."

"Just like that?"

"Just like that."

"Then what happened?"

"Little while later the guy that was with him—the guy that was with the one who got shot. He came in. Had been somewhere, I'm not sure where. But he come in the house and seen Steve sprawled across the bed all dead and everything and he started hollerin' and screamin.' And saying shit like, 'You stupid idiot. Why did you do that?'"

"Steve was on the bed?"

"In that first bedroom," Tinker said. "You been down there to the house?"

"Yes."

"Okay. The dead guy was in that first bedroom. Right there by the kitchen. That's where it all happened. Nick was in there when the guy come in. Then they got into it and the guy started saying all that and calling Nick names. Tony was in the kitchen and heard them arguing. He came in and he had a pistol, too. Shot the guy in the head. He fell almost the same place as the first one."

"And then what?"

"Nick wasn't too happy about that. He didn't seem to care about the first guy. But the second one, he didn't like it. Said that would cause trouble."

"And Tony was the one who shot the second guy?"

"Yeah. Nick did the first one. Tony did the second."

"What did they do after that?"

Tinker took another long draw on the cigarette. "Nothin' right away. They just left them both in the bedroom."

"Well, one of them was missing when the storm hit. What happened to that one?"

"Next day Nick—"

"After the shooting?"

"Yeah. They next day, Nick took me and Tony down there to clean the place up. Put Steve in a blanket, loaded him in the truck."

"You saw all this?"

"Well … uhm. I don't know if I should say I saw it. I'm just tryin' to help Tiffany."

"Tiffany?"

"Yeah."

"What do you mean by that?"

"I'm not admitting to nothing." Tinker grinned as if it were a game. "Tiff just said if I told you what happened, she could get them off her back."

"Get who off her back?"

"Nick. Tony. They've been after her since that guy broke in the house."

"After her for what?"

"Nick thinks she put that guy up to robbing the beach house. The guy they arrested for taking that stuff. He thinks that was all her idea."

"Nick thinks Tiffany put Dibber up to looting the house?"

"Yeah." Tinker nodded. "He thinks it was Tiffany's idea and that the whole point was to steal his money."

"Whose money?"

"Nick's."

"Did she? Is that why Dibber was in the house that night? Because she sent him in there to get Nick's money?"

Tinker glanced across the room at Tiffany. "You'd have to ask her. I can't say."

Connolly thought for a moment, then said, "Who else was around that house?"

"What do you mean?"

"How many times have you been to the beach house?"

Tinker shrugged. "I don't know."

"Ten?"

"Yeah." Tinker nodded his head. "Sure. I'd say more than ten times."

"A hundred?"

"I don't know. Could be."

"In all those times you were down there. Before the hurricane. Before Steve was shot. Before the other guy was shot. Who else have you seen?"

"Well ... Nick's mama was down there once or twice. A man they said was Nick's father was down there."

"Are you sure he was Nick's father?"

"They said he was."

"What did he look like?"

Tinker focused on Connolly as if studying him. "About your height. Heavier, though. And the time I saw him he had on blue work clothes and one of them funny hats like welders wear. You know. Short bill in front. Fits right against your head."

"Anybody else?"

A frown wrinkled Tinker's forehead. "One time we come down there, there was this—"

"At the beach house?"

"Yeah. There was this car parked down there. We was in Nick's truck. He saw it and just kept on going. Turned around at the end of the road."

"You mean, he saw this car at the beach house, and he didn't want to stop?"

"Right."

"Did he say why?"

"Didn't say nothing. I asked him about it, but he didn't say a word. Just kept driving."

They sat in silence, each one looking past the other. Finally, Connolly said, "Now, about Stephen Ellis."

Tinker shook his head. "I can't tell you no more about him. If I do, they'll know exactly where it come from."

"Well, that leaves us with a problem."

"What problem?"

Connolly gestured toward Tiffany. "If you want to help her get away from them, you'll have to testify."

Tinker's eyes opened wide. "Testify? You mean like in court?"

"Yeah."

"No way." Tinker shook his head and waved his hands in protest. "I ain't testifying in court about nothing." He gave a nervous laugh. "Nick would kill me."

"There's no other way for them to know what happened."

Tinker thought for a moment, then a knowing smile appeared. "Wait right there." He stood and pointed to Connolly. "Wait right there. I got something might do the trick."

Tinker scurried down the hall again. Connolly heard him open a drawer, then slam it closed. A moment later he was back. "Here." He offered Connolly a prescription bottle. It was about two inches high with a white cap on top. "This will prove it." Connolly hesitated. Tinker was insistent. "Go on." He gestured with the bottle. "Take it. Open it up."

Connolly was wary as he took the bottle. "What's in here?"

"Open it and see for yourself."

Connolly held the bottle at arm's length and twisted the cap off. A vile odor rushed out. The smell of it made him sick but he held his breath and tipped the bottle at an angle to see inside. There was a lump of something that filled the bottle to the rim but he couldn't quite make out what it was. Connolly frowned at Tinker. "What is this?"

Tinker grinned. "His finger," he said, gleefully.

Connolly's chin dropped. "His finger? Whose finger?"

"That guy. The one you was talkin' about. Steve."

Connolly glanced inside the bottle once more. As his eyes focused on the contents, he saw a fingernail surrounded by swollen, putrid flesh. He twisted the cap back on the bottle and did his best not to vomit.

"Man, you need some air," Tinker cackled. "You don't look so good."

"Yeah," Connolly groaned. "I don't feel so good."

"You don't look so good, either. You're white as a ghost. You gonna hurl?"

"I hope not." Connolly thrust the bottle toward Tinker. "You can keep it."

"No, no, no." Tinker backed away, gesturing again with both hands. "You take it. Better it goes to court than me."

"It's not much good without you."

Just then, the sound of a baby crying came from somewhere down the hallway. Tiffany shifted positions in the chair. "You got to do it, Tinker," she said. Her eyes were open, and she glanced in their direction. "You've got to go to court, if that's what it takes. I need you to."

Tinker's shoulders sagged and he sank back in the chair. Tiffany moved past them and disappeared down the hall. Connolly looked over at him. "I'll see what I can do with this." He gestured with the bottle. "But if it comes down to a hearing in court, you'll have to appear to explain what it means."

Tinker closed his eyes. "Then I'm already a dead man."

CHAPTER 44

With the medicine bottle at arm's length, Connolly made his way down the steps toward the Chrysler. Halfway to the driveway he heard a noise from behind and saw the bulldog standing near the pine sapling. The chain attached to its collar rattled as the dog took a step forward, gave a low growl, then charged toward him. Near the corner of the house the dog reached the end of the chain and its head jerked up violently, lifting its front paws off the ground. The rest of its body continued forward as the dog flipped upside down into the air, then came down with a thud on its back. Undeterred, it jumped quickly to its feet and lunged toward him. This time, mindful of the limits imposed by the chain, it struck a defiant pose and barked at him viciously.

Connolly opened the car door with his free hand and slid past the steering wheel onto the front seat. He closed the door and opened the ashtray on the dash beneath the radio with his free hand, then stood the bottle upright inside the tray and pushed the tray closed against it, lodging the bottle between in place. He jiggled it once or twice to make sure it wouldn't fall over, then started the engine and backed the car into the street.

As he drove back to town, he glanced at the bottle, wary of its contents, hoping it didn't come loose from the tray and roll around on the floor. That bottle gave him a serious problem. If it really contained someone's finger, he couldn't keep it. The finger was part of a human body. He was supposed to take it to Ted Morgan. The coroner was the official custodian of human remains, especially remains found under suspicious circumstances. Actually, he should have phoned someone immediately and at least given them an opportunity to bring a forensics team to the location where it was found. That was impossible, of course, but all the same, Morgan would want to know where it came from and how he came to possess it and then there would be an investigation.

Other options came to mind. He could take it to McNamara. The look on McNamara's face might be worth the trouble it would cause. Or he could give it to Toby. That would be better than giving it to Hodges. Maybe Morgan was the best choice after all.

Whatever he did with it, that finger was going to cause problems for Dibber. Morgan would identify the person from whom it came. Might take a few days, but he would find a way to identify it. And when they found out it belonged to Stephen Ellis, McNamara would charge Dibber with another count of murder. Never mind that he didn't have the whole body, or a cause of death, or even proof that Ellis was dead. He would charge Dibber and sort out the details later. Any momentum pushing this case toward an amicable resolution would be wiped away and it would happen as a result of evidence Connolly was compelled to disclose. Evidence with a negative impact on his own client.

At Government Street, a stalled car blocked traffic in the right lane. Connolly brought the Chrysler to a stop and checked the mirror. A line of cars moved past him to the left. While he waited for traffic, he glanced at the bottle. For the first time he noticed the name of the pharmacy was printed on the cap in blue letters. Embry's, a drugstore on the corner near St. Alban's Cathedral. He turned the bottle and gave it a closer look. A label had been attached on the side. Most of it had been peeled away leaving a thin film of glue that was tacky and smeared, but one corner of the label was intact.

Connolly checked the mirror for traffic once more and steered around the stalled car, then came to a stop in the parking lot at Zippadelli's Market. He took the bottle from the ashtray and examined the remains of the label. Only one corner of it remained intact, the rest was gone, but traces of a number were visible. A partial number, perhaps. He couldn't be sure. A prescription number, perhaps. Using that number, the pharmacy could determine the name of the person to whom the bottle belonged. A glimmer of hope seemed to appear. Then, just as quickly, it vanished. "They won't give out that kind of information." Still, it was worth a try.

After a search online with his smartphone, Connolly obtained the number for Embry's and called them. A friendly female voice answered. Connolly took a breath and began. "I need to get a prescription refilled."

"Yes, sir. Do you have the number?"

Connolly read the numbers from the label. "934275."

He heard the clerk typing the numbers on a keyboard. "Mr. Marchand?"

Connolly felt his heart jump. "Yes."

"This is your wife's prescription."

Connolly's heart jumped again, but his mind raced ahead. "This one's for Inez?"

"Yes, sir." Now he needed to end the call, without raising her suspicions. "Is that a problem?"

"No, sir, but it's expired. She doesn't have any more refills left on this one."

"Oh."

"We can call her doctor and see if they'll authorize it."

"No. That's okay. I thought it was mine."

"Okay. I can look right here and find what we have for you if you—"

"No." He cut her off. "That's okay. I'll call you back later." Connolly ended the call and laid the phone on the seat, then backed the car from the parking space.

From Zippadelli's, Connolly drove to the guesthouse. In the kitchen, he found a Ziploc bag in the drawer by the sink. He placed the prescription bottle in the bag, sealed it closed, and set it in the corner of the freezer compartment of the refrigerator. With that out of the way, he took a bottle of ginger ale from the lower compartment and took a long drink from it.

By then he had had time to think about his options from every angle. The pluses and minuses. Ups and downs. Pros and cons. And he was convinced he needed to deliver it to Ted Morgan, the county coroner. But before he did that, he wanted to talk to Hodges. To try his theory that someone else was involved. Someone Hodges was protecting. Someone on the inside. He wanted to know that before he lost control of the finger. Use it for leverage, if he had to. Insurance. He grimaced at the thought. But that's the kind of case this was and he was ready for it to end.

CHAPTER 45

The following morning, Connolly left the guesthouse early and drove downtown to St. Pachomius Church for morning prayer. He took a seat near the back and sat quietly, thinking, wondering, waiting. Thirty minutes later, the sun was above the tops of the trees in the east. Sunlight streamed through the stained-glass windows sending shafts of red, blue, and green across the pews. He watched as the intensity of the color changed, each shaft of light moving slowly across the room, tracking the path of the sun. The appearance of it captured his imagination and he did his best to remember the things he had learned in school about light and refraction, but none of it explained the mystery of the moment. The wonder. Light traveling through the universe, reaching the window, reaching him. Always present. Always becoming. He hadn't thought like that in years. Decades, even. He liked it.

An hour later, others began to enter and take their seats. Their presence interrupted his thoughts and he felt irritable from it. This was his space. His moment. His world. They were an intrusion. But he knew better and by the time Father Scott entered, he had moved on to think of other things. The page in the prayer book. The readings for the day. The responses they would give.

When the service ended, Connolly avoided Father Scott and the others and moved quickly outside. The sheriff's office was across the street and he made his way in that direction. Hodges worked from the building and Connolly meant to see him first thing. He had questions about Edwin Marchand, but more importantly, about the undercover operative he was sure Hodges had been using.

It still was early when Connolly entered the building. Hodges had only just arrived when Connolly reached his office. He glanced over his shoulder as Connolly appeared in the doorway. "You're out mighty early." Hodges set a Styrofoam coffee cup on the desk and moved around to his chair. "Something we need to talk about?"

Connolly leaned comfortably against the door frame. "Yesterday, when Gayle Underwood asked you about Edwin Marchand."

Hodges shook his head. "She shouldn't have brought that up in front of you."

"Maybe so," Connolly conceded. "But that was the first time she'd heard about Edwin Marchand. Until that moment, she had no idea Edwin Marchand's prints were in the beach house. And she had no idea what he'd said about it, either."

Hodges took the lid off the cup of coffee and poured in a packet of cream. "That's her problem."

"Yeah, well, I spent some time thinking about it."

Hodges shot Connolly a look. "You're solving her problems now?"

"No, but I am looking out for Dibber Landry. And if she didn't know about Edwin Marchand, I have to ask myself what else she doesn't know about."

Hodges smiled. "You don't have time for me to tell you all the things that woman doesn't know." He took a sip of coffee. "But that's not anything for you to worry about. Dibber's got enough to keep you busy without getting into her business."

"This is my problem. Not hers."

Hodges raised an eyebrow. "Oh?"

"I went back and checked the reports."

"What reports?"

"When I met with her and Henry, they gave me a copy of your report about the fingerprints. The report you gave them. It's not the same as the one you gave me."

Hodges seemed perturbed. "They gave you a copy of my report?"

"Yes."

"When?"

"The first time I met with them. Right after I took Dibber's case. A day or two after you arrested him."

Hodges didn't seem to like what he'd heard. "She should have asked me for an update, before she talked to you."

"Maybe. But you never followed up with Edwin Marchand, either."

"I talked to him."

"No." Connolly shook his head. "You didn't."

Hodges cocked his head to one side. "Are you calling me a liar?"

"Edwin Marchand denied being in that house. He denied ever being there. He denied ever even seeing the place. If you had a report from the FBI that said his prints matched prints from the house, his denial would have made him a suspect in this case. And it would have caused you to double-check the prints, too."

"So?"

"He was never a suspect in this case. And there's no indication anyone made a second inquiry about the prints."

"How do you know he wasn't a suspect?"

"Because I know you arrested Dibber from the records on the jet ski he sold to that pawn shop. You didn't arrest him on the fingerprints. And if you had conducted an actual investigation, you would have had seven other potential suspects."

Hodges' forehead wrinkled in a frown. "Seven? Where'd you get that number?"

"Your report says there were prints from seven different people found in that house."

Hodges sighed. "Whatever."

"Who are you protecting?"

Hodges glanced at something on the desk. "I'm not protecting anyone. And if I was, I sure as hell wouldn't tell you about it."

"This is a capital murder case," Connolly argued. "I'm entitled to know the names of any witnesses you know about who have any-thing to say about what happened in that house."

"Says who?"

"Alabama Rules of Criminal Procedure and about a million court decisions."

"You're entitled to evidence that tends to exonerate your client."

"I'm entitled to know the names of the people who were present in that house. You can't protect someone just because they're under-cover."

Hodges smiled again. "You think we had somebody under-cover?"

"I think you're looking for a major meth lab somewhere in the county. I think you think the Marchands are running one out at that nursery. And I think you had someone on the inside."

"And you think I lied about the prints to conceal that person's identity."

"Yes."

Hodges took another sip of coffee. "Well, maybe we have some-body in there, and maybe we don't. Either way, I'm not giving you any more names."

"We'll see about that." Connolly stepped away from the door.

Hodges came from his office to the hallway. "What does that mean?"

"You know exactly what it means," Connolly shouted.

"Cahill will never give you anything on this."

"You don't know Judge Cahill. He hates a liar more than I do."

After talking to Hodges, Connolly went to the guesthouse, took the medicine bottle from the freezer, and carried it to the car. Once again, he wedged the bottle into the ashtray, made sure it was securely in place, then backed the car away from the house. Minutes later, he was at Mobile General Hospital. He parked near the entrance and hurried inside.

As he came through the double doors at the end of the hall, he saw Ted Morgan in the autopsy suite. A corpse lay on the examination table. Morgan wore a surgical gown and mask. From the equipment and tools laid out beside him, he was about to begin an examination. Connolly entered the room.

Even with the mask obscuring his face, Morgan looked puzzled. "Mike? You want to help me with this one?"

Connolly placed the medicine bottle in Morgan's palm and squeezed Morgan's fingers closed around it. Morgan pushed down the mask from his face. "What's this?"

Connolly looked him in the eye. "I came into possession of this yesterday. That's all I can say. I came to have it. It's been in my possession ever since. I'm giving it to you." Without more, he started toward the door. Morgan called after him. "But what is it?"

"Open it and find out." Connolly waved over his shoulder and started up the hall toward the double doors. As the doors banged closed behind him, he heard Morgan gag. Connolly smiled. "I think he knows what it is now," he said to himself.

Down the corridor a little farther, Connolly took the cell phone from his pocket. He checked to make sure he hadn't missed any calls, then pressed a button to switched it off. The screen on the face of the phone went blank. Lights that illuminated the keys went out. He slid the phone back into his pocket.

For the next thirty minutes Connolly drove the city streets, aimlessly wandering from block to block, doing his best to avoid contact with anyone. Morgan would call the district attorney's office. Someone would piece enough of the circumstances together. They would find McNamara. And McNamara would call Connolly's office. Then he would try Connolly's cell phone. If Connolly answered, McNamara was sure to shout and scream and demand an explanation. Whose finger was it? Where did it come from? How did you come to have it? Questions Connolly didn't want to answer. It was much easier to avoid them. Let McNamara rant and rave to someone else. Get a good head of steam. File something in court. That would be okay. Connolly wouldn't mind explaining everything to

Judge Cahill. In fact, that would be the best outcome. Then maybe he would finally get some answers. But for now, he would avoid the issue.

Before long, he reached the Loop. Crenshaw Street was just ahead. When he left the hospital, he hadn't intended to go there. He hadn't intended to go anywhere. Certainly not there. But seeing the street sign put him at war with himself. Part of him wanted to drive by the house for one more look. Part of him wanted to drive in the opposite direction. An argument raged back and forth in his mind. *She's nothing but trouble. She's your mother. I hate her. She needs help. The place is a mess and it's her own fault. You could fix it for her. She doesn't deserve my help.*

Without resolving to do anything, Connolly made the corner onto Crenshaw Street. A moment later, he was in front of his mother's house. In his mind, he imagined knocking on her door. No. Kicking it down. Barging inside, demanding answers. Or sitting on the steps until she came out. But that might take a long time. From the look of the yard, she hadn't been outside in quite a while. The grass was almost knee high in places. Not really grass any more. Just weeds. Barbara was right. The lawn needed to be mowed.

Suddenly, he knew what to do. Something that would solve both their problems. Hers and his. At least, their immediate problem. He pressed his foot against the gas pedal. The car moved past the house and he made the block, coming back to Government Street.

Within minutes, he was back at the guesthouse where he changed from his suit to a worn pair of blue jeans, a T-shirt, and scuffed topsiders. As an afterthought, he grabbed a baseball cap from the closet near the door, then headed outside.

A shack stood on the far side of the property. He walked quickly to it and pulled open the door. Inside, a wheelbarrow leaned against the corner to the right. Rakes and hand tools rested against a cabinet. A lawnmower sat to the left with a gas can beside it. He picked up the can and gave it a shake to make sure there was gas in it, then loaded both into the trunk of the Chrysler.

A few minutes later, he was back at the house on Crenshaw

Street. He sat there a moment, the Chrysler idling at the curb, the sun shining through the windshield. Weeds in the front yard swayed in a gentle breeze, but the air was hot and humid. In no time at all he would be sweating from every pore of his body. Sweating. For her. The woman who abandoned him. And his brother. Years of anger boiled to the surface and he snatched the steering wheel to the right, as if to drive away. She didn't deserve it. Didn't deserve his help. Didn't deserve— He sighed.

No one deserved anything. He'd learned that from morning prayers. Everyone had issues. Instantly images from his own past flashed through his mind. Family gatherings endured through a drunken haze. Other missed entirely. The shouting. The fights. Nights spent with— He switched off the engine and came from the car.

In a hurry to get started before he changed his mind, Connolly didn't bother with knocking on the door to ask for permission. He simply lifted the mower from the trunk, filled it with gas, and gave the starter chord a pull. The engine sputtered to life.

Sweat trickled past the corners of his eyes as he pushed the mower into the tall weeds near the street and made his way across the lawn. By the time he reached the bushes on the far side, his shirt was soaked through. As he started in the opposite direction, he glanced at the house. His mother stood at a window in the corner where his bedroom had been. Their eyes met but only for a moment, then she stepped away.

From somewhere deep inside, a sense of loneliness rose up and seemed to overwhelm him with an aching sense of despair. As if the center of his soul had opened into a deep dark hole and he was teetering on the edge. Memories of the first night he and Rick had been there by themselves rushed out. He shoved the mower across the yard and quickened his pace, as if he could outrun the sensation, the memory, the moment.

Before long, the loneliness became anger but as it built to rage, it suddenly evaporated. Burned away by the heat. It was too hot to be angry. Too hot to be much of anything except wet with sweat.

Back and forth he went across the front yard and soon the monotony of the effort overtook his emotions. His body pushed the machine without any need of conscious thought, freeing his mind to wander, to escape the misery of the heat. His thoughts drifted from the yard and his mother to Dibber and Tiffany.

Dibber and Tiffany. A strange pair. Dibber was a drifter and at least ten years older. She was a waitress at a barbeque joint. "A straight up manipulator," Lutie had said. Buying money orders for Nick each week with money he made selling drugs—money laundering in its most basic form—yet no telling how much she ripped him off. Money from the sale of crystal meth Nick and the boys cooked in that barn at the nursery. The same barn where Nick's mother shot his grandfather. There would be a lot to tell a jury if Dibber's case went to trial, but Connolly wasn't sure any of it would help Dibber. A thug stealing another thug's money, at the behest of another man's girlfriend. The whole thing was a sordid mess.

The front yard didn't take long, then he moved to the back and started near the garage. Still, his mind continued to whirl.

And what about this Tinker fellow. Meeting in a restaurant bathroom. Talking to him from behind a toilet stall. He grinned at the thought of it. The aesthetics of that would be difficult to explain, too. Still, Tinker had some important things to say. They needed to finish that conversation. Maybe McNamara would get mad enough over the finger to force it all out in a hearing before Judge Cahill.

From the garage, Connolly moved across the yard in a rhythm. Past the steps by the door to the bushes along the property line, back to the garage, do it all again. After a while, his mind moved on to think of nothing more than putting one foot in front of the other. But no one can think of nothing for very long. Something always rushes in to fill the void and for him it was an image of Gayle Underwood.

The curve of her hip beneath a skirt. Her torso outlined by the fabric of her top. The sound of her voice—always a hint of laughter, even when she was serious. Like that day she was talking to Hodges outside the hospital. The conversation played through his mind. She told him the prints weren't on—

The back door opened and his mother appeared with a glass of ice water. He switched off the mower and crossed the lawn to the steps. She handed him the glass. "Don't cut down my flowers," she said. Tears came to his eyes. He started to say something in response, but she was already inside. Instead, he watched as her frail hands pushed the door closed.

When he was a boy, he and Rick took turns mowing the lawn. Rick always did a neat job. Trimmed around the trees. Pulled the weeds from the flowerbeds as he went by. Put everything in order. Connolly cut down everything in sight. When it was his turn, she always reminded him. "Don't cut down my flowers."

He drained the last drops of water from the glass, then set it on the top step and started the mower. She knew who he was. She remembered what happened. And she confirmed it with that parting comment.

CHAPTER 46

Connolly finished mowing the grass at his mother's house shortly before one that afternoon. He thought about knocking on the door to tell her goodbye. Perhaps try again to talk to her about the other things. But when he glanced toward the door, he had second thoughts. The lights in the kitchen were off and the house seemed dark.

Rather than pressing the matter further, he loaded the mower in the trunk of the car and drove to the guesthouse. He put the mower back in the garden shack, then went inside for a shower. As he passed the living room, he noticed the answering machine on the table by the sofa. He could see from the light on the top that there were no messages.

After a shower and change of clothes, he walked out to the Chrysler and started down the driveway. It seemed days had passed since he saw Hodges and Morgan and he had to remind himself it was only that morning. McNamara might not be looking for him yet. Or at all. But he didn't want to risk being found right then so he had to keep moving.

As he drove down the driveway toward the street, he felt his stomach growl and realized how hungry he was. Breakfast had been hours ago, and he'd burned that away pushing the mower across his mother's lawn. A sandwich from Port City Diner would taste good right then so when he reached Government Street, he pointed the car in that direction, then he thought better of it. Everyone knew he ate there. "That's the first place someone would look if they wanted to find me." Mentally, he ran through the list of places to eat. Ed's Seafood. Couldn't go there, half the lawyers in town ate there. And not Bluegill, the other half would be there. Roussos. The Original Oyster House. Wintzell's. Each one seemed more obvious than the first. Instead, he made a U-turn and drove in the opposite direction. A few minutes later, he reached the Superior Oil Truck Stop on the western edge of the city.

Built at a time when Highway 90 was a major thoroughfare, the truck stop consisted of a garage with three service bays on one side and a café on the other. A pile of used tires lay at one end of the building. Rows of trailer trucks lined the parking lot at the other. Six well-worn fuel pumps stood between the highway and the building. A fishing boat was parked in one of the service bays. Another was full of cardboard boxes. The third was empty. But the café was open and that was all Connolly cared about. He parked the car in front and went inside.

A counter stood between the kitchen and the dining room. Tables filled the space between the counter and the windows in front where a row of booths lined the walls. Sunlight cast shadows across the room at a noticeable angle, as if noon had passed a while before and the afternoon was moving on. Evening wasn't approaching but the lunch crowd had come and gone, and the place had a sense of quiet about it.

Connolly took a seat at a table near the corner. A menu was tucked between the napkin holder and a crusty bottle of catsup. He opened the menu and scanned it quickly. Before he finished, a waitress appeared. She was older, with gray hair that was pulled behind her head in a bun. She wore thick makeup that left a line below her jaw and seemed to flake along the creases of her face. She'd seen a lot of life, most of it the hard way, but there was something about her that suggested it hadn't all been bad. "What could I get you to drink?" she asked.

"Tea," Connolly replied. "Do you still have the special?"

"Yeah. Meatloaf," she said with a dour expression. "You don't want it."

Connolly grinned. "What do I want?"

"Fried catfish."

"Nah." Connolly shook his head. "I had fish the other day. Twice, actually. Not in the mood for it right now. What else?"

"Fried chicken is the next best thing."

"Okay." Connolly nodded. "Fried chicken."

"You get two sides with it."

Connolly shrugged. "You choose."

"Me?" She seemed surprised.

"I have faith in you."

"You don't even know me."

He grinned. "Just figure it out and bring it to me." The waitress scribbled something on her pad. "Okay," she said. "But no complaints."

She disappeared behind the counter and in a few minutes, the men at the counter left. Connolly had the dining room all to himself. He watched the parking lot through the front window and thought about his mother, the morning, and cutting the grass for her. He had been so long without her, he wasn't sure what to do or how to act or think about her now. And he was even less certain about what to do next. Maybe she would make that next move. Maybe he should have gone back to her house instead of coming to the truck stop. Maybe he should have gone to see Barbara—

A boy riding on a bicycle pedaled past the window. Connolly wondered why he wasn't in school, then couldn't remember if school had started yet. Before he finished that thought, a truck came from the highway to the parking lot. It had a flat tire and blue smoke rose from the flapping rubber as it came to a stop a few feet beyond the fuel pumps. Before the smoke had dissipated, the cab door creaked open, and the driver stepped down. He stood staring at the wheel with both hands on his hips. The boy on the bicycle coasted to a stop next to him and said something to the driver. The driver responded in an angry tone, most of it directed toward the tire, then gave the tire a kick and walked away. Connolly could see his lips were still moving as he came toward the building.

A minute or two later, an old man came from the garage side of the building dragging a large floor jack behind him, holding the handle of it with one hand. With his free hand he carried two wooden blocks that were stained with oil and scuffed from years of use and neglect. About the time the old man had the jack positioned under the truck, the waitress appeared at Connolly's table with a plate of fried chicken, mashed potatoes, and green beans. She set it on the table with a glass of tea and a plate of cornbread. "Is that what you wanted?" she asked.

Connolly smiled. "That's perfect." She stepped away as he spread a napkin across his lap and began to eat.

Outside, the driver of the truck with the flat tire noticed the Chrysler and moved around it, admiring it from every angle. When he had a good look at the exterior, he cupped his hands against the glass and peered inside. After studying the interior, he ran his fingers over the door, grasped the door handle, and gave it a tug. When it didn't open, he continued down the side to the rear fender, touching it lightly.

Connolly felt uneasy about the man's intentions and moved the napkin from his lap to the table in anticipation of standing. The man stared at the car a moment longer and when he didn't move on, Connolly scooted back from the table. As he was about to stand, the man outside stepped away from the car and started across the parking lot toward the truck. Connolly watched a moment longer, making sure the man was really leaving, then placed his legs back beneath the table, put the napkin in his lap again, and focused on the chicken.

When he finished eating, Connolly paid and walked outside to the car. By then the truck with the flat tire was gone. The boy on the bicycle was nowhere to be seen. The parking lot was quiet. He opened the driver's door of the Chrysler, started the engine, and backed it away from the building.

In midtown, Connolly made his way to Barbara's house. The realtor's sign was still in the yard. The thought of going inside and being trapped by all the memories sent a chill up his spine. But the thought of selling the house, of never being able to come back there, left him sad, too. As if selling the house meant selling the past and as bad as some of it had been, he didn't want to part with it.

After a moment, he opened the car door and stepped outside. He thumped the sign with his knuckle as he walked past it to the front porch. Barbara greeted him at the door. "Did you take the afternoon off?"

"No," he replied. "Why do you ask?"

"Mrs. Gordon called here looking for you."

"I'm sure she did."

"She said you had a call you needed to return."

Connolly grinned. "Can't be everywhere at once."

"Are you avoiding someone?"

"Something like that."

Barbara stepped onto to the porch and pulled the door closed behind her. "We could sit out here, but I think we'd be a little warm."

Connolly glanced toward the steps. "I think you're right."

"Want to come inside?"

Connolly shook his head. "Not today."

"You really have a problem with that, don't you."

"I really don't want to go back to who I was."

She moved closer and slipped her arms around his waist. "You aren't who you used to be, and you aren't going back to it merely by coming inside the house."

"Maybe not." He put his arms around her. "But I don't want to give it a chance."

She leaned against him and rested her head on his chest. "We could go over to your house."

"We could walk around back and sit out there."

She raised her head to look at him and smiled. "Okay."

They walked together down the steps and sauntered around the house to the back steps where they sat in the shade. For a long time neither of them said a word. Then Connolly took her hand in his. "Are you really going to sell this house?"

"I'm really going to sell it," she said with conviction.

"Has anyone made an offer?"

"Not yet."

"What does the realtor say?"

"She says it'll sell."

He stared across the back yard. "Do you remember the time we put dish detergent in Rachel's pool?"

"I remember the time you put it in there."

Connolly chuckled. "We'd been washing the car. She wanted to play in the pool. Seemed like a good idea."

"She had soap suds from head to toe."

"I miss her."

"Me, too."

"Why did she have to move so far away?"

"Tallahassee isn't that far."

"Seems like a long way." He sighed. "Have you talked to her this week?"

"Yes."

"How is she?"

"She's fine."

"Everything is okay with her job?"

"Yes. It's a good job. Physical therapists make good money these days."

Connolly shook his head. "Physical therapist. Seems like a title someone made up just to give someone a job."

"They help."

"Oh, I know," he agreed. "It just seems like life has changed so much."

"Not as much as you."

"Me?"

"We've spent more time talking in the last three years than we talked the entire time we were married."

"You think?"

"I know."

"I guess you're right. Maybe we should move to Tallahassee."

Her eyes opened wide. "Move to Tallahassee? What for?"

"Start over. Get it right with the grandchildren."

"Grandchild," Barbara corrected.

"She won't be the only child."

"Probably not."

"Think they'll come back for Christmas?"

"Maybe. I suppose that will depend on her work."

"Yeah."

"Are you just filling up the afternoon?"

He was caught off-guard. "What?"

"You've never rambled like this before. Are you just filling up the afternoon?"

Connolly had a sense of satisfaction from the comment. "No," he said. "Just talking." He leaned over and kissed her.

She straightened herself. "You better call Mrs. Gordon. Where's your cell phone?"

"In the car."

"You didn't answer it when she called."

"I turned it off earlier."

Barbara had a disapproving expression. "Mike, that poor woman's been scouring the earth trying to find you. She called here twice."

"Couldn't be helped."

"What's going on?"

"Dibber."

"What about him?"

"I think we're about to bust his case wide open."

"What'll it be this time?"

"I don't know."

"Is that why you wanted to sit back here?"

"No." He slipped his arm around her waist and pulled her close. They kissed again. "That's why I wanted to sit back here."

After dinner with Barbara, Connolly returned to the guesthouse. As he went inside, the beam of headlights shone through the front window and washed across the room. Connolly recognized the car as Mrs. Gordon's. He walked outside and waited at the end of the driveway as she brought the car to a stop. The door flew open. She started talking before her feet hit the ground. "Where have you been?" she demanded.

"Around."

"I've been looking for you all day."

"I heard."

"The least you could do was return my calls. Do you know how difficult it is to run an office without being able to reach you? What are you doing?"

Connolly leaned against the Chrysler. "I just got back from dinner and was thinking of having a ginger ale. "Want one?"

"No," she roared. "I don't want a bottle of ginger ale. I want to know how soon you can find a replacement."

He frowned. "A replacement?"

"Yes. A replacement. For me. I quit."

"You quit?"

"I quit," she repeated.

"Quit what?"

"My job."

He gave her an amused look. "But why?"

"I sit at my desk all day deciphering cryptic notes you scribble on the files. I answer calls from people you haven't bothered to contact in weeks. I juggle appointments, court dates, discovery, depositions. And you don't even bother to come to the office. You don't even bother to return my calls. Do you know how long it's been since you spent a day at your desk?"

"No. And I hope you don't either."

"That's just it. I don't."

"Good. I'd hate to spend so much time at my desk that either of us could remember it."

"Where have you been?"

"I wanted to be unavailable."

"Well, you accomplished that. But why cut me out?"

"So you wouldn't have to lie."

She hadn't expected that response. "You didn't want me to lie?" Connolly nodded. Mrs. Gordon kept going. "I've lied for you before."

"I'm sure you have, but it wasn't because I asked you to."

"No. You didn't come right out and say, 'Tell them a lie.'"

He gave her a deadpan look. "When did I ever imply you should not tell the truth?"

"What was I supposed to say? 'He's drunk out of his mind right now. Can he call you back?'" Connolly shrugged and looked away. Mrs. Gordon stepped closer and tapped him on the chest for emphasis. "You asked me to lie for you every time you drank yourself into oblivion and passed out on the floor."

"I'm sorry."

"I know you are. But why didn't you call me today?"

Connolly cleared his throat. "Did Henry McNamara call?"

"Yes."

"What about Walter? Did he call?"

"Yes."

"Do they have a hearing set in the morning?"

"Eight o'clock," she replied. "How did you know?"

"I went over to Tiffany's house yesterday. Her friend Tinker was there."

Mrs. Gordon frowned. "Tinker?"

"The guy I talked to at The Whistlin' Pig."

"What did he have to say?"

"A lot. And then he gave me a prescription bottle with a finger in it."

Her eyes opened wide. "A finger?"

"Yes."

"Whose finger?"

"Tinker said it belonged to Stephen Ellis."

"Inez Marchand's son."

"Right." Connolly nodded. "I took it to Ted Morgan this morning."

"And you didn't want to answer any questions about it today."

Connolly looked over at her. "Are you really quitting?"

"No." Mrs. Gordon sighed. "But don't do this again." She opened the door to her car. "I'm the person you call." She got in behind the wheel. "You understand? Whatever happens, whatever's wrong, whatever mess you make—I'm the person you call."

Connolly smiled at her. "Okay."

She slammed the door closed. He watched as she drove toward the street.

CHAPTER 47

The hearing set with Judge Cahill was about McNamara's motion to admit the finger as evidence and to compel Connolly to provide further information about it. Connolly saw it as a suggestion that he had done something wrong. He arrived a little before eight the next morning in Cahill's courtroom. Walter, the bailiff, was at his desk next to the judge's bench. He glanced up as Connolly came through the doorway. "When did you stop returning phone calls?"

"Sorry."

"We've been trying to find you since yesterday. The judge wanted to do this yesterday afternoon."

"Is he upset?"

"He's not too happy." Walter nodded over his shoulder. "Go on back there and see him. Get it over with now." There was a twinkle in his eye when he said it. Connolly knew it couldn't be that bad.

When he entered Judge Cahill's chambers, he found Cahill standing at the coffee pot. "Where were you yesterday?"

"Sorry I missed you."

"Walter called your office two or three times. I called myself."

"I was out of reach."

Cahill chuckled. "More like you didn't want anyone to find you."

"How's Henry?"

Cahill took a sip of coffee. "Henry is Henry. He'll be up here in a minute." He brushed past Connolly and stepped into his office. Connolly poured a cup of coffee for himself and walked out to the courtroom.

Ten minutes later, Henry McNamara arrived. Gayle Underwood followed a few steps behind. A moment later, the court reporter entered. McNamara's voice boomed. "Where were you yesterday?"

Connolly grinned. "Good morning, Henry."

McNamara glared at him. "You think this is funny?"

"I have no idea what you're talking about."

"You think you can just hand Morgan something like finger in a medicine bottle and no one will want to know where it came from?"

"I think anyone could figure out where it came from."

"Your client should have—"

The door behind the judge's bench opened. Everyone stood while he took a seat. Cahill settled into place and opened the file. "Walter, where's the defendant?"

"I thought you wanted to talk to the lawyers," Walter replied.

"We have a motion from the state in a capital murder case. I think the defendant has a right to be here." Cahill looked to Connolly. "Mr. Connolly, has your client waived his right to be here this morning?"

Connolly stood. "No, Your Honor. He hasn't."

Cahill slapped the file closed. "Walter, call me when he gets over here." He bounded from his chair and disappeared through the door into his office.

Walter left the room on the way to the jail to get Dibber. McNamara whispered something to Gayle, then left the courtroom, too, and the court reporter disappeared through the door behind the judge's bench.

When they were gone, Connolly asked Gayle, "Did Morgan examine the finger?"

"Yes," she said.

"Whose is it?"

"Stephen Ellis." She smiled. "But you didn't hear that from me."

"The real Stephen Ellis or the other Stephen Ellis."

"The real Stephen Ellis," she said. "Bobby Junkins had all ten of his fingers."

"Is Henry mad, or just putting on an act?"

"He's pretty angry."

"I don't know why. I did exactly what I was supposed to do."

"He doesn't see it that way."

"He thinks I should have brought it to him?"

"I'm not sure what he thinks."

"But you're certain the finger was Stephen's finger?"

"Yes. They checked the fingerprints."

Connolly arched an eyebrow. "Didn't someone try that before?"

"We got it right this time."

"Did you get the report yourself?"

Gayle shook her head. "Morgan got it."

"Not Hodges?"

Gayle gave him a smirk. "Not this time."

Twenty minutes later Walter arrived with Dibber, handcuffed and wearing an orange jumpsuit. Walter guided him to a chair beside Connolly. "Don't get up without asking me first," he said. "You understand?"

Dibber nodded. Walter moved away. Dibber leaned toward Connolly. "What's this about?"

"Tinker gave me a bottle with Stephen Ellis' finger inside."

"His what?" Dibber blurted.

Connolly gestured for quiet. "Not so loud," he cautioned. "His finger. I took it to the coroner. They want to know where I got it."

"Where did you get it?"

"Tinker."

"He had it?"

"Any reason why I shouldn't tell them?"

"About Tinker?"

"Yeah."

"What'll they do?"

"Probably arrest him."

"I don't care about Tinker," Dibber said. "But what about Tiffany? Will they arrest her?"

Connolly shrugged. "I don't know."

"What's the choice?"

"Tinker's not my client. Cahill will probably order me to tell them where it came from."

"And if you don't?"

"He'll put me in jail."

Dibber grinned. "You ever been in jail?"

Connolly avoided the question. "I'm no good to you in there."

The door behind the bench opened and Judge Cahill entered. He took a seat and once more glanced around the courtroom. "Are we ready now?"

"Yes, Your Honor," McNamara answered. "The state is ready."

Connolly stood. "We're ready, too, Your Honor."

Cahill leaned over the bench to the court reporter. "Ready?"

"Yes, Your Honor," she replied.

"Very well. We are here on case number 25919197. State of Alabama versus Dilbert Landry. This is a capital murder case, and we are here today on the state's motion for discovery. We normally just argue these motions among the lawyers but, this being a capital case, I think you have a witness, Mr. McNamara?"

"Yes, Your Honor."

"Very well, call your witness."

"Your Honor, the state calls Dr. Ted Morgan."

Morgan entered from the jury room and took a seat on the witness stand. Cahill placed him under oath and McNamara began. "Dr. Morgan, we are here on State versus Dilbert Landry. Are you familiar with that case?"

"Yes, I am."

"How are you familiar with that case?"

"I did a post-mortem examination associated with the case."

"Now, yesterday, did you receive some material relevant to that case?"

"Yes."

"What did you receive?"

"I received one human finger."

"From whom did you receive that finger?"

"I received it from Mike Connolly."

"And you are referring to the defendant's lawyer, who is present with us today in the courtroom?"

"Yes."

"Did you analyze that finger?"

"Yes."

"What did you find?"

"I found that it was the index finger from the left hand of—"

"You could tell from looking at it which hand it came from?"

"Yes."

"Whose left hand was it?"

"You'd have to ask the detective about that," Morgan replied.

"The detective?"

"Yes."

"Which detective?"

"Brian Hodges. He did the check on the fingerprints."

McNamara seemed confused. "I was under the impression you did the fingerprint check."

"No, sir. I called Hodges. He came over and took the prints."

"You didn't request them?"

"I do that sometimes when we have an unidentified body that's not associated with an ongoing case. But when something comes up in a case like this, I prefer to have the detectives take care of it."

"Do you know whose finger it was?"

"Yes," Morgan said. "I mean, Detective Hodges told me what the report said."

"And what did he tell you it said?"

Connolly stood. "Objection, Your Honor. This is hearsay."

"The rules allow it," McNamara countered. "If we can produce the witness at trial, the rules allow a witness to testify to this way."

"The rules allow it at a preliminary hearing," Connolly argued. "But this isn't a preliminary hearing. This is a hearing on his motion for discovery. He has the burden of proof here and he can't meet it with hearsay."

Cahill turned to McNamara. "You don't have Hodges here?"

"I can get him."

Cahill threw up his hands in frustration. "This is a capital murder case, Henry!" he scolded. "Do you need anything else from this witness?"

"No, Your Honor."

Cahill turned to Connolly. "Mike, do you have anything for him?"

"Just a couple of questions."

While Connolly approached the witness stand, Cahill said to Walter, "Get Brian Hodges up here."

Connolly spoke up. "Judge, could I get a ruling on my objection?"

"The objection is sustained, Mr. Connolly. Proceed with this witness. We'll find Hodges. But whatever you want from Ted, get it now."

McNamara took a seat. Connolly moved closer to the witness stand. "Dr. Morgan, you said you examined a corpse associated with this case."

"Yes."

"That corpse was found in a beach house on Dauphin Island."

"Yes."

"And that corpse is the one regarding which Mr. Landry is charged with capital murder."

"Yes."

"Now, since the time you did that autopsy, has anyone come to claim the body?"

"Yes," Morgan said. "Several have come to identify it."

"Who were they?"

"Billy Ellis came first."

"And what happened when Mr. Ellis saw the body?"

"Everyone thought the corpse was that of Stephen Ellis, but when Mr. Ellis looked at it, he identified it as someone named Bobby Junkins."

Connolly nodded. "And who else looked at the body?"

"Mr. and Mrs. Junkins."

"And what did they say about it?"

"They identified it as the body of their son."

"So, the body in the beach house was actually Bobby Junkins."

"Yes."

"Do you know how his body was first identified as someone else?"

"They used his fingerprints."

"Who took those fingerprints?"

"I believe they were taken by Detective Hodges."

"So, a body was found at the beach house, Hodges took fingerprints from it, sent those off to wherever they go, and the report came back that the dead man was Stephen Ellis—is that correct?"

McNamara stood. "Objection, Your Honor."

Morgan answered anyway. "Yes. They used the report to give him a name."

Judge Cahill glanced at McNamara. "Objection overruled."

Connolly continued. "Did you examine any other human remains in regard to this case?"

Morgan grinned. "Just the finger you brought me yesterday."

"You already told us you analyzed it. What exactly did you do?"

"The finger was covered with some sort of black soot. We took samples of it and analyzed that. And we found some material under the fingernail, so we tested that, too."

"What did you find?"

"The black substance on the exterior was soot from a fire."

"What kind of fire?"

"Wood, mostly. Nothing uncommon about it."

"So, the finger had been in a fire?"

"Yes."

"Were you able to determine anything about the soot?"

"Like I said, nothing out of the ordinary. The general composition was consistent with that of woody material, but there were traces of any number of combustible materials. Cardboard, cotton, the typical things one might expect to find."

"What about under the fingernail?"

"That was a little more interesting," Morgan noted. "We found a mixture of sulfur, nitrogen, traces of ammonia. Traces of a material used to make gel caps. And traces of pseudoephedrine."

"Like you might find from someone who's been in a meth lab?"

"Yes."

"Did you find anything else?"

Morgan shook his head. "I think that's about it."

Connolly looked up at Judge Cahill. "That's all, Your Honor."

Cahill look over at Morgan. "Ted, you may go." He glanced over at McNamara. "Any other witnesses?"

McNamara stood. "We call Mr. Connolly."

Cahill's eyes opened wide in a startled expression. "Do what?"

"We don't need Detective Hodges," McNamara said. "We can get what we want through Mr. Connolly."

Connolly spoke up. "I object, Your Honor. I'm not testifying in a hearing about a case involving my own client."

Cahill turned to Walter. "Call me when Hodges gets here." He stepped from the bench and disappeared.

When he was gone, Connolly called across the room to McNamara. "Nice try, Henry."

"Why don't you just tell us about the finger and get this over with?"

Connolly ignored the question and took a seat next to Dibber. "Make it look like we're talking," he whispered.

CHAPTER 48

Hodges arrived at the courthouse a little before ten. By then, Cahill's courtroom was filled with attorneys, spectators, and witnesses for the morning docket. Hodges came to the table where McNamara and Gayle were seated and huddled with them for a moment, reviewing something from a file that Hodges brought with him. After a moment, though, Hodges took a seat in a chair behind them, near the rail, and waited.

Not long after that, the door to Judge Cahill's chambers opened and he appeared. There was a rustling noise while everyone took a seat. Cahill looked to the others in the room. "We are in the middle of a hearing on a capital murder case. Y'all get comfortable and hopefully this won't take all morning." He turned to McNamara. "Mr. McNamara, I see Detective Hodges is here. Are you ready to proceed?"

"Yes, Your Honor."

"Mr. Connolly, are you ready?"

Connolly rose from his chair. "We're ready, Your Honor."

"Very well. Detective, come on up."

Hodges came to the witness stand carrying the same file he reviewed with McNamara. He took a seat and placed the file in his lap. When he was ready, McNamara began. "Detective Hodges, Ted Morgan testified earlier that he called you to come to his office yesterday. Do you recall doing that?"

"Yes. I went to the hospital yesterday morning. He had a severed finger he was trying to identify."

"What did you do?"

"I scanned the finger to get an image of the fingerprint."

"What did you do next?"

"I e-mailed the scan to the FBI."

"You e-mailed it?"

"Yes."

"You can do that with enough clarity to get a match?"

"Do it all the time," Hodges said. "We use a handheld scanning device. Uploads it like a cell phone. Their system is fully automated. All of their prints are digitized."

"Were they able to identify the print?"

"Yes."

"Whose was it?"

"The finger was from Stephen Ellis. White male. Age forty-four. Last known address was in Lawrenceville, Georgia."

"Did you inquire as to how Dr. Morgan came to have this finger?"

"He told me he got it from Mr. Connolly."

"The same Mr. Connolly seated at the defense table?"

"Yes."

"Did you attempt to contact Mr. Connolly about the finger?"

"No. I called your office and spoke to you about it."

"Nothing further from this witness."

Connolly came from the counsel's table and approached the witness stand. "Detective, this isn't the first set of prints you've lifted in this case, is it?"

"No."

McNamara stood. "I object, Your Honor. We're here about this finger and how Mr. Connolly came to have it and who gave it to him. We aren't here about fingerprints in general."

Connolly faced Judge Cahill. "This hearing is about a fingerprint from a finger in a case in which this detective is the lead investigator. He has matched other fingerprints prior to this one and those matches proved to be incorrect. I think I have a right to ask him about that."

"Overruled," Cahill said. "For now."

Connolly turned back to Hodges. "Detective, tell us about those other prints you found while investigating this case."

"We lifted several prints from the beach house. There were some on the medicine bottle the finger was in. And we took an image of the finger itself."

"Is that all?"

"Yes."

"How many different prints did you find in the beach house?"

Hodges opened the file in his lap and glanced at a page inside it. "Eight," he said.

"And how many of those prints were you able to identify?"

Hodges was backed into a corner now on the question Connolly had tried to get him to answer earlier about the prints. From the expression on his face, he didn't like it. "Five," he said.

"Five different prints. Five different people?"

"Yes."

"And who were those five people you identified?"

"Your client, Dilbert Landry. Nicholas Marchand. Inez March-and. Edwin Marchand. And Bobby Junkins, the man whose body we recovered from the house."

"You took fingerprints from the body that was in the beach house?"

"Yes."

"You sent those to the FBI."

"Yes."

"And what did they say?"

"The FBI gave me the information I just gave you." Hodges looked over at Judge Cahill. "Your honor, I can—"

"We'll get to that," Connolly said, interrupting. "Tell me about the body from the beach house. When you sent the FBI prints from the body, initially, when you were just beginning the investigation, who did the FBI say that person in the beach house was?"

"Stephen Ellis."

"But that was incorrect, wasn't it?"

"Yes. Apparently. The FBI never said."

"Do they ever acknowledge that sort of thing?"

"I don't know." Hodges shrugged. "I guess so."

"Have they ever told you in any other case that they made a mistake?"

"No."

"But the dead man wasn't Stephen Ellis, was he?"

"No."

"Who was he?"

"He was Bobby Junkins."

"But his fingerprints are on file with the FBI under a different name."

"Yes."

"And you had other prints from the house."

"Yes."

"And you sent those to the FBI for identification, too, didn't you?"

"Yes."

"After you received the results back from the FBI about those prints, you created a memo that detailed all of that, didn't you?"

"Yes."

"And that memo said, among other things, that you had identified one set of prints from the house as being those of Edwin Marchand."

"Yes, but——"

"Did you talk to Edwin Marchand about that?"

"Yes."

"What did he say?"

McNamara stood quickly. "Objection, Your Honor. This has nothing to do with my motion or the purpose of this hearing."

Cahill waved him off with a nonchalant gesture. "Overruled."

Connolly continued. "What did Edwin Marchand say?"

Hodges was angry. "He said he had never been in the beach

house."

"Is that all he said?"

"Yes."

"Didn't he actually say that he had never even seen it."

"Something like that," Hodges conceded.

"Did you ask him to account for his time?"

Hodges looked puzzled. "What do you mean?"

"You had a time of death for the body, didn't you?"

"Dr. Morgan said he had been dead about a week before they found him. He couldn't say specifically what day, but it had been about a week. That was as close as he could put it."

"Did you ask Mr. Marchand where he had been during that time?"

"Not really."

"In fact, you knew he wasn't in that house, didn't you?"

"I can explain all of that."

"I'm sure you can," Connolly noted. He took two pages from his file. "Do you recall talking to me in your office about this case?"

"Which time?"

"The first time."

"Yes."

"You gave me a copy of a report." Connolly asked the court reporter to mark the pages with an exhibit number while he continued. "Do you remember giving me that report?"

"Yes," Hodges sighed.

Connolly offered the documents to Hodges. "I show you what I've marked as Defendant's Exhibit A. Do you recognize this?"

Hodges glanced at the paper. "It's a copy of my memo to the file."

"You prepared it."

"Yes."

"And what does it say?"

"It says what I just told you. That we identified five of the prints from the house."

"The five you mentioned just now."

"Yes."

Connolly showed him another page. "Take a look at what I've marked as Defense Exhibit B. Do you recognize that?"

"Yes."

"What is it?"

"It's another memo to the file."

"You prepared it?"

"Yes."

"What does it say?"

"It says we identified two prints."

"And those two were?"

"Dilbert Landry and Nicholas Marchand."

"Can you explain the difference?"

Hodges frowned. "The difference?"

"Between the two reports," Connolly said. "Why does the first memo say five and the second says two?"

"I—"

Connolly interrupted. "At the time you created that first memo, you knew Edwin Marchand's prints weren't in that house, didn't you?"

"I knew—"

"And after you talked to him, you knew he had never even seen that house, didn't you?"

"I—"

"And if this were any other investigation, and you found Edwin Marchand's prints in the house, his statement that he had never been in that house would have made him a suspect, wouldn't it?"

"I don't think—"

"Whose prints were actually there?" Hodges didn't respond immediately. Connolly pressed the question. "What did the FBI report actually show about the prints you found in the house?"

"I can't—"

"You have a file in your lap," Connolly said, pointing to it. "You referred to it during your testimony for Mr. McNamara. Look through that file and show us the actual report the FBI sent you."

"They e-mailed their report."

"And you printed it for the file," Connolly argued. He didn't know that for certain but Hodges seemed like a paper kind of guy. "Show us your copy of that e-mail."

Hodges was obviously uneasy, and McNamara seemed to take a cue from it. "Judge, again, we aren't here on the question of finger-prints in general. We're here about the finger Mr. Connolly gave to Dr. Morgan. That's all. And I think——"

"Hold on, Henry." Cahill sat up straight in his chair. "I think Mr. Connolly has raised enough of a question about the accuracy of the work on this file." He turned to Hodges. "Do you have a copy of the e-mail from the FBI?"

"Yes, Your Honor."

"Let's see it." Cahill held out his hand as if beckoning. Hodges took a copy of the e-mail from his file and handed it to him. Cahill looked at it, then handed it to Connolly. Connolly glanced over the document. None of the names surprised him except one, Clyde Ramsey. And then he remembered his conversation with Toby, who told him that Hodges had married Ramsey's daughter.

Connolly had the court reporter mark it as an exhibit and handed it to Hodges. "Detective, I show you the document which has been marked as Defense Exhibit C. Can you tell us what that is?"

"It's a copy of the e-mail I received from the FBI office in Vir-ginia."

"The one we were just discussing."

"Yes."

"What does it say?"

"It says...." Hodges took a deep breath, then continued. "It says they had a match for three of the prints."

"And what were the names?"

"Nicholas Marchand. Inez Marchand. And——" Hodges paused again.

Connolly prodded him for an answer. "Go ahead, detective. Tell us the third name."

Hodges seemed shaken. "I didn't think it would matter." He had a plaintive tone.

Connolly was incredulous. "You didn't think it would matter?"

"No."

"That wasn't for you to decide, was it?"

"Everyone knew Edwin Marchand had nothing to do with this case."

"Everyone? How would they know that?"

Hodges looked away. Connolly pressed the point. "You knew he had nothing to do with this case, didn't you?"

"Yes."

"How did you know that?"

"I'd rather not say."

"You knew Edwin Marchand had nothing to do with this case because someone told you he had nothing to do with this case, didn't they?" Connolly was going out on a limb, but he didn't care. Hodges had falsified information in his file and tainted the investigation. He meant to make him pay for it.

"Yes," Hodges said weakly.

"Who told you?"

Hodges looked down. "My father-in-law."

"And who is your father-in-law?"

"Clyde Ramsey."

"The third name on that report from the FBI."

"Yes."

"Clyde Ramsey is your father-in-law."

"Yes."

"And you found his prints in the beach house, not Edwin March-and's."

"Yes."

Connolly wanted to ask many more questions. Grill Hodges endlessly about how he had shaped the case to focus on Dibber rather than conducting a real investigation. And he did it all to avoid implicating Clyde. But he was also sure Cahill understood all of that and, after all, this was a hearing on McNamara's motion, not a preliminary hearing or a trial. So, he glanced over at Cahill. "Nothing further, Your Honor."

Hodges gathered his file and stood to leave but Cahill stopped him. "Wait a minute," he said. "Sit down. You're not getting out of here just yet." Hodges took a seat. Cahill continued. "You deliberately mislabeled information relevant to this case."

Hodges' shoulder sagged. "I didn't think it would matter."

Cahill erupted. "You didn't think it would matter?!" His voice was loud and full and angry. "This is a capital murder case, and you didn't think it would matter?!" Hodges looked deflated. Cahill continued. "Do you know why your father-in-law's prints were in that beach house?"

Hodges did not reply. Cahill's voice grew even louder. "I'm asking you a question. A direct question. And I want a direct answer. Do you know why his prints were in that house?"

"He was, I believe, seeing Mrs. Marchand."

"He was having an affair with Mrs. Marchand?"

"Yes, Your Honor," Hodges said. "That's my understanding."

"And you covered it up by mislabeling the information in your file."

"I didn't think it would matter."

"Well," Cahill snapped. "You thought wrong."

Walter, who knew how to read Cahill's cues, was already standing at his desk with a form in his hand. Cahill took it and filled in the blank spaces with a pen. He found a pre-printed stamp on his desk and stamped the form with it. When he was finished, he signed it and handed it back to Walter. "Detective Hodges," he said, "I find you in criminal contempt of court and sentence you to five days in the county jail. Walter, take this man into custody." Cahill looked over at Hodges. "Did you leave a weapon downstairs?"

"Yes, Your Honor."

"Do you have any weapons on you right now?"

"No, Your Honor." Hodges tried again to defend himself. "Honestly, Your Honor, I didn't think—"

"You're in custody, Mr. Hodges," Cahill growled. "Are you sure you don't have a pistol on your ankle?"

"No, Your Honor. I left it at the office."

"Alright. Walter, cuff him and take him to jail."

As Walter led Hodges from the courtroom, Gayle stood and began gathering papers from the table where she and McNamara were seated. Cahill glared at her. "Take a seat, Ms. Underwood. We aren't through here yet." She took a seat quickly. Cahill shot a glare in Connolly's direction. "We'll get to you in a minute, Mike."

Cahill waited while Walter and Hodges made their way out the door. When they were gone, Cahill looked to Connolly. "Now, about this finger."

Connolly stood. "Yes, Your Honor."

"What do you have to say for yourself?"

"I came into possession of a prescription bottle. The bottle contained something that appeared to be human remains. I took it to Ted Morgan, the county medical examiner. That's all I can say."

"You don't know who gave it to you?"

"Any information I may have developed about the contents of that bottle were developed in the course of representing my client," Connolly replied. "Whatever I may know about that bottle, if anything, is protected by the attorney-client privilege."

Cahill slapped the bench and shouted. "I'm not asking you to tell me what your client told you! I'm asking about that bottle."

After years of appearing in Cahill's court, Connolly had come to understand that not everything the judge said had equal weight. However, distinguishing his degree of seriousness wasn't always easy. Connolly suppressed an urge to smile. "Your Honor, if the court finds that the information I may or may not know about the contents of that bottle did not arise from a privileged communication with my client, then I assert that it is information developed in the course of defending my client. As such, it is work product and is not subject to disclosure."

Cahill glanced over at McNamara. "What about that, Henry?"

McNamara stood. "Judge, I'm not interested in what his client said to him. I just want to know where he got the finger. Either he cut it off Mr. Ellis' hand himself, or someone gave it to him. I'm rather certain he didn't cut it off himself. So, as long as the person who gave it to him wasn't Mr. Connolly's client, I'm entitled to know who that person is."

Cahill had an expression Connolly had seen many times before. "Did you get this finger from your client?"

Connolly glanced over at Walter. A pair of handcuffs lay on the desk in front of him. Walter tapped them with his index finger and smiled. Connolly glanced down at the floor, thinking about what he should say.

If he gave them Tinker's name, Tinker would be arrested before sundown and Tinker would be in jail, charged with whatever crime McNamara could dream up. The duty judge would appoint a lawyer to defend him, and he would be lost as a witness in Dibber's case.

Cahill was serious. "Easy way, or the hard way, Mike."

Connolly said finally, "Judge, I received the finger from a potential witness. And if I—"

"What's the witness' name?!" Cahill shouted.

Connolly nodded toward McNamara. "I'll give them the name and address, but I'm not telling them anything else."

Cahill smiled at McNamara. "Better than nothing."

McNamara sighed. Cahill closed the file and stood. "You two get together and talk." He started from the bench, then spoke to the others still seated and waiting in the courtroom. "We'll take a short recess. I'll be back in ten minutes for the regular docket."

As Cahill disappeared through the doorway into his office, Connolly leaned over to McNamara. "You want the name now?"

McNamara reached for a pen. "I can't believe you did this." He grabbed a notepad from the table. "What's the name and address?"

Connolly smiled. "His name is Tinker Johnson."

Despite his anger, McNamara laughed. "Tinker?"

"Tinker," Connolly said.

"And where does Tinkerbell live?"

"I talked to him at 3965 Staples Road."

McNamara jotted down the address.

CHAPTER 49

It was eleven o'clock when Connolly left the courthouse and walked back to the office. He worked at his desk until noon, then went up the street to the Port City Diner for lunch. When he finished eating, he came back to the office and spent the afternoon returning calls and working on files. By five, though, he could stand it no more. He slipped on his jacket, scooped up a stack of files from the desk, and took them to Mrs. Gordon.

"This ought to meet with your approval," he said as he deposited the files with her.

"Work like that every day," she responded, "and you could make some money at this business."

"Work like that every day and they'll cart me out of here on a stretcher." He opened the door but paused before leaving. "I really didn't mean to make you mad yesterday."

With the flick of her wrist, Mrs. Gordon sent the pen in her hand sailing toward him. "Get out of here," she said playfully. The pen struck him on the shoulder and fell to the floor as he stepped into the corridor.

From the office building, Connolly drove to the guesthouse. He parked the car at the end of the driveway and went inside. It was early, but he was tired. The past few weeks had been draining. Stephen Ellis' finger. Earl Givens' abuse. Finding his own mother. It was more than he expected.

In the guesthouse, he ran a hot bath and sat in the tub reading the newspaper. The water was cold by the time he reached the sports section. He warmed it up while he read about the Braves and their chase for another pennant. When he finished with the sports section, he threw the paper on the floor and slid low in the tub. Water covered all but his nose and mouth. The heat from it eased the tension in his neck and he began to relax.

An hour later, Connolly climbed from the tub and made his way to the bedroom. He crawled into bed, pulled the covers over his head, and was soon fast asleep. After what seemed like only minutes, though, he was awakened by the sound of someone pounding on the door. He flipped back the covers and looked around. The room was dark. The hour was late, but he couldn't decide how late and still, the pounding on the door continued. He found his cell phone on the table beside the bed and pressed a button. The display showed the time was two in the morning. The pounding on the door grew even louder and more insistent.

Connolly forced himself from the bed, found his pants from a chair across the room, and started down the hall. When he reached the door, he called out in an impatient voice. "Who is it?"

A voice from the other side answered. "It's Tiffany. Let me in."

Tiffany. He groaned. She was the last person he wanted to see, and certainly not in the middle of the night. When he didn't respond immediately, she pounded on the door again. "Open up," she insisted. "I have to see you."

Reluctantly, Connolly unlocked the door. Tiffany pushed her way past him. "You gotta help me," she said.

"What's the matter?"

"They got Tinker."

"Who?"

"The cops. They came to the house and got him."

"When?"

"Tonight."

"Just now?"

"A few hours ago," she said. "They came to the house. Got him. Started going through everything. You gotta help him."

"Where is he?"

"In jail."

"Did they say anything about arresting you?"

"No. They just told me to get out of the way. Then they cuffed him, put him in the car, and started searching through the house like they was looking for something. They kept me outside. I got tired of waiting for them to leave and walked up the street to my sister's house. She let me use her car to come find you."

"What did they charge Tinker with?"

"I don't know."

"Have you talked to him since they took him in?"

"No. I just know he needs somebody to help him."

Connolly was still holding the door open. "I can't," he replied.

"Why not?"

"Because I already represent Dibber."

"What's that got to do with it?"

"Tinker's involved in Dibber's case. It would be a conflict for me to represent both."

"I don't know how they ever found him. How did the police know about him?"

Connolly avoided her gaze. "Well, they have their ways."

She glanced around the house. "I need a place to stay tonight."

Connolly felt uneasy but by then Tiffany was by the sofa. She sized up the living room, then gave him a smile he was certain she had used on a thousand guys before him. "Think I could stay here? Just tonight. I ain't got no place to go."

"I think you should stay with your sister," he replied.

"No way." Tiffany shook her head. "I ain't staying over there. Her husband is always feeling me up and rubbing on me and trying to get me in bed. Can I stay here? Just for the night."

Connolly sighed and closed the door. He didn't want her there. No telling what she'd steal. But he was too tired to argue, and she wasn't going to leave regardless of what he said. "You can sleep on the sofa," he offered.

She dropped her purse on the floor near an end table. Connolly moved up the hall. "But stay out of the kitchen."

"What do you mean?"

"You know exactly what I mean."

He heard her giggle as he walked toward the bedroom.

When Connolly awakened the next morning, Tiffany was gone. He stood near the sofa and sniffed the air. The room smelled like cigarette smoke, but nothing more. A quick glance told him nothing was missing, so he went to the kitchen for a cup of instant coffee. He drank it leaning against the counter by the sink.

An hour later he was showered and dressed. Somewhere past Houston Street his cell phone rang. The call was from Mrs. Gordon. "Somebody said you have an office downtown," she said.

He checked his watch and saw it was already ten. "Good morning, Mrs. Gordon."

"More like good afternoon."

"I had a late start."

Her tone changed. "Gayle Underwood called two or three times."

"What did she want?"

"For you to call her back."

"Okay."

"Are you coming in today?"

"I'll be there in a few minutes."

"I'll believe it when I see you." She ended the call before he could respond.

Connolly checked the call list on his phone and found the DA's number. After two rings, Juanita answered. It took her a few minutes to find Gayle. By the time she came on the line Connolly was on Royal Street. "We arrested Tinker Johnson last night," Gayle said. The sound of her voice made him remember the laughter in her eyes.

"I heard." Connolly propped his elbow on the ledge of the car door. "Did he tell you anything you didn't already know?"

"We searched the nursery this morning."

"Did that include the barn?"

"Yes."

"What did you find?"

"A meth lab."

"How big?"

"Haz-mat team's still in there. It's a mess. And we found the rest of Stephen Ellis' body."

"Where was he?"

"In a burn pile behind the barn."

Connolly had seen that burn pile the morning he talked to Nick. Stood just a few feet from it. The realization of it hit him hard and he found it difficult to concentrate on anything except the image of the burn pile and boxes and knowing that Stephen Ellis' body was beneath it.

The phone was still against Connolly's ear and after a moment he heard Gayle's voice calling to him. "Are you still there?"

"Yeah," he said. "Was there anything left of him that you could recognize?"

"Just his bones. They don't burn too well in a typical fire." Her voice sounded solemn. "At least, that's what someone said. Ted Morgan says we found all of them except the one you brought him."

"Are they sure it's Ellis?"

"He thinks so. Though I'm not sure how they could determine that."

"Did you arrest the Marchands?"

"Not yet. We're still looking for them."

"When you get them, make sure you run their DNA against a sample from Ellis."

"Right."

"So, what does this mean for Dibber?" Connolly asked.

"Dibber?"

"Landry."

Gayle's voice found its laughter again. "They call him Dibber?"

"Short for Dilbert."

"That's the other reason I called you. If he'll plead to theft of property, we'll drop the murder charge."

"What kind of sentence?"

"Year and a day. If you ask for probation, we won't oppose it."

"I'll talk to him today." Connolly parked the car on Dauphin Street and reached for the door handle.

"I showed Henry the results on the forensic report for the bullets," she added.

Connolly let go of the door handle and settled back against the seat. "Forensics?"

"I had the lab compare the bullets from this case to the ones from that old case you asked about. Earl Givens."

"What did the report show?"

"The lab says both bullets came from the same gun. A thirty-eight-caliber revolver."

"I thought they might."

"We still can't find the pistol, though. It was checked into the property room with all the other stuff on that Givens case but it's not there now."

Connolly frowned. "Is that going to cause us a problem?"

"Not for your client. He might be able to loot houses in a hurricane, but I don't think he could get something from the evidence room."

Connolly grasped the door handle once more. "Okay. I'll talk to Dibber and get back to you this afternoon."

"Alright. Listen, any idea where we might find Nick Marchand?"

"He wasn't at the nursery?"

"No. And his mother, Inez? She's missing, too. Any idea where we could find her?"

Connolly chuckled. "Is Hodges still in jail?"

"Yes."

"Maybe you should talk to him. He probably knows."

"I don't think he will talk to us. Certainly not to me."

"Send Henry."

"Henry doesn't talk to prisoners at the jail anymore." Her voice had a derisive tone.

Connolly laughed. "I think you'll have to solve the rest of this case on your own."

"I figured."

When the call ended, Connolly placed the phone on the seat, put the key in the ignition, and started the engine. This case was over. He might have to cajole Dibber into pleading to a theft charge for the jet ski, but that wouldn't take long. And if he plead guilty, Judge Cahill would give him probation. Assuming they could get to court this afternoon, Dibber would be back at home in time for dinner. The case was over for Dibber. But not for Connolly.

Some called it insatiable curiosity. Others called it being nosy. Whatever the trait, he had never been able to walk away from a case while questions remained unanswered. It wasn't a sense of duty. It wasn't a sense of loyalty. It was personal. Connolly wanted to know. Not for the good of a client. Not for the good of the community. Not for the sake of humanity. Just for Connolly. He had no idea where Nick Marchand might be, but he knew how to find Inez. And he was pretty sure where to find the missing pistol, too.

CHAPTER 50

After talking to Underwood, Connolly drove to Clyde Ramsey's house on Crenshaw Street. He stood on the porch and, with his hands cupped around his eyes to shield them from the glare, peered through the front window into the living room.

A newspaper lay on the floor beside a chair near the sofa. Next to the paper was an empty coffee cup. It seemed quiet and dark, as if no one was home, but something about it left Connolly feeling Ramsey was in there. Lurking just around the corner. Listening from the hallway. He jabbed the doorbell button with his finger. When no one answered he rang the doorbell again and again, then pounded on the door with his fist. When still no one appeared, he pounded on it again and shouted. "Clyde! I know you're in there!"

Sure enough, Clyde Ramsey appeared in the hallway and called in a loud voice. "What do you want?"

"Where's Nick Marchand?"

Ramsey came closer and stood near the sofa by the window. "What are you talking about?"

"Where's Nick Marchand?"

"I haven't seen him."

"They searched the nursery. Cops are looking for him and Inez."

Ramsey shook his head. "Go away and leave me alone."

"I know all about you and Inez. Everyone knows."

Ramsey glared at him. "You don't know anything."

"Is she here?"

When Ramsey didn't answer, Connolly goaded him. "She's here. I can tell. She's here, isn't she?"

Ramsey unlocked the door and stepped outside to the front porch. "Listen to me," he said. "All I have to do is make one phone call and you'll be in jail. So get off my porch and leave me alone."

"Make the call," Connolly said as he pushed past him and stepped inside. "The game's over, Clyde."

"You don't believe me?"

"Brian Hodges is in jail. The police are looking for Inez and Nick. This whole thing is falling apart. The sooner you come clean on what you know, the better it'll be for everyone." Connolly glanced around the room, then moved toward the kitchen. "I know you were covering for her. And most people would understand you wanted to spare Nick the pain of a trial when he was a boy." He faced Ramsey. "But now we're talking capital murder. Two people are dead. The DA's coming for Nick and Inez and when they find them here, they're gonna haul you in, too." Connolly saw the look in Ramsey's eyes. "They are here, aren't they? Both of them."

Ramsey looked away. "Why the sudden concern for me?"

"You're Toby's friend and you've had a long, successful career. Even a successful life. And, in spite of everything, you're a likeable guy. I'd hate to see it end for you in prison."

A noise came from the hall. Connolly glanced in that direction as Nick appeared in the doorway, holding a revolver. "Ain't nobody going to prison," he said.

Connolly glanced over at Ramsey. "That's the pistol?"

Ramsey smiled. "Couldn't let them keep it for evidence. Not after you started asking questions."

"But how'd you get—" Suddenly Connolly knew. "Hodges gave it to you."

Ramsey's expression became hard. "Why did you do that to him?"

"Do what to who?"

"Why did you humiliate Brian on the stand like that?"

"Hodges was trying to pin everything on Dibber Landry. What was I supposed to do? Look the other way and let my client go to prison just to hide your affair with Inez?"

Ramsey grinned. "That's what you think this is about?"

Connolly knew there was more to the story than that. He just wanted to keep everyone talking while he searched for a way out of the room. "You spent a lifetime enforcing the law," he continued. "Why would you get mixed up in something like Nick and his meth lab?"

"I spent a lifetime as a cop," Ramsey said. "But I didn't get paid two percent of what it was worth."

"So, this was about money?"

"It's about getting paid. My daddy was a deputy. Worked hard all his life. Got shot three times. Stabbed twice. And died without a thing to show for it. Besides." Ramsey glanced in Nick's direction. "It ain't like he's selling the stuff to school kids."

"Don't matter now anyway." Nick gestured with the pistol toward the back door. "Let's go."

Connolly was still looking at Ramsey. "You would send a man to prison—maybe see him executed—for this?"

"Somebody has to die," Ramsey quipped. "Ain't gonna be me."

Inez appeared behind Nick. Connolly kept talking to Ramsey. "Edwin knew it was you in that beach house." Ramsey had a sheepish expression. Connolly continued. "He knew you were sleeping with his wife."

Inez spoke up. "He's always known."

"That's why he was angry about the fingerprints."

"He's been angry a long time about a lot of things."

Connolly frowned. "So, if everyone knew, why did Hodges lie about the prints?"

Ramsey gave him a knowing look. Connolly's eyes opened wide. "You were trying to get Edwin for it and Dibber happened to wander in."

Ramsey shrugged. "It was a good plan."

Nick took a step closer. "This is a nice conversation but we ain't got time for it." He gave Connolly a shove toward the back door. "Let's go."

For the first time, Connolly looked Nick in the eye. "I'm not going anywhere."

Nick had a cynical expression. "You ain't that tough." He shoved him again. "Get moving."

Connolly stood firm. "Tell me something," he said. "Did you and your buddies kill Stephen Ellis before you knew he was your brother, or after?"

Before Nick could respond, Inez lunged toward them, reaching over Nick's shoulder to grab for the pistol. "I've had enough of this," she snarled. "Give me that gun. I'll take care of him right now."

"Not here," Ramsey retorted. "The neighbors will hear it." He groped for her arm.

"I don't care." Inez shrugged him off and grappled for the pistol all the more. "I just want it all to stop." Nick did his best to avoid her. "Give it to me," she insisted. "I've had enough." While they fought among themselves, Connolly scooted past all three and ran toward the front door. Behind him he heard Inez shouting. "Give it to me! He's getting away."

At the door, Connolly glanced over his shoulder as Inez wrested control of the pistol from the others. She pointed it in his direction and a shot rang out. The bullet whizzed past Connolly's head and struck the door frame as he stepped through.

From the porch, he looked through the window and saw Ramsey clutch his chest, then tumble to the floor. Connolly didn't wait to see what happened next but bounded down the steps, ran to the street, and took cover on the far side of the Chrysler. He heard Inez screaming from inside. "Clyde! No! Call an ambulance! Please! Somebody! Call an ambulance!"

Just then, Connolly heard a car in the driveway on the far side of the house. He raised up high enough to look through the Chrysler's windows and saw a yellow sedan backing up the driveway toward the street. Nick was at the steering wheel. Connolly dropped low and moved around the opposite end of the Chrysler to keep out of sight. The yellow sedan bounced across the curb into the street, then sped away.

Moments later, a patrol car screeched to a halt a few feet away. An officer jumped out, pistol drawn and ready. Connolly stood motionless, hands at his side, still holding the cell phone. The officer was all business. "Did you make the call?"

"No, sir."

"Somebody heard a gunshot. Where's the shooter?"

"Inside," Connolly said, pointing toward the house.

"Who was that in the yellow car?"

"Nick Marchand. The shooter's son."

A second patrol car arrived and stopped behind the first. Two officers got out. Connolly recognized one. The officer approached him. "What we got, Mr. Connolly?"

"The lady inside tried to shoot me. A man who was in there tried to get the gun away from her. I think she shot him."

The officer frowned. "You think?"

"I didn't wait around to find out."

"Are you armed?"

"No." Connolly shook his head.

"Wait here."

The first officer started toward the porch. The other two hurried around the end of the house. As they moved into position, the first officer crouched at the steps and shouted toward the house. "This is the police!"

Inez screamed in reply. "Get an ambulance!"

"Put down your weapon and come out!"

"I can't!"

The officer crept onto the porch and peeked through the open doorway, then seemed to relax. He stood and went inside. In a few minutes one of the officers who had gone around back appeared near the front window, talking on a cell phone.

Connolly moved to the driver's side of the Chrysler and sat sideways on the front seat. With his feet propped against the curb, he lay back and closed his eyes. It was going to be a long afternoon.

When paramedics arrived at Ramsey's house, they were accompanied by three additional patrol cars and a firetruck. The medics worked with Ramsey for half an hour but there was little they could do to save him. The shot from the pistol had torn a gaping hole in his chest.

An hour after they finished, Ted Morgan arrived with a team of forensics technicians. After they finished, Morgan's assistants carried Ramsey from the house in a body bag. Connolly watched from the front seat of the Chrysler.

When the body was gone, the first patrolman came from the house and walked over to the Chrysler. "I need to ask you a few questions," he said.

"Sure," Connolly replied.

"Did you know the decedent?"

"Yes."

"Did you know the woman?"

Connolly nodded. "Inez Marchand." He was sure they already had that information and wondered why the patrolman asked, but he didn't argue.

"Can you tell me—"

A pickup truck screeched to a halt a few feet away and the driver's door flew open. Edwin Marchand came from the cab, calling in a loud voice. "Inez!" He continued shouting as he ran toward the house. "Inez!"

A patrolman stopped him at the front door. "You can't go in there yet."

"Where is she?"

"You'll have to wait out here," the patrolman said.

Edwin spotted Connolly and started toward him. "What happened?" Before Connolly could respond, the patrolman who had been questioning him intervened. "Sir, you need to calm down."

Edwin shoved him aside and continued toward Connolly. "Where is she?" he demanded. "Where's Inez? Where's Nick?"

Three patrolmen appeared from nowhere and wrestled Edwin to the ground. Connolly moved out of the way. As Edwin struggled to get free, he called out to Connolly. "Where is she?!"

One of the patrolmen turned to Connolly. "Do you know this man?"

Connolly nodded. "He's Edwin Marchand. That's his wife inside."

The officers placed Edwin in handcuffs and lifted him to his feet. Edwin glared at Connolly. "Where is she? What did you do to her?"

"She's inside," Connolly said. "And I didn't do anything to her."

"Is she alright?" Edwin asked.

"I think so."

"What about Clyde?"

"I think he's dead." Connolly knew he was dead, he just didn't want to say so.

"What happened?"

"You'll have to ask Inez."

"What do you mean?"

"I mean I can't help you," Connolly said. "You'll have to talk to her."

A patrolman pushed Edwin toward a patrol car. "Let's go."

As they placed Edwin in the car, the front door of the house opened, and two patrolmen led Inez down the steps. She was in handcuffs and her dress was covered with blood. Edwin stared at her and called out to her, but she seemed not to notice him.

In the commotion of handling Edwin and getting Inez from the house, the patrolman who had been talking to Connolly was called away to help. Toby LeMoyne appeared, though, and Connolly was glad to see him. "Are you taking over for Hodges?"

"Not hardly," Toby gestured to the car with Inez inside. "Hard to believe she shot him."

"I think it was an accident."

"You don't think she wanted to kill him?"

"Nah," Connolly said.

"How do you know that?"

"Because she wanted to kill me."

Toby had a look of surprise. "Why did she want to kill you?"

"Because I found out the truth."

"That's enough of a reason for some, I suppose."

"It is if your whole life has been built on a lie."

"Which was?"

"For one thing, she and Clyde were having an affair."

"You mean, they had an affair. Once upon a time. When they were younger."

"No." Connolly shook his head. "I think it was still going on."

Toby looked perplexed. "Not really possible, is it? He's got to be—"

"Eighty."

"At least."

Connolly grinned. "Age doesn't have anything to do with it."

Toby shook his head as if to dislodge the thought of it. "I don't need these visuals in my mind."

Connolly laughed. "I think they really were. You know. Active."

"So, that's part of it. What's the rest about?"

"What do you mean?"

"You said, for one thing, they were having an affair. What's the other?"

"That's the part I'm still wrestling with."

"You mean about Dibber?"

Connolly grimaced. "Dibber just happened to be in the wrong place at the wrong time."

"He saw what happened?"

"No. That man in the beach house was dead long before Dibber came around."

"So, how'd he end up with a murder charge?"

"Hodges."

"Hodges was doing more than hiding Clyde's fingerprints?"

"Hodges found Clyde's prints in the beach house. And he knew about Clyde and Inez. But I'm pretty sure he knew about the meth lab and about who really killed the dead guy they found in the beach house."

"You heard about that meth lab?"

"Gayle Underwood called me."

"It was huge, man. Bigger than anything we expected."

"The super lab."

"And it really was super." Toby said. "So you think Hodges was covering up the lab and a murder?"

"Two or three murders, actually." Connolly opened the driver's door of the Chrysler. "But you'll have to figure that one out. I've got to get my client out of jail." He took a seat behind the steering wheel and started the engine. Toby pushed the door closed and leaned through the window opening. "They'll want a statement from you."

"They can give me a call when they're ready. I'm sure they know where to find me."

As Connolly drove down Crenshaw Street, shadows from the trees that lined the street covered the pavement. The rearview mirror above the windshield caught the reflection of the blue lights from the patrol cars. The glare made him blink his eyes. Up ahead, was his mother's house. He stared at it as he rolled past.

The lawn was mowed. The bushes trimmed. The dead branches that had littered the walkway were gone. The house was dark, but it no longer looked threatening. A sense of freedom washed over him. She hadn't made him cut the grass and she hadn't forced him to pick up the dead limbs. He did it on his own. And not because she demanded it, but because he had wanted to. Because of who he was, not who she had been. He would have stopped, perhaps, and knocked on the door to try and talk to her again, but he had other things that needed his attention, so he pressed his foot lightly against the gas pedal. The Chrysler picked up speed.

CHAPTER 51

Getting Dibber out of jail took longer than Connolly expected. Dibber was reluctant to admit he stole the jet ski and convincing him to say so was more difficult than Connolly imagined. Judge Cahill took his plea as the last case of the day and placed him on probation immediately. By the time the jail released him, it was almost dark. Carl met them in the lobby to take Dibber home. Connolly walked with them from the jail to the street, then made his way to the Chrysler. The day had been long and stressful. His wanted to get home quickly, collapse across the bed, and sleep, but there was still one more thing he had to do.

It took five minutes to reach Barbara's house on Ann Street. He brought the car to a stop out front and hopped out. The "For Sale" sign was still at the end of the walkway near the curb. He snatched it from the ground and rested the stick against his shoulder like a picket sign at a protest rally. When he reached the steps, he bounded up to the porch and rang the bell. After a moment, he rang it again, then knocked on the door with his fist, but no one answered. He walked to the end of the porch and leaned over the rail to check the driveway. Barbara's car was gone.

Disappointed, he took the cell phone from his pocket and called her number. The call went to her voice mail. He left a message, then carried the sign down the steps to the Chrysler and tossed it onto the backseat.

It was almost dark when Connolly arrived at The Pleiades. As he passed the main house the headlights from the Chrysler fell on a pickup truck—a 1963 Chevrolet pickup, to be exact, and Connolly smiled at the sight of it. Hollis was back.

Connolly brought the car to a stop behind the truck and switched off the Chrysler's headlights. As he opened the door to step from the car, the driver's door of the truck opened, too, and Hollis Toombs stepped out. Connolly came from the car with a broad grin. "Is everything alright?"

Hollis had a sheepish look. "Yeah." He nodded. "Everything's fine."

"Have any trouble?"

"Nope. No trouble at all."

"Did Victoria see enough of Disney World?"

"Oh, we saw a lot of it."

"Where is she?"

"She's over at Mrs. Gordon's. Had some stuff over there she wanted to get."

Connolly glanced at his watch. "Did y'all just get back today?"

"A few hours ago. I tried to tell her it could wait 'til tomorrow, but you know women."

"Yeah." Connolly nodded. "I know how they are." Then he corrected himself. "Well, actually, I don't know anything at all about them, but I try to fake it as best I can. Did they get your house ready?" Hollis had lived in a shack on Fowl River for years but that hardly seemed appropriate now that he had a wife. The new house wasn't quite ready when they left on their honeymoon.

"Yes." Hollis nodded. "The house is ready." He leaned against the truck. "I still got my shack down there on the river, though." He looked away. "Just in case."

Connolly sensed there was more to the situation. "Something you want to talk about?"

"Nah." Hollis shook his head again. "We're fine."

"Being married isn't much like dating someone."

Hollis smiled. "No, it isn't."

"Barbara and I fought nearly every day the first year we were married." Connolly looked down at the ground as if in thought. "Towards the end, we didn't fight at all."

Hollis took a deep breath and let it slowly escape. "The language barrier is a little more than I expected."

"Probably more than she expected, too."

"And sometimes … it's like she's a wild animal trapped in a cage, trying to figure out if she should bust loose or stay put."

"You probably feel the same way."

"Yeah. I do."

"It'll all work out, if you keep working at it. It'll all even out. Want to come inside?"

"Nah," Hollis replied. "I better get back over to Mrs. Gordon's. She'll be ready to go before long." Hollis opened the door of the truck. When he was seated behind the steering wheel, Connolly pushed the door closed. They talked through the window. "I'm glad you're back."

Hollis had an expectant look. "Got something you need me to do?"

"Yes, but we can talk about it later."

"Did you have any good cases while I was gone?"

"One."

"Who was the defendant?"

"A guy named Dibber Landry."

Hollis looked surprised. "I know Dibber."

"Yeah?"

"Me and him used to go fishing all the time. Then he took a job in Virginia. He's back?"

"Yeah."

"What happened to the job in Virginia?"

"I think he got in a fight with the foreman."

Hollis looked puzzled. "And that was your case?"

"No. He was living in his uncle's house on Dauphin Island. They said he killed a guy down there during the storm."

"During the hurricane?"

"Said he was looting a beach house. Surprised somebody. Killed him."

"That don't sound like Dibber. Looting a house during a storm, yeah. But not killing somebody. Unless someone was about to kill him."

"We got it all straightened out."

"Good."

Hollis started the truck's engine. "Hear anything from Raisa?"

"She left a message from the airport in Atlanta, but that was a couple of weeks ago, I think. I haven't heard from her since then."

Hollis gave him a look. "Do you miss her?"

Connolly felt uncomfortable with the topic. "I did at first."

"She had it bad for you. Think she'll be back?"

"Not for me."

Hollis nodded. "Just as well." He put the truck in gear. "I'll see you later."

Connolly stepped away. "Come by the office tomorrow."

"Okay." Hollis backed the truck from the house. Connolly called after him. "I'm glad you're back." Hollis tossed a wave out the window as he started down the drive.

Connolly stood there watching as the truck reached the end of the driveway and made the corner into the street. Night had fallen while they talked. The garden behind the main house looked dark and mysterious. The sultry night air invited him into the shadows. He glanced up through the trees toward the sky. A cluster of stars was visible through the haze. Sweat trickled down his back.

Just then, his cell phone rang. The call was from Barbara. "Where's my sign?" she asked.

"What makes you think I know where it is?"

"The neighbors saw you."

"You got any iced tea?"

"Yes. Where's my sign?"

"Pour me a glass," Connolly replied. "I'm coming over."

"It's too hot."

"Your air conditioner doesn't work?"

"It works fine," she said. "But it's too hot to sit outside."

"I thought we could sit in the den." Barbara fell silent. Connolly grinned. He knew by the silence she understood what he meant. "Are you still there?" he asked.

"Yes." Her voice seemed to catch. "I'm here."

"Pour the tea," he said. "I'm on my way." He ended the call and stepped toward the Chrysler.

Other fiction by Joe Hilley:

Sober Justice

Double Take

Night Rain

Electric Beach

The Deposition

What the Red Moon Knows

The Legend of Dell Briggers

The Art Dealer's Wife

For more information visit Joe's website at: www.joehilley.com

CPSIA information can be obtained
at www.ICGtesting.com
Printed in the USA
BVHW030752140621
609522BV00005B/64

9 781736 410523